"JOHNNY, JOHNNY."

Etta's lips sought his, found his, adored his. Cheyenne's heart expanded with emotion sweeter than wine, and for a startling moment he thought he might cry. But it passed, leaving him shaken. All she'd said was his name, but it was the first time she'd called him Johnny, and somehow, it meant so very much. It meant everything.

"You ever dream of me, Etta?"

She smiled. "All the time."

"In your dreams, do you call me by my first name?"

"Yes."

"I think I'd like it if we saved that for times like this when we're all alone. You can call me Johnny, and I'll call you . . . what I call you in my dreams."

Praise for Deborah Camp's previous book
MASTER OF MOONSPELL

If You've Enjoyed This Book,
Be Sure to Read These Other
AVON ROMANTIC TREASURES

CHEYENNE'S SHADOW

DEBORAH CAMP

An Avon Romantic Treasure

AVON BOOKS ◆ NEW YORK

CHEYENNE'S SHADOW is an original publication of Avon Books. This work has never before appeared in book form. This work is a novel. Any similarity to actual persons or events is purely coincidental.

AVON BOOKS
A division of
The Hearst Corporation
1350 Avenue of the Americas
New York, New York 10019

Copyright © 1994 by Deborah E. Camp
Published by arrangement with the author
Library of Congress Catalog Card Number: 93-90642
ISBN: 0-380-76739-2

First Avon Books Printing: March 1994

AVON TRADEMARK REG. U.S. PAT. OFF. AND IN OTHER COUNTRIES, MARCA REGISTRADA, HECHO EN U.S.A.

Printed in the U.S.A.

RA   10   9   8   7   6   5   4   3   2   1

Respect is like a shadow.
The harder you chase it,
the faster it moves.
Stand tall, and it will grow on you.

—Cowboy Saying

CHEYENNE'S SHADOW

Chapter 1

The streets of Clearwater, Texas, were quiet on this Saturday afternoon. Quiet as death.

Henryetta Hollister moved away from the door of the general store and shook off an ominous feeling as she joined her ranch hand at the front counter.

"Where did Andy get off to?" she asked.

"No tellin'," Whitey Malloy answered with a chuckle. "He might be down at the blacksmith's. You know how he loves to watch Jessup hammer out shoes." He screwed up one light blue eye and focused on the store proprietor. Placing a gnarled hand on top of one of the grain sacks, he leaned over the counter toward the round-faced man. "How many cows we gotta slaughter to pay for this mess of goods, Clarence?"

"Not more than one or two, I reckon," Clarence Allred answered in the same teasing vein. "By the way, Etta, I got some pretty, blue hair ribbons in yesterday. The ladies have been fighting over them. They will look pretty in your blond hair. You interested?"

She looked at the chubby man and bit back her sharp retort. Hair ribbons and other such man trappings were about as natural to her as a side-saddle was to a pig, and Clarence Allred darn well knew it. She eyed him, wondering if he'd heard about the railroad deal the Brickmans had cooked up. Maybe he was thinking she'd be needing to pretty herself up and snag a husband before she was put off her land. His pink face flushed coral under her scrutiny.

"No, thanks." She reached for the handkerchief in the back pocket of her pants. Mopping her brow with it, she resisted the urge to dip the hanky down the front of her shirt where a trickle of sweat ran between her breasts. After replacing the red calico bandanna, she tipped her head in the direction of the open door. "Hardly a soul stirring out there today."

"Probably too danged hot." Whitey slipped a new tin of chewing tobacco into his front shirt pocket. "We'd better enjoy it while we can. Fall is just a couple of weeks away, and then winter will be on us before we know it."

"Town was bustling just a few minutes ago." Clarence paused in adding the purchases to Etta's previous bill and craned his neck, trying to see outside. "Huh. That's peculiar. Wonder where every—"

Andy Dobbins came skidding around the door facing and barreled into the store, his slick-soled boots providing little traction. The fifteen-year-old reminded Etta of a marionette, the way his skinny arms and legs worked up and down. His body was growing—he'd added another three inches to his height in the past six months—but his shiny black face still bore the mark of youth.

"Lordy, son, who put a bug in your britches?" Whitey asked, chuckling.

"There's gonna be a gunfight!" Andy said, gasping for air. His scrawny chest labored under a shirt he'd outgrown. "Guess who!"

"Not you, I hope," Whitey drawled.

Etta frowned at the news. Men and their endless battles to prove themselves. When would it ever stop? "I don't care who it is," she said, glancing at the figure Clarence had come up with for the supplies. She winced, wondering if she'd be able to pay it come spring.

Andy rubbed his floppy hat off his head and nodded shyly at Clarence. " 'Lo, Mr. Allred. Beggin' your pardon for busting in here, but—"

"Which two are going to face each other, boy?" Clarence interrupted.

"It's Brickman and—"

"Brickman?" Etta whirled around to face Andy, suddenly interested. "Blaine Brickman's going to—" She stopped as Andy shook his head. "Ben? Ben's in a gunfight?" She felt a twinge of disappointment. God forgive her, but she would have paid what little money she had left to see Blaine Brickman lose a gunfight.

"Yeah, Ben and . . ." Andy drew in a chestful of air, his dark eyes huge with excitement. "Johnny Cheyenne, the gunfighter!"

Etta's heart stopped; then anger started it up again. Johnny Cheyenne, that no-good, gunslinging, gutless snake in the grass! She reined in her temper with difficulty. If he were facing the other Brickman, she thought with a derisive twist of her lips, it would be easy to choose sides. As it was, she couldn't decide whom she wanted dead once the smoke cleared.

"Johnny Cheyenne? No kiddin'?" Clarence came around the counter. He untied his bib apron and pulled it over his head as he edged Andy aside to peer out the door. "No wonder everybody's off the streets. I didn't even know he was in town. What happened? What did Ben do to make Cheyenne want to plug him?"

"It's over a saloon girl, I think," Andy said breathlessly. "One of them insulted her, and the other come to her rescue."

Whitey smiled. "Bet it was over Meg O'Rourke."

Andy nodded. "You win that bet. Meg's bawling her eyes out and grinning, all at the same time. She's scared, but she's kinda happy about it, too."

"Probably scared that Ben will kill Cheyenne and then beat the living hell out of her," Whitey said, stuffing a generous pinch of tobacco into his mouth. "I don't reckon she has much to worry about. My money's on Cheyenne."

"How much?" Clarence asked, glancing back at Whitey. "Would you put a dollar on that bet?"

Whitey shook his white head. "Nope, but I'll spot you two bits."

"Done." Clarence faced the street again.

Etta glared at Whitey for wasting money they didn't have, but the old cowpuncher only grinned mischievously.

"Still no sign of them. Where they gonna shoot it out, boy?"

"In front of the saloon," Andy said, standing on tiptoe to see past Clarence. "I ain't never seed a gunfight before. Have you, Miss Etta?"

"No, and I don't figure I've missed anything." She swallowed hard against the revulsion tightening her throat.

Whitey, slouching against the counter, straightened. "You recall Johnny Cheyenne, don't you, Etta?"

"Surely." She began poking their smaller purchases into a burlap bag. "He's one of the dirty outlaws Hank took up with."

"That so?" Clarence asked. "Your brother was one of the Nelson gang, wasn't he?"

"Cheyenne made a trip here to tell us about Hank being tried in Fort Smith," Whitey explained. "If it hadn't been for him, we wouldn't have known a thing about it. Hank sure wasn't about to get in touch with us. He was too proud."

"Us knowing about it didn't do much good," Etta groused.

"Well, now, that lawyer you hired kept Hank from swinging at the end of a rope. A twenty-five-year prison term is better than dying."

"He'll be an old man by the time he gets out," Etta said, her heart aching with the thought. *"If* he ever gets out of that stink hole." Tears burned the backs of her eyes.

"Now, take it easy," Whitey said, laying a comforting hand on her shoulder. "You might not like Cheyenne, but he did us a good turn, sister girl."

Etta ducked her head to hide her tender smile. *Sister girl.* As far back as she could remember, that had been Whitey Malloy's endearment for her, and she treasured it. Maybe because her father had never called her anything but Henryetta or Etta. He'd called Hank "partner" and "pal." Etta had been jealous of that. She sighed away the memories. Hollisters had always prized their sons. Their daughters were . . . well, only procurers of more sons, with any luck.

"Miss Etta, Miss Etta!" Andy yanked at Etta's

shirtsleeve to get her attention. "We're staying in town long enough to watch, ain't we?"

Etta confronted the hope in Andy's eyes. "It means so much to you to see two men try to kill each other?"

Andy averted his gaze and his fingers slipped from her sleeve. "Well, dadgum it, Miss Etta, when you put it that way—"

"I think everyone should see a shoot-out once in his life," Whitey drawled, giving Etta a warning glance. "Makes you appreciate minding your own business. Besides, seems we got a stake in this here shoot-out."

"You do, with your silly bet," Etta pointed out. "Not me—or Andy," she tacked on.

"We *all* got stakes in it. We know both gunfighters. Now if Ben Brickman wins, he and Blaine will feel even more powerful. If Johnny Cheyenne wins, we're shed of one Brickman, which will make our lives a mite easier. Seems to me you'd want to know the outcome, Etta."

She shrugged. "If y'all want to watch, it's okay by me." She refused to admit that Whitey was right, and that she was interested in who'd be left standing after the gunfight.

"There they are," Clarence said, already moving outside. "They're facing off in front of the Scarlet Rose, just like you said, boy."

Andy scrambled after Clarence, but paused to look back at Etta and Whitey.

"You-all comin'?"

"We're slower, but we'll be right behind you." Whitey lifted a snowy brow. "Well, Etta, you gonna watch or stay hid in here?"

"I was thinking of loading the wagon while you

and Andy gawk. Y'all can tell me all about it on
the way home."

He cupped her elbow in one hand. "Come on,
you know you want to. Lord, sister girl, you are a
stubborn cuss. You just hate to admit that you got
human feelings like curiosity and sympathy for
others and love for an old man and a Negro boy."

"I don't know what you're yammering about,"
Etta complained, letting him guide her outside
onto the boardwalk, which was already crowded
with onlookers.

Some folks stayed behind the windows of their
businesses, afraid to venture out for fear of being
plugged by a stray bullet. Down by the saloon,
Meg O'Rourke was caterwauling and being comforted by her fellow fallen angels. Whitey maneuvered around the other people, leading the way
for Etta. Andy had secured a place in front of the
saloon, and Whitey managed to wedge himself
and Etta next to him. Etta sent an irritated glare
over her shoulder at the wailing Meg, but the saloon girl was too busy being distraught to notice.

"I wish she'd shut her trap," Etta muttered. "Everybody in Clearwater knows she doesn't give a
hoot or holler for either one of these men."

Etta glanced at Ben Brickman, a hulking bear of
a man with a full beard and mustache the color of
chewed tobacco. He didn't look anything like his
twin brother, but they both shared a penchant for
evil. She swung her gaze across to the other man
and her heart stuttered.

She'd forgotten he was so handsome.

Well, that wasn't *entirely* true. She'd made herself not think of Johnny Cheyenne in those terms.

After all, she hated him. Him and his whole heinous lot.

Johnny Cheyenne stood over six feet, and his shoulders were broad enough to attract any woman's eye, so Etta didn't feel bad about admiring them. A double-breasted, faded red shirt covered his impressive torso, and fringed leather pants hugged his long, muscled legs. Like any saddle bum, he wore boots, but he was hatless. His blue-black hair hung just past his shoulders and had been pushed back off his broad forehead. Several long strands at his left temple had been braided, the ends wrapped with a strip of yellow leather.

His face was a testimony to a mixed heritage. High cheekbones and an aquiline nose came from his Cheyenne ancestry, while dark blue eyes and a heavy whisker-shadow came from his white forebears. A half-breed, Etta thought, glancing at dark-skinned Andy. Half-breeds were thought to be a rung lower on the ladder than even Negroes, although Etta didn't cotton to such nonsense. She didn't judge folks by their color, but by how they treated her. On *her* ladder, Andy Dobbins was on one of the top rungs, and Ben and his twin brother, Blaine, were hanging on the lowest one— Ben by a finger and Blaine by a fingernail.

She looked around, but didn't see Blaine anywhere. He doesn't know about this, she thought, or he'd be here otherwise. Cheyenne's lucky Blaine hasn't gotten wind of this, because Blaine would have made sure his brother won, even if that meant shooting Cheyenne himself.

Studying the infamous gunfighter, she couldn't see one sign of nervousness. He hadn't even broken a sweat. He could have been facing a harmless boy instead of a man bent on killing him. In contrast, Ben was sweating like a custard pie and twitching all over. Etta suspected he was liquored up, and if she was right about that, then she was looking at a dead man. Ben might have a ghost of a chance against Johnny Cheyenne sober, but drunk? She noticed the rapt expression on people's faces. Somebody ought to start digging Ben's grave.

Johnny Cheyenne had gained fame as one of the quickest draws in the West. Etta had no idea of how many men he'd killed—nor did she care to know—but she figured it was more than a couple, seeing as how his reputation had spread like wildfire.

"I'll just *die* if he gets hurt or k-killed," Meg announced between sobs.

Etta twisted around to her. "Which one?"

Meg's brown eyes rounded. "Johnny Cheyenne, of course! I don't care nothing about . . ." She squinted nervously at Ben, then whispered, "Ben Brickman or his brother."

Etta smiled and shook her head. "Meg O'Rourke, you spread yourself around so thin, I do believe I can see right through you."

Meg narrowed her eyes at Etta, but then shrugged off the comment. A wry expression brought out the dimples in her rouged cheeks. "You got yourself a sharp tongue, Etta Hollister, but I got no fuss with you, 'cause I understand you." She gave a wink. "Better than you think I do, honey."

Etta tensed under the other woman's scrutiny. She faced the street and wondered if Ben or Blaine had said something to Meg about what had happened in the past.

"You ready, Injun dung?" Ben shouted, twenty paces away from Cheyenne, and a hush fell over the area as if a lid had been shut tight.

Etta's heartbeats boomed in her ears, steady as the ticking of a clock. She looked from Ben to Cheyenne and her palms grew moist, her knees unreliable. She reached out, found Andy's hand, and gripped it hard in both of hers.

"You wanted this, Brickman," Cheyenne said, his deep bass voice carrying easily. "So make your move."

Meg sobbed, breaking the tense silence that followed. "I can't watch," she wailed.

"Then don't," someone muttered, and a nervous twitter erupted, followed by that deadly silence.

Late afternoon shadows spread across the street and onto the boardwalk where Etta stood, her legs trembling, her pulse slowing until she wondered if she was about to faint. All horses and conveyances had been removed from this block, making the street seem unusually wide. The edge of the sun dipped behind the rooflines, throwing the street into total shadow. Etta wondered if that was an advantage or a disadvantage.

She found she couldn't take her eyes off Cheyenne, although she could read precious little in his impassive face. His body appeared relaxed and loose. His gun hand hovered above his revolver, his long brown fingers slightly curled, ready to caress the pearl-handled weapon. His eyes glinted in their deep sockets, and Etta knew that he was examining Ben's face as intently as she examined his.

Tension built in Etta's chest, crowding her heart

and lungs. *Someone do something!* her mind screamed. She ripped her gaze from Cheyenne to glance at Ben, and in that second the world exploded.

Gunshots roared and the acrid scent of spent gunpowder burned Etta's nostrils. Her heart lurched at every shot—three in all—and then that terrible silence descended again. Death's hand gripped the town. Life returned in the small, insignificant sounds of a child crying for his mother, a man clearing his throat, a woman sobbing uncontrollably. Etta let go of Andy's hand and wiped the moisture from her eyes.

"Is he dead?" Meg O'Rourke asked, her voice high and thin.

When Etta's vision cleared, she found herself staring at a crumpled body in the street—a body that didn't move. Ben Brickman's. Despite her hatred for the man, Etta sent up a prayer that he wasn't dead.

Lester Craw, Clearwater's excuse for a sheriff, strode toward the body, bent down, and turned it over. Ben stared lifelessly up at the blue sky. Lester tore open Ben's bloody shirt, then looked around at the people crowded on the boardwalk.

"Looks dead to me," he announced. He passed a hand over Ben's face, closing the deceased's eyes.

The action seemed to release everyone from an evil spell. People moved. Some crossed the street to examine Ben's body more closely, while others hurried away to spread the news or try to forget what they'd witnessed. Etta looked toward Johnny Cheyenne. He still held his gun pointed at Ben. Blue smoke drifted from its engraved barrel.

"Anybody know where Blaine is?" the sheriff asked.

"At the ranch." Gerald Powell, the bank president, looked down at Ben. "Who's going to tell him about this?" He shifted his gaze pointedly to Lester.

"Me?" Lester straightened up and wiped his hands on the front of his trousers. "I think it would be better if it came from you."

"Why does anybody have to tell him?" Whitey piped up. "He's fairly intelligent. I reckon he'll figure it out for himself eventually."

People laughed nervously. Etta jabbed Whitey in the ribs with her elbow.

"You looking for trouble, old man?" she whispered to him. "Don't you know those two-faced weasels will break their blamed necks trying to get to Blaine first and tell him what you said?"

Whitey grinned. "I only stated a bald fact. Nothing sinister about that." He squinted, looking toward the gunman, who was still standing. "Hey there, young fella! Looks like you got winged."

Etta swung toward Johnny Cheyenne again. Sure enough, blood dripped from his gun hand. A sound of dismay escaped her before she could stop it. She glanced at the people near her, hoping no one had heard. She sure shouldn't be worrying about Johnny Cheyenne, she told herself crossly. If it weren't for him and his saddle pals, Hank would be home instead of doing hard labor at an Illinois prison. However, her heart constricted when she noticed the droplets of blood falling from Cheyenne's hand to mark the dusty street.

He moved with unhurried grace, settling his gun back into its sleeve. Lifting a strip of leather tied to his belt, he removed a knife from his back pocket and notched the strap with weighty significance. Even from a distance Etta could count five notches. Six now. Someone gasped. Someone else whispered, "Did you see what he just did?"

Savage, Etta thought. What kind of animal would take pride in such achievements? She knew she should turn her back on him in a show of disgust, but she found herself moving along the boardwalk, getting closer and closer to him. Whitey reached his side, and Etta saw a flash of recognition cross Cheyenne's face.

"Can I help you?" Whitey asked, indicating Cheyenne's hand with a nod. "Maybe you should soak that in some kerosene or whiskey. We don't have a town doctor, so—"

"I'm a doctor." A man came forward. His silver hair was parted in the middle and slicked carefully into place. As he passed Etta, she caught the scent of toilet water.

Lester Craw hurried to shake the man's hand. "You a doctor, huh?"

"That's right. I'm Dr. Alvin Steinbrenner. I came in on the noon stage from back East and I'm leaving tomorrow for Tucson."

"Steinbrenner," Lester repeated, rubbing his whiskered jaw. "You a Jew doctor, huh?"

Etta winced at the sheriff's bad manners. The doctor eyed the runty man with clear disdain before directing his attention to Johnny Cheyenne.

"I'd be pleased to look at your hand and see what I can do. Is the bullet still in there?"

Cheyenne raised his injured hand and turned it over, eyeing the damage. "It's just a flesh wound."

The doctor shook his head. "More than that,

young man." He turned toward the Scarlet Rose.
"Let's go into that saloon and I'll see what I can
do for you."

"Much obliged."

The doctor hesitated, his attention captured by
the lifeless man in the street.

"Can't do nothing for him," Lester said. "And
you don't have to do nothing for this here gunslinger either. In fact, I think it would be better if
he just rode out of town. We don't want your kind
in Clearwater, Cheyenne."

Etta seethed inwardly at the sheriff. The worm.
He had allowed Cheyenne to risk his life and rid
the town of a troublemaker, but now that the dirty
job was over, Lester was throwing his weight
around and ordering Cheyenne out of town.
Spineless, she thought. Just like the rest of the
townspeople.

Meg O'Rourke bustled forth. "The doctor is going to fix Cheyenne up, and you got no say in the
matter."

"Who says?" Lester demanded, puffing out his
chest.

"Me." She thrust her painted face close to his.
"You remember what me and you did the other
night, Lester? You want me to tell all these folks
about it?" She marched two fingers up his shirtfront. "I was the schoolmarm and you were a
naughty little boy, and I had to throw you over my
knees and tan your little—"

"Hey there, shut your mouth!" Lester slapped
her hand aside. His face blazed crimson as the
other saloon girls released peals of laughter.

Smiling, Etta looked around at the other amused
expressions until her gaze collided with Chey-

enne's. He narrowed his midnight-blue eyes, and Etta sensed he was trying to recall where he'd seen her before. She looked away, flushing hotly to the roots of her blond hair. She hoped he didn't remember. Probably wouldn't. Men like him didn't see women as individuals, but as mere diversions.

The sheriff cleared his throat and addressed the smiling doctor as he pushed Meg aside.

"Take the gunslinger into the saloon and bandage him up, but I want him out of town by morning!" Lester grabbed Gerald Powell by the elbow. "Me and you are going to tell Blaine about this—together."

"That's your job, not mine," Gerald protested.

Lester grinned, displaying a mouthful of yellow teeth. "He's the chairman of your bank, Powell. He won't like it when I tell him you wouldn't come along and help break the bad news."

Powell jerked his elbow from Lester's grasp. "I have to get my horse."

"Meetcha at the bank." Lester winked, cackled like a setting hen, and strutted away on legs not much longer than his arms.

"Does this hurt?" the doctor asked, pressing Cheyenne's bloody hand.

Cheyenne shook his head. "I don't feel anything." He flexed his fingers slowly. "Feels funny. It's hard for me to make my fingers move."

"That worries me. Could be nerve damage." The doctor slung drops of blood off the tips of his fingers.

Instinctively, Etta stepped forward and offered her bandanna. Dr. Steinbrenner accepted it with a grateful smile.

"Keep it," Etta said, shrugging. "It's just a rag."

"Thank you, young lady." The doctor wrapped the square of red calico around Cheyenne's hand.

Cheyenne's gaze drifted over Etta's face, and his brows met in concentration. He couldn't jar her from his memory, she thought. Good. Etta stepped back among the others, removing herself from his sight and regretting her act of mercy.

"Let's get you inside, where you can sit down and I can clean this," Dr. Steinbrenner suggested.

They headed for the saloon and parted the crowd like a bullet through tender skin. Whitey tagged along behind them, but Etta snagged his sleeve as he went past her.

"Just where do you think you're going, old man?"

"Inside . . . just for a minute. I want to see how bad the boy's been hit."

"Why? He's nothing to you. We've got to get back to the ranch while there's still daylight."

Whitey patted her hand, then firmly removed it from his sleeve. "Now, Etta, don't be uncharitable. You could come inside and help, you know. You're good at nursing."

"No." She folded her arms. "And I don't know why you care what happens to that heartless killer. He's the reason Hank's in prison!" She realized too late that her voice had risen and everyone else's had fallen silent. The hairs on the back of her neck lifted, and she knew she'd drawn Johnny Cheyenne's attention again. He stared at her, his eyes diamond-hard, then bobbed his head in a cool acknowledgment. The tip of his tongue raced across his full lower lip, leaving it glistening. Etta shivered and started to turn away.

"Miss Hollister?"

She paused and reluctantly brought her gaze back to him. His voice made her think of suede—soft and warm, but tough. Everything about him was tough. Even his heart, she told herself. If he had one.

"I didn't put your brother in prison. The law did that."

She wanted to rail at him, beat him with her tight fists, stomp him with her bootheels. To her, he was what was wrong with the world. He was just another man bent on getting his way, no matter if others were hurt or their lives were ruined. But words dried on her tongue. She felt conspicuous and vulnerable and frightened. Recoiling from him, she reached blindly for Andy and clamped a hand on his thin forearm.

"Come on," she mumbled to the boy, then turned and hurried away from the gawking crowd and the enigmatic gunfighter.

"You okay, Miss Etta?" Andy asked, striding ahead of her a little so that he could peer into her face.

"Yes, I'm just . . . where's Clarence? I need to sign our bill. You go ahead and start loading the wagon." She stepped inside the general store and seized a few moments to gather her composure while Andy carried out sacks of feed. She laid an open palm against the side of her face, feeling the heat of embarrassment, and cursed her inability to stand her ground. She would have given that gunslinger a piece of her mind if everyone hadn't been staring at her. Why couldn't people mind their own business and leave her be? Why couldn't she quit worrying about what people thought of her . . . what people had heard about her?

She slammed a fist down on the counter, angry at her own timidity and at the twist of fate that had taken her brother. Never had she been so in need of a formidable champion, and Hank was gone. Gone for twenty-five years.

"Sorry to keep you waiting, Etta." Clarence's footsteps sounded heavily in the quiet store. He grabbed his bib apron and tied it on as he rounded the counter. "Let me see . . . ah, yes. Here you go—just sign here." His eyebrows dipped in sudden concern. "You think you'll clear enough to pay all your bills by March, Etta? That's only six months away."

"I know that, Clarence. I've always paid my bills, haven't I?" Etta hedged, scratching out her name on the slip of paper. She pinned on a smile. "Besides, I just know that next year will be better than this one." Her gaze slipped to the wall calendar behind Clarence. By the time 1883 dawned, she'd know whether or not she could keep hold of her ranch.

Andy came in for another sack of feed. "Where'd they put Brickman's body, Mr. Allred?"

"Carried him over to the undertaker's. I'll tell you something else. Johnny Cheyenne had better get out of Clearwater before Blaine finds out what happened. Blaine will be loaded for bear." Clarence sighed heavily. "Can't say I'll miss Ben much, but his death isn't going to make life any easier around this town. Blaine will be in a rage over this, and there will be hell to pay for all of us."

Etta made a contemptuous sound. "If folks would stand up to him, he wouldn't act like he's the king of Clearwater."

"Etta, you know he owns most of the town.

How are we supposed to treat him? If you get on Blaine Brickman's bad side, you might as well pack up and move, because you won't have any life in Clearwater, that's for sure."

"I'd rather move than kiss that skunk's backside."

Clarence glanced sharply at her, then shrugged. "Guess that might come to pass, Etta. I heard about the railroad making plans to claim your land. Blaine told me he offered to buy you out, but you turned him down. If you're going to lose your land, you ought to at least get something for it so that you can ... well, settle your accounts and pay your way to another town."

Etta slapped the counter with the flat of her hand, making Clarence jump. She leaned close, eyeball to eyeball with him. "Don't you worry, Clarence, I'll settle my accounts. And the next time you and Brickman are discussing me, you can tell him that I wish he'd shove a stick of dynamite up his pants and light it."

Andy doubled over laughing, getting a smirk from Etta and a scowl from Clarence.

"Big words, Etta, but you know you can't win against Brickman. He's got this Texas county in his back pocket."

"He doesn't have *me* in his pocket." Etta straightened and rocked her wide-brimmed cowboy hat more firmly over her pale blond hair. "The day Brickman gets my land, you can start digging my grave, because he'll have to *kill* me to get it."

Clarence frowned. "Etta, you don't mean it."

"Oh, yes, I do," she assured him with a definitive nod and a narrowing of her green eyes. "Blaine Brickman has taken all he's going to take from me. He'll never get the Flying H. Not from me anyway. I'd rather die than let him have it." She arched a honey-colored brow. "You don't have to tell him that, Clarence. He already knows it."

Chapter 2

The sounds of gunfire came back to her as they had countless times since yesterday. Squatting beside a sagging barbwire fence section, Etta closed her eyes and let the memory of the gunfight overtake her. Maybe if she relived it, the haunting sights and sounds would finally go away.

What troubled her was that she'd been secretly thrilled by the confrontation. Johnny Cheyenne had looked invincible and manly standing in the middle of the street, showing not one twitch of fear or doubt. Then in a blaze of smoke and bullets, Ben Brickman was gone, like a splinter being plucked from a swollen finger. Etta felt good to be rid of him. She smiled to herself. If only Cheyenne could extract her other splinter—Blaine Brickman—she might be able to finally heal.

His eyes are dark, dark blue. Like a night sky.

Etta's own green eyes popped open. Now, where had *that* come from? she wondered with irritation. Why would she recall the exact shade of Johnny Cheyenne's eyes, for heaven's sake? Silly to remember something like that.

And he'd licked his lips like he'd wanted to taste her.

Etta jerked her mind from such thoughts. She felt her skin heat, the warmth creeping up her neck and into her cheeks. Great goblins, she was embarrassing herself! She laughed under her

breath and grabbed the sagging string of barbwire,
tough leather gloves protecting her hands. Pulling
hard, she tightened the three-strand wire and
wrapped it around the heavy nail in the post. She
reached into the cowhide pouch tied to her belt for
another nail, then hammered it into the post, securing the valuable wire more tightly.

Looking down the fence line at the flat land
that gave way to heavily wooded hills in the distance, she saw a vision of men working to build
a railroad. Etta blinked away the mirage and set
her jaw. Not on this land, she vowed. All she had
left was the two thousand acres of the Flying H,
and she was determined to keep it. However, a
feather of doubt floated through her. What if
they couldn't round up enough cattle for market?
She stared at the humpbacked hills, remembering all too clearly last fall when she and Whitey
had run less than half of her herd from among
those piney woods.

They'd have to do a sight better than that to
save the Flying H this year. Last year's bills had
piled onto this year's and those owed had spent
all their sympathy toward her. Come spring, they
wanted their money. The bill collectors had backed
off when her father had died suddenly, giving her
a year to get on her feet. She figured they all
thought she'd put the ranch up for sale and pay
them off. When she hadn't done that, folks had
lost patience with her.

Then the railroad had decided to put a spur
across the neighboring Double B, but Blaine
Brickman had talked them into waiting until
spring, assuring them that Etta would lose the Flying H by then and that they could run their track

on her abandoned ranch land. Brickman, of course, would gobble up what land the railroad didn't claim by eminent domain. He'd finally get what he wanted, or so he thought.

For as far back as Etta could remember, the Brickmans had coveted the Flying H because of a treasure in the foothills—a treasure so important a town had been named for it: the mouth of Clearwater Spring. Amos Brickman, Blaine's papa, had tried to buy the land from Henry Hollister many times and had passed his desire on to his twin sons. Water in Texas was as valuable as diamonds. Clearwater Spring meandered through the Double B, but its birthplace was on the Flying H, and that made the Brickmans vulnerable. They knew that the Hollisters could dam up the spring if they were of a mind to, cutting off the water source for the Double B's three thousand head of cattle. Of course, Henry Hollister hadn't been that kind of man. He'd always tried to be a good neighbor, even when his neighbors were a jealous, blackhearted lout and his two cutthroat sons.

Roy Powell, the railroad agent, had offered Brickman a chance to finally lay his hands on the Flying H jewel. Eminent domain. Lord, how Etta hated those words. And to think that Roy would agree to wait like a vulture for her to fold her hand! Once, not so many years ago, Roy had told her he loved her and wanted to marry her. Now he'd thrown in his lot with Brickman to snatch her land away from her.

"Never, never, never," Etta swore as she pushed herself to her feet. She turned toward her horse, recognized the man blocking her way, and her blood froze in her veins.

"Good afternoon, Etta," Blaine Brickman said, removing his flat-crowned black hat and giving her a belittling smile. "I'm so sorry to have startled you. I believe you were talking to yourself." He ran a forefinger across his thin sable mustache and down his neatly trimmed beard. "You should place yourself in the company of others more often, Etta. A woman as lovely as you surely can't be wanting for companionship."

Etta surveyed her situation quickly. Her horse was a few feet off to her right, but Brickman could get to her before she could get to it. His horse was behind him, munching on grass. She sighed. She was trapped.

"What do you want, Brickman?"

Blaine frowned. "I've asked you numerous times to call me Blaine, same as you've called me before. We've been close for too long to be so formal with each other, Etta."

"I'm busy." She jerked her gloves more snugly over her hands. "You should get off my land. Nobody invited you here."

"I came by because I'm perplexed."

She glared at him, unsure of what he meant. From the corner of her eye she judged how many steps it would take her to reach Southpaw, her rust-colored gelding.

"I just came from my brother's funeral. Why weren't you there?"

Stunned speechless for a moment by his utter gall, Etta released a breathy laugh of incredulity. "Why would you expect me to go?" She shook her head. "You didn't. You just used that as an excuse to come looking for me."

"I don't need excuses, Etta, dear." He gazed past her to the green hills. "I suppose you rejoiced when that outlaw killed my brother."

"Not really. Brickman, I've more important things—"

"It's a shame you're going to lose this land."

Etta set her jaw. "I'm not losing it. The railroad is going to run their track on *your* land, just like they planned before you talked them into waiting to see if I could pay my bills next year."

"Which you won't be able to do." He tucked his thumbs under his belt. As usual, he was dressed in his Sunday best: black suit, white shirt, black string tie, polished boots, and a belt with inlaid silver so shiny it rivaled the sun.

Studying him, Etta remembered how handsome he had seemed to her when she was a girl. His tailored clothes, soft, cultured voice, and effusive flattery had charmed her. Outward appearances had intimated that he was a gentleman, but Etta knew better. She knew what he was capable of. She knew of his black, calloused heart.

"The deal I made with the railroad was a business proposition, Etta. It wasn't personal. However, the proposition I'm about to make you *is* personal."

Etta's knees began to shake. She glanced at Southpaw again as her heartbeats accelerated and sweat beaded on her spine and between her breasts. Should she make a run for it? Maybe she could fight him off.

"I want you to do what you should have done five years ago. I want you to marry me."

A twisted smile captured her lips. "You're crazy."

"I'll buy up what the railroad doesn't take of the Flying H and give it to you as a wedding present." He simpered, his thin lips spreading his narrow mustache. "You'll want for nothing as my wife, Etta. I promise you that."

"Nothing except your death," Etta said, and his smile vanished. Fury snuffed out the lights in his eyes. "I told you to get off my land, Brickman. You getting hard of hearing?"

"I'm waiting for your answer," he said with cold patience. His black eyes perused her slowly, contemplatively.

Etta continued to shake and sweat. Fear clouded her reasoning and she dashed toward Southpaw. She gripped the saddle horn and raised her foot, missing the stirrup. That frantic moment was all Brickman needed. He clamped a hand on her shoulder and slung her around to face him, pressing her back against Southpaw's side. Etta stared into his face and recognized lust in his eyes.

He spread one hand along her throat; his other held both of her wrists captive between their bodies. At six feet, he was slender, his physique defined by long, ropy muscles. His hands were strong, easily holding her still while he inched closer until his legs pinned hers. Southpaw shifted. Etta prayed he'd bolt and run, but the gelding stayed put, just as he'd been trained to do.

"You're beautiful, Etta." Blaine's gaze moved over her hair, her lips, her flushed cheeks. "When you were a girl, I thought of you as a rosebud about to bloom. Now that you're in full blossom, you're magnificent. You try to hide your beauty under those work shirts and pants, but you can't hide, Etta. Every man who looks at you wants you." He caressed her throat. "But I'm the only man who will ever have you, Etta. No matter what you say or do, you're mine."

She whimpered as his mouth came down on hers, rubbing and osculating. Sealing her lips together tightly, she forbade him entry. His member stiffened, poking at her. Etta cringed as painful memories swept through her like ghosts. Something wild snapped inside her, lending her a burst of strength that somehow gained her freedom. She shoved him away and whirled. Her boot slipped neatly into the stirrup and she was astride Southpaw and racing with the wind. Brickman's maniacal laughter scampered after her, but she outran the sound. When she could hear nothing but Southpaw's thundering hoofbeats, she tugged on the reins and he slowed to a canter. Etta glanced over her shoulder, relieved to see that no one followed.

"I'm okay, I'm okay," she whispered, consoling herself, assuring her laboring heart that it could resume its normal pace. "He didn't hurt me, didn't hurt me."

She drew in a head-clearing breath and released it through her pursed lips. Her lips felt sticky. She wiped them across her shirtsleeve. She knew she hadn't escaped; Blaine had let her go, this time. What about next time? Would her luck hold out? She tugged Southpaw into a trot, needing to regain her self-control. She didn't want to alarm Whitey or Andy. She'd tell Whitey about this run-in with Blaine in her own time and in her own way. Whitey was getting on in years—Lord, he must be over fifty!—and he wasn't as spry anymore. He wanted to protect her, and she was afraid he'd confront Blaine and get hurt—or killed.

A few months ago, she'd promised Whitey that she'd tell him if Brickman threatened her or confronted her, and she'd keep her promise. She'd tell Whitey about Brickman's "proposal," but she'd water it down some so it'd be easier to swallow.

Bitterness tasted harsh on her tongue as she judged her chances of beating Brickman at his game. She felt so alone in her struggle, even though Whitey and Andy were on her side. They weren't family, and the Flying H was the ranch they worked, not the ranch they owned. When it came right down to the bottom line, Etta had everything to lose—her ranch, her way of life, her security, her family roots.

"Damn you, Hank," she whispered, picturing her brother's grinning, boyish face. "Why couldn't you have stayed here where you belong? Why couldn't you have thought about somebody besides yourself just once?" She jabbed her heels into Southpaw's sides and gave him his head.

"So I told him to get off my land, and I rode off," Etta said with a casual shrug. "That's all there was to it."

Whitey rode beside her astride the brown-, white-, and black-flecked pony he called Piebald. He squinted one blue eye, his expression that of disbelief. "That's all, huh? He asked you to marry him, you told him to get, and that's that."

"That's that." She bobbed her shoulders again.

"You didn't expect me to invite him to supper, did you?"

"No, but I get the feeling you ain't telling me everything."

Etta stared down at the ground to keep from facing Whitey and spotted bootheel marks and flattened grass. She jerked on the reins. Southpaw stopped and pricked his ears forward, then swung his head sideways to regard a grouping of tall cottonwoods.

"That's funny . . ."

"And don't go changing the subject," Whitey said. "What did Brickman do? Did he try anything?"

Etta flapped a hand, hushing him. "Somebody's been around here." She angled him a glance. "Are you sure you didn't check fences out this way before?"

"I'm sure. What'd you see?"

"Boot tracks."

She drew on her memory of the land. They were east of the ranch house, out where the country undulated toward the hills. Etta stared at a V-shaped copse of cottonwoods growing at the base of the foothills. They sheltered the mouth of Clearwater Spring. A few cattle mooed at them. The soft nicker of a horse floated from the trees, and a heifer swung her head toward the sound. A faint scent of woodsmoke teased Etta's nostrils. Her sixth sense kicked in.

"Somebody's camping around here," she whispered to Whitey, then directed her voice toward the trees, calling loudly, "Come on out! You know you're trespassing, so show yourself!" She reached back, resting her hand on the butt of the double-barreled shotgun hanging from her saddle.

Not a leaf stirred, but Etta knew she wasn't wrong. She could *feel* a presence. The cattle moved farther away from the cottonwoods. The horses shifted, stamping the tall grass and late-summer wildflowers. The breeze sailing in from the hills smelled dank and mossy, like autumn. Etta realized she was holding her breath and she let it out before she got dizzy.

Shadows shifted among the trees. Southpaw flung his head up, startled. Etta didn't see the man standing between the two tallest trees until Whitey issued a sound of surprise.

Etta's fingers tightened around the shotgun as the man moved from the shelter of the trees, but she relaxed when she saw that he held no weapon. Whitey urged Piebald toward him, but Etta held a tight rein on Southpaw.

"Well, hell, son, where'd you come from?" Whitey called to the man and from his tone Etta realized that he recognized the trespasser. In the next moment, so did she.

Johnny Cheyenne.

A thrill lit her heart before she could douse the flame. Placing a frown on her face, she glowered at him. Cheyenne looked from Whitey to Etta, and a smile tipped up one side of his wide mouth. Slowly, his gaze drifted to where Etta's hand lay on the rifle butt. She snatched it away. Cheyenne grinned broadly, his teeth showing white against his mahogany skin.

She should have known him instantly, she thought. He still wasn't wearing a hat. Everyone wore them nowadays, even Indians. Coonskin caps, wide-brimmed cowboy hats, ten-gallon styles, and flat-topped ones. Nobody went bareheaded; nobody except Johnny Cheyenne.

"I thought you were long gone," Whitey said, pushing his own sweat-stained hat back off his forehead so that Cheyenne could see his big, welcoming grin. "You been camping out here?"

Cheyenne nodded. He'd stopped a few feet from their horses. He wore the same clothes Etta had seen him in before, but they were wrinkled now and streaked with dirt. Bits of grass studded his blue-black hair. His gun belt hung low on his hips.

"Hell, son, why didn't you come up to the house and be civil?" Whitey chuckled, reaching out to tap Etta's shoulder with a playful fist. "We ain't got much, but we still got our hospitality, don't we, Etta Lou?"

"This land is for cattle, not trespassers," she said, steeling herself against Whitey's chastising scowl. "You pack up and move on," she told the gunslinger. She thought he'd give her a go-to-hell look, but he continued to smile cockily. "I mean it. I don't want any trouble from you, you hear?"

"You going to plug me?" he asked, smirking. Reaching around, he tugged something from his back pocket. He held it out in front of him, and Etta realized the fluttering cloth was her red bandanna. "I washed it in the stream. Most of the bloodstains came out."

The gunfight came back to her, filling her with that odd mixture of excitement and revulsion. She kneed Southpaw, and the gelding pranced forward a few steps. Leaning down, Etta took the proffered hanky. Her gaze moved to Cheyenne's wounded hand, which had been bandaged by the doctor. He held it awkwardly, as if it pained him. Then she noticed other things—a lack of luster in his eyes, an unhealthy pallor, ragged breathing, a stiff, un-natural stance.

"Are you sick?" she asked, and he shook his head quickly. Etta glanced from him to Whitey. The old man nodded, agreeing with her assess-ment. She turned toward the trespasser again. "You ought to get to another doctor. There are some in Amarillo. Or you could try the barber in Clearwater, although I can't vouch for his work. I hear he's a fair dentist and can sew up wounds in a pinch."

"Son, when did you eat last?" Whitey asked.

Cheyenne's smile seemed to be an effort now. "It's been a few hours."

"Days, maybe?" Whitey let loose a stream of to-bacco juice. "Etta, don't you think we could give him something to eat? If you don't, I will." He looked at her from beneath his snowy brows, his mouth set in a stern line.

She sighed, knowing she was whipped. "I guess, but then he should get gone from here."

Whitey grinned. "Let me help you pack up your things, partner." He swung out of the saddle and approached Cheyenne. "You look right peaked. That hand giving you trouble?" He walked into the shadows.

Cheyenne stared at Etta for a few moments longer before turning away and ducking under the lower tree limbs.

Etta swallowed hard, fighting off her flutter of nerves. Cheyenne made her uneasy just by looking at her. Of course, she could say the same about

nearly every man, but the way she felt around
Cheyenne was different. It was a flighty nervous,
like she didn't know for sure if she was about to
giggle or faint. Normally, she felt a wary nervousness around men because she'd learned not to
trust them—except for Whitey and Andy, of
course.

She listened to Whitey's jovial chatter and Cheyenne's occasional grunt and single-word answers.
When the two men emerged from the copse, Cheyenne led a big black horse with white socks and a
blazed face. Whitey strode to stand in front of
Etta's horse. He stroked Southpaw's brown nose
and angled a sly look up at Etta.

"I was thinking, sister girl . . ."

"Uh-oh. That means trouble," Etta drawled.

"Now, hold on and let me talk before you start
sassing." He glanced over at Cheyenne, who lev-
ered himself into a tooled saddle carefully, as if he
were saving what energy he had left. "Me and this
fella was talking, and I come up with a right smart
idea. Cheyenne's winged pretty bad, Etta, and it's
his gun hand. He needs a place to hole up while
his wound heals. If he stays in town, some damn
fool will come looking for him to make a name for
himself by drawing on Johnny Cheyenne, don'tcha
see?"

"That's *his* problem. He chose his life, and now
he's got to face the consequences of it." Etta kept
her expression stern, refusing to show any pity for
a man who had enticed her brother away from the
Flying H. Even so, her gaze flickered to his bandaged hand and she wondered about his wound.
Would it ever heal completely? Did she sense

worry in him? She suspected his haggard appearance could be blamed on more than hunger.

"I was thinking it would be mighty fine if Cheyenne stayed with us at the Flying H. We could use an extry cowboy."

Etta's gaze snapped back to Whitey. "Yes, we could use another cowboy, but what's that got to do with him?" She wagged her head in Cheyenne's direction. "I want the cattle roped, not shot. He won't be any use to us."

She sensed, rather than saw, Cheyenne's intense regard. She could feel his slow burn, his damning gaze, his bitter frown.

"Don't let your mouth run free until you know where it's headed," Whitey said, aiming a stubby finger at her.

Etta sighed. "What's that mean?"

"It means that you don't know anything about this fella, so you should listen before you spout off. Cheyenne used to work cattle ranches. It's been a while, but working cattle is something you don't forget how to do. Besides that," he said, raising his voice when Etta opened her mouth to protest, "his reputation will keep ... well, the wolves away from our door." He cut his blue eyes in Cheyenne's direction. "I told him about Brickman bullying you, Etta."

She sucked in a noisy breath. Color exploded in her cheeks. "What did you do that for? It's none of his business!"

"Don't get your britches in a twist, sister girl. Use your head. Having a fast gun on the ranch— especially the fast gun that killed one Brickman already—will discourage varmints from trespassing on the Flying H. We could all breathe a little easier, and we'd have another cowpoke helping us with the roundup. Don't be so proud and pig-headed that you won't even 'fess up that we've got to have another wrangler helping us this year. We got cattle up in the hills that ain't seen a rope for two years, and you know it." Whitey turned his head to spit. "Brickman knows it, too."

"I don't want to keep company with one of the outlaws who got Hank thrown in prison for bank robbery." She tipped her nose into the air. "I'm surprised you'd want to befriend him, Whitey."

"Well, I'm not surprised you're as stubborn as a jackass, but it pains me, nonetheless." He stepped around to Southpaw's side to rest a red-knuckled hand on her knee. "Etta, we got a hard winter ahead of us," he said softly, and his light blue eyes implored her, touching her heart. "I'm not a young rooster anymore, and Andy's not seasoned enough to be put in charge of the roundup. Brickman's going to do what he can to make sure you fail, and I can't fight him alone. It'd break my heart in two if something happened to you on my watch."

He paused, his lips twitching with emotion. He cleared his throat and spit tobacco juice on the ground between his dusty boots. "Now, Cheyenne needs a place to lie low and heal up, and we need a young buck to make the skin crawl between Brickman's legs. Not many bucks can do that, but Johnny Cheyenne can because he already sent one Brickman to an early grave." He winked and gave her a lopsided grin. "Do this for me, sister girl."

Etta pursed her lips in consternation. She glanced upward for guidance, then over at Cheyenne. He sat astride his spirited gelding, head bent, but shoulders proudly squared. She figured he was listening to every word. Probably gloating, too, she thought. Whitey squeezed her knee, pressing for her answer.

"Oh, great goblins and goose fat," she blurted out, hating to admit that Whitey's idea had merit. They could use another cowpuncher, and Brickman just might keep his distance from the gunslinger. She eyed Cheyenne again, catching the slight tremor in his injured hand as he stroked his horse's black mane. Her heart melted. "He can stay—as long as he earns his keep," she tacked on quickly. "I run a ranch, not an infirmary."

Cheyenne's deep-socketed eyes shifted to her. He dipped his head ever so slightly. "Don't you worry. I'll earn my keep. I've never accepted charity and I'm not likely to start now."

"And I don't want you bringing more trouble down on our heads. If any marshals come snooping around, I expect you to get."

"I'm not wanted for any crime," Cheyenne said, crossing his wrists on top of the saddle horn. Etta noticed that the bandage on his hand needed changing. It was no longer white, but gray, and a rusty stain had seeped through the top of it. "Any fight I've been in, I've won fair and square."

Etta stared at him dubiously. "He can stay in the tack room with you and Andy," she told Whitey.

The old man chuckled, slapped Etta's knee, then swung up into the saddle of his own gentle mare.

"Let's get back to the house. It's suppertime, and this young fella's got an empty gullet."

Etta motioned for them to go on. "You feed him. I'm going to check on the rest of the fences out here."

Whitey's bushy brows met in a frown. "We can do that tomorrow."

"Or I can do it now, and I'm going to do it now," she said sharply, then tapped her heels against Southpaw and rode away before Whitey could continue his objections.

"Damn nuisance," she muttered, thinking of the infamous gunfighter. "He'd better know how to rope and ride or I'll send him packing, no matter how Whitey feels about it."

Wonder what Brickman will think when he hears that his brother's killer is riding for the Flying H, Etta mused, then grinned. Lordy, she hoped it put a hitch in his get-along and a big old knot in his gut!

She reined Southpaw on a rise and looked back. Whitey and Cheyenne rode side by side in the direction of the ranch, their shadows moving ahead of them. Cheyenne's stretched a lot farther and was twice as wide as Whitey's.

Casts a big shadow, she thought, then reflected on how nice it would be to hide in it from Brickman for a spell. Her shoulders sagged with weariness. It had been so long since she'd felt safe, secure; not since before her father had died nearly a year ago. She tore her gaze from Cheyenne and denied the soft yearning within her.

She couldn't trust that gunfighter, she reminded herself. Why, he was no better than Blaine

Brickman! They were both bullies who solved their problems with bullets and bloodshed.

I'm just fighting fire with fire, she told herself with a confident nod. And as long as she stayed well clear of Cheyenne, she wouldn't get burned.

Chapter 3

The tack room was fairly roomy, but it wasn't meant to sleep three grown men. Cheyenne examined the narrow cots. He'd sooner sleep on the floor. Hardly listening to Whitey's idle chatter, he sensed Andy's keen regard. The youngster filled the corner like a shadow. His dark skin gleamed with sweat, and his brown eyes reminded Cheyenne of a curious deer. Cheyenne moved toward him. The boy twitched and squeezed his skinny body more tightly into the corner.

"He don't bite, Andy," Whitey said with a broad grin. "Andy's just learning how to cowboy, and he's coming along right nice."

"Got any Indian in you?" Cheyenne asked. "Creek, maybe?"

Andy shook his head. His throat flexed and the knob in it slid down and back up like a cork. "Not th-that I know of, Mr. Chey-Cheyenne."

"Cheyenne will do me." Cheyenne yanked the three-point Hudson Bay blanket off the bunk.

"H-how many men you killed?" Andy asked, his gaze slipping to the notched strap hanging from Cheyenne's belt.

"Enough," Cheyenne answered, folding the blanket and tucking it under one arm. "Tight quarters in here, and I'm a big man who needs a big space. I believe I'll sleep in the hayloft."

"You're a big fella for sure," Whitey agreed. He

39

motioned to one of the four bunks attached to the walls. "Just remember, you're more than welcome in here with us. We'll be glad for the company."

"Thanks, but I'm used to being on my own." He hoisted his saddlebags over his shoulder with his good hand. "I'll leave the rest of my tack in here, if it's okay."

"Sure thing." Whitey gave a wink. "How about some vittles? You look like you might drop where you're standing, son. You hungry, sick, or both?"

"Food will fix up me."

"I got some stew inside the house." Whitey planted a hand on Cheyenne's shoulder. "Glad you decided to stay for a while. Etta would never admit it, but she needs a young buck like you around."

Cheyenne darted a look at him. "I'm only staying until I'm healed up. After the roundup, I'll be on my way."

"I hear ya."

Cheyenne walked alongside the old man, noting his rocking, stiff-legged gait. "You've ridden so many rank nags, you've sprung your joints, old-timer."

Whitey wheezed a laugh. "That's for sure, young fella."

"How long have you been riding this particular range?"

"Twenty-two years, off and on. Mostly on."

"That makes you part of the family, I guess."

"Yep. Etta and Hank are the onliest ones I think of as family, now that Henry's gone. Henry was their father. He passed on about a year ago."

A long-haired yellow dog ambled toward them,

her belly full of puppies. Whitey spoke softly to the bitch dog, and she wagged her tail.

"Looks like she's about ready to drop her litter."

"Yep, she's due any day. This is Butter. Bounder is around here somewhere." He straightened from petting the dog. "Bounder's part bird dog and part sheepherding dog. Helluva mess, but good with cattle and horses. Hank brought home Butter and Bounder when they was pups. He got them from one of his girlfriends. Thought he'd breed them and make money. Hank's always dreaming up ways to make money without breaking a sweat."

"How long has it been since you've seen him?"

A shadow passed over the older man's face. "The day he was sentenced to prison. That was the last time. The trip to Illinois is so long and hard, and we've got so much to do here all the time . . ." He shrugged. "Besides, I don't think Hank much wants us to visit him at the prison. He ain't proud to be there."

The house Cheyenne approached was as plain as a brown wrapper. He looked up at the second floor with its narrow windows and black shutters, then down at a square porch that jutted from the front of the house. Three rockers stood in a line like soldiers. A stained spittoon was set discreetly behind an empty flower box. Cheyenne stepped up onto the bare-board porch and glanced inside the box. A few brown vines stretched across the dry dirt. He turned to take in the view. Not much, he thought of the flat, featureless acres. A red-roofed chicken coop off to one side provided shelter for a couple dozen hens and a red-combed rooster. A windmill turned slowly in the breeze, crying out for gear grease.

"She lives here by herself now?" Cheyenne asked.

"Etta?" Whitey glanced over his shoulder to catch Cheyenne's nod, then pulled open the screen door. "Yep. Lives a right quiet life. All she does is work like a pack mule all day and read books most of the night. Gonna put her eyes out if she don't watch it."

Cheyenne stepped inside the dark house. He smelled lilac water first, then parchment. His eyes grew accustomed to the dim interior, and he blinked in amazement. Books. So many books, Cheyenne couldn't imagine where she could have gotten them all. They lined shelves built on three walls of the front parlor. They formed stacks on and under every table. They lay open beside candles and oil lamps and windows. Beside him, Whitey chuckled, and Cheyenne realized he'd come to an abrupt halt.

"Ever see so many in all your born days?" The old man laughed and whacked his knee with an open palm. "And she's read every last one of 'em. Some more than once! I can't figure why she keeps them after she's read them, but she says she can't part with even one because she might want to read it again someday. Most of them are love stories. Some are bunches of poems. She calls them collections, I think." He flapped a hand, dismissing the literature. "Woman stuff."

Cheyenne reached for the nearest volume and turned the spine to catch the feeble light from the window. *Love's Lost Flower.* He replaced the book on its stack, and revised his opinion of Etta Hollister. He wouldn't have pegged her for a bleeding-heart romantic. He caught the aroma of food and sniffed. A weakness stole through him. He gripped the arm of a dingy medallion-backed sofa.

"Stew's hanging over the fire in the kitchen back here," Whitey said, motioning for him. "Got some bacon and biscuits left over from breakfast, too. You sit yourself at the table, and I'll dish some up."

Cheyenne swung a leg over the back of one of the chairs and sat before the linen-draped table. He grabbed a biscuit and a flap of thick bacon, his mouth watering, and made a sandwich. The first bite was so good he thought he might faint. Godamighty, he was hungry! His teeth tore at the biscuit and bacon; then he stuffed the rest of it into his mouth. His eyes watered. His stomach tightened, desperate for the morsels. He made another sandwich and ate it before Whitey placed a big bowl of steaming stew in front of him.

"I'll fetch you some water," Whitey said, moving to the dry sink.

Cheyenne couldn't remember food ever tasting so good. The stew was thick with beef and vegetables, seasoned with ground pepper and mustard seeds. He hunched over the bowl, intent on shoveling one spoonful after another into his mouth. Whitey set a mug of water at his elbow, but Cheyenne didn't stop to drink any of it until he'd finished the stew.

"Want more?" Whitey asked.

"If you don't mind."

"Don't mind a'tall." Whitey grinned, his mustache bristling. "Your gut was plumb empty, wasn't it?"

Cheyenne drank the water in six long swallows.

He passed the back of his sleeve over his mouth and closed his eyes. His arms and legs tingled as the strength began to return to them. His injured hand throbbed with his heartbeat. His head cleared. When he opened his eyes, his vision had sharpened to reveal that Whitey wasn't as old as he'd first thought. No more than fifty, he decided. The old boy's face had as many lines as a thumbprint, but his pale blue eyes were youthful.

Whitey replenished the stew bowl, then sat across from him to watch him eat. He sipped at a steaming mug of coffee, and those dancing blue eyes missed nothing.

Cheyenne took his time with the second helping, chewing each slice of lean beef and chunky potato and carrot thoroughly, giving the old cowhand a good show.

"Did you make this stew?" he asked around a mouthful.

Whitey chuckled. "Shoot, no. I don't cook up nothing but tall tales. Etta threw it together. She's a good pot cooker. You know, things like beans and stew. Makes a fair breakfast, and most holidays she whips up some mighty fine pies. She just don't have much time for fancy meals."

"Why doesn't she sell out and go somewhere else where life is easier?"

"And where is that? I ain't never seen that place."

Cheyenne bobbed an eyebrow in agreement. "Maybe not easier, but better for a woman."

"All she's ever known is this ranch. I reckon she can't bear to think of leaving it. Henry was always so proud of the place." Whitey stared into the stained mug. "Etta would feel like she'd failed him if she lost the Flying H. Besides, she's happy here."

"She is? She sure doesn't act happy. She ever smile?"

"Sure." Whitey scratched at his whiskers. "But not much lately. How about you? You ever smile? And you can't count that sneer you're so good at."

Cheyenne pushed himself back from the table, laying a hand on his stomach. "I've been accused of smiling now and then." He leaned on his elbows, going eye to eye with the older man. "Say what's the other Brickman like? Is he as scant-brained as his brother?"

Whitey's face tightened, and some of the sparkle left his eyes. He looked away, but Cheyenne had seen enough.

"Blaine's a braggart like Ben, and he loves to throw his weight around. But he ain't never been accused of being scant-brained. Nope. Smart and mean, that's what he is."

"That's a bad combination. Worse than dumb and mean."

Whitey nodded. "Much worse. You tread on him, you done stepped on a rattlesnake, boy."

Cheyenne sprawled in the chair. "Well, I killed his brother, so I guess I've riled him." He reached into his pocket for a matchstick and clamped his teeth down on it. He noted that Whitey had fished out his tobacco pouch.

"I thought you was gonna smoke."

Cheyenne shook his head.

"Wanta chew?" Whitey offered the stained pouch.

Cheyenne shook his head again. "Never acquired a taste for it."

"Not even in a peace pipe?" Whitey grinned, taking the sting from his words. "You raised Indian or white?"

"Indian."

Whitey lifted his bushy brows in surprise. "I woulda thought white. You ain't got any accent."

"My mother's parents spoke English. Her father was a white missionary. I was taught the Cheyenne language, English, and French."

"Shoot. You got more education than anybody around these parts." Whitey squinted one eye. "Can you write and do figures?"

Cheyenne nodded.

"Holy smokes, son. You're the town genius!"

Cheyenne bit down hard on the matchstick to keep from grinning, then wondered why. Habit, he surmised. Playing everything close to the vest and not revealing his true feelings had become second nature. He let go of the grin, feeling it grow on his lips and crinkle the corners of his eyes.

"Say, how well did you get to know Hank?"

"Pretty well, I guess. We rode together for a couple of months before they pulled that bank job."

"You weren't along on that one?"

"I never went along on those. I earned a good enough living with my gun. I didn't need to rob banks and stages."

"How come you took up with the Nelson gang, then?"

"Jeb Nelson taught me the fast draw. He's pretty fast himself, but I took to it like a duck to water. We became friends." Cheyenne tried to wiggle his fingers again. Fiery pain raced up his arm. "But we had a falling-out over Hank. They could have watched out for him better. He was green, and they knew it."

Whitey ran a hand over his bristling whiskers. "Yep, but he was growed, too. He knew there would be a price to pay for breaking the law."

The front door squeaked open and slammed shut. Cheyenne smelled Etta before she came into the kitchen. Does she know that she has her own scent? he wondered. Leather and lace. Leather from the hours she spent in the saddle, and lace from the toilet water she must splash on after her morning wash. Or did she wash up at night? He glanced from the corner of his eye at her shining blond hair and freckled nose. Morning, he decided. She probably rises a couple of hours before the sun so she can take her time with her toiletries.

He noticed that she tried hard not to look in his direction. She poured herself a glass of water and drank it thirstily. Cheyenne saw stubborn pride in the squareness of her shoulders and the stiffness of her spine. But he also saw vulnerability in the slight tremor of her hand when she touched the back of it to her wet lips.

"Did you two finish off that stew, or did you remember to save some for me and Andy?" She kept her back to them and stared out the kitchen window.

"We saved you a spoonful or two." Whitey stuffed a pinch of tobacco into his mouth. "I didn't eat any yet. I was waiting for you. Check those fences?"

"Sure did." She flung her long braid over her shoulder. The rope of light blond hair swung against her back like a clock's pendulum. "I'll feed the horses, then I'll come in for supper."

"I'll feed them." Whitey started to stand, but Etta clamped a hand on his shoulder and shoved him back into his chair.

"No! I'll do it. You ... you see to ... this ... him." She gave a curt nod toward Cheyenne. "The new hand."

Cheyenne rolled his gaze toward her, irritated with her long pauses. "Saying my name would save your breath, Miss Etta. *Cheyenne.*" He finally caught her gaze. Her eyes were dark green. "It won't break your jaw to say my name, will it?"

Her lips formed a formidable line. "Cheyenne." It sounded like blasphemy when she said it. She strode out of the room. The slamming front door signaled her departure.

"She don't mean to be so snippy," Whitey said. "She's just got a lot on her mind."

"Don't we all." Cheyenne flexed his gun hand against the burning pain shooting up his arm. His fingers barely moved, although he sent urgent messages for them to make a fist. "Don't we all."

Etta set aside the book of poetry she'd been reading, and rubbed her eyes with her forefinger and thumb. Quiet settled around her like a cloak—a heavy, oppressive cloak. The poems she had read tonight had spoken of family, love, and security. Tears stung her eyes as self-pity welled in her chest. It had been so long since she'd felt sheltered by family that it seemed a lifetime ago.

Her mother, Maridell, had been a serene beauty, but Etta could barely recall her. She'd had long blond hair that she'd worn in a braided crown atop her small head. Her voice, Etta recalled, had been as soft as goose down. But Maridell had died young, giving birth to the son whom Henry Hollister had wanted at all costs. Even if it meant the boy would be raised motherless.

Looking back on it all now, Etta figured Hank was what writers called "poetic justice." He had refused to be molded into the son Henry Hollister had dreamed of for so many years. Wild and restless, Hank was the opposite of his staid and straitlaced father.

Etta was more like Henry, but her father had never been interested enough to really look at her and recognize his influence in her responsible attitude and cool head. He never saw that she loved the land and the ranch life, that she loved him with all her being, that she was born to a saddle and with a rope in her hand. Of course, after Brickman had ruined everything, all Henry had seen when he looked at her was her betrayal and his shame.

She turned down the wick in the lamp next to her, then pulled her braid around and began loosening it. Her fingers worked automatically, the simple task calming her. For a few moments, she imagined a man's fingers performing this ritual, and smiled at how the image transformed the mundane into something incredibly sensual. Silly to indulge in such frivolity, she told herself. She would never have a man to call her own. Nobody of any account would have her.

But the need to dream persisted. She closed her eyes, relaxing, letting it come. In her mind's eye she saw his hands moving through her hair, combing out the tangles, caressing the shiny strands. Big hands with blunt-tipped fingers. Her vision moved up to his wrists and muscled forearms.

Black hairs lay against his sun-weathered skin. Up, up to bulging upper arms and gleaming shoulders. Finally, his face. Hawk-nosed, night-blue eyes, straight black hair.

With a startled gasp, Etta opened her eyes and sat up. She covered her heart with her hands, alarmed at its rapid pace. Why in the world had she imagined *him* unbraiding her hair? Johnny Cheyenne, of all people! Why, he was no better than a common murderer or thief.

Etta smoothed her hair back, trying to compose herself, while her mind bedeviled her with flashes of Johnny Cheyenne's enigmatic face, muscled arms, blue-black hair, and the sound of his deep, rumbling voice. She stood and crossed the book-crowded room to the front window. Looking out on the moon-splashed porch and yard, she found herself wondering who had raised Johnny Cheyenne and whence he'd sprung. She fancied he'd been born in a tepee on a windswept prairie, born of an Indian maiden, sired by an Indian brave.

No, that's wrong, she thought, recalling his dark blue eyes. Where'd he get those? He had white blood in him. Maybe more white than Indian.

"Oh, why am I wasting my time thinking about him?" she grumbled, whirling away from the window and grabbing up a lantern. "I surely have better things to do."

She pushed open the screen door and let it slam behind her. Swinging the lantern, she hopped off the porch and walked briskly toward the barn to check on Butter. The retriever might have her pups tonight, Etta thought, remembering how slowly Butter had been moving earlier.

The barn door was cracked open. Etta hooked a

hand around the edge of it and gave a yank. It opened with a rumble of hinges and rattle of chains. Inside, she heard Butter whine. Lifting the lantern, she located the canine. Butter slapped her tail against the hay and panted. Etta crouched beside her to lay her hand against the dog's bulging belly. Puppies moved against her palm, but Butter didn't seem to be in distress.

Etta clucked her tongue against the roof of her mouth. Butter tried to lick her face, but Etta dodged her, laughing quietly. Suddenly Butter lifted her head and pricked her ears. She looked up, alerted to something behind Etta. Etta swiveled around on the balls of her feet to see what had captured Butter's attention. Sometimes snakes wound themselves in the rafters and—

Her thoughts stumbled to a halt as her eyes widened. Johnny Cheyenne stood in the loft, legs apart, lit by a lantern hanging in the crook of his fingers. He wore nothing except a curious expression, and Etta couldn't take her eyes from him. She was barely aware of straightening to stand, head tilted back, lips parted.

Magnificent came to mind as she admired his bronzed body. A thin flame ran under her skin. She felt as if her tongue was broken because she couldn't speak. Nor could she move. She could only stare, her mouth slightly agape, her breathing shallow and fast.

She could tell by his expression that she'd startled him. He moved his free hand, the bandaged one, toward his exposed self instinctively, but then he stopped himself. She saw him relax, saw his expression change from alarmed to expectant.

Knowing she should turn away, Etta found she

couldn't. Never had she seen such perfection, and she studied him as she would a statue in a museum. She perused his massive shoulders and wide chest. She beheld his taut stomach, ridged with muscle. She scanned the slick black hairs swirling over his chest, legs, and arms. She heeded his man's organ, thick and veined, bobbing slightly in response to her avid attention.

He looked so comfortable, so capable, so utterly unconcerned with her bold appraisal. She had seen the nude male body before, but never one so beautiful, so virile. A trembling commenced within her. Her eyes burned. Yearning, strong and forbidden, coiled in her stomach and wound around her heart.

Slowly, teasingly, he reached for a blanket hanging from a peg near him. He set the lantern at his feet and wrapped the wool blanket around his waist, covering himself. A smile touched his wide mouth.

"Did you get what you came for?" he asked, his voice husky. "Or is there something else on your mind?"

His questions galvanized her. She looked away and retreated toward the open barn door.

"I was just . . . just . . ."

"Just what?" he prodded.

"Checking on the dog. She's going to have puppies."

"I know. I'll keep an eye on her for you."

She looked at him again. He was still smiling. The lamplight reached up, stroking his shoulders and chest with amber fingers. Her heart boomed in her chest, so loud she was certain he could hear it, too. "What are you doing up there? Why aren't you in the tack room?" She spoke too loudly, trying to be heard above her heartbeats.

"I'm going to sleep here, if that's okay with you." His voice was soft and caressing.

Etta shrugged, suddenly desperate to remove herself from the situation before he recognized how nonplussed she was to have so boldly examined him. She should have looked away. She should have scolded him severely for showing himself to her. Any lady would have behaved with more alarm, more affront. Lady? Etta scoffed inwardly. Well, it had been a while since anybody had thought of her as a lady. She guessed her behavior just now proved everyone right.

"I don't care where you sleep," she said tersely. "Might get cold in here, though."

"I'll be fine." His voice held amusement. "I don't want you to worry about me, Etta, you hear? Don't you lose a wink of sleep over me."

She jerked back her head, sending him a dark glare. "I won't, and if you think I might, then you're a bigger fool than I thought."

He chuckled, laughing at her. "I'm no fool, boss lady."

She swung her gaze to Butter, who was still slapping the straw with her tail. " 'Night, sweetie," she said.

"Good night."

Frowning, she moved outside. "I wasn't talking to you," she groused. "I was talking to the dog." She closed the door behind her with a disgusted grunt.

Cheyenne listened until he could no longer hear her footsteps; then he removed the blanket and spread it on top of the pallet he'd made earlier. He sat on it, laughing softly. What a foul-tempered porcupine of a woman! But then again, she was a constant surprise to him. He would have bet money that she would have shrieked and fled from the sight of his nakedness. But not Etta Hollister. Nope. She'd stared at him long and hard, taking inventory, committing him to memory. He liked that. And despite her glowering and snappish ways, he liked her. She had grit.

Quite a woman, he thought with a chuckle. Yes, she was quite a woman. He lay on his back and released a long sigh. Too bad she hated his guts.

Chapter 4

Swinging down from the saddle, Cheyenne rubbed the small of his back. His butt was numb. The rest of him burned and ached from the hours he'd spent in the saddle. After just one day of rounding up cattle on the flat Texas range, he felt like he'd been dragged behind his horse. He removed his gloves, tucked them under his fancy belt of linked silver disks, and inspected the calluses on his good hand. The bandage on the other was streaked with dirt and grime. The skin around the stitches throbbed. He wondered if the wound was worse instead of better. Maybe that's why his fingers were so stiff and nearly useless. He couldn't even throw a rope with it.

Etta rode into the corral on her feisty red-brown gelding. Sweat made her checked shirt stick to her back and breasts. Her brown felt hat showed sweat stains, too. Cheyenne had tried to keep up with her since sunup, and she had ridden him ragged. She had to be tired, because he was plumb tuckered out. He knew his wound had depleted his usual vigor, and he was still a little weak from the loss of blood and going without food for a couple of days, but he refused to use those as excuses. If ever there was a woman who could run a ranch as well as a man, it had to be Etta Hollister. She rode and roped better than any man he'd ever known. And he'd ridden with some legends.

Cheyenne forced one boot in front of the other, advancing toward her. She ignored him as she swung her leg over the saddle, her back to him. He reached up and spanned her waist. His fingertips found her ribs, and his palms and thumbs discovered the suppleness of her back. She stiffened and wrenched herself from his grasp. Irritation sparked in her forest-green eyes. She pushed her hat off and it dangled against her back from the chin strap. The hair around her face was honey-blond and damp.

"Just what do you think you're doing?"

Cheyenne held up his hands in surrender. "I was only helping you off your horse."

"I don't need help," she said, almost spitting the words at him. "I've been getting on and off a horse by myself ever since I was a tadpole. Keep your hands to yourself."

"You sure make it hard for a man to be nice to you."

"I'm not interested in you being nice. All I ask is that you earn your keep around here." She yanked off her gloves and slapped them in one palm. "And I think you should be more careful."

"Careful?"

"You shouldn't be parading around in your altogether. It's not decent."

He bit his lower lip to keep from smirking. "Maybe you should announce yourself before you sneak up on a man."

"Sneak?" she repeated, slashing him with a cutting glare. "That barn is mine. I can go in there anytime I like. You're supposed to be bedding down in the tack room."

"Well, now you know different, so don't come

snooping around late at night unless you want another look at me, bossy."

Her eyes threw fire at him. "My name is Etta."

"Right. Henryetta Louise."

"Who told you my given name?" she demanded, glancing toward Whitey, who had just ridden up with Andy.

"Hank. Louise was your mother's mother. You and Hank are both named after your old man. Some would say that was a mark of vanity on his part."

"At least I have a *real* name, and not some outlaw's version of one. I guess you figured that 'Johnny Cheyenne' would look good on a Wanted poster." She delivered a wincing smile, then let it drop. Looking at him through the veil of her sable lashes, she cleared her throat nervously. "You don't talk Indian. You sound more like a Johnny Reb than a Johnny Cheyenne."

"Would you like me better if I talked funny?" He tapped the center of his chest with his fist and fixed a stern expression on his face. "I Cheyenne. I no like woman with tongue as sharp as serpent's tooth. If she wantum Indian brave to work plenty much for her, she better start talking to him like him is man and not stray dog." He bent his knees to witness the beginning of a genuine smile hovering at the corners of her mouth. "Do I fit your idea of a half-breed now? Maybe I should paint my face and carry a tomahawk."

"Maybe you should quit putting words in my mouth." She shouldered past him. "I was just making an observation. You can grow horns and a tail for all I care."

He gathered up the reins of her horse. "I'll see to the horses. You see to the grub."

"I give the orders around here."

She was damn pretty with red flags flying in her cheeks and her eyes spitting fire. He caught the end of her braid in his free hand and gave it a playful tug. "You might be a man-eater, boss lady, but you'll find me a tough piece of gristle to chew."

She flung back her head, and the braid slipped from his fingertips. Whitey joined them, giving both of them long, calculating looks.

"My backside's dragged and my stomach's growling. How about something besides stew?"

"We got enough stew left over for one more night."

"Some other night, Etta. My mouth's hankering for chicken. I'll catch one and pluck it for you."

She gave him a curious look. "Chicken? It's not Sunday. We never have fried chicken unless it's Sunday."

"I'll say a prayer before I wring the hen's neck. Will that suit ya?"

Cheyenne grinned, liking the old boy's wit and the way he always managed to get Etta's goat.

Whitey turned Etta in the direction of the house and gave her a push. "Go on, now. Nobody's going to hell for eating chicken in the middle of the week."

"All right, all right." She stomped toward the house, arms swinging, her hat bouncing against her back.

Watching her, Whitey chuckled. "Ain't she a rip-snorter?"

"She sure knows how to ride, rope, and bitch."

Cheyenne loosened the saddle on his horse and rocked it back and forth to give Lariat a bit of relief. "She goes around puffed up like a green bronc on a cold morning."

Whitey chuckled. "Damn if you ain't right! Well, I gotta strangle a hen. See to my horse, won't you, son?"

Cheyenne nodded, grabbing the reins of Whitey's piebald mare and his own black gelding. He led the horses to the barn, where Andy was already brushing down his brown pony.

"That little broomtail of yours is as fast as greased lightning," Cheyenne noted as he guided the horses into their stalls. "Brush down Piebald while I see to Lariat and Southpaw."

"Yes, sir."

"And call me Cheyenne." He glanced sharply at the boy. "Don't make me tell you that again."

Andy gulped. "Okay . . . Cheyenne."

Cheyenne nodded, satisfied. He slid the saddles off Southpaw and Lariat. Ironically, Etta's saddle was of the Cheyenne style. All business. His was Texas style with Mexican and Indian influences. All flash.

Her brown saddle sported little tooling—a simple rose etched in the padded seat and some leaves running up the cantle—and minimal fuss of ties and rigging rings. His black saddle sparkled with silver disks, each decorated with bits of turquoise in the center. Eagle and hawk feathers trailed from them. Indian beadwork in black, white, and red dangled from studs and silver rings. Intricate Cheyenne beading edged the latigo and horn. His initials had been scored in the leather fenders. A saddle fit for a famous gun-slinger, not for a cattle-drive cowboy.

"Who was the first man you killed?" Andy asked from the next stall.

Cheyenne ran a hand down Lariat's wet back. His horse wasn't used to driving cattle either, but Lariat had held up better than the man who had ridden him. Cheyenne's backside tingled and burned. His spine felt like it was made of broken glass.

"Cheyenne? Did you hear me?" Andy persisted.

"If you and me are going to be saddle pals, we need to get something straight. I don't brag about men I've killed. I leave that for other people to discuss. Doesn't interest me one lick."

"Okay. I was just wondering . . ."

"How long you been working on the Flying H?"

"A little over a year. My folks got thirteen other kids, and I needed to make my own way. Etta and Whitey took me in. They're teaching me cowboy-ing."

"Looks like you learn fast." Cheyenne grunted as he bent to massage Lariat's front legs.

"You sore?" Andy asked, stepping around into the same stall. He grinned, showing off healthy, square teeth.

"Sore as a saloon tart after her first night up-stairs." Cheyenne laughed softly as the boy ducked his head. "You ever been with a girl, Andy?"

"Nah." Andy leaned back against the bare-board wall. "I'm too busy."

Cheyenne released a harsh laugh. "I hope I never get that busy."

"Ain't many darkies around here. The only Negro girl I know of works as a maid in the hotel. I think she's five or six years older than me. And I ain't seen any Indian girls in Clearwater."

"I'm not picky about colors. They're all the same shade in the dark, pal." Cheyenne sent him a wink as he moved from Lariat to Etta's Southpaw. "I don't care if they're white, brown, black, or yellow. If they're double-breasted and warm-blooded, I'll hop right on and give them a good ride."

Andy's eyes bulged in their sockets. He turned away, grabbing a brush and going back to Piebald and his own Nugget.

Cheyenne smiled to himself, tickled at the youngster's embarrassment. He'd been just like him when he'd taken up with Quint Donahue, a fur-trading liar of repute. Cheyenne recalled Quint's barrel-chested laugh and booming voice. He'd taught Cheyenne how to joke and poke fun, and he'd given him his first female. She'd been a friend of Quint's, some twenty years Cheyenne's senior, but no matter. She'd been patient and generous, never once laughing at him or making him feel inadequate.

Bless her heart, Cheyenne thought with a warm chuckle. She'd surely had reason to complain, but she hadn't. She'd guided him, instructed him, and whispered encouragement as he'd groped and panted and pulled his trigger almost at the same second he'd entered her.

Of course, time and experience had changed all that. Now he didn't worry about leaving a woman unsatisfied. He always left them smiling and asking him to come again and again. He grinned at his thoughts and felt his manhood stir.

Southpaw shifted restlessly. Cheyenne patted

the gelding's russet rump, then reached for the feed bucket. He poured grain into the trough, and Southpaw and Lariat came forward to inhale it. While the horses chomped, Cheyenne unwrapped his wounded hand. He held it up to catch the late afternoon light. The skin around the stitches was purple and yellow. A clear fluid oozed from one corner. He tried to make a tight fist, but couldn't.

He cursed, hearing the doctor's warning again, circling in his head like a mad wasp.

There's a chance you might not gain complete use of this hand again. Nerve damage . . . time will tell.

Andy sidled up to him. "Can I have a look at it?"

Cheyenne shrugged and held out his hand. "Not much to see. Hurts like hell."

Andy knitted his brows. "It don't look good. You ought to have Etta tend to it."

Cheyenne shook his head. "I value my skin. No telling what that gal would do to me."

"Awww, she wouldn't do nothing but help you. Etta talks tough, but she's a good person. She don't like for anything to suffer." Andy gave him an earnest look. "You ought to let her see to it, no foolin'. She's got all kinds of salves and medicines. She can fix you up."

Cheyenne waved his hand back and forth, cooling the fevered flesh. "I'm going to leave the bandage off for a while and see if that helps it."

"Whitey says your hand might not heal up all the way. Your gun hand, ain't it?"

"That's right." Cheyenne turned away from the boy. Doubt shadowed his soul. "By the time we get the cattle rounded up and branded, I'll be well and fit and on my way to Mexico and Rosalita."

"Who's that? Your gal?"

"One of them. She runs a cantina in Chihuahua, and she's holding some money for me."

"Ain't you worried about Mr. Brickman?"

"Why should I be worried about a dead man?"

"I mean the live one. Mr. Blaine Brickman. You killed his brother, and I bet he ain't too happy 'bout it. He might come looking for you."

"Let him come. If he pulls his sharpshooter on me, I'll fill him so full of lead, you can melt him down for bullets."

Andy's eyes grew round; then he snickered and covered his grinning mouth with both hands. He stumbled out of the stall and toward sunlight, his eyes tearing with mirth. "I got to tell Whitey what you said. He'll bust a gut." He loped toward the chicken coop.

Cheyenne smiled, feeling good until he looked down at his useless hand. His smile slipped and his humor faded. What in hell would he do if he didn't get his gun hand back? He'd be just another no-account half-breed.

He could bluff a gullible boy, but he sure couldn't fool himself. If someone drew on him right now, Cheyenne would have to be put to bed with a pick and a shovel. He couldn't even hold a gun properly, much less shoot one.

And if such news ever spread, he'd have all the gun-toting saddle bums from here to the Rockies looking for him and calling him out so that they could make their reputations off him.

Thinking about that diminished his pride enough to allow him to ponder how he'd ask Etta Hollister to doctor his hand. He'd have to approach her during dinner, before she banished him

and the others to the barn and tack room. It
wouldn't be easy. He'd learned one truth about
her—nothing concerning Etta Hollister was ever
easy.

Cheyenne stared across the table at the spine of
the book. *Sweet Passion's Song.* He could barely see
the top of Etta's blond head. She gripped the book
in one hand while she ate with the other. The fried
chicken, potatoes, gravy, and sweet corn were going fast. Whitey and Andy were downing their
third pieces of chicken. Cheyenne grabbed his second drumstick.

So far, since they'd sat down at the table, Etta
hadn't lowered her reading material. She had
mumbled a halfhearted apology/explanation for
her rudeness—"Y'all talk. I'll read. Don't pay me
no mind"—and had disappeared behind the pages
of *Sweet Passion's Song.* Cheyenne wondered what
she'd do if he suddenly ripped the book from her
hand and threw it across the room. He was
tempted, but he figured she wouldn't want to doctor his hand afterward.

"Lord have mercy, this is good grub," Whitey
said, spilling another spoonful of kernels into his
tin plate. "You got a good scald on this corn, Etta.
Nothing tastier than skillet-fried corn." He received a grunt from Etta. "You getting enough to
eat there, Cheyenne? Help yourself or starve.
That's the Golden Rule at this here supper table."

Cheyenne rested his injured hand alongside his
plate, then inched it closer to the center of the table and closer to Etta's tin cup. He'd noticed that
she never looked when she lifted the cup, drank

from it, and set it down. If he could time it just right ...

She groped, found the cup, and brought it up and around the book to her lips. He heard her slurp; then the cup came back around. She lowered it. Cheyenne repositioned his hand. The cup settled squarely on top of his wound.

"Owww, damn it to hell!" he squalled, and the literary wall came tumbling down. He thought she'd be contrite and full of apology, but he forgot he was dealing with Etta Hollister.

"Why in tarnation is your bad hand sticking way over here on my side of the table?" she demanded crossly. "It'll never heal if you don't keep it out of everyone's way."

"Why don't you watch what you're doing instead of burying your nose in that book?" He cradled his hand, which felt as hot as a flatiron. "My wound isn't healing like it should, and you sure didn't help it any just now."

Etta dropped her gaze to his injury. "Why isn't it bandaged?"

"I took that off. I thought it needed air."

"Air? Dirt, you mean. Before you know it, it'll rot off. You'd better keep it covered."

"It needs more than a bandage. The skin's looking sick. Do you keep a medicine bag around here?"

"Medicine bag?" she parroted, cocking her head to one side. "You mean, like Indians?"

Impatience blazed through him. "No, I don't mean like Indians," he mocked. "I mean like a doctor. If I wanted Indian medicine, I wouldn't be asking *you* for it, would I?"

"You don't have to be so grouchy."

"Neither do you." He matched her, glare for glare.

Whitey stood and went to the cupboard above the dry sink. He pushed bowls and cups aside and pulled out a black tin box with a red lid. Without a word, he placed it on the table next to Etta, then resumed his seat.

"I don't reckon Cheyenne will rope too good if his hand rots off. Guess you'd better see to it, Etta. Come on, Andy, let's feed the dogs these leavings." Whitey scraped the bones into his plate, then the few kernels of remaining corn and slices of potatoes.

He and Andy plucked their hats off the hall tree and took their leave.

Etta folded her arms and sat back in the chair to study the man seated across from her. The one thing she'd tried to avoid had happened. She was alone with him. Damn Whitey! He knew good and well that she didn't want Johnny Cheyenne's company. And she sure didn't want to touch him, which she would have to do to doctor his maimed hand.

She didn't like the prideful glint in his eyes or the smirk poking at one corner of his mouth. She knew she shouldn't be so obstinate, but she felt that she was compromising her principles by administering to him. He was nothing but a heartless gunslinger. He'd given his word to stick around until the end of the roundup, but she honestly didn't think he'd stay more than a week or two. A killer's word was about as sound as Confederate bonds.

She glanced at his injury, and in that glance, she saw that he was right. The wound looked sick.

Concern broke through her icy resolve, and she knew she was beaten.

Etta flipped up the latches on the box and lifted the red lid. Tubes, bottles, and bandages lined the interior, plus tiny scissors, tweezers, catgut string, and sharp needles. She turned up the wick of the lamp and brought it closer.

"Come around here and sit beside me," she said, keeping her voice as bland as paste.

He rose, so tall and broad that his shadow completely engulfed her. A corner of her heart fluttered with awareness. He came around the table, moving with that liquid grace that so attracted her. Oh, *why* was she so drawn to him? Why couldn't she blot out the things she liked, and concentrate on the many, many things she disliked about him? His gunslinging ways. His murdering heart. His callous disregard for the young men following in his wake and ending up in prison.

Those things faded and dimmed in the sultry light of his midnight-blue eyes and the scent of lye soap on his freshly scrubbed skin. He straddled a chair, rested one arm along the back of it, and extended his injured hand.

Etta drew in a deep breath before she took his fingers between her own. His were hot, hers cold. His were big, hers small. He was steady, but she trembled. Man, woman. Woman, man. She clamped down on that equation and concentrated fiercely on the festering wound.

"You're right," she said, unable to speak above a whisper. "This has fever in it. I'll clean it first. I've got some medicine that ought to take the fire out of it. I'll try not to pain you any. You try to hold still."

"Do what you have to do." His deep baritone stroked her frazzled nerves.

She glanced up. He wore no hat, not even on the range. Instead, he'd tied a leather thong lengthwise around his head to catch rolling beads of sweat before they could sting his eyes. He parted his straight black hair on the left side and it hung to his shoulders in back, but had been trimmed at his temples and ears. He'd braided a few inky strands behind his left ear. Tiny red beads circled the end of the braid. Like him, it was part white man's haircut and part Indian's. His clothing reflected his mixed heritage as well. Soft leather pants and fringed chaps, a lightweight Indian blanket vest of bright colors, fancy-stitched boots, and a linsey-woolsey shirt. Contrast. Conflict. Did this reflect his inner composition as well?

"You look nice in that dress. Do you always dress for dinner, or just when you serve up chicken?"

Etta took a deep breath, trying not to react to his compliment and gentle teasing. She had changed from her dusty work clothes into a dark blue housedress, which she protected with a white apron. She liked to wear dresses whenever possible. She spent so much time in pants and work shirts that it was a pleasure to slip into something feminine. And he'd noticed.

Well, it was only fair. She'd certainly noticed every little thing about him—his fancy saddle and the way he sat astride it, the little Indian yips he emitted when he rousted heifers from the piney woods, the blue-black sheen of his hair when it was struck by sunlight. Yes, she'd noticed.

She could feel his eyes on her like a flame leap-

ing across her skin. He never flinched from her
cleaning of the wound. Although she was gentle,
she knew the proud flesh pained him something
awful.

"Should the stitches come out?"

"No, not yet. This needs to knit a whole lot better before we mess with those. I'm going to smear
on this medicine now. It'll burn like hell's fire."

He nodded. Stoic.

Etta bit down on her lower lip, then squeezed
the greasy ointment out of the tube and onto his
swollen flesh. She rubbed it in with a tender forefinger, and he earned her respect and awe by not
showing any discomfort. Lord, he was tough! She
would have been howling like a rabid coyote, but
not him. In fact, he even managed a smile of
thanks when she reached for the roll of bandages.

"You must be carved out of wood instead of
skin," she noted, rolling out a length of the soft
cotton and snipping it free with the scissors. "With
the work you'll be doing around here every day,
we'll need to change this dressing often—two or
three times a week until your wound is well on
the mend."

"I can do that, I guess. I hate to trouble you . . ."

"It'll be more trouble if your hand gets so in-
fected I can't do anything about it. As it is, I think
we've caught it in time. Another day or two, you
wouldn't have been so lucky." She wrapped the
white cloth around his hand, thoughtful. "What
were you doing out there by the stream?"

"When?"

"Yesterday when we found you."

"Just biding my time."

"Until what?"

"Until I started feeling better. I was hoping to catch some fish and fill my gut."

"How come you hadn't eaten in so long? Did you run out of money before you came into town?"

He nodded. "Lost most of it in a crooked poker game. I'd won some back and was asking for directions to the nearest plate of good food when Brickman recognized me and called me out."

"So you're a gambler, too."

"When I have to be."

"Ever think of working for a living?"

"I'm not much good at anything. Do you know anyone interested in hiring a half-breed who's good with a gun? Besides you, of course."

She secured the bandage with a tight knot. "Wiggle your fingers."

He removed his hand from hers. "Thanks. Feels better already."

Etta tipped her head sideways, examining his shuttered expression. "You can't, can you?"

He stood up, towering over her, throwing her into shadow again.

"Do you have any movement in that hand?"

"Some."

"Any feeling?"

"Lots." He trailed his fingertips down the side of her face.

Etta jerked back, panic clutching her heart. She stood up and into the light, her hands balled into tight fists, her senses aflame. Her panic subsided, replaced by something more fearsome—the spark of desire.

"I felt that." One corner of his mouth lifted in a lopsided smile. "Felt good."

Etta slipped one hand across the table and grabbed a butter knife. "Don't you take liberties with me. You keep your hands to yourself."

"Lord, woman, you sure get fired up over nothing. What's wrong? You afraid some dirty Indian might rub off on your lily-white skin?"

"You might have been my brother's idea of a big man, but you don't mean spit to me. You just do your job and keep your hands to yourself."

He laughed under his breath and picked up the book she'd escaped into during supper. "*Sweet Passion's Song.* Is it singing to you, Etta, or are you tone-deaf?"

"Give me that—" She reached to snatch it from his fingers, but he moved it aside and grabbed her wrist with his other hand—the one she thought he had no strength in. She'd been wrong. He was still stout enough to hold on, his fingers tightening to cut off the blood flow. Her fingers grew numb and the butter knife fell to the table with a loud thud.

He pulled her against him. She looked up, finding herself so close that she could see the black pinpoints of beard dotting his jawline and chin. Etta tasted fear, even as her heart betrayed her by soaring on wings of unfettered yearning.

"I see the fear in you," he whispered. "And I see the passion. Which should I heed?"

"Let go!" she ground out between her gritted teeth.

He opened his fingers, one by one, releasing her from his trap. She bolted across the room, her eyes as big as silver dollars, her breath sawing in her throat.

"If it weren't for you, my brother would be

working this ranch with me instead of breaking up rocks in a prison quarry."

He shook his head, smiling at her narrow view of the world. "If you believe that, then you don't know your brother." Moving toward the back door, he afforded her one more glance. The lantern light caressed the soft lines of her face and graceful neck. Her hair, woven into a shimmering braid, lay across her left shoulder. Her breasts rose and fell with her shallow breathing. He wondered if she was green or seasoned. He submitted her to his thorough inspection, his gaze touring every curve, each enticing attribute. He saw her tremble.

"You ever lie with a man, boss lady?"

The book came flying, and he had too few seconds to duck. One corner of it nicked his cheek. Cheyenne scooped up the volume and tucked it under his arm.

"Much obliged. I'll read it and underline my favorite parts for you." He winked and slipped out the door before she could throw something else.

Chapter 5

The past three days had been hard ones. Usually Etta wouldn't contemplate quitting hours before sundown, but her body felt so stiff and her skin so sticky that all she could think about was getting out of the saddle and filling her stomach. The others hadn't put up any fuss when she'd called it a day at four o'clock, a good three hours before sundown. She figured they were all just as sore, as tired, and as hungry. Besides, tomorrow they had to go into town to get some horses shod, so they'd all need to clean up and be presentable come sunup.

They'd washed off the surface grime and devoured a quick meal of beans, greens, and corn bread. The men had gone to feed the livestock while Etta had washed and dried the dishes. Now she stepped out on the porch to watch the sun begin to dip below the horizon. A sharp pop startled her; then she realized it must be Cheyenne. It seemed that every free moment he had was spent on target practice. What a waste of time, she thought, moving to the side of the porch to peer around the corner at him.

He'd set different-sized tin cans along the top fence rail. He stood with his back to her, his legs braced apart, his bandaged hand hovering stiffly above his holstered gun. He made a grab for the pearl-handled pistol, wrestled it from the holster, and almost dropped it. He had to hold the revolver in both hands to steady it enough to get off a shot that went wide. She heard him curse viciously as he slipped the gun back into the holster.

Etta shook her head, thinking him a fool. She hopped off the porch and sauntered toward him.

"You ought to let that hand heal before you expect much from it," she called to him, making him turn around to face her. "You're rushing things a mite."

"Maybe, but this doesn't hurt me any more than throwing a rope does. You don't seem to think that's rushing things."

She ignored his comment since he was on target. Damn him. He still wore his chaps, and Etta counseled herself not to stare. She'd seen men in chaps her whole life, but when they were worn by Johnny Cheyenne, they titillated. The way they stopped at the juncture of his thighs, cupping and framing his privates ... and with his trousers being black and his chaps brown ... well, that accentuated his obvious endowments. With a mighty effort, she directed her attention to the cans. Orangy sunlight speared through no more than half a dozen holes.

"I've always heard that quick draws aren't necessarily sure shots. Whitey says that the average sheriff can outshoot most gunslingers in target practice."

"He's right, but I'm quick and I'm true." He flashed a grin. "That's why I'm so good."

She looked away, feeling lightning-struck by his blazing smile. Not wanting him to get the idea that she was the least bit dazzled by him, she glanced at the cans again and gave a short laugh. "You're not so good today."

The cloud that descended over his features made her regret her sharp tongue. Worry tugged at the corners of his mouth. Etta shoved her hands into her apron pockets and stared at the tufts of grass between her shoes, her mind racing to find a way to appease him.

He caressed the butt of the gun, then tried to draw it as he'd done so many times before, effortlessly, smoothly. The gun fell from his hand to the dirt.

"Damn it to hell!" He scooped it up and wiped the dirt from the white handle. "It's hopeless." He reached around and shoved the gun into the holster strapped to his right side.

His anguish tapped into her sympathy. To her continued consternation, she found herself drawn to him and wanting to ease his discomfort, his dread of what tomorrow might bring. She knew that ailment intimately. All her tomorrows loomed before her like soldiers of doom.

"You know what ..." Etta looked from his bandaged right hand to his strong left hand, remembering when Southpaw had gone lame a few years back. "That reminds me ..."

"What?" He threw her a surly, impatient glance.

"Can you write with your left hand?"

"No, I can't do anything much with it. Why?"

"When Southpaw was a foal, I noticed that he favored his left side. He was always pawing in the dirt with his left hoof, and he led with it, too. That's why I called him Southpaw."

Cheyenne massaged the palm of his injured hand, a scowl firmly fixed on his face. "You got a point, or are you just yammering to take my mind off my troubles?"

She bit down on her rising temper. "Hold your horses and quit interrupting me. Like I was saying, Southpaw's a lefty and—"

"He's also a horse, and I'm a man. And I'm not a lefty."

"I know all that," Etta snapped, irritated with his grumpiness. "Kindly let me finish. I'm trying to tell you that Southpaw got his left front leg caught between rocks a couple of years ago. Pulled his muscles and made him lame for a few months. During that time, he learned to favor his right leg and still does, even though his left one is all healed up. He's a better horse since that injury. He's stronger and more sure-footed." She walked to the fence on the pretense of examining the tins atop the fence rail and to give Cheyenne a chance to catch her meaning.

"Well, I'm glad for Southpaw, but I can't ever see a day when I'll be a fast draw with my left hand," he said, so low she could barely hear him.

"And I bet that a few months ago you couldn't ever see a day when you'd be riding the range and roping cattle again either."

He ran a hand over his jaw to hide his smile. "That's true enough. Maybe I'll try using my other hand."

"It works a sight better than your right one does for the time being. Andy's good with leather. He could make you a left-handed holster. You ought to ask him. He'd be tickled to do it. He's always wanting to make harnesses and belts and the like."

He was looking at her in a jarring fashion—his eyes all glittery and his lips curving into a devilishly attractive grin. If she didn't know better, she would have sworn he liked her—a lot.

She grew uneasy under his steady gaze. "Well, I'll be getting back to the house," she said, flustered.

"Got a book to read, I guess."

She lifted a haughty brow, wanting to ask him to return her book, but not bad enough to give him an opening to tease her about it. "I've got chores," she said brusquely. "You'll be wanting to practice while there's still light. 'Evening to you." Sweeping past him, she hurried to the house, feeling as if she were escaping instead of merely leaving him to his target practice.

Sometimes she felt like a schoolgirl around him, and she hated it. She was twenty, and far too old to feel such things, and he certainly wasn't the type of man any decent schoolgirl would have a crush on!

He's bad, she told herself firmly so that she wouldn't be tempted to forget. Bad to the bone.

Cheyenne had been stared at all his life, and he thought he was used to it—until he rode into Clearwater, Texas, the next day with the rest of the Flying H outfit.

People gawked at him as if he were a ghost or a damn fool looking to be one. He tried to take no notice of them, but it was difficult. A boy of about ten ran toward them, out into the middle of the street. Cheyenne had to rein in his horse to keep from bumping into the lad.

"You came back!" the boy said, his eyes as round as saucers in his freckled face. "Everybody said you wouldn't. Said you'd be too chicken to stick around after killing a Brickman. But you came back! You gonna kill the other one now?"

"I'm not going to kill anyone." Cheyenne shifted uneasily in the saddle. Did the whole town think he'd come back spoiling for another fight?

"Move aside, son, before one of these horses damages your goods," Whitey said, reaching down to snag the boy by his suspenders. He chuckled, sending the youngster on his way with a gentle pull and push. "I do believe folks are thinking you've come to save the day, Cheyenne."

Cheyenne resisted the impulse to rest his hand on the butt of his Colt. He knew it would give him comfort, but it also might give the wrong impression. "They're in for a disappointment. If they hate Brickman so much, why don't they hire a sheriff who will stand up to him?"

Whitey scratched at his bristling whiskers. "That's easier said than done, seeing as how Brickman does the hiring and pays the sheriff's salary."

Cheyenne glanced around at the curious onlookers. One or two waved. Others smiled hopefully at him. He faced front, refusing to acknowledge the furtive greetings. "They could change that if they wanted to. They could form a town council to hire a sheriff and collect from all the townsfolk for the man's salary."

"It would take backbone for something like that," Etta said, "and there's a shortage of spine in this town."

Cheyenne glanced at her, glad she'd spoken up, since that gave him an excuse to inspect her. She looked mighty fine in her suede riding skirt, calico blouse, and "town hat" of straw and velvet flow-

ers. Leather and lace. He admired the feminine
clothing and the strength evident in her erect posture and tipped-up chin. If she didn't have such a
rapier tongue and stay-away-from-me demeanor,
he didn't doubt she would have more than her
share of starry-eyed suitors.

"All these people know how to do is step and
fetch it for Brickman," she added. "Oh, they belly-
ache, but they do whatever he tells them to do."

"You gonna come with us to the blacksmith's?"
Whitey asked Etta.

"No, you go on. I'm going to the church to say
howdy to Pastor Reed, and then I've got to stop in
at the dry goods store. Tell Jessup to be gentle
with that roan filly when he shoes her. She's got a
tender place above her left knee."

"I'll tell him," Whitey said, waving her off. "I
been having horses shod more years than you've
been alive."

Cheyenne rode on, flanked by Andy and
Whitey, while Etta veered Southpaw away from
them and headed for the white, steepled church.

Watching her, Cheyenne felt a smile in his heart
when he recalled last evening and her suggestion
that he try shooting with his left hand. She'd
shown him a glimpse of the compassion he knew
she possessed in abundance. She's been burned
like me, he thought. At some time in her life, she
had reached out to someone and that someone
had set her world on fire. Her scars were on the
inside, but Cheyenne could see them, clear as day.

"Is she real religious?" he asked, watching her
rein in Southpaw in front of the church.

Whitey wheezed a laugh. "She's been known to
pray and she's read the Bible all the way through,

but that's not why she's going to the church. Pastor Reed has more books than Etta, and he loans them."

"Ah." Cheyenne grinned, seeing the light. "They share a passion."

"There you go." Whitey removed his floppy hat and swiped at his forehead with his shirtsleeve. "I wish she'd strike up a passion with a man interested in more than reading about it, though. Etta needs herself a husband. She don't think so, but if she could find herself a provider, I'd breathe easier."

Cheyenne pretended to polish one of the silver disks decorating his saddle, thinking that Whitey might be measuring him for a husband's yoke and collar. Not me, old man, he thought. While Etta had caught his eye, he wasn't aiming to marry her—or any woman, for that matter. He liked the free life just fine. Once his hand was healed, he'd be making tracks.

The blacksmith stepped outside his big barn to greet them. He weighed nearly three hundred pounds, and the canvas apron he wore would have made a good-sized tent.

"Hello there, Whitey Malloy. Hey there, Andy." The smithy wiped his blackened hands on the smeared front of his apron as he eyed Cheyenne. He nodded a greeting, his small eyes lost in folds of loose skin. "You must be Johnny Cheyenne. I was out at the Cox farm when you gunned down Ben Brickman, but Lone Deer told me all about it." He looked back at a gray-haired Indian emerging from the shadows of the structure.

Cheyenne raised a hand in greeting, recognizing the old Indian from the day he was shot. Lone

Deer had stood near while the doctor had stitched up Cheyenne's hand. A serenity emanated from Lone Deer, a peacefulness that Cheyenne envied. It seemed that the older tribesman had found answers to questions that bedeviled Cheyenne.

He was dressed in white man's clothes—brown shirt and trousers, butter-colored boots—but he wore his hair in braids, and a rope of colored beads and grizzly teeth hung around his neck.

"Where's Etta?" the smithy asked.

"Seeing to her own errands." Whitey jerked a thumb at the seven horses trailing them. "We need shoes for these, Jessup. We're in the market for some bridles and halters, too, if you ain't wanting a sack of gold for them."

"I got some broke-in bridles in a trade the other day. As for halters, I only got a couple I can spare. Got some leather I'll send you. Andy can make you some halters. He's mighty talented, I hear."

Andy beamed. "I can do that, Whitey. Won't be no trouble for me."

"Well, we'll see." Whitey scratched at his chin whiskers. "Depends on how much Jessup wants for that there leather. I didn't come to town to get held up."

A pained expression settled on Jessup's fleshy face. "Why do you talk like that about me, Malloy, when I ain't never done wrong by you? Get down off that nag and come in here out of the sun."

Grumbling under his breath, Whitey dismounted and went inside with Andy at his heels, leading the horses. Cheyenne eased off Lariat and moved toward Lone Deer.

"How's the hand?" Lone Deer asked in his native tongue.

"Not so good," Cheyenne answered in English.

"You don't speak the ancient tongue?" Lone Deer asked, still in Cheyenne.

"No. Not anymore."

Lone Deer walked to a bench placed in the shade of a hickory tree. He sat down and waited for Cheyenne to join him. Cheyenne sat on the other end and surveyed the commerce around him. The Brickman name cropped up on three businesses—Brickman Land Office, Brickman Surveying, and Peters, Alsup and Brickman Law Office.

"Which Brickman is a lawyer?"

Humor entered Lone Deer's dark eyes. "Neither. The one who still lives owns that building, so he made the lawyers put his name in with theirs." Lone Deer shrugged. "This is what I've been told."

"Looks like he owns most of the town."

"He does." Lone Deer switched to the white man's language. "What he does not own he controls. Even this place. The blacksmith owes nothing to Brickman, but he does what Brickman tells him and asks for no money in return." Lone Deer cut his eyes at Cheyenne. "You have made a powerful enemy, my young brave."

Cheyenne lifted a brow, accepting the truth and dismissing it. "You work here for the blacksmith?"

"No. Sometimes I sleep here. I work at the saloon."

"Doing what?"

"Whatever needs to be done. Pouring fire water. Sweeping floors. Keeping the lanterns burning."

"Why did you leave your tribe?"

Lone Deer gazed down the dusty street, but Cheyenne thought he looked into the past instead of at the passing wagons and horses. "My world changed. The white men kept coming, and many of my people were killed. I took my wife and son and went to where there were more buffalo and deer, but my family died in a flood."

"And you didn't want to go back to your band?"

"We are from the high country, and there are not many of us left. It is a long journey back. I decided to stay here."

"You like this town?"

Lone Deer didn't answer for a minute. "I am old. Going to a new place would shorten my time. I will stay here until I'm called to the spirit world. Then I will join my wife and son." A smile nudged his lips. "You don't like what you see here?"

Cheyenne surveyed the boxy buildings and the narrow street. "I think this place is full of cowards. Brickman swaggers around like a king, and they all let him. Except for Etta," he amended. "She's got courage."

"She is more afraid than anyone."

Cheyenne shifted sideways to face the Indian. The man's profile harkened him back to his own band of Cheyenne. In fact, Lone Deer looked a lot like Yellow Wolf, the chief of his mother's tribe. The same large nose, square jaw, and smooth, teak-colored skin. "You know Etta?" he asked.

Lone Deer shook his head. "I have seen her, watched her. And I have listened when others have talked of her. Brickman and the railroad have plans for her land."

"What makes you think she's afraid?"

"She is a woman with a good head. Only a fool

would not be afraid of losing what is dear. She is also not blind, and she can see how Brickman looks at her."

"How's that?" Cheyenne leaned closer, interested in the man's answer.

"Like he would like to lie with her," Lone Deer said, reverting to the Cheyenne language again.

Cheyenne sat back against the bench to mull this over. Whitey had told him that Brickman had threatened Etta, and Cheyenne had thought he'd meant that Brickman had threatened to take Etta's land. But maybe he'd been wrong. Maybe Brickman had threatened to take Etta, whether she cooperated or not.

"If ever a man needed killing, it sounds as if Blaine Brickman is that man," Cheyenne said.

Lone Deer folded his arms against his chest. "You haven't killed enough men yet? How many must you kill before you can turn to a different life?"

Cheyenne heard the censure in the old man's voice. He was used to it. People either respected him or lectured him. "I don't have a number in mind. I don't draw on anybody who doesn't draw on me first."

"What if you refused?"

Cheyenne laughed shortly. "Then I'd be dead."

"You get money for this?"

"Sometimes. People make bets and I get a cut of that money. I've gunned down two outlaws and collected the rewards on them. I'm good at the gaming tables, too." He rested an arm across the back of the bench. "I don't need much money to get by, and I do okay for myself." He realized that the older Indian was staring at his wounded hand.

"I'm helping out at the Flying H for food and lodging while I heal up."

"I heard the doctor say that your hand might never again do what you ask of it."

"It's getting better," Cheyenne lied. "The doctor was wrong."

"It is good that you try to believe this until your heart is ready to hold the truth."

Cheyenne crossed his arms over his chest defensively, but kept his temper reined. Speaking harshly to an elder was bad manners. The teachings of the Cheyenne were hard to shake, he thought with a rueful smile. "Who was the chief of your tribe?"

"Red Sky. He was my mother's brother. He has been dead many, many years."

"You remember the time before the white settlers came?"

"Yes. It is clear in my memory." Lone Deer rocked forward and withdrew a silver flask from under the back of his belt. He tipped it to his lips and drank. Cheyenne smelled whiskey as Lone Deer offered him a sip.

"No, thanks."

Lone Deer nodded and replaced the flask. "In the days of my youth, we lived a simple life. We moved to different hunting grounds, sometimes having to fight others who thought they owned the land. Sometimes a chief needed to show his strength and tried to force others to another camp. There would be fighting. Then there would be sworn enemies."

"Same as now," Cheyenne noted.

"Some, yes. But there is so little land to fight for now. Almost all is claimed by the white man. Hatred lies in many hearts. It poisons all men." He looked hard at Cheyenne. "You have many white ancestors in you. They are in your eyes and in the hair that covers your body."

Cheyenne tensed. "Yes. My father was white."

"And what of your mother? Cheyenne and . . . ?"

"White. Cheyenne and white. Her father was a missionary and her mother was a Cheyenne widow. Her father died of the fever when she was a babe, so her mother took another Cheyenne husband." He sighed wearily. Might as well tell the whole story. "My mother was raised in the ways of the Cheyenne, but her eyes liked to look upon white skin. She spurned Cheyenne suitors and lay with a cavalry officer. He left before she even knew she was with child. She sent word to the fort, but never heard from him. A fur trader told her that my father had a white wife in Philadelphia and three children."

"Did you ever try to find him?"

Cheyenne shook his head, his heart hardening as it always did when he discussed his parents. "I have nothing to say to him. He isn't to blame for my being here anyway. My mother was not forced, and he wasn't the only white man she opened her thighs for."

The older man nodded. "And you have suffered because of this."

A sudden burst of anger broke over Cheyenne like a clap of thunder, but he managed to keep his voice low and steady. "Suffered? Not me. I left the tribe as soon as I was able, and I haven't looked back. I never belonged there."

"They did not accept you?"

He shrugged. "They tried to include me, but I never felt much like an Indian."

"Or much like a white man?" Lone Deer ventured. He smiled suddenly, his dark eyes twinkling. "I have been Cheyenne all my life, but I don't know how it feels to be one." He rested one dark hand on Cheyenne's knee. "No need to be so angry with this old man."

"I'm not angry at you." Just at the whole damn country, Cheyenne thought.

"I think anger is so much a part of you that you will think something is lost once the anger's fire has died out. Or maybe you will be lucky and love will come into your life and replace that anger. Then you won't feel empty."

Cheyenne studied the old fox and wondered if he might be touched in the head. "They treat you well in this town, my father?" he asked, using the traditional words of respect for elder Cheyennes.

"Well enough, but you are a marked man here. You will need eyes in the back of your head and the guidance of the spirits." He patted Cheyenne's knee. "You wait here. I have something to show you."

Cheyenne watched the man's slow, dignified gait. Lone Deer went inside the blacksmith's and emerged a minute later carrying a short, thick stick, carved and decorated with beads and feathers.

"A coup stick," Cheyenne said, taking it from Lone Deer to admire it. "Yours?"

Lone Deer nodded. "And now it is yours."

Cheyenne looked at him in surprise. "No. I can't take it." He held it out, waiting for Lone Deer to reclaim it.

"You do not take it. I give it. It has served me well and kept me safe all these many years. You take it now. When the bitterness crowds your heart, look at it and see your heritage. Think not on the scars and wounds, but on the beauty and courage of the People flowing in your veins." Lone Deer ran his fingertips along the carvings. "My father's father did these. The eagle's talon, the sun's face, the sign of the lightning bolt. All symbols of strength. All symbols of the People."

Cheyenne knew the old man was offering him more than a coup stick—he was offering friendship and respect. Tradition demanded that Cheyenne accept the gift and give something in return. He glanced down at himself, wondering what he had that could symbolize his life and his trust. His gaze fell on the leather strap, notched six times. He untied it from his belt and held it out to Lone Deer.

"This is one of my most treasured possessions, but I want you to have it. The cuts in the leather represent the men who have drawn against me and died."

Lone Deer took the strap and ran a fingertip along each notch. "Six." He gripped the leather in his fist. "I take it, and maybe you will not have to kill again."

Cheyenne nodded, though he didn't put much faith in Lone Deer's idea. He stood, and on impulse, he embraced the old man. Lone Deer hugged him back, his arms strong around Cheyenne's waist. When Cheyenne stepped away from Lone Deer, emotion clutched his throat as memories of his boyhood among skin lodges and open prairie came back to him.

"Remember the beauty," Lone Deer whispered, then turned and walked away.

An uncommon peace lay upon Cheyenne's heart.

Chapter 6

Observing the end of the exchange between Cheyenne and Lone Deer, Etta hung back, not wanting them to know that she'd seen them. Cheyenne had given that old Indian his leather strap, the one he notched after each kill, and then Cheyenne had *hugged* him! If she hadn't seen it with her own eyes, she would never have believed it.

Etta turned away from the blacksmith's and walked back toward the dry goods store. She'd planned to fetch the supplies list from Whitey, but she'd just try to remember what was on it. She didn't want to barge in on whatever brewed between Lone Deer and Johnny Cheyenne.

She crossed the busy street to the false-fronted building. Hester Pitch stood behind the counter, patiently counting out a penny's worth of gumdrops for a young boy. Hester was Clarence Allred's sister. Her husband, Dan, emerged from the back room, his arms full of mops and brooms. He started to smile at Etta, then he recognized her, and the pleasantry disappeared. Etta drew in a quick breath, trying to dispel the knot of tension in her chest. Damn it all! For all he knew, she'd come in to pay what she owed. Although he was probably too smart to think that.

"You back in town already, Etta?" Hester said,

taking the boy's penny and giving him the bag of gumdrops.

"Yes. I forgot some things last time, and we needed to get some horses shod." She stepped aside, and the boy barrelled past her. "Good morning, Dan. Nice-looking brooms you got there."

"They cost a dollar apiece."

Etta bit her tongue, wishing she could tell him to wrap up six for her while she pulled a wad of bills out of her purse that could choke a horse. But she couldn't. All she could do was wish ... and get ready to crawl on her stomach. She directed her gaze to Hester, the softer touch.

"Whitey's got my list, but I think I can remember ... I'm needing a sack of oats, and another of flour. Oh, and a bushel of potatoes if you can spare them."

Dan stepped forward. "You gonna pay on your bill today, Etta?"

Hester sent her husband a sharp glance, and Etta a sympathetic smile.

Etta turned to Dan. "No, I'm not. When I sell my herd, I'll pay you in full, just like all the other ranchers you have in your books."

"You didn't pay all you owed last time. I had to hold over twenty-three dollars from last year." He went around the counter and flipped through the pages of his brown ledger until he found the Flying H's entries. He ran a long, skinny finger down the far-right column. "You owe fifty-one dollars and some cents already." He squinted at her from behind the thick, square panes of his glasses. "You want me to add even more to that figure, Etta?"

"Dan," Hester admonished, snapping his shirtsleeve garter. "Don't be so harsh." Her brown eyes implored him and soft wrinkles appeared at the corners of her mouth. "The Hollisters have always paid up. You know that."

"*Henry* Hollister did," Dan corrected, swinging his gaze back to Etta. "You really *need* those extra goods, Etta?"

Anger smoked in Etta like a branding iron. How did he dare to lecture her, question her! What gave him the right? She didn't owe that much more than any other rancher. She gathered in a breath to use in telling him that he could take his words of advice and stuff them down his gullet, but just then Lone Deer entered the store and divided the sparks flying between her and the proprietor. He looked from one flushed face to the other, then pretended to be fascinated by a roll of barbwire.

Hester leaned close to her husband. "Let her have the things on credit, Dan. Brickman won't find out. It's only a few more dollars."

"What's Brickman got to do with this?" Etta asked.

"Nothing," Dan mumbled, glaring at his wife before peering at Lone Deer. "What do you want? Is the Scarlet Rose out of cigars again?"

Lone Deer nodded and held up a single finger. "One box." The Indian greeted Etta with a nod. "Word is you have a big herd this year, Miss Etta. That cowboy you hired should round up even more before winter sets in."

Dan whirled around, tossing the box of cigars on the counter. "What cowboy? You got money to pay another cowboy?"

"He'll be paid after the roundup . . . not that it's any of your business." Etta directed a sly smile toward Lone Deer. "Guess you can't keep good news to yourself these days. Yeah, I got a big herd," she lied as winningly as the Indian had. "More head than my pa rounded up in the last two or three years he rode the range. And I'm going to have more spring calves than ever before."

"That's wonderful, Etta," Hester said, her eyes shining. "Did you hear that, Dan? Etta's doing real well out there on the Flying H."

"I heard, I heard." Dan removed his eyeglasses and polished them on the hem of his wife's apron. He hooked the wires over and behind his jug ears before running his finger down the long column of numbers on Etta's page again. "You can have the flour and oats, but not the potatoes. Those are for *paying* customers only, until I get in another load."

Etta gripped the edge of the counter, but managed a tense smile. "Thanks. The men will be along to load the sacks onto the horses, so you won't have to put yourself out none."

Dan hunched over his ledger and added the items to Etta's list. Etta winked at Lone Deer, and the old Indian's dark eyes smiled at her.

"Etta, come with me a minute," Hester said, rounding the counter and taking Etta by the arm. "I want to show you the new lamps we got in. I know you don't need any, but they're so unusual . . ."

"And expensive," Dan added loudly. "Two and a half apiece! The ones with colored shades are three dollars even."

"Don't pay him any mind," Hester whispered. "He's got dollars on the brain."

Etta noticed the new lamps, displayed on a high shelf, too high for youngsters' hands. "Those are pretty," she said, admiring the red glass shades on several of them. "Wouldn't put out much light, though."

"I didn't really want you to see those . . ." Hester shifted bolts of material aside and pulled out a large, folded square of forest-green linen. "I sold nearly the whole bolt of this for Mrs. Perrywrinkle to make draperies for her front parlor, but this much was left over. I saved it for you." She held it out to Etta. "Should be enough for a lovely dress. I thought of you because this color is nearly the same shade as your eyes."

Etta stepped back, stunned by Hester's thoughtfulness. "I can't. I owe y'all too much as it is."

"I'm not *selling* this to you," Hester whispered. "I'm *giving* it to you." She pushed the fabric into Etta's hands. "Take it. Dan doesn't know a thing about it. There's not enough to sell to anyone. I'd just add it to my quilt scraps. You take it. I know you haven't made yourself a new dress since your pa's funeral, and that one was black as coal. You'll need a new frock."

Etta smiled with a touch of bitterness. "I don't know what for."

"For catching a man's fancy, of course." Hester patted her arm. "Wear it when you come to town sometime so I can see it on you."

Etta squeezed Hester's big-knuckled hand. "Thanks. I believe you just earned yourself another jewel for your crown in heaven."

"Take this, too." She withdrew a length of sky-blue ribbon from her apron pocket and tucked it into Etta's shirt pocket. "You know, Dan isn't as selfish as he lets on. He's just worried Brickman might take it on himself to trade elsewhere. That would ruin us."

"Has Brickman threatened to do that? Is he telling the merchants they can't trade with me or else he'll close them down?"

Hester chewed on her lower lip for a moment. "Well, not in so many words ... but similar words are flying around town. We don't know if there's truth in any of it, but Dan doesn't like to take chances."

Frustration whirled in Etta like a dust devil. "I won't tell anyone that I'm owing you and Dan. If Brickman tries anything, you tell me. I'll pay y'all if I have to sell my soul to do it."

"Oh, don't do that!" Hester laughed softly. "And don't worry about us."

"Hester! We got customers up front," Dan yelled. "*Paying* customers!"

"Coming, coming!" Hester winced, then shared a smile with Etta. "Men! Most of them have the manners of a hog."

Etta removed her straw hat, made a tight roll of the material, and stuffed it into the crown. Hester nodded with approval, and Etta followed her to the front of the store. Lone Deer was gone, but two men stood at the counter and the butcher's wife was inspecting one of the new mops. Etta signed her name to the bill of goods under Dan Pitch's watchful eyes. Clutching her hat to her side, Etta left the dry goods store.

Once outside, she pulled the material free from her hat and wedged it under her arm. She replaced her hat over her fair hair, feeling for the pins and sticking them through to hold the straw creation atop her head. The brim was short, but shaded her face. Looking up, she tensed involuntarily when she spotted two of Brickman's ranch hands. Oh, no, she thought with a sinking feeling. Just walk on past, boys, she told them mentally. We don't want any trouble now, do we?

Clyde Smith's long legs were so bowed that his knees angled way out to the sides when he walked. Barney Timmons, shorter and meaner, had a full beard of greasy black hair and eyes that made Etta think of a coyote's—slanty, wild, furtive. She wondered if his mother had yipped at the moon.

They stopped in front of her, blocking her passage. When Etta edged left, they followed. When she moved right, they moved with her. She crossed her arms against her chest, hugging her purse, the folded material, and the fragments of her courage.

"My dance card is full up, boys," she sassed. "Y'all are going to have to take your box step somewhere else. Now, excuse me. I got errands to run."

"You ain't much longer for these parts, and me and Barney here was thinking we ought to get friendly with you while we still can."

"That's right," Barney joined in, wiping a hand across his woolly mustache. He scratched furiously at his beard, and Etta thought she saw fleas spring from it. She stepped back, eyeing the men with disgust. "Hey, where are you going?" Barney snagged her by the arm. "That ain't the way to be friendly. Step into the Scarlet Rose, and me and Clyde will buy you a drink or two." He glanced up at the swinging sign above Etta's head. His fingers tightened on her elbow.

"No, thanks." Etta tried to jerk her arm from his biting fingers, but failed. Her heart crowded into

her throat and she glanced around nervously. A
few people watched from across the street, but
made no move in her direction.

Clyde grabbed her other elbow and pressed
close to her side. His breath was hot and foul,
spreading over her face like pond scum. "A stiff
drink will do you a world of good, Etta Hollister.
I hear you can show a man a pretty good time
when you set your mind to it."

Rage shattered her composure and she twisted
furiously, freeing herself of the clutching hands,
only to be captured again in Barney's spine-
crushing embrace. He squeezed the air from her
lungs, and Etta thought she might faint. His coyote eyes blazed, and his lips drew together in a
sickening semblance of a pucker.

Suddenly the tip of a revolver sprouted from
Barney's ear, and the two men fell as still as death.
Etta cut her eyes sideways past the bandaged
hand holding the Colt, and straight into cool, calm
eyes of sapphire blue. Her heart slipped down her
throat and settled in her bosom again.

"Let her go," Cheyenne said, his tone soft, com-
pelling. "Let her go . . . now."

Barney's arms fell to his sides. His hands trembled, and his wild eyes stared straight ahead.

Cheyenne made a *tsking* sound of regret. "Pal,
you done stepped in a pile of trouble." He tipped
his head to one side, regarding the fit of his gun's
barrel in Barney's ear. "I've never shot a man this
close up." He looked past the shivering Barney to
Clyde. "Fella, you better move away, or your bud-
dy's brains might fly all over your shirt when I
pull the trigger."

Clyde stumbled backward, and Barney released a high-pitched whine.

"What the hell are you doing?" Barney wailed, his eyes searching wildly for Clyde. "Help me, for God's sake!" Then his frantic gaze found Etta again. "Call him off, Miss Etta. Please? I was only funning. I was only trying to be nice by buying you a drink. No harm done." He extended his hands, palms up, beseeching, begging her to intervene.

" 'Call him off'?" Cheyenne repeated. "You calling me a dog, fella?"

"No! I ain't callin' you nothing. I don't know you from Adam." Barney gulped. "Miss Etta . . . please?"

Power was hers, and she reveled in it. She glanced at Cheyenne, thankful for his timely appearance. In a startling instant, she felt what he felt, and she knew why he'd chosen the life of a gunslinger: to make men quake in their boots, to demand respect from those reluctant to give it, to be able to walk down the street unmolested! Oh, yes. She understood. It took everything she had in her not to draw the moment out, not to allow Barney to suffer and cry, not to make Clyde run like a jackrabbit.

She looked away from Cheyenne's tempting offer of redemption and realized that she'd dropped her purse and the green fabric.

"You pick up my belongings like a gentleman, Barney Timmons, and you and Clyde apologize to me. Then I might ask Johnny Cheyenne to spare your worthless lives."

"J-Johnny Chey-Cheyenne?" Barney sputtered.

"Holy shit," Clyde muttered, retreating another step. "Mr. Brickman said you was long gone."

"He's wrong . . . obviously." Etta tapped her foot. "Well? I'm waiting, and Johnny Cheyenne's patience is about as long as your gut, Barney." She lifted her hand, eye-level with Barney, and held her finger and thumb within an inch of each other. " 'Bout that long, I'd say."

Cheyenne's lips twitched in a near smirk. He angled the gun back just enough to clear Barney's ear cavity. "Better do as she says, pal. One signal from her and you're going to have less between your ears than you already do."

Barney stooped down and picked up Etta's velvet purse and the material. He handed them to her with trembling hands.

"Sorry, Miss Etta." He wiped his brow with his dirty sleeve, then looked toward Clyde. "Well, tell her!"

"Oh, right." Clyde removed his sweat-stained hat. "Mighty sorry, Miss Etta. We didn't mean no offense." He eyed Cheyenne. "Will that do you?"

"You're asking the wrong person." Cheyenne nodded at Etta. "She's the one you should be talking to, not me."

"Miss Etta?" Clyde questioned. "What do you say? Me and Barney can be on our way and no bad feelings. You just say the word." His gaze strayed to the gun Cheyenne still pointed at Barney's head.

Etta sighed, satisfied that she had her pound of flesh. "Get along, both of you." She shook a finger at them. "But don't ever try anything with me again, or I won't be so forgiving. You hear?"

"Yes, we sure do." Clyde grabbed Barney by the

shirt collar and hauled him backward. In two swishes of a cat's tail, the two men had skedaddled out of Etta's sight.

Etta turned slowly, aware that she should say something nice to Cheyenne. He angled his body so that he could holster his gun without anyone on the street seeing the slow, painful process. Sympathy squeezed her heart. Great goblins! She was getting all soft for him!

Part of her wanted to thank him in a cold voice, while another encouraged her to drop her shield and let him see how much his rescue had meant to her. As she looked into his eyes, the nicer side of her won out—almost.

"I suppose I should thank you." The words felt odd coming from her. It had been a long time since she'd felt beholden to any man other than Whitey.

A smile lifted one corner of Cheyenne's mouth. "Don't do anything against your religion or upbringing."

She forced back the blunt retort that sprang to her tongue. She *had* been raised better. Why, her pa and Whitey were two of the kindest people on earth. Of course, that kindness had sometimes been used against them.

"Those two work for Brickman?"

She lowered her shield even farther, deciding to try a little kindness. "Right. Saddle bums. Clyde Smith's been riding the Double B for about ten years, I guess. Barney Timmons was hired last year. I appreciate your help with them. They ... well, they had me worried for a minute."

Three town girls approached them, all done up in starched skirts and petticoats and holding fancy parasols. Etta moved closer to the buildings, allowing the girls to pass, and wondered what they did all day besides stroll up and down the main street as if they were in a parade.

They sashayed past, twittering and flirting with Cheyenne with their eyes and dimples. Cheyenne smiled and turned clean around to admire their backsides. Etta frowned at his obtuse behavior. Didn't he know that those gals wouldn't wipe their noses on him, much less be seen in public with him? Oh, yes, they'd flirt, but they sure wouldn't take up with a half-breed gunslinger.

"Hey there, Johnny Cheyenne." Meg O'Rourke held open the batwing doors of the Scarlet Rose Saloon. She offered a bright smile and pushed out her chest, giving Cheyenne a good look at her ample breasts, partially revealed by the low neckline of her tight dress. "You wanna look at some gal's rear, then come on inside here and look at mine." She reached out and snagged one side of his vest. "Buy me a drink and I might show you my room upstairs."

Etta cleared her throat. "Hello to you, too, Meg."

Meg didn't even bother to glance in Etta's direction. "Hello. I didn't see you standing there, Etta."

"You still don't," Etta fired back, then deliberately stepped in front of Cheyenne and into Meg's line of vision. Meg's brown eyes glittered with malice. "I didn't know you lived here at the Scarlet Rose."

Meg frowned. "I don't."

"But didn't you just tell Cheyenne that you've got a room here, upstairs?" Etta widened her eyes. "Whores are up there, aren't they?"

Meg's eyes narrowed to slits. She stepped forward, letting the doors swing shut behind her. "You callin' me a whore, Etta Hollister?" She pushed up the sleeves of her dress and lifted a fist. " 'Cause if you are . . ."

Cheyenne's hand landed on Etta's shoulder and his fingers curled into her skin. Even through her clothes she felt the heat of him. She would have pulled away, but she noticed a flash of jealousy in Meg's eyes, so she stood her ground. He remained beside Etta, but reached out with his other hand to touch his fingertips to Meg's rouged cheek.

"I'll have to take you up on that offer some other time. Here come Whitey and Andy."

Etta edged away from him to look down the street. Sure enough, Whitey and Andy rode toward them, leading a string of freshly shod horses.

"Blaine Brickman's real put out with you, honey," Meg told Cheyenne, grabbing his hand before he could move away from her. "You be careful. I don't want anything to happen to you. I couldn't stand it if Brickman hurt you—or k-killed you!" She raised herself up on tiptoe, her pink mouth whisper-close to Cheyenne's smiling lips, her hands clutching the sides of his vest. "Hon, you're keeping bad company. You don't want to rile Brickman any more than he's already riled. Believe me, honey, you need to cut loose from the Flying H quick as you can."

"Let's go, Cheyenne," Etta ordered, delivering a hateful glare to the saloon girl. "You've got nerve talking to him about bad company, Meg O'Rourke. Why, you've been sleeping with Brickmans ever since you hit town."

Meg released Cheyenne and treated Etta to a

harsh smile. "But not as long as you've been sleeping with them, from what I hear."

The world seemed to tip sideways. Etta grasped the hitching post behind her and felt her face drain of color. She wanted to dig a hole and crawl into it. Instead, she turned blindly and stepped out into the street. She almost walked into Whitey's horse.

"Whoa there, little sister." Whitey held out Southpaw's reins to Etta. "Here you go. You're ready, ain't ya?"

From the corner of her eye she saw Cheyenne lean toward Meg and say something—something that caused Meg to gather her lips in a pout and flounce back inside the saloon.

"You finish your errands?" Whitey asked again.

Etta nodded. "We need to stop off at Pitch's for a load."

Whitey pushed back his hat, eyeing her with interest. "You didn't run into any trouble, did you?"

Etta's gaze met Cheyenne's briefly. "No. No trouble." She pressed her knees into Southpaw's side and rode toward the dry goods store. What must he think of her after what Meg had said? she wondered, then shook off the worry. What did she care what Johnny Cheyenne thought? He was nothing to her. Nothing at all.

But she flinched every time she caught his gaze straying to her on the ride home, and her heart felt like a dead weight in her chest. He thinks I slept with the Brickmans, she acknowledged. And he probably thinks I liked it.

She looked ahead at the gently rolling land, and tried to lift her spirits with the promise of a tub of water and a bar of lilac-scented soap. But she knew that she could never scrub hard enough. Anytime she thought of Blaine Brickman, she felt dirty. And when she allowed herself to remember that evening by the stream—well, she'd never be able to wash that out of her head, her heart, her soul. Never.

Chapter 7

Eight damp balls of fur squirmed blindly, seeking sustenance, their tiny noses leading them to the exhausted bitch dog's teats. Cheyenne crouched in the straw beside Butter and patted her smooth head.

"Good timing, girl. You've guaranteed yourself a lazy winter. No roundup for you. You'll be staying behind with your young ones."

Butter began cleaning the newborns with the broad flat of her tongue. Cheyenne counted five males and three females. Three of the males had long golden hair like Butter, and there was a long-haired white one, too. The other male looked more like Bounder with his long black-and-white fur. Two of the females were black with blond markings, while their other sister sported a solid black coat. Etta would be thrilled. Well, maybe not thrilled, he amended, remembering the tight rein she kept on her emotions. But she'd at least be pleased.

She'd been worrying over Butter for days, afraid that the dog would give birth after they'd all left the ranch house for a couple of weeks out on the farthest reaches of the Flying H. No telling how long they'd be gone. At least a week. Maybe two. Then they'd have to hurry back because winter would be setting in and there was still so much work to be done to get the herd ready for market.

He rose to his full height and moved outside to check the stars. From them, he gathered it wasn't quite ten. He looked toward the house and saw a light in the bedroom. Maybe she was still awake.

He ran his hands through his hair, pushing it back from his forehead, then reached into his pocket for his bandanna. As he moved toward the house, he twisted the cloth into a thin band and tied it lengthwise around his head. He tightened the knot until the cloth fit snugly across his forehead. As he gained the porch, he fastened the bottom two buttons on his shirt, but didn't bother to tuck the tails into the wasitband of his soft buckskin pants.

Raising a fist, he hesitated, listening for a moment for any sounds within. There were none. He knocked lightly against the screen. When there was no response, he opened the screen door and tapped his knuckles on the wooden door. He heard a shuffling within and the swish of bare feet on the floorboards near the door.

"Who is it?" Etta called from inside.

"Cheyenne. I've got something to tell you."

"Tell me in the morning."

He shrugged. So be it. Turning away, he started to step off the porch when he heard the grumble of hinges.

"Tell me what?" Etta asked, peeking at him through the crack in the door.

Cheyenne leaned a shoulder against the support post. "Butter had her pups."

The door opened wider. Etta wore a nightdress of virginal white with a pink ribbon at the neck, the ends of it trailing down over her breasts. Her hair was loose and soft around her face. Cheyenne felt the skin tighten between his legs. He wanted to see her better . . . in the light. Stepping off the porch, he sent her what he hoped was a friendly smile.

"Come see for yourself. There are eight of them."

"Eight!" She pushed open the screen and walked barefoot out on the porch. Grabbing the post, she prepared to leap off and follow him, but her senses returned. She looked down at her thin nightdress and pink toes. "Wait. I've got to— Wait." She darted back inside.

"Hell," Cheyenne muttered, kicking at a bent horseshoe that glinted in the fading grass. He tipped back his head and filled his lungs with air that carried a mixture of autumn's dying breath and winter's first frosty sigh.

He ambled toward the barn, trying to recall every detail of the gown she'd been wearing. He knew she'd come out dressed in day clothes and with her boots on. She would pile her hair up on her head, too, or maybe she'd braid it. Either way, she'd be back to the untouchable Etta Hollister.

Inside the barn, he lit another lantern and placed it close to Butter and her pups. He smiled, watching the puppies squirm and suckle while Butter nosed them, licked them, sniffed them. He gathered the soiled straw and replaced it with fresh. Butter wagged her tail as if thanking him.

Bounder crept around the edge of the barn door, ears standing straight up as he listened to the snuffling and squeaky whimpers. Cheyenne stepped aside so that Bounder could get a look at his new family, but Butter showed her teeth, and Bounder backed off.

Etta hurried inside, out of breath and nearly bursting with excitement. To Cheyenne's utter amazement and joy, she had left her hair loose and had thrown on only a pale pink wrapper and stuck her feet in brown velvet slippers. His blood thickened and then flooded his organ. God, she was pretty, with her blond hair flowing over her narrow shoulders and her eyes shining like emeralds.

She fell to her knees in the straw to admire the puppies. Laughter, soft and feminine, bubbled from her. "Oh, look at them," she whispered, a catch in her voice. "Butter, they're beautiful."

No, you are. He had to fight to keep the words from spilling out. He cleared his throat of them. "Butter scared off Bounder. She wouldn't let him near them."

"She's probably afraid he'll hurt them. It happens sometimes. The stud tries to tear out the throats of the pups. Jealousy, I guess. Or maybe he knows that Butter won't let him near her until the pups are weaned, so he figures he'll get rid of them and shorten the waiting time."

"Or maybe," Cheyenne drawled, "she's just being a bitch."

Etta angled a glance up at him, saw his smile, and shrugged. "Why didn't you come get me sooner?"

"I wasn't here when she was whelping. When I came into the barn, she'd already finished."

"Where have you been?" she asked. "Did you sneak back into town?"

He drew his brows together, trying to sort her out. "Town?" He shook his head. "No, I was playing poker with Whitey and Andy in the—" Realization struck him a blow. "You thought I'd gone back to Clearwater to be with Meg O'Rourke, didn't you?"

She shrugged again. "Don't care if you did or you didn't. I was just . . . never mind." She stroked the head of the black pup with her fingertip. "I wonder how many of each she's had."

"Five males and three females," he told her. The lantern light changed her hair from sunny blond to deep gold. It looked soft and thick, and he wanted to bury his hands in it.

"Oh, you sweet, sweet thing," she cooed, picking up the black-and-white pup. "What a pretty face! You look just like Bounder. What's wrong, sweetie? You want your mama? Poor baby. There, there, poor baby."

Her voice, lilting and soft and so sweet it made Cheyenne hurt inside, rolled over him and swept through him. He fisted one hand and stood spread-legged, throbbing and pulsing and aching. Christ, if only she'd talk to him that way! Her voice reminded him of everything feminine—curling lashes, creamy breasts, heart-shaped backsides, soft thighs, and slim ankles. Her voice teased him with dulcet tones and nonsense words that made his heart puddle in his chest. Her voice wrapped him in a velvet fist that moved up and down, up and down, until his whole body trembled and shook.

"Christ Almighty!" He spun away, feeling hot and ready to burst.

"What the hell's wrong with you?" she asked, her voice no longer sweet as honey now that she was addressing him.

"The question is, what the hell's wrong with

you?" he asked between gritted teeth. "Why are you sweet-talking puppies when you should be using that voice on a man?" He glanced over his shoulder. She averted her gaze and bent over the puppies.

"I don't care what you think or what all you've heard, but ... I'm not a whore."

He stared at her, wanting to kiss her and shake the life out of her at the same time. "I know that, damn it!" He strode past her and out into the night air.

Etta watched him go, then turned back to the squirming puppies, her eyes brimming with tears. She wiped them away, sniffed, swallowed, took a deep breath. What's wrong with me? she wailed inside. She couldn't control her emotions anymore, especially with Johnny Cheyenne.

And why did he have to go around half naked? His hand wasn't so bad that he couldn't button his shirt all the way up to his neck. She closed her eyes and saw him bare, as he'd been that other night in the barn. Her eyes popped open and her skin grew hot and moist. Lordy, she had to get control of herself again or there would be hell to pay.

She concentrated on the puppies, checking them over. They all seemed healthy, and she figured she'd keep one or two. The others would be easy to find homes for, since they were all pretty and would be good herding dogs.

She listened to Cheyenne pacing outside, and wished she could read his thoughts just as she did a book. She would love to open the cover and leaf through the pages of his life; to know his history, his secrets, the truth and fiction of his heart of hearts. She would love to know what he *really* thought of her.

Disgusted with her silly absorption in him, she made herself remember that he was one of the men who had led her brother astray. That's all she needed to know about him.

She sensed his return and looked up to see him filling the opening to the barn. Her mouth became so dry she thought she might choke. His shoulders were so broad, his waist so lean, his legs so powerful. Her gaze strayed and she saw the bulge. She jerked her gaze away, but too late. She'd seen. She knew. Saints be sinners, she'd placed that stiffening in him!

"I'm sorry I yelled at you," he said in a voice that made her go all soft inside. "It's just that . . . well, hearing you talking so sweet to those pups made me want—well, want."

"There's always that room upstairs at the Scarlet Rose," she said, then sent him a quick smile to show that she was pulling his leg. "You've got an open invitation, so I hear."

He nodded, a smile pushing up one corner of his mouth. "You've got fire in you, Etta. I admire that."

Admire? He admired her? She squinted one eye. "Who's sweet-talking who here?"

"No fooling." He crouched beside her.

Etta swore she could feel the heat of him envelop her like a puff of steam from a locomotive. She was glad for the deep shadows concealing her furtive glances his way. His skin made her think of copper, all shiny and taut, and his chest muscles drew her gaze like a bee to a blossom. She'd never seen a flesh-and-blood man so perfectly sculpted.

He brought to her mind the pictures in one of her books, *Greek Statuary of the Old Masters*, and she decided she would find that book among her collection and have another look at it. She'd been fascinated with it the first time, but now that she had proof that such bodies existed . . . well, that would make it doubly more interesting.

"Whitey told me that Brickman threatened you."

She settled on her knees in the hay and pulled her wrapper more tightly around her, although she was burning up with a strange kind of fever. "That's right. He's full of threats. I don't pay him any mind."

"You're lying. He's on your mind more than you want to admit, even to yourself." He slanted a forearm across one knee and twisted around to look at her. "Did he threaten to take more than your land? Did he say he was going to take you?"

She gasped softly before she could stop herself. "He did. But like I said, he's always threatening to do things to people."

"And from what I hear, they aren't idle threats. He's a dangerous man."

"And I'm a dangerous woman," she said, glaring at him and thrusting out her chin.

He smiled. "There's that fire again." He chuckled, and the sound rumbled up from his chest like a cat's deep purring. "You'll get no argument from me, Etta Hollister." He smoothed a fingertip over his leather-covered knee, making a trail in the nap. "I don't know much about him, but it's easy to see he's got the town of Clearwater shaking in its boots. You should probably heed his words and keep your eyes peeled. It would be good if you didn't go anywhere alone, too."

"Did Whitey tell you to follow me? Did he put you up to this?" She sighed. "He worries himself sick over every little thing and someday he'll—"

"This is my idea," he interrupted. "After talking to people in town today, I realized that Blaine Brickman is someone to be reckoned with."

"I've reckoned with him my whole life. I can handle him." Etta hoped she sounded firm and unconcerned. Glancing at Cheyenne, she saw that she hadn't convinced him. "All he's really interested in is this land."

"I don't think so." He rubbed a palm over his leather-covered knee. "Lone Deer told me that Brickman looks at you as a man looks at a woman he hopes to bed."

"Oh, you mean like you just looked at me?" The moment the words escaped, she wished them back. Her heart stopped beating for long, suffering seconds, and then tapped frantically. She didn't dare look at him for fear he'd laugh at her. Probably thinks I'm asking for it, she decided, shutting her eyes tightly against the pain. Stupid, stupid, stupid . . . !

The full press of his mouth on the side of her neck sent her sprawling backward into the hay. Liquid fire shot from the moist place on her neck straight down her spine. She shivered as if she were caught in a snowstorm.

Supporting herself on stiff arms, she witnessed his sensual smile and gleaming eyes with renewed shock. On all fours, he started toward her. "No!" Etta held up one hand in a flimsy shield. "None of that. I didn't . . . I shouldn't have said that. I don't want you thinking that I . . . that I want anything to do with you."

"Oh, you've *tried* to make that clear," he said, his voice low and growly. "But I don't believe you, Etta. Like I said, there's fire in you. Passion's fire." He grinned. "Sweet passion's fire."

"Song," she corrected, then realized he knew he'd been incorrect. "And I want my book back."

"But I haven't finished it yet."

"You probably can't even read."

"Yes, I can. In three languages. How about you?" He crawled forward one step.

"Stop." She shook her hand at him, palm facing his grinning visage. "Three languages? You're lying." She studied him carefully. "You're not lying?"

"No. I'll return the book soon. I'm savoring all the good parts. Did you like that scene when the young lady was kissed by the knight and swooned in his arms? I don't think you'd swoon. I think you'd kiss him back. I think you'd give him your tongue."

"Stop!" She realized he'd moved closer still, and she scrambled back by digging her heels into the hay and pushing. Her nightgown and wrapper tangled around her legs. One of her velvet slippers fell off her foot. Before she could even think of retrieving it, Cheyenne had snatched it up and grabbed her ankle in his free hand.

"Let me help you." He paused. "Or perhaps I should remove the other one?"

She tried to jerk free, and he tightened his grip.

"No? All right, all right." He positioned the slipper onto her foot, then kissed her ankle before letting go. "Back to that book—"

"No. Back to the house for me." She sprang up and started to dart past him, but he was as quick as a striking copperhead. His arms snaked around her waist and she found herself pressed against the hard length of him, her head thrown back so that her gaze locked with his.

"Not so fast, Etta," he whispered, his clean-smelling breath wafting over her face like a sun-warmed breeze. He dipped his head and his lips touched her throat. His whiskers were rough against her skin, and she squirmed in his embrace. 'Shh, shh. Steady now. I'm not going to hurt you."

She reached back, trying to balance herself, and felt the rough plank wall behind her. Her fingers touched cold metal and she grasped at it. A handle. A metal handle. Her tactile senses identified the object—a shovel. His mouth felt wonderful on her throat, skimming down to the V neckline of her wrapper and to the swell of her breasts. So wonderful. Too wonderful.

His hold on her loosened as his roving mouth continued to explore in her gaping neckline. Etta felt her insides soften and that old feeling ... that helpless, unstructured feeling, stole through her. With a burst of panic, she wrenched away from him and brought the shovel around and up. Shock registered in his eyes.

"Back off," Etta warned. "I'm going to the house."

He retreated, giving her a clear path. "Go right ahead." Lowering his brows, he stared at her warily as she advanced, the business end of the shovel held high. "Before the week's out, you're going to kiss me back."

"You're crazy." She sidestepped her way out of the barn, keeping him in plain sight.

He laughed under his breath. "You think that

shovel is keeping me from you?" He laughed again, louder. "The only thing keeping me from you is me." He jerked a thumb at his chest. "I don't take what isn't offered."

"And I'm not offering. You touch me like that again and I'll—"

"Next time, you'll kiss me back." He pointed a finger at her and gave a wink. "Before the end of the week. Mark my words."

"You're loco." She dropped the shovel, then turned and ran for the house. Her nightdress and wrapper clung to her legs, but she didn't trip. Bounding up onto the porch, she glanced back to see if he followed. He didn't.

He stood in a pool of moonlight, leaning on the shovel and watching her, his white teeth blazing against his dark skin. She felt foolish, giving him such a show. She hated feeling foolish.

"And I want my book back," she yelled at him with impotent fury. She wagged a finger for emphasis. "By the end of the week. Mark my words," she added in a needling tone. With a quick lift of her chin, she whirled and waltzed into the house. She tried not to care that he was laughing at her.

Cheyenne flung back his head and stared at the cool moon. She has fire, he told himself. And she's a challenge. Any man who wanted her was in for the fight of his life, that was for sure.

He squared his shoulders. He'd never backed away from a fight worth winning, and Etta was worth it. Yes, no doubt about it. Turning, he strolled toward the barn. He could hear the soft whimpering of the puppies and felt a corresponding sensation deep inside him. A vulnerability. A wonderment. A need to be touched and comforted.

It was new to him, this sensation. And he wasn't quite sure he liked it. But it persisted, whether he liked it or not. He had a sinking feeling that Etta had put it there. Damn her green eyes. Her forest-green eyes.

Chapter 8

During the whole damn week, he hadn't touched her. Hadn't even looked at her all that much. It was unnerving. By the end of the week, Etta was as jumpy as a bitten-up cow near a swarm of flies.

Not that she *wanted* him to make any advances, she thought, bending over to place her head beneath the spout of the pump behind the house. She worked the handle and cold water poured over her head, wetting her hair to the scalp. Why had he promised to get a kiss off her by the end of the week if he had no intention of following through on it? she wondered crossly.

Grabbing up a bar of Castile soap, she rubbed it into a lather and applied the foaming suds to her hair. Her back ached from the long hours of bending over squirming calves, and she straightened while she massaged her scalp. Soap bubbles rolled near her eyes. She shut them tight and continued the brisk washing of her waist-length hair.

Seven whole days of waiting and wondering when he'd make his move on her, and for what? Nothing. Not one suggestive glance or accidental brushing of his body against hers. Ooh, she hated Johnny Cheyenne for baiting her! He was a mangy coyote of a man.

Leaning over, she rinsed the suds from her hair, then wrung out the water. Her shirt stuck to her, having gotten soaked. She plucked at the front of it as she trudged to the house to start supper. Seven whole days and nothing. There was nothing worse than a silver-tongued devil. She was beginning to think that Johnny Cheyenne was more of a threat to her peace of mind than Brickman or the doggone railroad!

Standing at the corner of the barn in deep shadow, Cheyenne watched Etta wash her hair. He had a good view of her heart-shaped backside. When she straightened to work the suds into her fair hair, he admired her curves and long, firm legs. He thought of how good those legs would feel wrapped tight around him while he drove hard and fast into her. He ran a hand down his sweaty face. Good God, he ached for her. Seven days. He'd lived through seven days of hell because she was as stubborn as she was spirited.

He could only hope that she was half as miserable as he was.

At the first of the week he'd thought she'd cave in by about Wednesday, but that day had come and gone without even a howdy-do from Etta. She'll come calling by Friday, he'd assured himself. Somehow, some way, she'd give him a come-hither smile and her eyes would sparkle with promise and he'd be on her like a young bull after his first heifer. But nothing. No glance, no smile, no encouragement.

Sunday had dawned with little hope. She'd read her Bible during breakfast, holding the black book high so there was no chance for her to meet his gaze. Then she'd ordered him and Andy to rope and drag calves to the pen, where she and Whitey cropped, cut, and branded them. It had been a busy, dusty, frustrating day of grunts, groans, and occasional curses as the calves ducked, dodged, and kicked with uncanny accuracy.

Cheyenne had left Lariat in the pasture and had ridden one of Etta's quick-footed cattle ponies, named Cutter. The dun-colored gelding had proved himself a match for the frisky calves, and Cheyenne had found himself sitting in the saddle and admiring the horse's skill.

But now he admired another frisky critter as Etta rinsed her hair and then twisted it into a long rope, squeezing the excess water from it. When she stood up and turned toward him, he sucked in his breath, glimpsing the alluring outline of her breasts beneath the clinging dampness of her shirt. Her nipples showed pink through her chemise and checked shirt. He broke out in a thin sweat and heat built in his loins. She had the kind of body that gave a man wet dreams. Full breasts and a narrow, nipped-in waist. Slim, rounded hips, and legs that seemed to go all the way to her collarbone. Her hands, although roughened from roping, were slender and constructed of delicate bones. Hands made to create needlepoint pillows, plant flower gardens, bathe babies, and make a man beg for mercy.

She'd call him crazy if he told her how he often imagined her in a lady's parlor, perched on a velvet settee, bent over an embroidery hoop. How he got hot thinking of how sunlight shimmered over her pale gold hair, how the décolletage of her gown enticed the male eye, how she looked up from her handiwork to give him a special smile of intimacy. He was certain she never pictured herself in such a place, but he did. Maybe because such a scene was in that book he'd borrowed from her, and he'd noticed that those pages were dog-eared and finger-smudged from many careful readings.

Etta Hollister might have been born to the saddle, but like any woman, there was a side to her that wanted a more genteel life. Of course, being a man, Cheyenne also felt sure she needed something else, too—to be taken on a wild ride of uncompromising, overwhelming lust. God knew that's what he needed.

Her long legs took her to the house while Cheyenne writhed in an agony of his own making. All she'd have to do was give him a little sign—a puckering of her lips, a flutter of her lashes, just the hint of a knowing smile—and he'd be all hers for a few hours. He'd sworn he'd get her to kiss him, but it looked as if she had won this battle of wills. Squinting, he glared at the house while the swelling in his trousers bedeviled him. The whole damn week he'd been half hard and ready for action. He might just have to ride into town for some relief tonight. Damn Etta Hollister and her stubborn pride!

Standing by the sink with her arms in warm, soapy water up to the elbows, Etta let her thoughts whisk her away to earlier that day, when work had been interrupted by the midday meal of beans, bread, and apple cobbler.

The temperature being unusually warm during this first week of October, the men had sprawled in the grass after dinner to allow their food to settle and their bodies to cool. Etta had sat up against a tree, hat in hand, fanning herself and discouraging insects. Through slitted eyes she'd watched as Cheyenne had risen from the brown-and-green pasture grass to remove his shirt. He'd wadded the garment in one hand and wiped his gleaming torso with it, then spread the dark blue shirt out on a fence for the sun to bake the dampness out of it.

Etta had seen men do this all her life, but she'd never been entranced by it until that afternoon. Every mundane gesture took on new significance when performed by Johnny Cheyenne. She'd been made aware of how closely she watched him do this common task after yanking her gaze from him to find that Whitey was grinning like a drunken cat at her. There was no escaping Whitey. He saw everything, and he could read her like nobody else. She'd pulled a smart-alecky face at him, shrugged, and looked off toward the branding pen as if nothing at all were wrong with her. As if her heart weren't beating to the point of bursting.

She closed her eyes to examine the memory more clearly. Yes, much better. She could see the delineation of muscle writhing beneath Cheyenne's coppery skin. Unlike other Indians she'd seen, he had body hair. Straight and sparse, it dusted his lower legs, belly, and chest, darkening his coloring even more. And he moved with such easy grace, she thought. Like a dancer, he executed each motion with fluid precision. Even reduced to the more awkward use of his left hand, he managed to mesmerize with movement, to mystify with mobility.

Masculine also took on new meaning for Etta when she looked upon him. His masculinity rede-

fined her femininity, bringing out nuances and reactions in her that she'd never known before.
Watching as he plowed his fingers through his
thick, inky hair ... admiring his light-footed,
flowing gait ... smelling his spicy, manly body
scent ... observing the strong flexing of his throat
as he drank greedily from a canteen ... envying
the droplet that rolled from the corner of his
mouth, down his square chin, to the winged expanse of his clavicle—oh, it all made her squirm
with a keen restlessness.

She knew what her body wanted. It wanted his
body. She'd read enough books and lived enough
life to know desire when it crouched in her like a
caged animal waiting for the door to spring open.
And she knew what would trip the latch on that
door. Just one kiss. One kiss and she'd be his, any
which way and for as long as he wanted.

Etta lifted her hands from the tepid water and
covered her face. Suds eased down her wrists to
tickle her forearms.

Don't be ridiculous, she scolded herself soundly.
*You would not be reduced to a puddle of need with just
one kiss. Great gobs of goose fat, you've been reading
too many love stories!*

Instead of dwelling on Cheyenne and his masculine attributes, she made herself focus on poor
Hank rotting in a prison cell. She doubted if Cheyenne ever wasted a thought on him. Her brother
was merely a casualty of Cheyenne and the Nelson gang's. It had been a dark day when Hank
had ridden off to seek his fortune away from the
Flying H. He'd been goaded by Blaine Brickman
to head for the hills—another reason for Etta to
hate Brickman.

Within a month rumors had gotten back to her that Hank had joined up with an outlaw gang. A month later she'd received a letter from him that confirmed the awful truth. He'd written that he was traveling with some friendly fellows, among them one Jeb Nelson. Whitey had told her that Jeb was lead rider of the Nelson gang, along with his brother, who had died three months earlier in a shoot-out. Hank's letter had been full of Jeb Nelson—how funny he was, how he could draw a gun and shoot it before you could blink an eye, how he was free as a bird and didn't answer to any man. That, Hank had written, was the life for him. Free as a bird.

How free do you feel now, Hank? she wondered. Bet you wish you could push back the hands of time and make some different decisions. Etta knitted her brows as she dried her arms and hands on a towel. Come to think of it, Hank probably wouldn't change his mind about much. He was fool enough to believe that he could get away with that bank robbery, given a second chance. Even as a boy, he'd shown little remorse or inclination to change his ways. When he was bad and was caught, he grinned and took his lumps, never once saying he'd never do it again. Because he *would* break the rules Henry Hollister had set for him. He broke them every chance he got, which was daily.

Etta shook her head in frustration as she pushed open the back door and threw out the dishwater. Yessiree, her brother wouldn't ever change. No man did. And any woman who thought different was a damn fool.

Letting the door swing shut, Etta put away the

wash bucket and dishes, humming lightly under her breath. She was getting used to not having Hank around, but she still missed him, especially at night. He used to sing to her and play the guitar. Sometimes she'd read to him; other times he'd make up a wild story for her amusement. Despite his lazy, careless ways, he'd been good company.

In her bedroom, she brushed her clean hair until it crackled and shone like pale corn silk in full sun. Seven days. A week. She shut her eyes and wished she could stop thinking about Cheyenne's silly promise and feeling all droopy about it.

Fatigue softened her muscles. She shouldn't have stayed up so late last night to finish sewing this dress, she thought. She examined the frock she wore, admiring the simple, elegant lines and the lace edging the sweetheart-shaped neckline. The material Hester had given her had been just enough. She'd had only a couple of square inches left over, and those would be stitched into a quilt someday. Etta sighed, running her hands along the fitted waist. Cheyenne hadn't even noticed.

She shoved aside her melancholy. Maybe she'd check on the puppies before turning in. She stood up, liking that idea. Yes. She'd check on the puppies. Etta hurried toward the barn, a part of her acknowledging that puppies weren't pulling her toward the barn. He was. He and his cursed promise.

Cheyenne lay back in the sweet-smelling hay, eyes closed and half asleep. A dream wove through his subconscious, a dream of his boyhood among the tribe of Cheyenne. He saw his mother again, crouched over a stretched buffalo hide that she was tanning. She looked up and smiled at him. Then her face changed. Her hair lightened from black to blond. Her eyes changed from light brown to dark green. She became Etta, making cooing sounds at him in that tone of voice that never failed to make him hard with wanting.

A dog barked repeatedly, and Etta scolded it. She turned toward the black-and-white herding hound and shook her finger, a frown on her face.

"Hush that racket! You'll wake him up, you silly thing. Now go on outside, and I'll be out in a minute to pet you. Go on, I said. You'll get your petting, don't you worry. Get down, Bounder. Get!"

Cheyenne opened his eyes, fully awake and aware that his dream had dovetailed neatly into reality. He rolled to his feet and looked down from the loft at the top of Etta's blond head. She still wore the attractive forest-green dress she'd had on during supper, but—sweet Jesus!—she'd unbraided her hair. It fell full and shining to her waist. He remembered seeing her wash it earlier, and his passion for her caused him to swell even more.

"So if I go outside, you'll pet me?" he asked, grinning broadly to try to cut through his inner tension. She whirled to face him. She'd been doting on the puppies, but he captured her complete attention.

Etta stared up at him, and a traitorous part of her regretted that he was clothed. Bits of hay clung to his black hair, and the skin around his eyes was puffy. He'd been sleeping, she thought, running her gaze down his open shirt and unfastened work pants.

Lord have mercy, he looked good to her hungry

eyes. She went weak in the knees and dropped to them under the pretense of admiring Butter's litter.

"No answer to my question?"

Question? Oh, yes, he had asked her a question. She couldn't remember it. Seeing him had wiped her slate clean. "I wanted to play with the puppies for a while."

"I'd let you play with me, if you want."

Her throat constricted around her beating heart. Etta chanced a glance in his direction to find that he was descending the loft ladder. She recalled another time when a man had made her heart flutter in her throat and she'd felt dizzy with expectation. But this time was different. This man was different. For one thing, she was a woman now and knew what awaited her should she encourage him. For another, he would accept her decision should she refuse him. He wouldn't press or sweet-talk her. He'd retreat or advance, leaving the final decision to her. She couldn't say that she knew Johnny Cheyenne all that well, but she knew that about him. He didn't force himself on women. She sensed that it was a matter of pride with him.

He came to stand behind and to her right, hovering in her peripheral vision, daring her to turn and face him. But she found she couldn't. Her courage deserted her and she stared at the nursing puppies as impotent tears built in her eyes. She had trespassed on his territory, wasn't that enough? It would have to be, she realized, because she could do no more on her own. Her pride might be in tatters, but there was enough left to keep her from asking him outright to make good on his promise.

She heard the rustle of hay, felt the heat of him, and then his lips touched the nape of her neck. Pleasure ricocheted through her and she squeezed her eyelids and lips together to keep from swooning. His lips felt as if they were fashioned from velveteen, so soft and warm. He kissed her again along the back of her ear. The tip of his tongue traced the outer shell.

His lips opened against her skin and he breathed out, hot and damp.

"Etta . . ."

A moan worked itself past Etta's clogged throat, and in the next moment she had twisted around into his waiting arms. His mouth covered hers in a hard, masterful kiss that stoked her simmering desire into a raging firestorm. She tangled her fingers in his hair and opened her mouth to him. His tongue speared her, filled her up, shattered her previous notion that the best kisses were pure and celestial. His kiss was all fire and brimstone. Sweet as sin. The best she'd ever had. Better than anything her nimble mind had imagined.

Any other time, with any other man, she would fight like a wildcat, but tonight, with him, she was a kitten in his arms. Her tender, swollen breasts pressed urgently against his chest. He cupped her buttocks in his hands and pulled her closer, between his spread thighs, against the hard heat of him. She felt him move down there, a live thing wanting to get at her. She didn't care. All she wanted was for him to go on making love to her mouth with his big, bold tongue. She wanted his hands on her . . . anywhere, everywhere.

When he set her from him, she kept her eyes closed for a few moments, hoping he'd resume his torrid seduction. When he didn't, she lifted her lashes slowly. She thought he'd be smiling, but he wasn't. His gaze roamed over her face, searching, finding ... what?

"We've been sniffing and circling each other ever since that day in town when I sent Ben Brickman from this world." He brought up one hand to smooth it over her hair. He watched, his blue eyes traveling the path of his hand. He tugged at her blouse exposing her neck so that he could place a warm kiss in the curve of it and another on her freckled shoulder. "You can't deny it. You wanted me to do this all week. You came here hoping I'd make good on my promise. Well, I have. Now, what are you going to do about it, boss lady?"

Boss lady. Oh, Lord, how *would* she face him tomorrow? He'd expect ... what? For her to give over to him, go all shy when he spoke to her, break her blamed neck to do his bidding? No, no. Not that. Never that. She wouldn't be any man's tamed mutt, trotting at his feet and being faithful while he chased every female who flounced by. Besides, he was an outlaw, and not long for this ranch. She was letting a dirty outlaw love on her!

Struggling mightily, she broke out of his embrace and sucked in a deep breath like a drowning woman crashing through the water's surface for blue sky. He sat back on one knee and planted his other foot in the hay. Rubbing the lower half of his face, he surveyed her expression, and regret shadowed his eyes.

"You're going to run out of here like a cat with its tail on fire, aren't you?"

She shook her head and gained her feet. No, she wouldn't run. She'd walk . . . fast.

"Etta!"

His command stopped her, forced her to pivot and face him again. Her lips throbbed from his kisses, and her insides quivered like plucked bowstrings.

"You and me have to settle this between us, one way or the other. It won't just go away. It's far too strong for that. We'll either have to give in to it or decide to hate each other."

"I already hate you," she managed to say, and her voice sounded strained, her tone flat and unbelieving.

He grinned and shook his head. "Not yet, but soon, maybe. I hope it doesn't come to that."

"Sure. You want to sow your oats, and then what? You'll expect me to accommodate you every time you get to walking stiff-legged, and you'll expect me to keep out of your way otherwise. Well, I won't be your plowshare, Cheyenne. I think better of myself than that."

He grinned lopsidedly. "Etta, if all I was looking for was a field to plow, I'd pick one less rocky than yours."

She tipped up her chin. "Then what *are* you looking for, just a good time? You looking to kill an hour?"

He nodded, rubbing his stubbled chin again. "Yeah, I'm looking for a good time, but I want you for more than an hour, Etta. An hour will just get me started. It'll take me all night and maybe part of the next day to get around to all I've got planned for you." He lifted one black brow. "I don't suppose you're interested?"

Etta found she couldn't speak, couldn't even gather enough moisture in her mouth to spit. She spun around, her face feeling as hot as a griddle, and stumbled blindly toward the house.

Cheyenne let go of a long, shuddering sigh. "Nope, I didn't think so," he whispered, then looked forlornly up into the shadows of the loft, where only dreams of her awaited him. Just when he thought he might bellow with frustration, a pleasantry halved his inner pain.

He'd kept his promise! He'd gotten that kiss off her, and she'd let him. Hell, she'd pranced in here tonight to *encourage* him! He rubbed the ridge behind his fly and winced. Cold comfort, he thought, and a damned hollow victory.

Climbing up the ladder, he ruminated on his downfall. He'd shot himself in the foot when he'd called her "boss lady." Yep. That's when he'd lost her. When would he learn to keep his mouth busy loving a woman instead of trying to talk to her? Next time—if he were given a next time—he'd keep quiet and do what he did best: make love to her until she begged him to stop.

Chapter 9

"**H**ow long you figure we'll be in the hills?" Andy asked Whitey. The boy stacked short-handled tools and a tightly folded tarp at Whitey's feet, adding to the mound of essentials already there.

Glancing down at the items, Whitey frowned. "I forgot about those. Thanks, Andy. My old mule sure is going to be carrying a load. I might have to put some of this in the chuck wagon. How long will we be gone?" He repeated the boy's question. "Hard to say. A week, maybe two. All depends."

"Depends on what?" Cheyenne asked as he rode closer to the two cowhands.

Whitey squinted one eye and looked up at him. "On whether you two young bucks work or play at working. If I have to do all the chasing, roping, herding, and cooking, then we'll have to be out in those hills a spell."

Cheyenne gave a short, silent laugh. "It will be me and Andy doing all the work, old-timer. You just stay out of our way, or we might have to run you over. Right, Andy?"

Andy showed a mouthful of white teeth. "That's right, Cheyenne. Me and you is a team."

"Team, my Aunt Fanny." Whitey ran a hand over his drooping mustache and eyed Cheyenne's tack. "Where you off to on your fancy horse with his fancy saddle?" He touched a fingertip to a trailing eagle feather.

"Nowhere. I just wanted to ride Lariat a little while. I'll be leaving him behind when we head for the hills. He's a showboat and not much good with cattle."

"So I've noticed." Whitey stroked the gelding's black mane. "But he's a beauty. What's he got in him?"

"Arabian, mostly. But he must have some Tennessee trotter, because he sure likes to prance." Cheyenne leaned one arm on the high saddle horn. "Bought him off a Gypsy horse trader in Laredo. He knows lots of tricks and nothing much spooks him. The Gypsy said he was a circus horse."

"Is that right?" Whitey turned his head to let go of a stream of tobacco. When he swung his head back around, his gaze sharpened. "Here comes Etta at a fast trot. She's been going at full steam since before sunup." He stepped into the path of Etta's horse. "Hey there, sister girl." He laid a hand on Southpaw's sweaty neck. "Look at this. This poor hayburner is plumb tuckered out and the day ain't half over yet. Where you off to now, Etta?"

She pushed back her curved-brimmed hat. Her hair curled damply around her flushed face. "I'm riding over to the south corral to look over the horses we've rounded up so far and winnow out the best ones. Y'all got any favorites you want me to bring back?"

"I want that buff-colored gelding with the brown tail and mane," Andy spoke up. "He's as fast as a snake on a slick rock."

"Yeah, and I'd like to try out that pure white mare we lassoed out by the north pond." Whitey scratched between Southpaw's ears, and the horse butted him gently. "That mare will throw off some pretty foals. We ought to pin her up with a stallion this winter and see what we get."

Etta nodded and shifted toward Cheyenne, her gaze playing lightly over the festooned saddle. "What about you? Got any favorites?"

"Favorite what?" He widened his blue eyes in feigned comprehension when the other cowhands laughed. "Oh, you talking horses, aren't you?" He lifted a swath of Lariat's inky mane and let it run through his fingers. "Yeah, I got favorites. But I'll pick them out myself. I'm riding there with you. Lariat needs the exercise. He's getting lazy being out to pasture for so long."

"That's a good idea," Whitey said, backing up from Southpaw. "You don't need to be riding by yourself anyway, Etta."

She made a scoffing sound. "I don't know why not. I've been riding by myself since I was no bigger than a minute."

"I'll tell you why," Whitey offered. "His name is Blaine Brickman. You recall him, Etta Lou?"

She frowned and pulled her hat onto her forehead. "He doesn't scare me. If he trespasses on my land, I'll send him back home with a blast of buckshot." She rested a hand on the butt of the rifle strapped to her saddle.

Cheyenne chuckled, earning her thunderous glare, and reined Lariat around, heading south. "Let's ride, Sure Shot."

"Yeah, and hurry on back," Whitey called after them. "I'm so hungry I could eat this folded tarp.

I'm hungry enough to eat my saddle blanket. Hell, I'm as hungry as a woodpecker with a headache! Hear me, sister girl? I want my chow afore dark tonight!"

Cheyenne gave a short laugh and glanced at Etta. She smiled, then turned her face away from him to laugh at Whitey's graphic lament.

"He's always got something to say," Cheyenne noted, grinning. "But he's right, Etta. You shouldn't ride by yourself until this railroad thing is settled. I've never met him, but Brickman strikes me as someone who would stop at nothing to get what he wants."

"I don't want to talk about him." She dug in her heels, and her russet gelding broke into a canter.

They rode in silence, side by side across the gold-and-brown land where hay had recently been cut. Cheyenne's shoulder muscles ached when he thought of the past three days he'd spent with a pitchfork in his hands, throwing mounds of hay high up onto the wagon driven by Whitey. Hellish work, but oddly satisfying. As he looked out over the pastureland, he felt a sense of accomplishment, a chest-ballooning burst of pride. They'd put up enough hay to weather the winter, and that gave him peace of mind. Why he couldn't tell, since he wouldn't be wintering on the Flying H and shouldn't give a damn if the stock was fed or not. But he did care. He'd been raised to tend and respect animal life. The teachings went deep into his heart and mingled with his blood.

Etta's devotion to her land was contagious, he thought, realizing that he had begun to take more care in the way he accomplished his chores and that he slept soundly each night, pleasantly exhausted. He awakened each morning with his mind full of plans for the day, making lists of the things he needed to do, and looking forward to joking with Whitey and Andy and teasing Etta until she smiled or blushed. It was all so different from the life he had been leading. His days before the ranch had been unstructured, and he'd spent most of the daylight hours in bed, rising just before supper to dress and mosey over to the town saloon. He'd played cards and traded lies until closing; then he'd bedded a saloon tart, counted his money, and slept with one eye open. He expected to die every day.

Realizing that he was perilously close to feeling sorry for himself, he swept aside his ruminations and told himself he wasn't cut out for ranching. Why, he'd go crazy living here! It was all right for a while, just until he had the use of his hand back again, but then he knew he'd be more than happy to ride away and never look back.

He looked back now at the shorn field and the brilliantly blue sky with its dusting of clouds. He heard a faint bawling and saw a cow near a section fence.

"I think that cow's down," he told Etta, reining Lariat toward it. "I'll go check it out. You go on ahead, and I'll catch up."

Etta shaded her eyes with one hand. "What's she doing out there anyway? She probably stepped in a hole, or maybe she's getting ready to drop a calf. Something's wrong, or she wouldn't be out here on her lonesome."

The cow tipped up her white-and-pink nose and released another long bellow. Lariat tipped his ears forward, and Cheyenne kneed him into a gallop.

The rope loop snaked out, gathered wind, then slipped neatly over the white horse's head. Etta gave a tug and the noose tightened around the steed's neck. Passing the rope behind her, she grasped it in her gloved hands as the frisky mare reared and tried to jerk Etta off her feet.

"Settle down, girl." Etta shortened the rope little by little until she could slip a halter over the mare's ears. She tied the horse with the others she'd culled from the herd, then surveyed the corralled horses again. One or two more ought to be enough, she thought, looking for sturdy hindquarters and wide chests. Roundup was hard on horses, so she'd need three for each rider, and she'd take a couple of extras in case tragedy struck.

She recalled one autumn a few years back when they'd gone to round up hill cattle and one stroke of bad luck after another had befallen them. They'd left the ranch house with nine horses and four mules. They'd come back with five horses and three mules. And they'd rounded up only half of their herd. That had been a lean year, one of their worst. Of course, since Hank had left and her pa had died, those times seemed downright prosperous. Seemed like all they had anymore was bad luck.

She heard a horse approaching at a fast clip, but she couldn't get a good look at the rider until she had sidestepped a couple of the milling horses. She expected Cheyenne, so her cry of alarm was out before she could stop it. Blaine Brickman.

Think about bad luck, and who rides up? she thought, wishing she could duck behind the horses and not be seen. But that idea was futile. Like a rabbit trying to hide behind a blade of grass, she'd been spotted by the hunter, and he wasn't about to show her any mercy.

"Are you hurt?" Blaine asked, throwing a leg over his saddle and dropping lightly to his feet, no more than arm's reach from her.

Etta retreated, giving herself more room to run. "No, but you're going to be in a world of hurt if you don't quit trespassing on my land. I've warned you all I'm going to, Brickman." She glanced around to find that all the horses had trotted to the other side of the corral, leaving her to fend for herself against this two-legged coyote.

"Getting ready to head for high land?" He strolled along the corral fence, running a black leather glove along the second rail from the top. "How many head you figure on rounding up?"

"More than I'll need," she answered with intentional ambiguity. "It was a dry summer. If it stays this dry next summer, I'll have to dam up the spring."

Brickman sent her a narrow glance. "You won't be here next summer, Etta, unless you show some intelligence. You could keep most of this ranch if you'd only listen to reason. You know, there are any number of women who would jump at the chance to be Mrs. Blaine Brickman."

Etta laughed harshly. "Yeah, they'd jump, right out a two-story window to be rid of you." She propped her hands on her hips and stared hard at him. "If you haven't noticed, the only women in town who look twice at you are the ones you buy at the saloon. It's been so long since you've attracted the right element, you've forgotten there's a difference between ladies and whores."

"I attracted you," he reminded her with an oily smile.

Etta winced. "Don't keep reminding me. I was just a girl without any sense where men are concerned. I know better now."

"Do you recall when we used to read passages of books aloud to one another, Etta? Remember when I wrote you a poem? I titled it 'Bursting Blossom.' You loved that poem."

"Like I said, I didn't have much sense back then. I recall it was a weak excuse for poetry. Didn't you try to rhyme *bower* with *cowherd?*" She laughed, genuinely amused at the memory of his attempts at poetry.

His eyes glinted like metal. "You have obviously ceased to appreciate the finer things in life. I don't suppose you ever read or write poetry anymore."

"I never did write it, but I read it all the time. It's because I've increased my knowledge of it that I can now tell you that you should stick to swindling people, Brickman, because you're about as successful at writing poetry as I am at tolerating your bad company." She had edged close to Southpaw, and now she made a grab for the rifle.

Brickman sprang at her, and there was a brief, heated struggle for control of the weapon. His tobacco-scented breath scorched the side of her face, and his hands closed bruisingly upon hers as she tried to jerk the rifle from its leather-and-canvas sling.

Suddenly a shadow blotted out the sun and Etta felt a bolt of alarm pass through Brickman. She released her breath in a slow hiss of relief. She didn't have to ask. She knew that Cheyenne sat astride his big, flashy horse somewhere behind her.

Surprisingly, Brickman let her go without a word from Cheyenne and stepped back from her. He straightened his clothes and ran a finger along his mustache, smoothing it. Etta didn't bother with the rifle, sensing that she'd gained the upper hand, thanks to Cheyenne's timely arrival. Brickman cocked a thin brow, waiting for an introduction.

Etta pushed damp strands of hair back from her temples and forehead and faced Cheyenne. He looked as cool and undisturbed as a pond on a windless day. With his wrists crossed on the saddle horn and his shoulders slightly hunched, he was the picture of self-assurance. Only the dark blue of his eyes and the muscles jerking in his jawline belied his calm exterior.

"What was wrong with that cow?" Etta asked, as if he hadn't come up on a fight over a rifle.

"She had her hind foot stuck in a gopher hole." Cheyenne spoke in a voice slightly above a whisper. "She's okay. I pointed her toward the herd and she went at a gallop."

"That's good." Etta nodded toward the tethered ponies. "I'm almost done here. Go ahead and pick yourself out a couple, and that should be enough. We'll have the mules with us, too." She eyed a blue Appaloosa. "That spotted-rump stallion might be a nice one. A little wild, though. You'll have to break him to the saddle."

Brickman cleared his throat. "Etta, you're being

rude. I haven't made this man's acquaintance. Won't you introduce us?"

"Cheyenne," Cheyenne told him. "Johnny Cheyenne. I killed your brother." A long stem of wheat bobbed between his lips. He removed it and tossed it aside. "And I'll kill you if you ever touch her again."

An unexpected thrill surged through Etta. She felt like a damsel in one of her favorite novels, and for a moment she could imagine Cheyenne wearing a glinting suit of armor. She blinked away the image and tugged her gaze away from him when a spear of sunlight glanced off the silver disks on his saddle.

"Johnny Cheyenne, the famous gunslinger," Brickman said, striding forward, one hand outstretched in a friendly gesture. "I'm Blaine Brickman. I heard you were riding for the Flying H, but I couldn't believe it. Why would a gunslinger become a cow herder? I asked myself. The only answer I could come up with was that either you've turned yellow or your injuries are worse than others believe." He stared at Cheyenne's hands, but like his own, they were gloved.

Cheyenne ignored Brickman's proffered hand. "Get on your horse and off this land. Miss Hollister doesn't cotton to trespassers. In fact, I've been given orders to shoot any I see. You want to be the first?"

"I'm not trespassing. I'm merely visiting my friend and neighbor." Brickman smiled at Etta. "Etta and I go way back. Isn't that right, Etta? Haven't you told your new hand how we have a past together?"

"You shut your trap!" Etta rounded on him, her

hands doubled into tight fists at her side. "And you *are* trespassing, and I won't have it. Cheyenne, if he doesn't settle his narrow butt in his saddle in the next minute, I want you to shoot the mangy dog."

Brickman eased the side of his forefinger beneath his mustache, his eyes laughing at her. "Mangy dog, is it?" He tipped back his head and laughed. "Seems like you're a bit mixed up. Looks to me like you've taken in another mongrel, hoping to make him into a lapdog." He stared boldly at Cheyenne. "I don't hold any grudges about what you did to Ben. I figure my brother asked for a gunfight and got one he couldn't handle." Brickman placed a polished black boot into the stirrup and pulled himself into the saddle.

Etta watched carefully, knowing he'd mounted up to be eye-level with Cheyenne. Nothing worse than having to look up to a man while insulting him. He maneuvered his big white stallion closer to Cheyenne's black horse with its white socks and blazed face.

"However, Mr. Cheyenne, I am not my brother. Fair fights are for fools. If you want me as an enemy, you've got it, but it won't be pleasant. As for touching Etta . . ." He glanced at her, then returned his steady gaze to Cheyenne. "I think you should know that my intentions toward her are honorable. I've asked her to marry me."

Cheyenne's eyes shifted to Etta, and she felt her face burn with embarrassment. He brought his gaze slowly, insolently, back to Brickman. "She doesn't seem overjoyed." He squared his shoulders, displaying his girth to the other, slighter man. "She was trying to get to her rifle when I rode up. I believe she was aiming to shoot you. I'd take that as a *no*, Brickman."

Etta charged forward. "He doesn't want me, he wants my land! He wants Clearwater Spring."

With some effort, Brickman tore his damning gaze from Cheyenne. "I want it all, Etta, dear. You included." He spurred his horse, and the stallion he'd named Dodger pranced a few steps toward Lariat. "Where'd you get that saddle, Mr. Cheyenne?"

Etta looked from the saddle to Brickman and caught him admiring his reflection in one of the shiny disks. The man was impossibly vain. Why hadn't she seen that back when it really mattered?

"Mexico," Cheyenne answered.

"I'd be interested in buying it."

One corner of Cheyenne's full lips lifted. "Would you, now?"

"What would you say is a fair price?"

"Thought you didn't believe in being fair."

Brickman snapped his fingers. "Come, come. Name your price."

"Your nuts on a stick."

Brickman's head rocked back as if Cheyenne had hit him. Etta squeezed her lips together to keep from gasping or laughing aloud. She felt like doing both. She looked at Cheyenne with quiet awe. He was the only man she knew who would talk like that to Blaine Brickman. In that moment he won not only her respect, but also her admiration. No wonder Hank had been so enamored of him. He was as grand as an Independence Day parade.

"So that's how it's going to be," Brickman said, all politeness swept from his tone. His face grew

taut with hatred. "Fine. You want me as your enemy?" He pointed a finger at Cheyenne. "You got
it." Then he reined his horse in a tight circle.
Dodger pranced and reared before settling on all
fours again. Brickman leaned down to speak to
Etta. "Collar your lapdog, Etta. Next time he snaps
at me, I'll nail his worthless hide to your front
door." Then he spurred the big white horse and
shot away, his black coattails flying, his body stiff
and erect in the saddle.

Etta released her pent-up breath.

"What's he holding over your head?" Cheyenne
asked.

Etta composed her features, realizing he'd
gleaned more than she'd thought from the tense
confrontation. She decided to veer him in a more
comfortable direction. "You're a gutsy cuss, I'll
give you that." She laughed under her breath.
"You had Brickman damn near tongue-tied, he
was so mad."

"You going to answer me?"

"Nope." She knocked dust off her chaps. "Pick
out a couple of horses and let's get back to the
ranch. Whitey's probably grazing with the cattle
by now."

"You know that he's lusting for you, right? He
was standing there with a hard-on, pretty as you
please. If I hadn't come up, he would have raped
you."

"No, I would have shot him."

"I don't think so. You're tough, but he's tougher.
How long has he been trying to get between your
legs?"

She hoisted herself into her saddle and shot fire
at him with her eyes. "Get your mind out of the

mud puddles, will you? How dare you talk to me like that! I'm not only your boss, I'm a lady, brought up right and proper. I won't listen to smut. You got that?"

He nodded, completely unruffled. "I got it. I'm just wondering if you get it. He's dangerous where you're concerned, Etta. He means to have you, whether you consent or not. Were you friendly with him at one time? Did he try something already?"

"It's none of your business, and I'm not discussing this with you." She waved an arm toward the bunched horses. "Choose a couple, I said, and hurry."

He shook his head in frustration and winnowed out the Appaloosa and a dapple-gray gelding, both as wild as hares.

"You'll have to saddle-break them," Etta said as he tied them to the string of others.

"I've broken my share. Guess I can break these, too."

"With a bum hand?"

He slanted her a speaking glance. "With it tied behind my back and the other in front of my back."

She looked away, laughing at his bravado. "I can see how you'd turn Hank's head and make him want to be just like you. He must have eaten up all your bragging words like candy. Me and this ranch wouldn't stand a chance against you and your big lies."

"I'm not what Hank was running to, Etta. He was running away from this ranch. He hated it here."

"That's another lie. You don't know what you're

talking about." She clucked her tongue against the roof of her mouth and led the eleven horses from the corral. "Close the gate behind you."

Riding ahead, she hoped to escape his unwanted advice and his ideas about her brother. However, he caught up with her in no time.

"I don't feel like talking," she snapped at him before he could utter a syllable.

"Fine. I'll talk. You listen."

"I don't feel like listening either."

"You might as well quit blaming me for Hank taking up with the Nelson gang. I didn't have anything to do with it."

"But you let him go to prison, didn't you?"

"And how in hell was I supposed to keep him out of prison once he was arrested?"

"You could have talked him out of robbing that bank."

"Oh, sure. Like you talked him into staying here at the Flying H?"

"He hero-worshipped you, not me."

"He loves you with all his heart. I was just another footloose fast gun. I didn't mean sawdust to Hank Hollister. Still don't."

"He would have come back home if you and the others hadn't made your life out to be something out of a penny novel. Don't you think I know that you could make Hell itself sound like a pretty, little hot spot? You and those other outlaws filled him with lies and then left him to rot in prison."

"You don't believe that," he said, chiding her. "You just want to believe it. You know as well as I do that Hank is as restless as the wind. The only way he'd ever stay put on the Flying H is to be buried on it."

Furious with his uncanny assessment of her shiftless brother, Etta threw the lead rope at him. He caught it, surprise registering on his face.

"I said I didn't want to talk or listen, didn't I? You take them in. I'm gone." She slapped the reins against Southpaw and he answered by plowing up earth and tunneling through air.

The tethered horses perked up their ears and tensed, ready to give chase. Cheyenne worked fast, calming them, making them forget the galloping horse and heed the sting of his voice. When he'd settled them sufficiently, he looked in the direction Etta had taken. She was a dot against purple sky and a thorn in his side.

Well, if she wouldn't talk, Whitey would. After supper, he'd offer Whitey a sip from his whiskey stash and the old boy would open up about Etta and Brickman. There was water under that bridge, and Cheyenne aimed to find out just how deep it went.

One thing he knew for certain already: he hated Brickman. Hated him on sight. Him and his spotless clothes and proper English. Cheyenne laughed humorlessly. Looked like he'd killed the wrong brother. But that could be set to right. He massaged the palm of his injured hand, wishing the numbness would fade. When he thought of Brickman's black eyes, his trigger finger itched. He smiled. Damn, it felt good!

Chapter 10

Fireflies blinked across the porch yard, and crickets chirped a twilight melody. Etta sat in the front-porch rocker and relaxed with contentment, while Whitey whittled and chewed. She glanced at the piece of tan wood he was carving on. A deer was taking shape.

"This is probably one of the last evenings we'll see lightning bugs until next summer," Etta said. "The mornings are getting cooler. Have you noticed?"

"Yep, and my arthritic bones have noticed, too." Whitey looked toward the barn. "Guess Cheyenne and Andy are working on the harnesses tonight."

"Guess so."

"I'm glad he was with you today when Brickman tried to make trouble." Whitey angled her a curious look when she laughed. "What's so funny?"

"Oh, I was thinking about what he said to Brickman." She laughed again, remembering Brickman's shocked look—almost as if he'd been goosed. "Brickman sure didn't expect Cheyenne to talk so disrespectful to him. I believe he thought Cheyenne would pussy-foot around him, seeing as how he'd killed Ben. You should have seen his face, Whitey." She slapped one knee and released a peal of laughter. "His mouth dropped open and

148

his eyes bugged out. It was all I could do not to bust out and bray like a donkey."

"Cheyenne asked me if Brickman had forced himself on you back when."

The delight she'd been feeling faded like a lightning bug's illumination. "I hope you told him to mind his own business."

"I told him the truth. That as far as I knew, Brickman hadn't ever forced himself on you." Sympathy flickered in his pale blue eyes. "He's not being nosy. He's just trying to get a feel for the lay of the land."

Etta rocked with agitation and the old chair creaked in protest. "He's full of questions and advice, and I get tired of it."

Whitey put down the knife and block of wood to replenish his chew of tobacco. "What kind of advice is he giving you? If it's that you should keep an eye out for Brickman and run the other way when you see him, I'd say you ought to lend an ear."

"Today he was lecturing me about Hank."

"Cheyenne was lecturing? He must talk a peck more with you than he does with me and Andy. He's a man of few words around us."

"He said that Hank would never have stayed here, no matter what."

Whitey shot her a piercing glare. "And that there surprised you? Come on, Etta Lou, you know deep in your heart that's true. Maybe you wish it wasn't so, but wishing don't change things. Hank was never long for this here ranch. He hated it with a passion."

"He didn't hate the ranch; he just didn't like

Papa always ordering him around like he was a dog."

"Bah!" Whitey spit out tobacco juice. "You and me talking about the same Hank Hollister? He didn't like taking orders from *anyone*, and he *did* hate the ranch life."

"The Brickmans filled his head with tales of the open road. He wouldn't have been so anxious to hit the trail if it hadn't been for them."

Whitey shook his head and took up his carving again. "Seems to me you're placing the blame everywhere but on Hank. I wish I had me a silver dollar for every time Hank told me he was going to leave as soon as he was able. I'd be a rich man." He paused to consider the block of wood before continuing. "It's plumb stupid to accuse Cheyenne of kidnapping your brother, Etta. If you've set your heart to hate him, then pick a reason that makes sense."

Etta clutched the chair arms and rocked back and forth, her gaze latched onto the horizon, her throat tightening with aggravation. He was right, she thought with great reluctance. Hank was about as reliable as a rusty watch. It had been only a matter of time before he deserted the Flying H.

"Why couldn't he have loved this place just half as much as I love it?" she asked, but she knew there was no answer.

"Here's a better one. Why are you bound and determined to hate Cheyenne?"

"I'm not bound and . . ." She let the rest fade as truth strengthened her voice again. "He makes me nervous. I don't want to like a man who makes his living by killing."

"He tells me he makes his living by separating fools from their money."

She slanted him a look. "And how's that?"

"Gambling, mostly. You know, Etta, you might decide to hate me, too, if you knew what all I've done in my life for some quick cash."

"I doubt that."

"Don't be so sure. In my younger years I did things I'm not proud of. Why don't you tell Cheyenne what happened between you and Brickman?"

Her breath whistled down her throat. She gripped the chair arms and leaned toward Whitey. "Tell him, you say? No, Whitey." She shook a finger at him. "And don't you *dare* flap your tongue about me to him."

"Where's the harm? If he knows what happened, then—"

"I don't want to talk about it to anybody." She sat back in the rocker and closed her eyes. "I want to forget it."

"Sister girl, you've got nothing to be ashamed of. None of it was your fault."

She let her head roll from side to side against the high carved back of the rocker. "Let's not talk about it, please? It haunts me enough."

"Okay. Sorry." He concentrated on the carving for long, quiet minutes. "I miss Hank, too, but if he were released from prison tomorrow, how long do you reckon he'd hang around here? The truth is a pill to swaller, but it can cure what ails ya. And as for Brickman, well, I do believe he's met his match in that Johnny Cheyenne. I hope Brickman never gets wind that Cheyenne's gun

hand is about as useless as a twenty-two cartridge
in a ten-gauge shotgun."

"Me, too." Etta closed her eyes. The night noises
grew faint and the air blew cooler against her skin.
"I like thinking that Blaine Brickman might be just
a mite worried." She enjoyed that image for a moment before another thought, this one disturbing,
cut through her amusement. She sat up straight.
"Whitey, you don't think Brickman will do something like ... well, send his men after Cheyenne,
do you? He might even shoot him in the back."

"Now, don't fret about Cheyenne. He didn't live
this long by being dumb. That young fella is as sly
as a fox and twice as quick." Whitey rested a
gnarled hand on her knee. "You okay? You look
plumb shook."

"Oh, I ..." She settled back in the rocker and listened to her heart booming in her ears. "I got a
feeling, that's all. All of a sudden I got a chill, like
something awful was about to happen." She
crossed her arms as the night seemed to close in
on her. "I'm going inside, Whitey. Good night to
you."

Whitey waved the short-bladed knife in response as Etta left him to the creation of his
wooden deer.

Sitting on the top rail of the corral fence, Etta
watched with gleeful anticipation as Cheyenne
gingerly mounted the quivering Appaloosa.

"He's green, son," Whitey called, standing inside the corral and leaning against the fence. He
glanced up at Etta and shared a knowing grin.
"Looks fast, too. Hell, that hoss's shadow probably
follows a mile behind him, he's so fast."

Cheyenne paid them no attention as he eased his rump down on the saddle. The Appaloosa snorted and skinned back his ears. Cheyenne spoke in a low, gentle voice that didn't seem to please the skittish horse any. Cheyenne gripped the reins and hugged the rank animal with his legs a split second before the stallion leaped into the air as if he had springs for legs.

"Yeehiiii!" Whitey swept off his battered hat and slapped it against his thigh. A smile split his face and his eyes glimmered with excitement. "Ride 'im, cowboy! Hang on to that back-bending bronc!"

Etta gripped the top rail and leaned forward, her insides taking every jump and jolt with Cheyenne as the snorting, kicking steed barreled across the corral and back again. How Cheyenne hung on was a miracle in itself. He let go of the saddle horn with his bandaged hand and extended it up over his head in a classic cowboy posture. Moving with the horse instead of fighting him, Cheyenne's body looked like it was filled with sawdust instead of bone and muscle.

"Stay with him," Etta whispered, then sank her teeth into her lower lip.

They'd been breaking horses all morning—she and Whitey and Cheyenne—while Andy had ridden into town for a tin of molasses. Whitey refused to go on a roundup without molasses for his morning flapjacks. They'd saved the big Appaloosa for last, since he would be the hardest to break. The others hadn't given them much trouble. A few bucks, snorts, and crazy-stepping, and they'd settled right down. But the Appaloosa was different. He wouldn't give up the free life so easily, and they had sensed it.

Bounder barked and ran in circles, his signal of an approaching rider. Etta looked east toward town and saw the lone figure, a dust cloud nearly blotting him out. She touched Whitey's shoulder.

"Andy's coming."

"Good. He'll want to see this." Whitey returned his attention to the bronco, who was losing some of his steam. "Attaway, Cheyenne. That hoss is getting tired of trying to chin hisself on the sun."

Etta divided her attention between Cheyenne and Andy. She wondered why Andy was riding as if the hounds of Hell were nipping at his heels.

"You got him, son!" Whitey broke away from the fence and approached the winded horse. "Woowee, this hoss is so lathered up it looks like he's waiting for a close shave." He reached up a hand to shake Cheyenne's. "Good riding, son. This here's gonna be a hell of a cow horse. What we gonna call him?"

"You do the honors. I'm no good at naming anything. Hell, I couldn't even think of a name for myself and had to let an old geezer lay a moniker on me."

"Let's see . . ." Whitey scratched at his chin whiskers while he circled the horse. "How about Cannon, since he was trying to launch you like a cannonball?"

Cheyenne chuckled, keeping a firm hand on the reins of the trembling horse. "That's a good one, Whitey. I think I'll ride him around the ring and take him through his paces."

"Good ideer." Whitey turned at the sound of thundering hooves and waved grandly. "Hey thar,

Andy! You missed a good show. Hell, it was better than front-row seats at an all-girl revue from Pair-ree!"

Andy didn't even wait for Nugget to come to a full stop before he slid out of the saddle. He ran toward the corral, his eyes big and red-rimmed.

"Something terrible's happened in town!" His head rocked back and forth as he struggled for breath. He motioned wildly for Cheyenne to ride closer. When Cheyenne had positioned the winded horse alongside the fence, Andy sucked in a huge breath to blurt out the rest. "Lone Deer's dead. Somebody killed him last night."

Etta threw her legs over the fence and dropped to her feet beside Andy. "Killed him?" Her feelings of doom from last night returned, haunting her. "Oh, my God. I knew something bad was going to happen. Who did it? Did they get him? Is he in jail?"

Andy shook his head, holding up both hands to ward off her questions. His hat fell off, landing near a mound of horse excrement, but he paid it no mind. "Ain't nobody been jailed, and nobody knows who done it."

"Was he shot?" Whitey asked.

"No. Hanged."

"Oh, no!" Etta rested a hand over her laboring heart as horror built within her. One name came blazing across her mind: Brickman. "Why would . . . what's the point? Lone Deer hardly ever spoke to . . . oh, wait." She remembered the day in the dry goods store when the old Indian had made up a pretty story for her benefit. "In front of Dan Pitch . . . he took my side . . ."

"What are you yammering about?" Whitey

asked. "Who said this had anything to do with you? Where'd they find him, Andy?"

"Out back of the saloon, in that hackberry tree. Nobody's talking. The whole town is tight-lipped about it."

"That means Brickman's behind it," Etta said, her hatred for her neighbor twisting her insides.

"What makes you say that?" Cheyenne asked, his voice as soft as the hiss of a snake.

"Because everybody would be talking about it if they weren't scared. They know Brickman's behind it, and they know why."

"Why?" Whitey asked, arms akimbo. "I sure don't see it."

Etta sighed and felt a quivering around her heart that threatened to shake her voice. "Lone Deer took up for me at the dry goods store. Dan Pitch wasn't going to let me put anything on the book until I was paid up, but Lone Deer did some fancy talking and made Dan think I was sitting pretty here on the Flying H." She smiled, remembering. "He didn't have to do that—why, I've never said more than ten words to that Indian all the time I've known him." She looked from Whitey to Cheyenne. "Why did he stick his neck out for me, I wonder?"

"The undertaker and the saloonkeeper are arguing about what to do with Lone Deer's body," Andy said before Cheyenne could venture an answer. "Nobody has claimed it yet. They don't want to be out a nickel on him."

"Goddamn it." Cheyenne said something else, something that sounded like Indian talk to Etta; then he reached down and unlatched the corral gate. "Move aside," he commanded the others. "I'll be back by tomorrow."

Before Etta could respond, Cheyenne kicked the wild-eyed Appaloosa into a flat-out gallop.

"Where do you think you're going?" she shouted after him, knowing she'd get no answer. Besides, it was obvious. He was headed for town. "Damn fool. He's going off half-cocked and he'll get his blamed head blown off. Then who's going to help me with the roundup?"

"The *roundup?*" Whitey flung his hat on the ground and glared at Etta. "Will you stop acting like Hard-Hearted Hannah? Me and Andy ain't fooled, sister girl. We both know you got feelings for that gunslinger. Maybe they ain't tender, sweet feelings, but they're feelings all the same. You ain't worried about the golldurned roundup. You're worried about him and what he's fixing to do." Whitey glared at her, his watery blue eyes sparking with challenge. "If you're going after him, take my horse. He's fresh and already saddled."

Etta hesitated for a few moments, stubborn pride nailing her in place. "Great goblins, I'm going," she blurted out with extreme frustration. It galled her to be stripped naked, even if it was just Whitey and Andy looking at her. She'd like to argue that they were wrong, that her feelings for Cheyenne were as shallow as a desert lake, but there was no time. He was already a dot with dust around him, a smudge on the horizon. If she didn't ride after him, she'd have to bury him. She stomped over to Piebald and eased herself onto the sun-warmed saddle.

"Don't just stand around waiting for me," she said before flicking the reins to get the horse go-

ing. "Load the wagon and grease the windmill!"
Then she bent over Piebald's long neck and let the
mare race the wind.

The air stung her eyes and dried her mouth and
nose. Piebald stretched out in a powerful gallop,
swallowing up acre after acre, mile after mile.
When Etta raised her head to see through the
horse's flowing mane, her heart bumped against
her ribs with joy as she saw Cheyenne dead
ahead. The Appaloosa was walking, his energy depleted by this new task of carrying a man on his
back. Etta reined in Piebald to a canter.

"Hey there! You should have hopped on a fresh
horse if you wanted to race." She rode up beside
Cheyenne, slowing Piebald to a walk. Etta studied
his shuttered expression, gleaning nothing from it.
"You going to call Brickman out? I should tell you
he's a pretty good shot. Fast, too."

"Am I wearing a gun?"

She glanced at his lean waist, then at the rifle
strapped behind his saddle. "Nope, but that re-
peater could blow a nice-sized hole in a man."

He adjusted the strip of leather he'd tied around
his head. "I'm not sniffing for blood. I'm going to
claim my friend's body." He swung his dark blue
eyes around to her. "That okay with you, boss
lady?"

She nodded. "I didn't want you doing something stupid. Did you know Lone Deer before?"

"No."

"How did you two become friends?"

"Same way anybody does." He stroked the Appaloosa's sweaty neck, then tugged the animal to
a stop. "Do you have any water in that canteen?"

Etta shrugged. "Don't know. This gear belongs to Whitey." She jiggled the canteen. "It's full."

"Good. I need to give this big boy a drink." He threw a long leg over the horse and dropped lightly to the ground. "Let me use your hat."

"Use it for what?" Etta asked, giving him the canteen.

"For a bucket."

"A *what?*" She had already started to hand it over, but she snatched it back. "Use your neckerchief."

"I'd let you use my hat," he said, a smile touching the corners of his mouth. "My horse needs a drink, Etta. You going to deprive it of some refreshment?"

"You should wear a hat."

"You think so?"

She couldn't help herself. Before she knew it, she was admiring the gloss of his thick black hair, noticing that it had grown until the blunt ends now brushed past his shoulders in the back. The side part was as straight and neat as an Amish farmer's corn row. Her senses recalled the cool, silky texture of his hair. She handed over her hat.

"No, you shouldn't wear one. Wouldn't suit you."

He grinned, and his teeth were dazzling against his dark skin. "At least we agree on something." He poured three inches of water into the crown of her hat and let the grateful Appaloosa slurp it dry.

"There you go, big fella," he crooned, shoving his blunt-ended fingers through the horse's forelock. "It's not much farther to town, and I'll let you drink your fill from the community trough." He removed his neckerchief and used it to line the inside of Etta's hat before handing it back to her. "Much obliged, boss lady."

She took it from him, oddly touched by his watering of the horse and the care he had taken with her hat. "Don't call me that," she said, then added, "Please."

Cheyenne stumbled back, his hand covering his heart. "Did you say 'please' to this no-account gunslinger? My, my. Lone Deer's death has surely rattled your brains." He mounted up again. The Appaloosa tried to buck, but Cheyenne controlled him with firm hands and a low, commanding tone.

Etta replaced her hat on her head and tapped one heel against Piebald. The big horse cantered and the Appaloosa matched the pace.

"You don't have to go all the way into town with me," Cheyenne said. "I'm going to claim the body and dispose of it properly. I'm not looking for a fight today."

Today. She glanced at him, wondering when he'd set out after Brickman. It was inevitable now, she knew. He wouldn't let Lone Deer die like a dog without making someone pay.

"I want to go," she said. "I don't think Andy remembered to get the molasses, and . . . I liked Lone Deer."

Cheyenne frowned. "Is that so hard to admit, that you liked an old Indian who did you a good turn?"

"No," she said hotly. "I liked him." She jutted her chin. "I didn't know him all that well, but I liked him. Are you claiming the body because he's one of yours?"

"One of mine?" He scowled at her. "You mean, an Indian?"

"No. A Cheyenne. That's what you are, isn't it?"

He nodded. "And white. Don't forget that. I've got more white blood running through me than Indian."

"Is that how you got your eyes?"

His mouth formed a straight, uncompromising line. "Yes." He spoke through clenched teeth. "My Indian name was Strange Eyes and I hated it. It only pointed out that I didn't belong with the tribe."

"That's not as good a name as Lone Deer. Why did you pick a white name instead of calling yourself by another Indian name?"

"I didn't choose my name. It was given to me." He shrugged. "At the time, I didn't care what anybody called me. Staying alive was my main interest." He shifted in the saddle. "Are you sure Brickman was behind this lynching?"

"I'd stake the ranch on it. I'm not saying he put the noose around Lone Deer's neck, but he sure as shooting paid someone to do it."

"Just because Lone Deer showed you a kindness? Brickman wasn't there at the store, so how would he know about it anyway?"

Etta laughed bitterly. "You don't know the lay of the land yet, stranger. I can tell you almost in detail what happened and why it happened. Brickman found out that Dan Pitch added to my bill and demanded to know why."

"Why does he care?"

Etta rolled her eyes. "Because he's trying to force me off my land, Cheyenne. If I can't get supplies, then I might have to pack it in sooner. That's what he's living for." She sighed. "Okay, so he

asks Pitch why he added the goods to my out-
standing debt, and Pitch tells him that Lone Deer
said I had me a blue-ribbon cowboy working the
ranch and that I'd already rounded up more cattle
than I needed for market."

Cheyenne furrowed his brow. "Am I supposed
to be the blue-ribbon cowboy?"

Etta giggled. "You're him." She sobered as the
rest of the scenario formed in her mind. "So
Brickman gave orders to teach Lone Deer a lesson.
They didn't have to kill him, damn them. He was
a harmless old man." She jerked her mind away
from what they might find in town. God, she
hoped someone had cut Lone Deer down from
that hackberry tree.

"You think Brickman should get away with it?"
Cheyenne asked softly.

Etta selected her words with care. "No, I want
him to get his due." She reached out and gathered
Cheyenne's shirtsleeve in one fist. She shook him
urgently. "But I need you to stay alive. Don't you
see? If you die, he wins."

He patted her hand reassuringly. Etta loosened
her hold and her fingers slipped out from under
his. She averted her face, unsettled with herself for
revealing how much she had come to rely on him.
After a minute, he cleared his throat.

"When we get to town, you go on to the store
for the molasses and I'll ride over to the saloon to
see what's been done about Lone Deer."

His understanding that she couldn't deal with
her feelings yet was a sweet surprise. "We should
have brought a travois," she ventured, dreading
the task ahead of them.

"I'll make one if we need it."

She nodded, glancing once more at his formidable profile, and wondered how many women had fallen in love with Johnny Cheyenne.

Chapter 11

⌒⌒⌒⌒⌒

The area he selected was flat and windswept. A band of fir trees circled the area, almost as if they'd been meticulously placed, each the same distance from the next. Beyond were small groves of cottonwood and oak. Beyond those lay blue-tinged hills.

Etta sat in the shade where the horses had been tethered to watch Cheyenne work quickly, building a funeral pyre. Lone Deer's sheet-wrapped body lay near him. Silence seemed to settle over the clearing as if all of nature felt and honored the sorrowful occasion.

Etta recalled the shoddy treatment she'd endured at the dry goods store, and her irritation returned anew. Dan Pitch had refused to put the tin of molasses on her IOU, and she'd known he was following Brickman's orders. One tin of molasses! If Whitey hadn't wanted that molasses so much, she wouldn't have bothered. She'd have marched out of the store then and there.

But for Whitey she'd haggled, trying to talk Dan into adding that one item. He'd been adamant; even when his wife had tried to intervene in Etta's behalf, he'd refused. He'd even said he wished Etta would pay her bill and then take her business elsewhere. Elsewhere! As if Clearwater had more than one dry goods store. She had been on the verge of begging when Cheyenne had stepped into the middle of her embarrassing dilemma.

Pride filled her now, and she dipped her head as a smile broke across her face. Oh, he'd been magnificent. The flash of fire in Cheyenne's eyes and the firm set of his mouth had told everyone not to cross him. He'd just been to the undertaker's and his pain was obvious. He'd kept his patience on a tight leash. Sizing up the situation, he'd thrown a coin on the counter and ordered Pitch to give Etta the molasses.

Dan Pitch hadn't argued. One look at the cold expression on Cheyenne's face and he couldn't get that tin of molasses fast enough.

Etta's upbringing had told her to refuse this charity, but a wiser inner voice had urged her to enjoy the moment. Smiling to herself, she had admitted that she liked being rescued. It was worth the earlier humiliation to see Dan Pitch back down and scramble to do Cheyenne's bidding.

She'd sensed the change in town within minutes of riding down the main street. Nobody looked directly at her or Cheyenne. Everybody turned away and ducked inside buildings. Brickman's law was in force, and Etta and Cheyenne were fugitives.

Etta had cautioned Cheyenne not to give the sheriff any reason to lock him up, but she'd been worried that he wouldn't listen. Profound relief had washed over her when they had ridden out of town. Clearwater hadn't been that friendly before, but it was enemy territory now. All because of Blaine Brickman. Etta hammered the ground with her fist. God, how she hated that man!

"You okay?"

She looked up and felt herself blush. "Yes,

I'm . . ." She swallowed, feeling silly. "I was thinking about Brickman. He makes me so mad. He's
got the whole town trembling."

Cheyenne came toward her, and Etta's heart
climbed into her throat. He'd removed his shirt
and his torso glistened with perspiration. His
chest was wide and muscled and smooth, except
for a dusting of hair near his dark brown nipples
and down the center of him. He reminded her of
a powerful animal striding toward her on soundless feet. She shivered uncontrollably.

He threw something into her lap. "This was
wrapped around Lone Deer's neck."

Etta picked up the leather strap and didn't understand until her forefinger moved over the
notches. She looked up at Cheyenne. "This was
yours."

He nodded. "I traded Lone Deer that for this."
He pulled a short club from under his belt and ex-
tended it toward her. "It's a coup stick. Lone
Deer's father made it, and it was treasured by
him. That piece of leather was my treasure.
Brickman must have known that."

Etta decided not to tell him that she'd witnessed
the exchange of gifts between him and Lone Deer.
Instead, she admired the club and handed it back
to him. She picked up the leather strap again.
"You made a show of notching this after you
killed Ben Brickman. It's no wonder word of that
got back to Blaine." She laid it aside and examined
his expression, trying to understand the devils he
wrestled with and the pain they inflicted upon
him.

His face went still and hard. His lips parted, but
looked as if they were carved from wood. "This is

a message to me. Brickman wants me to know that he has taken Lone Deer's life to get even for the one I took. But this isn't over. It's only beginning between me and him."

"I don't want you thinking this is your fight. The Brickmans and the Hollisters have never gotten along too well."

His eyes flashed blue fire. "You expect me to walk away from this, to do nothing? He killed that man." He pointed at the tightly wrapped body. "Lone Deer did him no harm." His gaze swung back to Etta, and she saw the specter of death. "He'll pay, Etta. I mean to see that Brickman pays."

"How?" She lowered her gaze to his right hand. "Are you going to call him out, Cheyenne? You're forgetting something, aren't you? Brickman's almost as good a shot as you used to be."

He spun away from her, and she wished she had curbed her tongue.

"You don't have to stay for this. Go on back to the ranch."

Etta stood up and brushed grass from the back of her split skirt. "I'm staying. Lone Deer was good to me. I want to pay my last respects."

"Suit yourself." He picked up the body and placed it on the platform he'd built of felled trees, grasses, and leaves.

Etta looked up at the position of the sun. It was four or five hours past noon, so Cheyenne had worked on the funeral pyre for at least three hours. She'd offered to help, but he'd told her to just stay out of his way. He knew how to build a pyre, had been taught as a young boy, and he didn't need her assistance. Stung by his abrupt dismissal, she'd retreated, remembering how hard she'd been to live with following her father's death. A soul needed solitude to heal.

Cheyenne lifted his face to the sky and spoke in his native tongue, which sounded beautiful to Etta. When he raised his arms, coup stick in hand, Etta thought she saw the track of tears on his cheeks, but they could have been from drops of sweat. His lips moved in a whispered prayer.

The finality descended on her. Lone Deer was gone. Murdered. And she wasn't blameless. Lone Deer had joined her camp and had paid with his life. Damn Brickman! How she wished he would join his father and brother in Hell!

Swiping at the hot tears standing in her eyes, she focused on the stirring image of Cheyenne as he passed a torch from one end of the pyre to the other. Flames leaped up, surrounding the body that had held Lone Deer's soul. Cheyenne stepped back from the heat of the fire, the torch still aflame in his hand. He looked wild and foreign to her, but she found herself moving closer, drawn by her need to share in this tragedy. As she approached, she saw his gaze flicker sideways. His face hardened and his eyes narrowed to smoking slits.

Alarmed, Etta spotted the lone horseman, a dark blotch against the pale sky. Brickman.

"What's he doing here?" she murmured, turning toward the horses. "I'll get rid of him."

Cheyenne clamped a hand on her shoulder to keep her at his side. "He's on his own land."

"No, he's . . ." She glanced around, realizing they were near the boundary fence. Cheyenne was right. Brickman was on the other side, on his own property.

"I *wanted* him to see this. That's why I chose this spot. It's close enough to his land for him to see the smoke and come nosing around."

Etta tore her gaze from the stark figure on horseback to the savage profile of the man beside her. His lips parted to show his even, white teeth, so startling against his dark, shining skin. The ends of his hair fluttered to caress his smooth, bare shoulders. He seemed indestructible, and she wondered if Blaine Brickman had enough sense to be afraid of him.

From the corner of her eye Etta saw movement near the trees. She spun around, afraid that Brickman had sent his men to ambush them, and she was dimly aware of Cheyenne's hand on her shoulder. He pulled her back and put himself between her and the moving shadows. He held a knife in one hand, and she wondered when he'd drawn it and from where. She held her breath, exhaling only when she saw the spiky horns.

"It's only a deer," she said, releasing a shaky laugh.

"So it is." Cheyenne's voice held a measure of wonder.

The stag walked out into the clearing, its rack sporting twelve points. The animal stared at the pyre, then swung its head to stare at Cheyenne and Etta. Expecting it to bolt and run, Etta peeked around Cheyenne and waited. Standing in the glow of the funeral pyre, its rack casting slashing shadows across the short grass, the deer displayed no fear. In that instant, Etta felt as if she were living in a strange dreamland that teetered on the edge of a nightmare. Life and death, dark and light, right and wrong all seemed to converge and set her head to whirling.

Cheyenne cast aside the torch and took up the coup stick again, clutching it tightly in his fist. He exchanged a long look with the stag, and then the corners of his mouth lifted in an odd smile. Etta looked back at the deer. The lone deer.

As the eerie realization struck her, the buck turned and melted back into the thick woods. Cheyenne turned slowly toward the slight hill where Brickman still sat astride his white horse. He lifted the coup stick high, straight up over his head, in a gesture of pride and defiance. Etta watched, enthralled. He seemed more Indian now than white, more exotic than any far-off land she'd ever read about.

He released a booming cry that echoed and rippled across the land. A war cry. A cry of freedom. A harsh sound of pent-up fury and blazing redemption. Etta shivered. Oh, he was magnificent! So proud. So brave. She knew why her brother had followed so willingly. Most men would seem pitifully small standing next to Johnny Cheyenne. She swung her gaze toward the rider on the hill, and a hateful grin twisted her lips. Why, Brickman was no more than a bothersome gnat!

Cheyenne cried out again, his voice hoarse and deep. The strange sound spooked Brickman's mount, and the white stallion reared and screamed. Brickman shouted to the animal, but that only made it more wild. He struggled to bring the horse under control, but it bolted down the other side of the hill, out of sight, with Brickman still fighting the reins and barely keeping his seat.

Etta stifled a laugh and looked back to the place

where the deer had disappeared. Nothing moved. Had it been a vision or real? She couldn't be sure. Perhaps it had been an omen, a message from a higher power.

She glanced at Cheyenne. He had lowered the coup stick and was staring at the pyre, which was fully engulfed in flames. The supports gave way and the platform fell in a shower of embers and sparks. Etta stepped back as ashes billowed out, but Cheyenne stood his ground and watched the flames grow weaker. The roar became a whisper, then a hiss.

In his face she saw sadness and triumph, regret and manly pride. Her feet moved of their own accord, and it seemed natural for her to curl her fingers around his hard biceps and lay her cheek against his smooth shoulder. His skin was warm and supple. He shifted to enfold her in his embrace. She pressed the side of her face against his chest and breathed him in as she would a bouquet's perfume. He smelled wild and musky, totally uncivilized. Her senses responded to him, coming to life after a long hibernation.

He spread one hand at her throat and lifted her face to his. Her heart stammered, even as she raised herself on tiptoe to welcome his descending mouth. His full lips parted over hers, taking her in, sucking softly. She brought her arms up and around his neck. Her inhibitions, her wariness, her hurtful memories were dry kindling for the searing heat of his kiss. The flame of passion engulfed her and she opened her mouth for the mating of his tongue. But after one satiny-slick caress, Etta pulled away and her eyes flew open. She struggled briefly, her fingertips tingling against his chest, her palms kissing his sun-warmed shoulders; then she sagged against him. God, what was she doing? Would she never learn?

"What's wrong?" he whispered, his lips moving against the hair at her temple.

"I . . . can't do this." She tipped her head forward and rested it against his square chin. "You make my head spin, and I have to keep my wits about me." She placed one hand against her chest. "My heart—it's thundering like never before! When I feel like this, it scares me."

"Scares you?" he repeated with a slight shake of his head. "You should never be afraid of what your heart is trying to tell you." He nudged her chin with his knuckles. "Your heart will never lead you astray."

Etta laughed, but without humor, and inched out of his embrace. "My heart has led me straight into catastrophes. I've learned not to listen to it and never to trust it. That was a hard lesson I'm not looking to repeat."

"You want to tell me about it?"

She drew in a deep breath and eyed him, finding no real curiosity in his expression. He seemed interested, not nosy, but she couldn't confide in him. "No. I don't know you that well." Feeling uncomfortable, she switched her attention to the smoldering embers. "Well, good-bye, Lone Deer. You were a good friend when I needed one. I'll never forget you." She glanced up at the cloudless sky. "Give him his wings, Lord. He's earned them."

Cheyenne chuckled, shaking his head when she sent him a quelling glance. "Sorry. I was trying to picture Lone Deer with wings sprouting from his back."

She moved toward the horses, and he fell into step with her. "You two sure got close quick," she said. "Did he remind you of someone?"

"He reminded me of . . . the People. I've lived so many years among the whites that I had almost forgotten the old ways." He held Southpaw's reins while Etta climbed aboard; then he mounted his own horse.

"Do you feel white or Indian?"

"Neither. I'm an outcast." He shrugged, his gaze lingering on the smoking remains of the pyre. "But Lone Deer didn't treat me that way. He understood the Cheyenne part of me and accepted the white part of me. I've met only one other man like him."

"Who?"

He smiled, and lines fanned out from the corners of his eyes. "An old whiskey-guzzling trader named Quint Donahue. He took me in when I was still a boy trying to be a man." He slanted her a chiding glance. "He's responsible for my name, which you so admire."

Etta gave a haughty sniff, but then grinned at him. "It's not your given name."

"Of course not. I hated my Cheyenne name—Strange Eyes. It pointed out that I was different. That I didn't belong."

"Your eyes aren't strange. I think they're kind of pretty."

He winced as if she'd insulted him. "You'd think they were strange in an Indian village. The elders named me that to further shame my mother. She was part white and my father was white."

Etta studied him from the corner of her eye, thinking that a few minutes ago he hadn't seemed white at all.

"Quint called me Cheyenne and then tacked on 'Johnny' after a while," he said, picking up his story. "He had a kid brother named Johnny, I think."

"And you kept the name."

His blue eyes sparkled. "I thought it would look mighty impressive on a Wanted poster."

Etta tapped Southpaw's flanks with her heels. "Sometimes I shoot off my mouth when I should keep it holstered."

He urged his horse slightly ahead of Southpaw and twisted around to eye her with drop-jawed shock. "Is that an apology? Is Etta Lou apologizing to the dirty half-breed?"

"I've called you some bad things, but never that," she informed him. "And I wasn't exactly apologizing. I was just explaining."

"Oh." He nodded gravely. "That's a relief. I'd hate to think you're getting soft for me."

She darted a glance his way. He stared ahead, but a grin tugged at one corner of his wide mouth. She thought of his fiery kiss and compared it to another's. Lord, there was a world of difference in the two! Maybe she could let him—no.

She shut the door on that possibility. She couldn't let him seduce her, woo her, or whatever he had in mind to do to her. The outcome would be the same as before. He'd have bragging rights and she'd be dirt under his fancy boots.

* * *

The Double B wasn't so much a ranch as a kingdom. Through shades of twilight, Cheyenne noticed the signs of wealth in the new strings of barbwire stretched between whitewashed posts and the fancy wagon-wheel gate with the Double B brand displayed prominently and in gold leaf.

Cheyenne pointed Lariat in the direction of the ranch house. The lane was wide enough for a carriage and lined with dogwoods and wildflowers. He placed a gloved hand on the butt of his revolver in an instinctive gesture of reassurance as the ranch house came into view.

Perched on a knoll, the residence was in the shape of a square with an open courtyard in the center. Built of logs and mortar, it looked old but well kept. Shrubs and low trees surrounded it, and a split-rail fence protected it from grazing cattle.

He knew he hadn't ridden onto Double B land without notice, so he wasn't surprised when three riders approached from the other direction and stopped near the house. Cheyenne twisted in the saddle and counted two more behind him. He rode on until he was within speaking distance of the three men guarding the front gate.

"I want to see your boss," he said, directing his request to the oldest of the three, a man younger than Whitey but not half as pleasant.

He heard the ones behind him ride past. He glanced at them. They were the two skunks who had tried to bully Etta in town. Their hatred for him was easy to see, but he lent it no importance. Hatred was something he'd known more intimately than love, and he had long since learned to shield himself from it.

"He don't want to hear anything you've got to say, half-breed," the head wrangler said.

"I think he will," Cheyenne countered, then turned toward the house. "Brickman! Come on out and face me!"

Almost immediately, the latch lifted on the door and it swung inward. Brickman stepped out onto the shadowed porch, carrying a lantern with him. The light swung crazily as he lifted the lamp and hung it on a peg. He tucked his thumbs into the waist band of his tailored black pants. A cheroot smoked between his thin lips. His black hair was slicked back and his sideburns reached to his jawline. He eyed Cheyenne with bored displeasure as he stifled a yawn.

"Good evening." His tone was modulated, his pronunciation precise. He tossed aside the cheroot and drew in a breath of air. "Ah, it's a beautiful night. The stars are just beginning to peek out." His gaze drifted back to Cheyenne. "What brings you to my home . . . uninvited?"

Cheyenne unwound the notched leather strap from his gloved hand and threw it onto the porch. It landed across Brickman's boots. "That."

Brickman stared at the strap for a moment, then kicked it aside. "That belongs to you, doesn't it?"

"It used to." Cheyenne kept his gaze pinned to Brickman, but he tuned his other senses to the men circling him. He knew they'd grab their side-arms with one signal from their boss. Caution forced him to move slowly. He propped a fist against his thigh and adopted the same sort of insolence he observed in Brickman. "You think the score is settled, but you're wrong. You've made me your sworn enemy by sping innocent blood."

"And you've never done that?" Brickman asked with a jeer. "If you're here to swagger and boast and bluster, then I must ask that you leave. I was spending a pleasant evening reading verse from some of the early Roman poets. I must ask Etta if she's familiar with them."

Cheyenne slid his hand up his thigh, closer to his gun. "I didn't want to tangle with your brother, but he called me out. It was a fair fight. Not like what you did to Lone Deer."

"Ah, yes. I heard about his death." Brickman yawned again, covering his mouth with the back of his hand in a gesture that struck Cheyenne as feminine. "Tragic. Is that what you were burning earlier today? I thought it was some sort of redskin celebration."

"You knew what was going on. You're not as stupid as you look."

Brickman no longer appeared bored or uninterested. His eyes sharpened and his stare was as keen as a newly honed knife blade. Barney Timmons, one of the men who had jostled Etta in town, snickered and covered his grinning, gaptoothed mouth with one hand. Brickman struck like a snake, grabbing the lantern off the peg and slinging it right at Timmons. The globe broke, spilling flame and kerosene across Timmons' shirtfront and one pant leg. His horse screamed and bucked him off, then bolted for the barn while Timmons shrieked and rolled on the ground to snuff out the flames.

"Gather your moldy belongings and clear out. If

I see you around after tonight, I'll shoot you as I would any stray dog scrounging on my property."

"You're crazy!" Timmons screamed at his boss as he patted his smoldering clothes. The stench of seared flesh and burned hair permeated the air.

Brickman winced. "Cork your shrieking, Timmons, and get out of my sight." His soulless eyes found Cheyenne again. "I'd like you to leave as well. Your company, I'm afraid, is lackluster."

Cheyenne adjusted the strip of leather bisecting his forehead. "You're a brave man when you're surrounded by a fortress, but I'll catch you out in the open someday, Brickman, and you'll be the one screaming."

"Is that so? Will you shoot me like you did my brother?" He laughed and lowered his gaze to Cheyenne's gloved hands. "I must admit you have a fine strut for a bird with a broken wing. You'll excuse me if I don't shake in my boots. I find your threats quite . . . lame." His smile was shortened by feigned sympathy.

Cheyenne hated Brickman with everything in him. For the first time in his illustrious career, he wanted to draw his weapon—not to defend his own life, but to end another's.

"Would you like me to strap on my gun and kill you now?" Brickman taunted. "We could cease all these empty threats and get down to business, so to speak."

Could he take him? Cheyenne wondered. Etta had said Brickman was fast, but maybe with a little luck he could beat him. He glanced around, remembering the other armed men.

"Not with your fortress around you," he said, shaking his head. "I'll wait until it's just you and me. In the meantime, you stay away from Etta Hollister."

Brickman ran his thumbs underneath his suspenders, up and down, up and down, as he raked Cheyenne with a contemptuous gaze. "I believe I'll go inside for my holster and Colt. I've listened to enough of your toothless growls and I think it's time I shut you up. We'll discover, once and for all, if the rumors are true about your injury being more than a matter of bruised and broken skin." He smiled faintly. "It will be quite interesting. Maybe even more interesting than the Roman poetry."

Cheyenne's gut tightened and he felt like a wild stallion chased into a box canyon. "I told you I wanted a fair fight."

Brickman gestured to the other men. "You boys go on about your business. Our famous gunfighter doesn't want an audience this time. Come back in a half hour for his body."

"The light's too bad."

Brickman had started inside, but he stopped and turned back to Cheyenne. "Are you desperate for excuses, gunslinger? You shouldn't be giving orders if you have no way of enforcing them. I'll get my gun."

If Cheyenne had been that cornered stallion, he would have reared and charged, hoping to break free of the predicament. As it was, he remained motionless, his thoughts in a whirl. Could he out-draw him? His hand felt tight . . . unresponsive . . . If he could drop to one knee as he shot, he might dodge Brickman's first bullet and give himself an extra second to squeeze off another . . . The timing would have to be perfect, and his hand ... his hand ... God, his hand ... useless ...

"Hey thar, Johnny Cheyenne!"

Cheyenne turned in the saddle and squinted against the fast-gathering dusk at a galloping speckled horse and the man astride her. The rider removed his battered hat and waved it grandly. Fading light touched his snowy hair. Whitey!

"Who is barging in *now?*" Brickman asked with exasperation. His eyes widened, then rolled up. "It's that old buzzard from the Flying H." He curled his upper lip. "If Etta weren't so fond of him ..."

Cheyenne whipped back around to bludgeon Brickman with his hard glare. "Don't even *think* it, Brickman, unless you want to wear your guts on the outside of your skin."

Brickman frowned. "More threats. This is so tiresome."

Whitey reined Piebald next to Cheyenne's horse. He grinned broadly and listed in the saddle. "'Evening to y'all. Is there a party over here or somethin'?" He sniffed the air. "I smell smoke. Y'all got a slab of beef on the spit?"

"That's coyote meat you smell, old crow," Brickman said, eyes glinting with sick humor. "If you don't want to be next on the spit, you'd better point that nag back toward the Flying H. I've better things to do than entertain windbags and drunks."

"I come looking for my saddle mate here," Whitey said, punching Cheyenne on the shoulder. "Let's get on back to the ranch, pal o' mine."

Cheyenne regarded him. He didn't smell whiskey, but it was obvious that Whitey had been busy varnishing his tonsils. "Easy there," Cheyenne said, reaching out to steady the old man. "You've been sucking on a bottle this evening, haven't you?"

"I 'fess up." Whitey belched, then chuckled. "Tomorrow we ride, so tonight we kick up our heels."

"Ride?" Brickman had moved toward the front door, but he stopped. His eyes gleamed with interest. "You're heading for timber tomorrow, are you?" He laughed lightly. "What a waste of time. If you two cared anything for Etta, you'd advise her to give up this futile roundup. The railroad's not going to take pity on her."

"Hey thar, Stickman." Whitey let loose a juicy burp. "You lonely now that your ugly brother is fertilizing the prairie?"

Cheyenne barely kept himself from moaning aloud. Now, why did the old man have to shoot his mouth off? From the fury infusing Brickman's face, Cheyenne figured Whitey was a minute away from getting pummeled or shot.

"Why, you worthless old saddle bum," Brickman said, his voice a low growl. "I always thought you were crazy as a loon and now I know it. A man with any sense wouldn't trod on a coiled rattlesnake."

"Let's get back home," Cheyenne suggested, deciding that Whitey's safety was more important than an ill-timed shooting match with Brickman.

Whitey turned Piebald around in a circle before settling in the right direction. "Etta'll be real irked if she finds out we winded up here." He chuckled and aimed a stream of tobacco at Brickman's porch steps. A drop or two painted Brickman's boot top before he could dance out of the way. "That thar's my calling card." Whitey roared with laughter and gouged Piebald with his spurs, making the horse take off like a jackrabbit.

Cheyenne couldn't keep himself from grinning at Brickman's smoking glare and snarling mouth before he chased Piebald's tracks.

Lariat was still two or three lengths behind Piebald when they crossed over onto Flying H sod. Whitey pulled Piebald to a prancing trot, letting Cheyenne and Lariat catch up. The first thing Cheyenne noticed was the change in the way Whitey sat in the saddle. He wasn't leaning sideways, and his expression was as sober as a judge's.

"You're not drunk."

Whitey gave a quick nod. "But you're plumb nuts to go to the Double B looking for a gunfight that'll get you killed. I thought you had some wits about you, son."

"I wanted to give Brickman something. I wasn't looking for a fight ... yet. That'll come in time."

"You're golldurned lucky to be alive. If it weren't for me, you'd be dead as Grandpa's pecker."

"I guess you want my thanks."

"Naw, I don't want your thanks." Whitey gave him a glare that made Cheyenne shift uneasily in the saddle. He'd never seen the old boy so disgruntled. "I want you to stay alive! You sure won't be any good to Etta dead."

"I'm not afraid of Brickman."

"Aww, quit being such a dagburned, stubborn Indian. I'm not so much trying to save your life as I'm trying to keep sister girl safe. You're the only thing standing in Brickman's way, don't you know that?"

Cheyenne shook his head, unable to follow Whitey's fussy explanation. "Standing in his way? The railroad—"

"I ain't worried about the dagblamed railroad. If Brickman is kept away from Etta, the railroad deal will fall through. Me, you, and Etta can see to that by rounding up enough steers to pay off the Flying H's debts. Brickman will do anything to make sure that don't happen. I figured we was washed up until you came along."

Whitey squinted, his pale blue eyes barely discernible in the failing light. He removed his hat and plowed his fingers through his thinning hair, then rocked the hat back into place.

"I ain't saying Brickman is scared of you or even real worried about you being around," Whitey continued. "But you've given him pause. You've made him take a second look, which is good."

"He killed Lone Deer. I wanted him to know that I wasn't going to let it pass. He'll pay."

Whitey cursed under his breath, releasing a string of obscenities that would have made a convict blush. "Son, you hearing me?"

"Yes."

"No, you ain't. Lone Deer is dead. Etta and her dreams are still alive." He pointed a gnarled knuckle at Cheyenne and shook it to emphasize his words. "I mean to keep them that way, even if I have to act like a damn fool and come riding to your rescue, risking my wrinkled hide." He leaned closer. "You hearing me now, big gun?"

Cheyenne poked at the inside of his cheek with his tongue to keep from grinning. He figured the old man wouldn't like being laughed at just now. "I understand. From this moment on, I'll think of Etta first and my personal revenge second."

Whitey turned his head to spit. He dabbed at his mouth with his shirt cuff. "Glad you got your hearing back. We won't mention this little journey to Etta. She'd be so irritated she'd fry our nuts for breakfast." With that, he whispered something to Piebald and the big cutting horse dove into the night.

Cheyenne watched him go, wondering if Etta had any idea how devoted the old boy was to her.

Chapter 12

❧~∞∞~❧

They camped the first night away from the ranch in a place they called Forked Tree Clearing. An hour before quitting time, Whitey was sent ahead so that by the time Etta, Cheyenne, and Andy arrived, the campfire was blazing and supper was boiling in the pot.

Whitey had fashioned a corral for the horses by stretching a rope among four trees. After driving the cattle they'd rustled into a shallow valley between two hillocks, Etta sent Andy to help Whitey with supper while she and Cheyenne unsaddled the horses. She felt awkward around Cheyenne after her vulnerable encounter with him at Lone Deer's funeral. She tried to appear calm, while her insides quivered with awareness.

During the day she'd caught herself admiring his control of horse and steer. He sat square in the saddle, using his muscled legs to guide the cutting horse she'd loaned him. Cutter was well suited to Cheyenne. Only a skilled horseman could ride him. He'd shed himself of Andy a couple of times with lightning-quick turns and breathless dives down hills and ravines. The ornery gelding had sent Etta sprawling in the dirt last fall when he'd raced beneath the low branches of a sycamore. One thick limb had caught her at chest level, knocking the wind out of her and bruising her pride. But Cutter hadn't been able to unseat Chey-

enne. "You and that pony got on pretty good today," she noted, ending the tense silence between
her and Cheyenne.

"He's headstrong, but he sure knows cattle."
Cheyenne grunted as he removed the plain saddle,
on loan from the Flying H. "He tried to run me
under some low branches, but I kicked the stuffing
out of him and he abandoned that idea."

Etta laughed. "That's one of his favorite tricks."
She debated whether to voice her admiration of
Cheyenne's roping skills and finally decided he
deserved the praise. "Where'd you learn to rope so
good? Even with your hand all mangled, you rope
better than most cowboys I've seen."

"I've got quite a few men to thank for that, and
your brother's one of them."

"Hank?" She paused in her rough brushing of
Southpaw's wet hide. "When did Hank ever rope
cows around you? I thought all you did with him
was rob banks."

He slanted her a warning glare. "I told you,
Etta, I've never robbed a bank." Picking up a
grooming brush, he pulled the stiff bristles down
Cutter's back. The horse nickered and shook all
over. "Easy there, son," Cheyenne murmured in a
low, raspy voice.

Etta shivered, her senses responding to his purring, growling tone. His blue shirt stuck to his
back, molding itself to his shoulder blades and
lean waist. His denim pants were faded blue
across his muscled buttocks, and his long legs
were encased in leather chaps. He was lean and
mean, and oh, so masculine.

Like the men in the books she read, she admitted to herself. But those men were attracted to

soft-spoken virgins, not to rough-talking ma-
trons. That's what she was, a matron. She
winced, hating the sound of that word. Worse
than being called a spinster, she decided, because
at least spinsters had saved themselves and their
reputations.

"Did you hear me?" he asked, breaking into her
musings.

"What? No, I . . ." Had he said something? She
shook her head. "I couldn't hear you."

He arched a dark brow. "I said that Hank and
me used to rope cactus when we were bored. He
showed me some tricks and talked a lot about cutting and roping."

So that's why Cheyenne's riding had reminded
her of how her father had sat a horse and pitched
a lasso. "Hank Hollister is a puzzle."

"Why do you say that?"

"He couldn't wait to leave this life, and then he
spends his free time showing a gunslinger how to
cut cattle and rope steers. I should think he'd be
practicing shooting and robbing."

Cheyenne barely managed to hold back a grin.
"Practicing robbing is pretty hard to do. Dry runs
can get you killed, same as the real ones. As for
shooting, we did hold some target practice, and
me or Jeb always won. Jeb was the fastest gun I've
ever seen."

He tucked the grooming gear into his saddlebag
and checked the water bucket. "I guess these
horses will hold until after supper. I'll fetch more
water for them before I bed down." He scratched
between Cutter's ears. The big gelding butted
Cheyenne and blew warm air through quivering

nostrils. Cheyenne smiled and patted the animal's sleek neck.

For an instant Etta saw in Cheyenne the son her father had wanted so desperately. Except, she reminded herself, Johnny Cheyenne hadn't made his name as a wrangler, but as a gunslinger. Henry Hollister wouldn't be too proud of that. When Hank had left, Henry had sulked for weeks, blaming everyone for Hank's restlessness but himself.

"Hank and Papa never got along," Etta said, not realizing she'd spoken aloud until she already had Cheyenne's attention. She shrugged, regretting her divulgence, if it was one. Probably hadn't come as any surprise to Cheyenne.

"What about you and your father? How did you two get along?"

"Just fine." She rubbed Southpaw's rump as she moved past the horse to duck under the rope Whitey had strung among the trees. "Papa related better to menfolk, though. He always figured Hank would take over the ranch, so he paid more attention to him."

"Do you remember your mother?"

"Not very much. She died giving birth to Hank."

Cheyenne stepped over the rope corral. "If your father doted on Hank, then who doted on you?"

A name sprang to her tongue, but she bit down on it. Turning away, she started toward the camp. She didn't hear Cheyenne follow her immediately; then she heard his tread behind her. His long legs brought him easily to her side.

"Whitey?"

"Whitey what?" she countered.

"Did Whitey dote on you?"

"Oh." She smiled, and some of the tension left her body. "I guess, sure." Sensing his regard, she adopted a more impersonal demeanor. "Bet you're hungry. You earned your grub tonight, Cheyenne. Go on ahead. Don't wait for me."

"Here, I've got something for you."

"For me?" She paused, glancing at him and the book he pushed at her. Her book. One of her favorite love stories. "It's about time you returned that. I guess you got a good laugh over it."

"I enjoyed it. I noted the juiciest parts, just like I promised."

"I hope you didn't mark it up! I value my books, and I don't want them written all over."

"I didn't write anything in it. I marked the pages with wildflowers."

"With . . . wildflowers?" She found the first one, pressed between pages, the pink blossom and tiny leaves flattened and crisp. An image of him plucking the blossoms and pressing them between the parchment pages sent an unexpected weakness through her. One glance, and she recognized the scene. In it, the hero professed his obsession for the heroine in words so eloquent that even now sentimentality burned the backs of her eyes. She snapped the book shut and her gaze bounced up to Cheyenne's. He was studying her as if she were a mystery he meant to solve.

"If you like the song so much, why not dance to it?" he whispered in that tone that sent delicious shivers marching along her limbs. "*Sweet Passion's Song.*" He rubbed a thumb down the book's spine, where the words were printed in gold. "You invade my dreams, Etta. When I close my eyes, I see you sitting in your bed, reading this book, and pining for a lover. Then I dream that I come into your room and you throw the book aside and embrace me. The love we make, it's—"

A cowbell clanked, and Etta jumped back from Cheyenne as if he had suddenly grown horns.

"Y'all come, y'all come!" Whitey called, and the bell rattled again. "Supper's on!"

With her face afire, Etta grasped the book in one hand and hurried toward the camp. Cheyenne strolled along, arriving a minute behind her.

"Pull up some dirt, pal." Whitey motioned him into the circle around the fire. "Food always tastes better than ever the first night out under the stars. Henry used to say it was the pine-scented air that gives a man a powerful hunger, but I think it's the smell of a campfire."

"I think it's 'cause we've been working like a mule team in a rocky field," Andy offered, and everyone laughed.

"And I think you're the wisest man amongst us," Etta told Andy, poking him playfully with her elbow. "Which probably isn't saying all that much."

Whitey chuckled and gave her a wink. "We rounded up more than a few fat heifers today, sister girl. Got some mighty nice-looking ponies, too."

Etta nodded and looked around at the men, each face so different from the next. Whitey, with his sparkling, faded blue eyes and white-stubbled chin and cheeks; Andy, his dark brown face beaming with youth and energy; and Cheyenne, his features an interesting combination of two races.

"Which one of us will take the first watch?" she asked before spooning savory stew into her mouth. She'd made it last night, knowing she'd be more tired the first evening out than on any other, and that a ready-made supper would be a welcome respite. She'd been right. The stew tasted even more wonderful since she didn't have to make it from scratch after a hard day in a harder saddle.

"I'll take first watch," Cheyenne volunteered, already getting to his feet, stew bowl in hand.

"You don't have to go now," Whitey said, reaching up to tug at Cheyenne's fringed chaps. "Sit down a spell. Them cows will be okay for a few minutes."

"Maybe, maybe not. We'd all be cussing a blue streak if something spooked them and they took off." Cheyenne spooned more stew into his bowl and slung his canteen over his shoulder. "I'll eat while I'm on watch."

"One of us will relieve you in a few hours," Whitey said, reaching for a can of peaches. "Don't you want a spoonful of these?"

Cheyenne shook his head, hoisting the wooden bowl. "This will do me." He strode off in the direction of the cattle, which could be heard in the distance, their mournful lowing carrying on the cool breeze.

"These peaches remind me of the time me and another fella decided to do some canning," Whitey said, settling back against his saddle to enjoy the golden, sweet treat. "I don't know what we did wrong, but the peaches turned black and so sticky we could have used them for wallpaper paste. One of the dogs ate some and had the runs for days ..."

Whitey's voice droned on, but his words were lost on Etta as she stared after Cheyenne and thought of his dream. Had he been fooling her, trying to turn her head with pretty words? Having tasted his kisses, she found herself fighting a feverish craving. He's just like these peaches, she thought, holding out her empty bowl for Whitey to spoon the sugary, golden slices of fruit into it. One taste and she wanted more. She wanted more.

An amorous bull reared up on a heifer and caused a ripple of excitement through the herd. From her lookout on the crest of the west hillock, Etta clucked her tongue against the roof of her mouth and whistled softly. The herd settled, and the bull curbed his passion. She smiled contritely, thinking of the single-mindedness of the male animal. She'd like a silver dollar for every time she'd seen a bull try to mount a heifer while the herd was being driven at a fast clip.

Stars blinked feebly, dying in the advent of dawn. The four horses they'd rounded up from the low hills had been cobbled together near the camp, and Etta could occasionally hear their nervous whinnies. One was a young filly and should bring a nice price at market.

Running her gaze over the small herd, she counted heads again. They'd rounded up thirty-two. She knew there would be days when they'd scare up half that many, maybe even less. But she prayed for days when they'd find fifty or sixty at

a time, roaming these thickly wooded hills together, already wearing their shaggy winter coats.
Of this herd, there were only a few underweight
ones. Summer grazing had been good in these
humped hills around Clearwater Spring. Canyon
land lay to the north and south. Clearwater Spring
meandered through hills before reaching what was
called the high plains.

Etta never tired of admiring the land. It seemed
different and yet the same to her. Like one of her
love stories, each time she visited it, she found
new things to explore, new horizons to ponder.
Following in her father's footsteps, she had fallen
in love with this land. But since his death and
Hank's imprisonment, she'd felt a gnawing loneliness. Even with Whitey and Andy around, she
missed having family. All her life she'd had family
to lean on. During the last years, when her father
had rarely spoken to her, he'd at least been there
for her. She'd known he wouldn't completely desert her. Blood was a bond so strong, it endured
bitter disappointment and unrealized expectations.

In the books she read, the heroines might be
princesses or duchesses, but they weren't happy
until they found good men to share their lives.
Her problem was in finding a good man around
Clearwater. The eligible ones were either dumb as
stumps, ugly as sin, or old as Moses.

Shadows shifted around her and she whirled,
bringing up the rifle and sighting it in the center
of a bare chest. She lowered the weapon and
frowned at a grinning Cheyenne.

"You fool! Don't you know better than to sneak
up on a person in the middle of the night?"

"Were you snoozing?"

"No, I was counting heads," she said, unwilling to tell him of her woolgathering.

"There are thirty-two head."

She looked up at him, surprised that he'd actually counted the number of cattle they'd herded. He sat beside her, bending his knees and propping his arms on them. Plucking a long blade of Johnson grass, he stuck it between his full lips and chewed on it.

"I thought I smelled rain, but I guess not. I've come to take over your watch."

"You don't have to." She looked toward the eastern sky, which was already pale gray. "The sun will be up in another hour."

He nodded. "That's why I'm here. I figured you'd like to get a jump on breakfast. Coffee's already made."

She hunched her shoulders against a breeze that had become more chilly as dawn approached. Gathering the ends of the saddle blanket she'd thrown around herself, she pulled it closer. She was miserably aware of his bare skin inches from her, and had to exercise extreme will not to stare at his bulging arms and chest muscles.

"You should have worn more clothes. It's cold away from the campfire."

He stretched and flexed his muscles. The movement sent his aroma to her. He smelled warm and spicy. His hair was ruffled from sleep, lying in tangles against his neck. He'd removed his headband, and several thick locks curled on his forehead. She wanted desperately to sweep them back with her fingertips.

"I'm not cold. It'd have to snow to get a shiver from me. When I was a boy, I ran around in noth-

ing but leggings and a thin buckskin shirt during
the winter months."

Closing her eyes, she imagined him as a boy,
young and free, his hair in long ebony braids, his
heart not yet tinged with bitterness.

"Were you a precocious youngster?"

"Precocious?" He shook his head. "No. Misun-
derstood, shy, a loner. My best friend was my
pony. The other children weren't mean to me, but
they shunned me. I was never asked to join their
adventures."

"How sad. I never had playmates either, other
than Hank. He was more personable than I was.
He went into town frequently and made friends,
but Papa frowned on that. I stayed at home, of
course. It's not proper for a young lady to go into
town without an escort, and Papa sure wasn't
going to be my chaperon. He didn't trust Hank
to watch over me, so my social life was . . ." She
laughed softly. "Well, it was hardly even there."

"Books became your social life."

She directed her attention away from him, staring intently in the opposite direction. He knew she
was trying to hide her feelings from him.

"There's nothing wrong with reading."

"Nothing at all," he agreed. "Nothing wrong
with a man courting a woman either, especially
when they're both willing."

The lightening sky afforded him a milky illumination with which to admire the lush, sable cres-
cents of her lashes. When he'd first seen her, he
hadn't noticed her attributes. All he'd seen was
her snapping eyes and frowning mouth. He'd
heard her brusque words and felt the sting of her
disapproval.

In the last gasp of night, he could see much more of her than he had that day in the bright sunshine. He could see her heart, warm and vulnerable and brave. He could see her spirit, bright and resilient. He could see her loneliness. He could see that he wanted her, that she wanted him.

"Dreaming of me?" he whispered, leaning closer to her.

Her eyes popped open. "No!" She swung around, her hair shimmering in the soft light. "I thought you were going back to camp."

"Not me. You go on."

She planted her hands flat against the ground as if to push herself to her feet, but she didn't. The sky had arrested her attention. Stars winked out, one by one, and pearly gray color gave over to pale pink.

"You ever miss the Indian life?" she asked after a while.

"Sometimes, but not often. It's a hard life, especially for women. With the whites moving in by the droves, the land is changing, and everything with it." He laid his cheek on his crossed arms to look at her. Her profile was clean, sculpted by a clever hand. He liked the rounded tip of her nose and the almond shape of her eyes.

"From what I've seen, life is hard for women all over, not just around the Indians."

"What do you think of Indians?"

"Not much."

Anger nipped at him with sharp, shredding teeth. He slammed his eyes shut and weathered a blaze of acrid disappointment. He had hoped she would be different.

"I made up my mind a long time ago not to

dwell on silly things like that," she went on. "I've got more important things to think about ... like keeping what's rightfully mine and staying one step ahead of men like Brickman."

He released his breath in a long sigh and his lashes lifted. A smile brimmed in his heart and poured onto his mouth. She *was* different.

"Etta?" Her name fell from his lips like a prayer.

She turned slowly, as if sensing his changed mood, his heightened awareness of her every breath and heartbeat. Plucking the sprig of grass from between his teeth, he tossed it aside. He reached out slowly, deliberately, and his fingers slipped under her hair to the back of her neck. She didn't move until he added pressure, and then she let him guide her mouth to his. Her lips were cool and unresponsive. He kissed them tenderly, plucking at them, gathering them into a submissive moue.

He splayed the fingers of his other hand at her neck. Garbled sounds vibrated in her throat and she pushed fretfully at his shoulders.

"Don't do this," she pleaded against his lips. "It's all so pointless. Can't you see that? We'll only hurt each other."

"This isn't pointless." Cheyenne rose up on his knees and gathered her into his arms. He crushed her against him, giving her no room to fight or squirm. With one hand he captured her long braid and tugged it gently until her head fell back and her mouth opened wider. Her eyes were green pools, deep and mysterious. Her hands flattened against his back and moved in a tentative caress.

He breached her lips with his tongue and explored the satiny warmth of her mouth. She melted against him, a moan of compliance seeping from her mouth into his. Breaking the kiss, he leaned back to appreciate her peaches-and-cream coloring and the stardust in her eyes.

"You're beautiful." He smoothed his thumbs across her cheekbones. "And I want you. I want you moaning beneath me. I want your hands on me. I want to hear you cry out my name as I spill my seed in you."

He took her mouth again, and she responded with surprising fervor. Falling back into the grass and leaves, he took her with him. Her weight was a sweet agony upon him. He ate at her lips, taking more and more of her. When her tongue touched his, he groaned and, moving his mouth from her lips, ran his tongue down her long throat to the warm, damp valley between her breasts.

Dreams became reality. Her fingers feathered through his hair, and she rained kisses upon his face. The tip of her tongue poked at the corners of his mouth and then slipped inside to seduce him with quick, light movements. He swelled to painful proportions and arched his hips, pressing himself against her. She lifted her mouth from his and her emerald eyes bored into him. An inner struggle brought a frown to her lips and a stiffness to her body. She rolled off him and faced the restless herd again.

"I can't do this, I tell you. I promised myself I wouldn't be a fool for a man again."

"I don't think you're a fool, unless you keep denying yourself the pleasure I can give you, that we could give each other." He sat up and drove his fingers through his hair in a gesture born of frustration. "What's wrong, Etta? Are you afraid?"

"Yes."

"There's nothing to be afraid of. It's wonderful when a man and a woman unite. I'll be gentle. I won't hurt you." He touched her shoulder, but she jerked away. "Did Brickman ruin you for other men?"

She narrowed her eyes, and the look she gave him was as deadly as a poisoned arrow. "I'm not *ruined*. I just don't want to take up with you in that way. You're a gunslinger and here just for the roundup. I've got enough troubles without adding more to them."

"Don't you ever want to leave your troubles behind for an hour or two?" He yearned to run a hand over her shining hair, but he knew better. He also knew he could take her in his arms, force a few kisses onto her lips, and her resistance would crumble under the crushing weight of passion. But he didn't want her that way. "Would you believe me if I told you I haven't wanted a woman this bad for a long, long time?"

She shifted her gaze in his direction. "Would you believe me if I told you I'd already been told that by a man?"

"I don't give a damn about any other man who came before me," he ground out, and she swung around to him, startled. "There might have been one or a whole army, but I don't give a good damn."

Disbelief colored her smile with ridicule. "You don't mean that."

"Quit fighting me, and I'll show you how much I mean it." He waited a heartbeat. "A coward, huh? You're afraid you'll like it so much that you'll have to admit you like me, too."

Her eyes burned with anger . . . and with banked passion. If he could coax only a little flame—

"Cheyenne? Etta? Where y'all at? Is somebody gonna fry up something for breakfast?" Whitey hollered, and the cattle stirred to wakefulness again.

"I'm coming!" Etta surged to her feet.

"Coward," Cheyenne murmured.

"Liar," Etta shot back. "There isn't a man alive who doesn't wonder who sowed the seeds ahead of him." She stamped him with an accusing glare, then plowed through the underbrush toward camp.

Cheyenne picked up a rock and heaved it at a squawking jaybird. He missed by two feet, but the bird flew off in a flutter of blue, black, and white. He breathed deeply, struggling to master his temper. Why he wanted such a sharp-tongued, foul-tempered female was beyond him. She always had to have the last word, and that galled him no end. Especially when the last words were right on target.

He did wonder, but how many or what kind of men didn't matter to him. What mattered was that whoever had been there before him had eroded her trust and leached her confidence. A hoot owl landed on a limb high above his head and asked its constant question, *Whoooo?*

Cheyenne watched the horned fowl against a pink-and-violet sky. He knew who. Blaine

Brickman. What had him baffled was why. Why in heaven would a woman with as much common sense as Etta Hollister take up with a snake like Brickman? *Why?*

Chapter 13

For three days Etta managed to avoid Cheyenne. She made sure she wasn't alone with him at any time and she never invited conversation. He was right. She was running scared.

On this fifth day of the roundup, they dismounted around noon for a quick meal of biscuits and sausage. Bounder raced around the cattle, keeping them herded in a meadow surrounded by the tops of rounded hills on three sides and by a steep incline on the fourth.

Andy grabbed a sandwich and an apple and mounted up again to help Bounder. Etta walked gingerly to the shade of a pecan tree and sat on matted grass and crushed hulls to consume her hard biscuit and greasy sausage patty.

The herd grew daily, and they already had thirty head more than they'd rounded up last year. Etta knew she had Cheyenne to thank for that. He worked like there was no tomorrow, as if the ranch they were trying to save were his own. At night he slept deeply, his soft snoring nearly drowned out by Whitey's rattles and wheezes. Etta slept fitfully, her dreams haunted by his lips, his hands, his assurances that he wouldn't hurt her and that he didn't care about who had been with her before him. Just like in the books . . . but a more unlikely romantic hero would be hard to imagine.

Thinking back, she could barely remember the first time she'd seen him. He'd ridden to the ranch in the dead of night to deliver the news of Hank's arrest. His reputation had preceded him, and Etta had hated him keenly and thoroughly. She'd lumped him in with all the bloodthirsty fools who littered the West.

The next time her path had crossed his was on the main street of Clearwater when he'd gunned down Ben Brickman. No tears had been shed on that day, she thought with a wry grimace. Ben wasn't as dangerous as Blaine, but he was mean and heartless. The kind who would kick a sick dog or slap a crying child. Blaine, on the other hand, paid others to do his dirty deeds.

Whitey approached her on legs that seemed even more bowed than usual. He removed his hat and poured water over the top of his head, then capped the canteen.

"Don't feel much like fall, does it?" Etta asked.

"Nope, but my old bones can feel it at night and in the morning. Betcha there's frost on the grass in another week." He fanned his red face with his battered hat. "We've done good, sister girl."

"There's still another hundred head up here."

"Shoot, I bet there's more than a hundred. We might roust up another fifty or sixty without too much trouble." He chuckled and scratched at his bristled chin. "That Cheyenne is some cowboy, ain't he? Guess you'll never call him a lazy, good-for-nothing gunslinger again, will you?"

"When did I call him that?"

Whitey ambled closer. "What *are* you calling him these days, Etta?"

She chewed her sandwich with gusto and refused to answer.

"He's asked me again about you and Brickman."

Dread coated her and she had trouble swallowing the food. "What did you tell him?"

"I told him to ask you."

She nodded, relaxing a little. "Good."

"He said he had asked and that you wouldn't answer. Why don't you tell him what Brickman did to you?"

"Why should I?" she countered. "It's none of his business."

"Now, Etta, you forgetting who you're talking to? Girl, I know you like I know myself. You and Cheyenne have swapped some kisses, so it's only natural that he would be interested in what made you so sore-hearted."

She bent her head and fumbled with the cork stuck in the neck of her canteen. Yanking it free, she tipped the canteen to her lips and drank the cool water. Some dribbled from the corners of her mouth down her throat. She thought of Cheyenne's lips there, soft as butterfly wings. The last gulp of water choked her and she coughed violently.

"You okay?"

"Yes," she managed to croak out as she wedged the cork back into the canteen.

"I guess you don't want to talk to this old cowpoke about your feelings for Cheyenne." He smiled encouragement. "Bet you think it's none of my business, too, but that don't stop me from wanting the best for you or from giving you some advice."

She sighed. "Whitey, you know you have a special place in my heart, but I don't want to—"

"You can trust him, Etta. I think he's an honorable man. He hates Brickman almost as much as you do, so you two ought to talk about him. Get it all out in the open so's you know where you stand with each other."

"What makes you think Cheyenne's so trustworthy? Just because he's working hard?"

"More than that. Brickman's his enemy now because of what happened to Lone Deer. You and Cheyenne could stand up against Brickman better if you were to stand side by side."

"How am I supposed to put it all behind me by dredging up the details for every acquaintance? You're always telling me to forget it. Well, I'm trying, Whitey." She finished the sandwich and stood up. "Let's get back to work."

"Etta . . ."

She shook her head, then reached out and squeezed his arm. "I can't tell him. I can't talk about it yet."

His mouth twisted and he looked away quickly, but not before Etta saw the buildup of moisture in his eyes. She collected Southpaw and mounted up again. Her backside tingled and her hands felt hot and raw as she pulled on her rawhide gloves again. Cheyenne had already returned to the herd.

Etta spurred Southpaw. She gestured for Andy to stay with the herd while she, Cheyenne, and Whitey rode for the timbered, rocky hilltops. Sliding between ash and sycamore, the horses ferreted out stray cattle. The ride was rough, jostling the body and rubbing bones together. Etta concentrated on a big heifer who was stubbornly trying

to avoid Southpaw's direction. She held herself in
the saddle with her thighs and her sense of balance while she let fly a loop of rope. The rope circled the heifer's neck and Southpaw dug in his
hooves, setting himself against the powerful tug of
the confused heifer.

"Come on, girl," Etta said between clenched
teeth. She wrapped the end of the rope around the
saddle horn and guided Southpaw around the
trees and down the slope. When they were within
sight of the herd, she loosened the rope and let the
heifer gallop down the hillside to join the others.

A garbled cry sailed on the air, and Etta looked
back, worry freezing her heart. Southpaw heard it,
too, and he pranced nervously.

"Etta!" Cheyenne's voice reached her, and she
sensed the urgency in it.

"Yaaa!" Etta whipped Southpaw around and
dug in her spurs.

Limbs struck her face, stinging and biting, but
she was hardly conscious of them. Southpaw
plowed through leaves and hard earth, his ears
skinned back, his big body moving with grace
and skill. Etta knew he'd take her to Cheyenne,
so she just held on. Was Cheyenne hurt? Broken
bones . . . or maybe he only got the wind knocked
out of him. That's it. Cutter ran him under a tree
limb and he forgot to duck this time. She let her
breath escape in a tension-relieving sigh. Then she
heard a horse scream in agony, and Southpaw
bucked and quivered beneath her. She laid a hand
on his neck to calm him while her own heart
thumped with fear.

Southpaw dodged around the massive trunk of
a Scotch pine and gave Etta her first glimpse of the

accident. Piebald lay on her side, kicking, grunting, then letting out another bloody scream. Cheyenne squatted beside Whitey, who was flat on his back. He held Cutter's reins in one hand, and the horse was trying to rear, spooked by Piebald's thrashing and shrieking. Cheyenne glanced up, saw her, and waved her on.

She didn't need the summons. She was already sending Southpaw toward them at a dangerous gait. Drawing near, she saw that Piebald would have to be put down. A bone in her right front leg stuck through the hide. A sob worked its way up her throat. She yanked at the reins and leaped out of the saddle before Southpaw had come to a full halt.

"Whitey?" Etta dropped to her knees on the other side of him. He was conscious, but pale and sweaty. "What did you break?"

"His right shoulder has popped out of its socket, and it looks like he's broken his other arm," Cheyenne told her.

"Fell on it . . ." Whitey gasped for breath. "Piebald stepped in a gopher hole. Is she . . . Etta?"

Etta shook her head, deciphering the old man's disjointed communication. "She's bad, Whitey."

Piebald let out another shuddering screech of pain, and Whitey's eyes filled with tears.

"Put her down for me, Etta."

She nodded and pressed the back of her hand against Whitey's sandpapery cheek. "I will."

"Do it now." He swallowed hard. "I can't stand hearing her. It's tearing at my guts."

She broke out in a cold sweat of dread, but she stood up and went toward Southpaw. She could tell that her horse wanted to buck and run, yet his training kept him from it. Removing her shotgun from the saddle sling, she cocked it.

"Stay put, Southpaw. It'll be over in a minute." She drew in a deep breath and turned toward Piebald. Moving a few steps closer, she tried to keep her tears at bay, but they blurred her vision. She wiped her eyes on her shirtsleeve.

"You want me to do it?" Cheyenne asked.

Etta shook her head. It was her duty, since Whitey wasn't able. Piebald was part of her ranch, part of her livelihood. Etta lifted the rifle and aimed carefully. One shot, she told herself. Make it true so she won't suffer another second more than she must. Her trigger finger curled, squeezed slowly, and the rifle slammed into her shoulder with a sharp crack and a whiff of smoke. Piebald jerked and fell motionless, silent, thankfully dead.

Etta wiped away her tears again, then turned back to the men. Cheyenne regarded her solemnly. Whitey's chest heaved, and Etta knew he was crying, not from his injuries, but from losing one of his best friends.

"We need to set his arm if it's broken," she said, adopting a brusque attitude to mask her grief.

"Right, but help me pop his shoulder back in place. You hold him down."

Etta sat on Whitey and pressed the heels of her hands against his bony chest. He smiled weakly at her. Before she could even think about what would come next, Cheyenne gave Whitey's arm a swift, clean pull. Whitey shouted and nearly bucked Etta off.

"Done," Cheyenne announced, then doused a handkerchief with water from his canteen and bathed Whitey's face with it. "You look like you'd like to bring up your guts, old man."

"I believe I do," Whitey agreed, his voice thin and thready.

Cheyenne motioned for Etta to slide off the fallen cow roper; then he gingerly rolled Whitey onto his left side, and Whitey promptly vomited.

"Feel better?" Cheyenne let Whitey roll onto his back and dabbed at his mouth with the wet cloth.

"A little. My arm pains me."

Cheyenne looked at Etta. "Can you set bones?"

"Yes. I'll need two pieces of wood for splints, each about two feet long. And leather ties or strips of cloth—either one." She faced Cheyenne. "You'll have to hold him down while I set the bone."

Cheyenne gave a short nod. "I'll get the things for the splint while you get an idea of what kind of break he's got." He trotted over to Cutter and leaped onto the horse's back in a surge of muscle and natural-born agility.

Etta turned back to Whitey. "It's a shame about Piebald. She was a good horse."

"Hell, she was the best I ever had." He sniffed. "How many places is my arm broke? It's hurting bad around my wrist."

"Let's see here . . ." She bent over him and pressed his flesh tenderly, feeling the misalignment. "Just one break. Right here above your wrist. You're lucky, old man. You could have killed yourself."

"Lucky, hell. I've let you down, sister girl. I sure can't be any good to you this way."

"You haven't let me down," she argued. "I swear sometimes you sound half crazy. We've got enough cattle rounded up anyway."

He narrowed his blue eyes, regarding her with undisguised irritation. "I broke my arm, not my common sense. We ain't rounded up enough, and you know it."

"Let's not fret about that now. You lie still and rest." She grabbed Cheyenne's canteen and drank from it, then gave Whitey a sip.

"Y'all need to go ahead with the roundup. Leave me here with some provisions, and I'll be fine."

"Hush that talk. I'm not leaving you here by yourself."

"I'm not asking you, Etta. I'm telling you."

"Is that so?" She leaned down until she was almost nose to nose with him. "You sure are brave-talking for a man lying flat on his back with a broken arm and no horse." She kissed his whiskered cheek, then straightened quickly as Cheyenne rode up, sticks and scraps of cloth in hand.

Firelight played over Etta's face, bathing her forehead and chin in amber, deepening the shadows under her eyes and at the corners of her mouth. Watching her, Cheyenne noticed that she only picked at the food she had prepared—fried rabbit, boiled potatoes, and turnip greens.

Andy had left to guard the herd. Whitey lay snoring, having eaten supper and succumbed to an eventful, pain-filled day.

Etta had been nothing but pure grit when she'd shot Piebald, Cheyenne remembered. He had gained a heightened respect for her, marveling at her iron will and tender heart. Every day brought him new insights into her character and a stronger bond. There was hardly an hour that went by that he didn't think about bedding her. She was no longer a puzzle to him or an interesting diversion. Etta Hollister had become his obsession.

Across the smoking fire, she sat cross-legged, her shirtsleeves rolled up to expose her slender, tanned arms. She'd released her hair from its confining braid and it shimmered around her shoulders and down her back to her hips. Her breasts weren't large or small, but in between; her hips were shapely, her legs long and alluring, the kind a man would give a month's wages to have wrapped around him. She released a little sigh, and his member stiffened and throbbed. Desperate to rid himself of the discomfort, Cheyenne stood and began to pace. He ran his fingers through his hair and passed his hands down his hot, sweaty face. Feeling her regard, he searched for something to say, something to explain his restlessness. He knew the truth would only draw her wrath.

"I figure we should let Andy take Whitey back home in the wagon. Me and you can round up some more strays and then follow them in a couple of days."

She shook her head immediately, as if she'd anticipated his suggestion. "No, we'll all start for home at first light."

Cheyenne stopped pacing and stood over her, his legs braced apart. "We don't have enough cattle, Etta. You want to save your ranch, don't you? Another couple of days and we can round up more than—"

"We've got enough. I ought to know better than you."

"Yes, you ought to, but it seems you don't. We'd be cutting it close. If you got top dollar, you'd be in the clear, most probably, but who knows what kind of price you might have to settle for. Don't you think you'd better round up twenty more head than you think you'll need?"

"I say we've got enough now," she snapped, looking up into his face. "I'm not leaving Whitey. We'll all go home together so I can watch over him and—"

"I don't need no wet-nursing," Whitey said, his voice full of gravel from his recent snoring. "Cheyenne's talking sense, sister girl. Andy can help me get home. You and Cheyenne keep on rousting out these fat cows. Hell, they need to be rounded up and brought to market before they get so old and tough they won't bring a plugged nickel from the cattle brokers." He patted his pockets with his left hand. "Where did my chew go?"

"I'll get you some out of your saddlebags," Cheyenne offered. He found the crumpled bag of tobacco and handed it to Whitey. He looked at Etta again. "You'll need to round up enough to give you a good start next year."

"I've been in the ranching business all my life" she reminded him, her green eyes flashing fire. She leaned back on stiff arms. "We've all done pretty good. It'll be good to get back home and—"

"Dadburnit, Etta Lou, will you quit being so golldurned stubborn?" Whitey yelled in a rare display of anger. "Me and Cheyenne are trying to do right by you. We want you to keep the Flying H, so why are you fighting us on this? You know Andy can get me home, so what's the problem? You afraid to be alone out here with Cheyenne?"

Her mouth dropped open, but before she could answer, Whitey continued.

"If so, then Andy can stay here and Cheyenne can get me home. But you know as well as I do that the sun rises in the east, the moon ain't made of cheese, and Cheyenne is twice the cowboy Andy is." He shifted his gaze from Etta to Cheyenne. "I figure you can handle him. He don't seem to be the kind of man to force himself on a woman. Am I right?"

Cheyenne leaned back against the supply wagon, crossing his arms and ankles. "You're right." He looked at Etta. "Well, what's it going to be? Are you going to listen to good advice or act like you've got goose feathers for brains?"

She bristled and surged to her feet to glare at him, her hands bunched into fists at her sides, her breasts straining against the front of her shirt. For a minute, Cheyenne wondered if he'd lied about not taking her by force. He wanted her so badly, desperation threatened to poison his better judgment. Maybe she should be scared to be alone with him. Maybe she knew him better than he knew himself.

"I'll answer for her," Whitey said. "She's going to—"

"No," Cheyenne interrupted. "Let her answer."

Etta hitched up her chin and her green eyes glittered with foolish pride. "I'm not afraid of you, Cheyenne."

His gaze wandered down the length of her, and he enjoyed the trip. "Good. I'm not afraid of you either."

Whitey chuckled and pulled his hat down over his eyes. "Sometimes the two of you scare the wits outta me. If'n you both accidentally grabbed hold of a stick of lit dynamite, you'd both let it blow up in your hands before either of you let go first. It's enough to make any sensible man afraid to be around you!"

Cheyenne thought Etta wasn't going to smile, but then she did, and his heart turned over and he throbbed down under. Etta *did* scare him—he was afraid he'd lost his heart to her.

Chapter 14

⌒◯◯⌒

The first day with just the two of them riding proved successful. Etta and Cheyenne rustled up seventeen head of cattle to add to the herd.

They hadn't moved the herd, but kept it in the same shallow valley with Bounder as a guard while Etta and Cheyenne wound their way among trees and thickets of brambly bush. But they moved their camp close to the herd so that they could watch them while they settled down for the night. Cheyenne had disappeared with soap and a wash rag in hand. Etta warmed up beans and fried a skillet of potatoes and sweet onions.

He worked like a Chinaman, she thought, stirring the potatoes so they wouldn't stick to the bottom of the iron skillet. Yes, he worked harder and longer than she would ask of him, and she figured he knew it. The man was full of pride. He wasn't much interested in pleasing anyone but himself, and that was enough because his expectations were lofty. Rounding up seven cows and a young bull wasn't good enough, although Etta had been ecstatic. No, he'd ridden Cutter until the horse's hide was black with sweat. He'd ridden tirelessly, ducking and diving among the trees to ferret out the reluctant cattle. Seventeen in all, and Etta could claim only eight of them.

A crazy notion buzzed into her head like a honey-drunk bee. Did he want to exhaust himself for reasons other than his pride? Was he anxious about spending the night with her alone? She poked at the potatoes. Great gobs of goose fat, he couldn't be any more anxious than she was! She'd caught herself several times that day staring at him, her gaze skipping like stones over the ripples of his muscles, the fluidity of his movements, the pools of his blue eyes. Her imagination had taken to forbidden pleasures—to cool hands upon hot flesh and tangled limbs and thrusting tongues. She had never entertained such thoughts before, never yearned for such carnal behavior.

The stench of burned food jolted her and she lifted the skillet away from the fire. She stirred the potatoes and picked out the few that had turned black. Tossing them toward Bounder, she laughed when he grabbed them as if they were prime beef. Wrestling for control of her own thoughts, Etta set the skillet of potatoes and the pot of beans near the fire, along with two tin plates and other utensils. She poured herself a cup of coffee and sat down to wait for him.

In the murky distance, past a break in the trees, the cattle grazed. Bounder lay a few feet from them, panting furiously, his tail wagging now and then. She'd already fed and watered him as she'd done with the horses, and he seemed thoroughly contented. She envied his simple pleasures.

A fat moon hung in the sky where stars blazed. The wind picked up. A wolf howled and yipped in the distance. Bounder whined in response. Anticipation quivered in the air like an approaching storm.

Cheyenne returned, his light tread barely making a sound, the scent of lye soap and damp skin preceding him. He walked past her. Etta sucked in her breath. He wore no shirt and his back was smooth, undulating with muscle. His black hair was wet and straight. He leaned over and plucked a clean shirt from one of his saddlebags. Drops of water rolled down the indentation of his spine. Etta wished she could lap them up with her tongue.

He didn't turn to face her until he'd slipped his long arms into the shirtsleeves. The material soaked up the moisture on his skin, sticking to him in interesting places. She imagined herself striding to him and ripping the shirt off his back, then dotting his bronzed skin with quick, sucking kisses.

"Supper ready?"

Etta couldn't have spoken right then to save her life. She nodded at the food.

"Looks good." He fastened the bottom two shirt buttons and abandoned the rest. Sitting near her, he picked up a plate and scooped beans and potatoes onto it. "I bet I washed off a pound of dirt. That creek looked muddy after I climbed out of it." He handed her the other plate. "Want me to wait on you?"

"No." Her voice emerged, breathy and foreign-sounding. "I . . . burned some of the potatoes."

He scooped some into his mouth. "Taste fine to me," he mumbled around the food.

Etta spooned servings onto her plate, then sat back against her saddle to eat. Her hunger superseded her nervousness at having him near, and she tucked into the food, even taking seconds. Cheyenne was equally ravenous, finishing off both the beans and the potatoes after Etta convinced him she'd had enough.

He retired to his pallet, made of Indian blankets and old saddle pads. Lying on his side, he propped his head in one hand. A long-stemmed wildflower of shocking pink bobbed between his lips. She'd come to expect that of him. Anytime he relaxed, he chewed on a blade of grass, a piece of straw, or a matchstick. She was glad he did that instead of chewing or smoking tobacco. Filthy habits. The wildflower shifted from one corner of his mouth to the other. Wildflowers. She smiled. He'd pressed them between the pages of her book. She'd found each one, reading the passages they marked, blushing privately with passion. Wildflowers.

"What are you thinking about—getting rich?"

She let go a scoffing laugh. "Oh, sure. Of course, my idea of riches and yours might be pretty different."

"Not as much as you'd think." He relaxed on his back to contemplate the star-studded sky. "In these parts, I'd think that Clearwater Spring is worth a pot or two of gold."

"More than that," she acknowledged. "Why do you think Blaine Brickman wants my land so much?"

"I thought the railroad wanted your land."

"They want any old land. They're just looking to lay tracks in the vicinity, and they aren't picky about who owns what. Brickman's another story."

"That's what I figured. Why don't you tell me a little of that story?"

She narrowed her eyes, realizing he'd led her

into a trap. "Did you ever meet your father?" she asked, setting a snare for him instead.

He glanced sideways at her. "What's that got to do with Brickman?"

"Nothing. I don't want to talk about Brickman."

"Fine. I don't want to talk about the bastard who fathered me."

She shrugged. "Suit yourself." Her nerves were firing again, sending tremors through her extremities. She felt twitchy, edgy, full of useless energy. "Pretty night." Had she said that aloud?

He rolled his eyes in her direction again. "Nice and cool. I was in Denver once and the air felt like this. Like it was coming off a block of ice. Cool and a little damp."

"Guess you've been lots of places."

"A few."

"Where's your favorite?"

"I like Texas pretty good and Mexico. I know some real friendly folks south of the border."

From the dreamy luster that entered his eyes, she assumed the folks were female. Jealousy, strong and unexpected, wormed into her consciousness. Etta folded her arms tightly against her chest and stared pointedly away from Cheyenne and at the moving shadows of the cattle. They were quiet, shifting and sliding against one another, nosing at the grass, chewing their cuds. Some of the older ones had moved to the outside of the herd to lie down and doze.

Bounder scratched fretfully at fleas, but remained faithfully alert. He saw Etta looking at him and thumped his tail against the ground. Etta's thoughts circled back to Cheyenne.

"What made you want to be a gunslinger? Did you know one before ... in Mexico, maybe?"

He laid an arm across his eyes, and she didn't think he would answer. She was about to push herself to her feet and go sit by Bounder when Cheyenne drew in a deep breath.

"I met up with Jeb Nelson, and he taught me how to handle a gun. I was faster than him, and he was damned fast. Word got around, and some jackass finally called me out. I shot him before he could clear his gun from his holster. Killed him." His voice was emotionless and cold. "I wasn't proud of what had happened, but then I noticed a change in how folks treated me. For the first time in my life, people respected me and left me the hell alone."

"You don't like to be around anyone?" She sensed he had a lonely heart, just like her, but she had trouble believing he was satisfied with his solitary life. "You want people to shun you?"

"Yes, if they're going to treat me like pig slop, which is how I was generally treated."

"You exaggerate."

He rocked onto his side in a swift movement, and bent one leg at the knee. His gaze pinned her. "No, I don't. I'm a half-breed. I'm lower than dirt. My mother was a filthy savage and my father was an Indian lover. Can't get worse than that." He slid his hand over the saddle in back of him and brought his ivory-handled Colt into view. Moonlight caressed the blue-black barrel. He examined the weapon as if it were a magic wand. "But when I'm packing this, I get respect. Folks step aside and keep their lips buttoned. Saloon gals swish their hips at me, and bartenders set me up drinks on the house."

"Aren't you mistaking fear for respect?" she ventured.

He smirked. "What's the difference?"

She shrugged, wishing she could reach him. "I've come to respect certain things about you which have nothing to do with that gun in your hand."

His smirk remained. "What have I done to earn your respect, boss lady?"

"Many things." She withstood his insolence with a lift of her chin and eyebrows. "I think that what a person holds in his heart is more important than what he holds in his hand."

The smirk faltered. "Is that so?" His tone had changed, and she was instantly aware of a certain sizzle in the air between them.

"Yes," Etta whispered.

"You really believe that, do you?"

She faced him levelly, her arms crossed against her, her back as straight as an arrow. "Yes, I believe it." Catching the merest flicker of mockery, she steeled herself against the sting of it. "I can see I haven't convinced you."

"No. Not yet." He laid down the gun and came to his feet in a lithe motion, then erased the space between them in two soundless steps. He knelt on one knee before her and gripped her wrists.

Etta stiffened until she thought her spine might snap. His fingers bit into her flesh as he exerted his power over her and uncrossed her arms. Flames danced in his blue eyes, and from the contact of his skin on hers, she knew that he burned for her. He wet his lips with the tip of his tongue and released her wrists to frame her face in his hands. The tips of his long fingers caressed her hairline. His thumbs probed the softness of her lips.

"You don't mind if I put you to the test, do you?" he asked, but didn't wait for her answer. His mouth swooped to hers, and Etta surged upward into his arms.

The intensity and mastery of his kiss both thrilled and frightened her. She struggled away from him in a near panic.

"Etta," he said, growling her name. He caught handfuls of her hair. "Don't deny me. I won't have it."

"I don't want you to hurt me." Her truthfulness pierced his mindless passion. "If we're going to do this, I want it done right."

A smile tipped up the corners of his wide mouth. His fists relaxed, and he stroked her blond hair gently. "Don't you worry, honey. We're going to do it, and it'll be done right. You have my personal guarantee."

She smiled back at him, tickled by his brassy assurance; then she emitted a little squeak when he gathered her into his arms as if she were a babe instead of a grown woman. He carried her to his side of the campfire and laid her down on his soft Indian blanket pallet.

He stood over her, a foot on each side of her waist, tall and bronze and . . . hers for the night. Etta swallowed hard and stared. She remembered his body in vivid detail from that night in the barn. The vision had fueled her dreams and awakened her longings for a man—for *this* man.

Her fingers felt awkward as she found each button of her shirt and slipped it through its slit. Cheyenne didn't move a muscle, except his eyes.

They followed. They watched. They darkened to the blue-black pitch of his hair. Etta opened her blouse and pushed the straps of her thin chemise off her shoulders. Aching to touch him, she placed a hand on his left knee and moved it up, up to his hard thigh, then in, in to his pulsating warmth.

He rasped something in his mother tongue and dropped to his knees, straddling her. He plunged his hands into her hair and tipped her head back. She parted her lips to receive his searing kiss. He was rough and tender, savage and courtly. She felt his battle for control even as she felt it crumble.

"God . . ." He glanced up beseechingly, then looked at her. "Etta, I want you . . . I want you . . ." He pushed her shirt off her arms and the chemise soon followed. He caressed her exposed breasts with his eyes, then his hands. "Your nipples are as hard as diamonds."

"All for you," she whispered, caught up in the feel of him beneath her wandering hands. She'd never known a man's skin could feel so wonderful—slick and tough like an exotic hide. She raised herself up, hugging him to her, and bit playfully at his shoulder. "I could just eat you up," she admitted. Now that she'd decided to give herself to him, she vowed not to hold anything back. If he wanted her, he'd get all of her: her body, her opinions, her needs, her demands, her expectations.

He removed his boots and socks, unfastened his trousers, shucked them down his legs, and kicked free of them. It took him only a few moments to remove his cotton underdrawers, and then he was on her in all his magnificence. Etta sighed, having caught a fleeting glimpse of his member. He was already hard and erect, looking as if that part of him were made of iron instead of flesh.

But she wasn't afraid or apprehensive. She parted her thighs and let him settle against her. It had been a long time, but she tried to recall the good things. There had been a couple of them before the world had come crumbling down on top of her.

Somehow he'd unfastened her denim pants and was sliding them down her legs. His lips moved upon her body, along her stomach, grazing over that thatch of golden hair, skimming the length of her right leg. He tugged off her boots, tore off her socks, and kissed her hot, pink toes. She giggled and squirmed.

He poised over her, his elbows locked, his lower body resting intimately against hers, his eyes a serious blue.

"I don't know what happened, but I figure Brickman has something to do with it." He stamped her mouth with his to keep her from talking. "Just know this. I mean to make you forget that son of a bitch. From this night on, when you think of loving, you'll think of me."

She would have called him insufferably vain if she hadn't believed every word he spoke.

Noticing that his gaze strayed from her face to her breasts, she was gripped by a seizure of shyness. "Don't look at me," she pleaded. "I'm no beauty. Just make love to me. It's been so long since a man kissed me like he meant it."

"I mean it," he pledged. "And I like to look at you. I love the shape of your breasts, Etta. Round and high with crests the color of a blushing rose."

He leaned lower and his tongue flicked at one of her taut nipples.

The simple caress created a tumult of feelings coursing through her. Etta arched involuntarily and clutched his silky hair in her hands. He opened his mouth wide around her breast and sucked hard. She cried out, the surge of rapture so great she thought she might faint.

She didn't remember it ever being so wondrous or her body so hungry for another's. She combed his hair with her fingers just as she had dreamed of doing for all these weeks. The weight of his body on hers set off sparks of awareness from head to foot. His thighs rubbed hers farther apart and she felt his thick arousal lying hotly on her stomach. Curiosity guided her hands down to explore him. His kisses grew wilder, his tongue thrusting against hers as her fingers measured his enormity.

Before, there had been pain and shame and little else, but she knew that nothing about this man would be little. His big hands gently kneaded her breasts, molding them for his hot mouth and flicking tongue. Tension expanded in Etta until breathing was an effort. She guided him between her legs, then moved her hands around to his tightly muscled hips.

He lifted his head to lock gazes with her. She raised herself up and settled her lips lightly on his. His hesitation was more touching than any of his compliments.

"Go on. I want you inside me," she whispered.

Cheyenne kept her gaze captive as he breached her and inched himself into a perfect union. He filled her emptiness with power and passion. Etta clutched his hips. Her eyelids refused to stay open. When the tip of him seemed to burn into her soul, she closed her eyes and released a shuddering sigh of completion.

He groaned and rested his forehead against hers. "It's even better than I dreamed of," he said, his voice a rough, husky sound. "First time that's ever happened." He kissed her forehead. "Tell me if I hurt you."

She smiled. "You're not hurting me."

He moved. She gasped. He retreated. She held him fast. He gripped her hips. She let him lead her. They created a rhythm, a friction, a mystical communication. His careful tenderness dissolved under the blazing flames of his passion. His lips scorched, his hands burned, his eyes smoked, his pace blistered.

Etta had never released every shred of control, every thread of self-consciousness, until that moment when a tremendous firestorm of tremors and trembling overtook her. She cried out his name, unsure of what was happening to her, unconcerned about cattle and railroads and every other trivial thing. Her mind let go and her body reacted to the tumultuous, delicious thrust and parry of Johnny Cheyenne.

Tears washed her eyes, tickled her temples, and dampened her hair. She wrapped her legs around Cheyenne as he touched off flashpoints deep inside her.

He moaned, stilled, then surged once more, lifting her hips off the blanket. Etta felt him buck inside her like a wild thing, and then his jubilant release. In this, too, he wasn't quick. She marveled at his stamina as he continued to rejoice in his own sweet reward. His eyes were tightly closed, his breath hissing through clenched teeth, his mouth drawn tight with the pain of his pleasure. She rubbed the small of his back with her heels as he finished. He eased himself down upon her, covering her like a blanket, cuddling her like a newborn. He remained inside her, softer but no less fulfilling. He nuzzled her hair.

"Am I too heavy?" he asked, his voice strained and husky.

"No." She embraced him with all her limbs. "You stay right where you are." She felt his lips spread in a smile against her neck.

Etta stared at the heavens, feeling infinitely closer to them. Gradually, she relaxed her hold as the world around her returned. She smelled the herd, listened to them snorting and scuffling, felt the gentle breeze dry droplets of perspiration on her skin. Cheyenne's chest hair tickled her sensitive breasts. She thought of when she had seen him in the loft, and of holding his naked body against her now. A dream come true. She'd read about them since she was a girl, never believing she'd ever experience such a miracle. Her reading material had probably contributed to her troubles with Brickman.

Brickman. She frowned and shut her eyes. Why did she have to think of him when she'd finally found the antidote to his poison?

Cheyenne shifted and slipped out of her. What did he think of her now? she wondered. He certainly knew she was no virgin. She winced inwardly, not wanting him to think she'd had many men before him. He must understand how special this had been for her, what a revelation he had given her.

"Cheyenne . . ."

"Yes?"

She swallowed hard, afraid she might retch. "Brickman had me when I was younger."

He lifted himself up, sliding off to one side, his head cradled in his hand. "The son of a bitch raped you, didn't he?"

Sadness enveloped her heart. She raised a hand and drifted a fingertip from the corner of Cheyenne's eye to the corresponding corner of his mouth. No man was as beautiful, Etta thought. Even when she'd tried her best to hate him, she had been entranced with his male beauty.

"Didn't he?" Cheyenne repeated, more forcefully.

Oh, how she wished she could agree with him and share his righteous wrath.

"No," she whispered, tears filling her eyes. "I let him. I wanted him." A fat tear rolled onto her cheek. "I was young and . . . starry-eyed."

"How young?"

She had to press her lips together for a few moments to keep from sobbing. When she was sure she could trust her voice again, she drew in a quick breath and expelled the answer as she would a distasteful morsel. "Fifteen."

His eyes widened. "How old was he?"

"Thirty-five."

Cheyenne rolled onto his back. "Damn. It's worse than I thought."

Her shame returned like bad company. Etta reached for her shirt and draped it across her breasts and stomach. Still she felt exposed. She turned her head to look at him and wished they could have held on to the dream for a few minutes more. But she wasn't surprised. Cheyenne wasn't the first man she'd lost because of Blaine Brickman.

Chapter 15

Etta reached for the corner of the blanket she was half lying on and tugged it across her nude body. She would have liked to curl up in a tight ball and sob her heart out, but her pride prevented such behavior while Cheyenne remained awake beside her. She glanced across the fire to her own pallet and thought about making her way to it. What was she waiting for? He sure wouldn't stop her. In fact, he was probably wishing she'd get the hell away from him so he could—

"He should have been strung up right then and there for taking advantage of a young girl."

Etta held her breath, afraid to believe what she'd heard. Was he taking her side? She looked at him. A frown pinched the skin between his eyes.

"Did Henry know the bastard was courting you?"

She cautioned her foolish heart not to rejoice too soon. She hadn't told the whole ugly story yet. "No. Papa thought Blaine was just being nice to me. He didn't know *how* nice." The memories— some faded, some all too vivid—swam behind her red-rimmed eyes. "I'm not making excuses for myself, but Papa never paid me much attention and I didn't have a mother around to guide me, to teach me the ways of men and women. Looking back, I see that I should have had more sense. I should have—"

"Hell, Etta, how much wisdom does any fifteen-year-old have?" He shifted onto his side again. "Hank was Henry's favorite."

She nodded. "Absolutely, and Papa never tried to hide it." Fidgeting with the fringe on the Indian blanket, she cast the line of her thoughts far, far back into the shadows. "I was looking for someone to show an interest in me, and I guess Blaine sensed it right off. He was the first to ever pick me a bouquet, and he bought me books and read poetry aloud to me. He even wrote me a love sonnet." She smiled. "It wasn't very good, but it worked its magic on me. He made me believe that he truly cared for me."

"Didn't it bother you that he was so much older?"

"At first, but then I stopped thinking about him like that. It seemed we shared so many things. To me he seemed younger than his years, and, of course, I felt I was a terribly mature fifteen-year-old."

Cheyenne smiled. "What fifteen-year-old doesn't?"

A wolf howled, sounding closer than before, and Bounder barked. Cheyenne found his feet and padded lightly across the ground toward the herd. Etta used the moments alone to escape to her side of the fire. She did it for him, not for herself. She would have liked to have his arms around her for the rest of the night, but she figured Cheyenne wouldn't be too amorous once she finished telling him the sordid details.

He returned, the sight of his nude form taking her breath away. He sent her a curious look, his gaze moving from his pallet to hers. Shrugging, he snatched up one of his blankets and wrapped it around himself like a cloak, then sat beside her.

Regarding her surreptitiously, Cheyenne tried to decipher her mood. She'd returned to her own pallet, which made him wonder if she was already regretting her surrender to him. She looked sad and lonely, her eyes dull, her mouth drooping at the corners.

"The herd?" she asked when the silence became oppressive.

"Everything looks fine." He eyed her, sensing her anxiety. Something told him her regrets had nothing to do with him. "Go on, tell me about Brickman," he urged, scooting closer to her. "When did you realize he was a snake in the grass?"

She drew her lower lip between her teeth. "Right in the middle of . . . well, when we did it." Her gaze slid to his sheepishly. "Halfway through, I wanted to stop him, beg him to leave me alone, but I had enough sense to know it was too late for such hysterics."

"Guess he did some powerful sweet-talking to even get you on your back."

She nodded. "I knew it was wrong, but he said he loved me. He said we would get married and join our ranches. He made it sound as if we'd be king and queen of Texas."

"I think he believes that even now," Cheyenne said dryly. "He's obsessed with you, Etta."

She looked alarmed. "No. He wants the land and the spring."

"And you," Cheyenne assured her. "He wants you."

She looked at him uneasily. "No, I don't think—"

"I know it. You're under his skin like a rash. He wants the railroad to cut through the Flying H, but he also wants to bring you to your knees. You spurned him, Etta, and it's clear he can't live with that."

"He wants what he can't have—again."

"Did he give you trouble afterward? Did he try to see you again?"

"I saw him all the time." She made circles in the dirt with her forefinger, round and round, joining and mingling. "In those days Papa and Hank went over to the Double B every Friday night to play poker."

"So they were all friends?"

Etta shook her head. "Not really. Just neighbors. Hank liked the Brickmans a lot more than Papa did. Blaine's the one who encouraged Hank to leave the ranch and seek his fortune. He filled him with wild talk about gold rushes, silver mines, quick money, and easy women. After me and him—well, after what we did, I made him promise that he'd never tell Papa. I was crying . . . real upset . . . and I told him we couldn't ever do it again. It was wrong. I was too young, and he was too old for me. He asked me to marry him, but I wouldn't. I knew Papa wouldn't allow it." She paused to calm herself, her chest rising and falling, her lips parted, her breath soughing past them.

Cheyenne laid a hand on her shoulder. "Easy. Take it easy."

She gulped and hunched her shoulders. It

pained him to see her in such distress over something that had happened years ago.

"He tried to change my mind, but I didn't much like doing it with him. It ... well, it hurt, and he wasn't too gentle or too concerned about how I felt." She gave Cheyenne a quick smile. "Not like you."

He nodded gravely. "Glad to hear it."

"Anyway, about that time Whitey talked to Papa and made him see that I was of courting age and needed a beau. I think Whitey suspected that something was happening between me and Brickman."

"Not much gets past Whitey," Cheyenne noted.

"Yes, and he watched over me better than Papa. So Papa looked around and found me a suitable beau. The banker's son, Roy Powell." She smiled bitterly.

Cheyenne tipped his head to one side, pondering. "That name rings a bell."

"Roy's with the railroad now, and he's the one who agreed to Brickman's wait-and-see plan. Even he sided with Brickman."

"Did you break his heart?"

She sighed. "If I did, I didn't mean to. We were engaged."

"Engaged?" Cheyenne rocked back, surprised by this turn of events. He hadn't imagined that she'd had a serious relationship with anyone other than maybe Brickman. He felt his eyes widen. "You and the banker's son?"

"Yes."

"When?"

"Let's see ... I was eighteen. Two years ago.

Seems like much longer than that. Roy's married now. Papa's dead."

"What happened with you and Brickman during those three years before you were engaged?"

"Nothing. He left me alone, mostly." She sighed. "Well, he was always hanging around. I remember avoiding him. Every time I saw him I felt dirty, and I was scared he'd tell somebody. When Roy started courting me, I just knew Brickman would say something, but he didn't. Not then."

Cheyenne leaned closer, peering into her face. "But he did say something, didn't he? Picked his time."

She glanced nervously at him. "That's right. He picked his time. He waited until I was happy and secure. He waited until I thought he'd forgotten all about it."

"He told Roy, and the stupid young buck thought the worst of you for it," Cheyenne guessed, skipping ahead to the next chapter. "Probably broke off the engagement without even hearing you out."

"No, he didn't tell Roy about what we'd done. I'm not sure Roy even knows today, unless his own father told him." She pulled the blanket up to her chin. The night had grown colder, darker. She shivered. He wanted to pull her into his embrace, but he was afraid she'd break into pieces if he did. She seemed so fragile, so brittle. As if her bones were glass and her skin creamy porcelain.

"Blaine and Papa got into a fight over Hank," she said, her voice strangely emotionless. "Hank had packed up and was heading for Mexico. Blaine had lent him money and given him the name of some old boy who owned a cantina down there. Said he could point Hank toward untold riches." She rolled her eyes. "Hank was never much for thinking things through."

"Hank wouldn't have stayed on the ranch. If Brickman hadn't staked him, he would have found another way to leave."

She released an achy little sigh that tugged at Cheyenne's heartstrings. "Blaine and Ben came by that night to talk to Hank before he left, and they all got into a yelling fight. Ben and Hank took off for town to get drunk, I guess. I was sitting on the porch listening to Blaine and Papa insult each other. I don't remember how or why they started talking about me. All I remember is Blaine telling Papa that things could be worse, that Roy Powell might find out before the wedding—which was a month away—that I was no virgin. That Blaine had already had me years ago."

"Godamighty." Cheyenne raked a hand through his hair and felt sick. "What a bastard. I hope Henry went for his gun and tried to shoot Brickman's balls off."

"No." Etta closed her eyes wearily. "He asked me to deny it. I couldn't."

Cheyenne stared at Etta's profile. A mixture of admiration and irritation brought a scowl to his face. "Etta, you're too honest for your own good. You should have lied your ass off."

"Maybe, but I didn't. Brickman looked right at me and told Papa how I'd been willing and eager, how I'd told him I loved him and wanted to marry him. Papa took me inside the house and shut the door. He'd never hit me before that night. He slapped me hard across the face, and told me he'd never be able to look at me again without being ashamed. And he never did."

Anger pumped through Cheyenne. Damn you, Henry Hollister. Look what you've done, you prideful son of a bitch. Your beloved son's in prison and your daughter has a lock on her heart.

"The next day Papa went into town and told Mr. Powell that he couldn't allow Roy to marry me because . . ." She drew a deep breath, her eyes tightly shut. "Because I wasn't good enough."

Cheyenne surged to his feet, wishing he could beat somebody senseless. He paced, holding the blanket in place around his hips with one hand. He had guessed that Brickman and Etta had played some slap and tickle, and had convinced himself that Brickman had probably raped Etta. His mind whirled, trying to piece the new picture together.

"I haven't talked about this in so long . . ." She wiped her eyes with the heels of her hands and sniffed. "It still hurts, you know? Papa died and I . . . well, he was so disappointed in me."

"Your father—I know you loved him—but what a stupid, puffed-up peacock!" Cheyenne bent at the waist to be at eye level with her. "He let the wolves devour his own flesh and blood!"

"He thought he'd raised me better than to—"

"And he never made any mistakes? He was perfect?"

"You have to admit that sleeping with Brickman was a giant of a mistake, Cheyenne. I should have . . . I was raised right. I read the Bible and I—"

"You were fifteen," he said, sitting down again. The blanket gaped open to reveal his thighs, but he didn't give a damn. "Henry should have beaten Brickman to a pulp and made him write in his own blood that he'd keep his mouth shut or Henry would cut out his tongue."

"Is that the Indian way?"

"That's the *family* way," he bit out. "Parents should defend their young against predators and scavengers. Hell, Henry threw you to them. No wonder Hank had few kind words to say about his father."

Etta's hands tightened on the blanket. "Papa adored Hank!"

"Yes, but Hank wasn't perfect, and Henry would accept nothing less."

She drew her knees up and rested her chin on them. "The worst part was that me and Papa had gotten kind of close. He had begun to see how good I was with a horse and a rope. I think he was sort of proud of me, and he was glad I'd landed a man with a future." She slid her cheek against her knee, hiding her face in shadow. "Roy was the most popular bachelor around Clearwater. He had no idea that I was, that I had been ... well, you understand."

"He ended it with you?"

"No, I did. Papa did. I never saw Roy alone after that. He went off to school a couple of months later."

"He never wrote you? He never even said good-bye?"

"No."

"He must have straw for a spine. Any man worth his salt would have talked to you face-to-face about why you'd decided to call off the wedding." He observed the sadness in her green eyes and the trembling of her lips. "Seems to me that all the men in your life—except for Whitey—have let you down real bad, Etta. It's a wonder you trust any of them."

"Trust is hard," she admitted. "I don't even trust myself."

He sat close to her, side by side. "Tell me why you moved over here. Didn't you enjoy yourself on my side of the fire?"

Pink color rouged her cheeks. "I thought you'd probably want to get some sleep—alone."

He crooked a finger beneath her chin and brought her gaze around to his. "Foolish woman. How can I sleep now that I've known the wonder of you? I want more, Etta. Much more." His brows met in a frown. "Or are you ashamed again? Do you wish you could take back the past hours?"

"I'm not ashamed. I'm not a starry-eyed girl anymore. I know what I want." Her lips twisted into a grimace. "And it's not as if I have a reputation to guard. I think everyone in Clearwater knows about me and Brickman. Ever since me and Roy split, the men in town have treated me as if I were common." Suddenly she sobbed, deep in her chest, and tipped her head down on her knees. "Oh, why did I let him destroy my life? I hate him. God, how I hate him!"

"Etta, don't waste any more tears over him." Cheyenne turned her and she sagged against him. He held her in his arms, the blankets falling away so that skin kissed skin. He moved his lips against her sunny hair. "It wasn't your fault. None of it. You were caught between one man's vanity and another's pride."

"I just wish I could go back and mend everything. Sometimes when I'm fixing fences, I wonder why a person isn't given a chance to go back and fix life that way. Mend the holes and shore up the weak places. Make it strong again so you can keep out the pain." She buried her face against his chest. "Papa died before I could win back his love."

"Etta, I don't know much about love, but I do know it's not winnings. It grows like flowers from seeds. The love with the deepest roots is supposed to be the love of parents for their children. You shouldn't have felt that you had to win your father's love. It should have been there all along, since the day you were born."

She raised her head and her tear-washed eyes glimmered in the moonlight. "Did your mother love you like that?"

"My mother had her faults and shortcomings. I can't say that we had a strong union. But she fought like a wildcat when the other children teased me about my eyes and coloring. She could see that I would never fit in, never belong to the tribe, so she didn't discourage me when I talked about leaving. In her own way, she wanted the best for me. In her own way, she was a better parent to me than Henry was to you. I never saw that clearly until now."

Etta stiffened and drew away from him. She wiped the tear tracks from her cheeks and thrust her chin up. She couldn't have looked more formidable if she had donned a suit of armor. "Well, we're not children anymore, are we? We have to bear our burdens."

"Which means?" Cheyenne probed, not liking the return of Etta's prickly, off-putting demeanor.

"Which means that I've had a good cry, but tomorrow nothing will have changed. If we don't get some sleep, we'll be dozing in the saddle."

When she would have twisted away from him to snuggle down onto her own pallet, he caught her shoulders and stopped her.

"No, you don't," he said, aggravation making his voice a growl.

"Cheyenne, it's late. I enjoyed being with you, but it's back to business now.

"Don't hide from me. Show me your heart again, Etta. Show me your heart."

Indecision trembled through her; then tears welled in her eyes. With a soft, yearning cry, she wound her arms around his neck and kissed him fully, lavishly. He circled her waist with his arms and angled her backward until she was lying on the pallet, her hair spread around her head like silky sunbeams.

Cheyenne was sure he'd seen a more beautiful woman in his time, but he couldn't remember when or whom. With moonlight and shadows playing over Etta's pale skin and her eyes shining with the fires of passion, she looked more like a dream than a flesh-and-blood woman. But her mouth sought his and her tongue courted his, and he knew it was real, a blessing from above. He kissed her neck and felt her rapid pulse.

"You still want me?" she whispered. "Even after what I've told you, you still want to be with me?"

"Nothing you told me has changed my mind about you, Etta. Sometimes I'd like to wring your neck because you're so stubborn, but mostly I want to kiss you senseless."

"What do you want to do now?" she teased, her breath hot against his cheek, her hands wandering freely across his buttocks and back.

"I want to bury myself in you," he told her frankly. "I want to lose myself in you. I want to be the best you've ever had or ever will have." He grinned and caught her earlobe between his teeth. "And I think I'm going to get it all, honey. Lucky you."

"You strutting rooster," she chided, then laughed. She clutched his buttocks and gave them a shake. "Let's see what you've got, gunslinger."

He was getting hard, so hard he could drive nails into bedrock. Her sexy talk worked like a potion on him. "I've got a big gun and lots of ammunition," he murmured.

"Yeah? Make your move, Sure Shot." Her teeth caught his earlobe and tugged. "We'll see who's still—standing erect—after the smoke clears."

Cheyenne moaned. "God help me. I'm a dead man." He opened his mouth over hers, and the movement of her tongue against his nearly took off the top of his head.

When her legs came around him, he knew he was a goner for sure. Primal need overtook him in a blaze of glory and he gathered her more completely beneath him, trying to touch all of her, every satiny inch.

Her skin was slick and smooth, his rough and hairy. She smelled faintly of lilac—how did she do that out here on a damned cattle drive?—and God only knew how he smelled. She tasted sweet, a lit-

tle salty, and her hair felt like ropes of satin in his
hands. He slanted his mouth over hers, then
slanted another way, then made a minor adjust-
ment until his lips seared into hers like a branding
iron against tender flesh. She moaned and he
swore her eyes rolled back in her head.

Bolstered by that, he suckled her breasts until
she pleaded incoherently. He entered her and she
pushed her middle against his to hurry him up.
He pushed in further and she sighed expan-
sively, her legs tightening around him like iron
bands.

She gloved him like no other woman, and he
enjoyed her murmurs of wonder and pleasure. He
knew he couldn't tell her without sounding stupid
or insulting, but he was glad she wasn't a virgin
and that she had a dab of experience. There was
no deflowering to execute, no pain to help her en-
dure. However, she wasn't a woman of the world
either, and so much of what he was doing to her
was a revelation to her body and senses. He liked
not being the first, and he liked being the first man
to matter, the first man to unite with the woman
she'd become.

And what a woman. Those romance books had
opened her up, made her bold and free. She released little mewling sounds as he moved in and
out of her. She clutched at his shoulders and nib-
bled on his chin, kissed his eyelids, laved his nipples. He knew damn well she hadn't learned any
of that from her unfortunate afternoon with
Brickman. She'd learned it all from those love stories. In fact, he'd discovered a few things himself
in the one he'd read.

He tried some out by raining light kisses across her lips and tracing the shape of her face with his fingertips. She smiled and almost purred.

Her muscles contracted around his throbbing organ, and all finesse blew out of him. He groaned her name and thrust hard into her. She quivered from the inside out. He lowered himself onto his elbows and pressed his face into the side of her neck as his release came in short jerks that seemed to rattle his brain around in his head. She trembled in his arms and he rubbed against the button of flesh that felt as hard as a pebble. She gasped, and her body convulsed around him as she panted incoherent words.

Then one word came through loud and clear.

"Johnny. Oh, Johnny."

Her lips sought his, found his, adored his. Cheyenne's heart expanded with emotion sweeter than wine, and for a startling moment he thought he might cry. But it passed, leaving him shaken. All she'd said was his name, but it was the first time she'd called him Johnny, and somehow, it meant so very much. It meant everything.

He smoothed her hair back from her face and dropped a tender kiss on her passion-pink lips. "You ever dream of me, Etta?"

She smiled. "All the time."

"In your dreams, did you call me by my first name?"

Some of the stardust diminished in her eyes. "Yes." Her voice was tiny, even meek.

He smiled. "I think I'd like it if we saved that for times like this when we're all alone. You can call me Johnny, and I'll call you . . . what I call you in my dreams."

"What?" she asked, her voice strong again. "What do you call me in your dreams?" She frowned. "I hope it's not 'boss lady' or 'bossy.'"

"No, that's what I call you when I'm ready to wring your neck. In my dreams I call you 'sweetheart.'"

She colored prettily and her lashes swept down demurely. "Nobody's ever called me that and meant it."

"Not even the banker's son?"

"Not even him." Her sable lashes lifted. "I suppose you've used that on all your women."

"You might not believe this, but I'm not a man given to flowery words and sweet nothings. They don't come naturally to me. But it seems right to talk to you about how your hair makes me think of sunbeams, and your eyes of leaves in the deepest part of the forest. And it seems right that I should whisper in your ear and call you sweetheart." He whispered it, his lips caressing her lobe. "Sweetheart."

"Johnny," she whispered back.

"The smoke has cleared, and you're the victor." He rolled off her, pulling her with him so that she draped herself against his side and upon his chest.

"I think we both got off our shots and hit our targets," she murmured, sounding tired.

He grabbed the edge of the blanket and spread it over her. She snuggled closer, flinging one of her long legs across his. He closed his eyes and was almost instantly asleep.

"Cheyenne?" Etta whispered. He didn't answer. She heard him snore softly. Turning her head slightly, she kissed his chest, near his dusky nipple. "I love you, Johnny Cheyenne," she whispered. "But it's okay if you don't love me back." She swallowed the tight emotion in her throat. "You've given me so much already."

Chapter 16

Expecting awkwardness the next morning, Etta was surprised and grateful that Cheyenne adopted an easy-going, work-comes-first attitude. After a quick breakfast, they saddled up, checked on the herd, then set off to round up more strays. Bounder remained behind with the herd.

At midday they stopped for a light meal and long drinks of water. They talked about Whitey's injury and how long it might be before he was completely healed. She told Cheyenne how Andy had come to her doorstep, half starved and looking for work. She'd been grieving for her father and had taken Andy in to help Whitey with the chores. She'd grown fond of the youngster, and thought he would be a fine cowboy.

Cheyenne didn't talk much, true to his nature, but he listened intently. Etta appreciated his attention to her conversation. So often women's talk was dismissed as unimportant chitchat. She liked conversing with him, watching his expressions change, hearing his occasional opinions or insights into her problems and frustrations with ranching, relationships, and the world in general. Mostly, she liked the way he made her feel—important.

During the afternoon they rounded up twelve head Cheyenne found huddled together in a copse of pine and a tangle of wild grapevines. She and Cheyenne worked seamlessly, weaving among the close trees, urging the cattle up and down uneven ground to reach the camp. The twelve brought the day's haul in at twenty-one. More than Etta needed to satisfy the bill collectors. She looked at Cheyenne, caught his gaze, and knew that he was thinking the same thing. She smiled. He smiled back. Etta couldn't remember feeling so good.

"We've done a good day's work, boss lady," he said, winding up his rope and hooking it over his saddle horn.

"I guess we can stop early." Her thoughts skipped ahead to the drapes of evening settling around them as she and Cheyenne scaled the peaks of passion.

"Stop?" He glanced at the sun. "Why? We've got three or four more hours of daylight."

She chose her words carefully, not wanting to let on that she was anxious for the night, the campfire, him. "We've got more than we need now."

"I know, but let's see how many more we can rustle up before sunset. I'll make it interesting."

"How's that?" she asked, noting the twinkle in his eyes.

"The one who brings in the most from now until sunset gets to be on top tonight."

She averted her face, feeling the surge of hot color in her cheeks. Smiling, she tugged her hat more firmly over her forehead. "We'll be so tired tonight we won't be thinking along such lines."

"The hell you say! Come on, Etta. Don't you want to be on top for a change?"

She jerked her gloves on more snugly, then gave Southpaw her spurs. "You're on, Cheyenne!" she yelled, laughing when he gave a shout of surprise.

In truth, she didn't care who herded the most cattle. Tonight, they'd both win.

Riding the crest of passion, Etta enjoyed each sizzling moment atop Cheyenne before she collapsed, her breasts flattening against his chest, which rose and fell with his bellowed breathing.

"I've never done that before," she said, panting. "It's different on top."

"You learn fast."

His breath cooled her hot face. Etta realized she was dripping with perspiration, so she peeled herself off him and lay on her back. The wind barely stirred and the air seemed heavy, oppressive. She opened her eyes and stared at a dark sky. No moon. No stars.

"You think it might rain?" she asked.

Thunder growled in the near distance. Cheyenne chuckled.

"Does that answer your question?"

"Hope it doesn't spook the herd," she said.

"We'll keep a close eye on them. They'll most likely welcome the rain. It's gotten too damn dry and dusty out here." He laid a hand on her thigh. "I'll put up a tent."

Etta rose to her feet and grabbed Cheyenne's shirt. "Okay, and I'll cover things that need it." She went toward the fire and grabbed up the skillets and small sacks of flour and sugar to stuff them back into the water-resistant parfleches.

Working with him had taken on a new significance. She allowed herself the luxury of thinking of them as real partners, husband and wife. She smiled at the image of them building a life together, of her asking him what he'd like for supper, of him telling anyone who would listen how clever she was and how she could cook rat and make it taste good. These were the everyday routines some women would scoff at, but they were uncommon in her life. So uncommon that they'd ceased to be insignificant. She yearned for them as some yearned for riches, fancy dresses, and new buggies.

Admiring his skill at pitching the tent, she wondered if there was anything he didn't do better than most men. Even his timing was perfect. She'd finished securing the camp amenities to find that he'd staked the last corner of the tent. A raindrop splashed on her nose, and she laughed.

"You're pretty good at that," she said, pointing to the small, oiled tarp construction. "Did you live in a skin lodge when you were with the Cheyenne?"

"Of course. I watched my mother erect our lodge, and could do it myself by the time I was eight or nine years old." He bobbed his winged brows. "Naturally, I never did."

"Why is that?"

He scowled good-naturedly. "That's woman's work. No man with pride would touch a lodge, unless he was alone with no woman to do it for him."

Etta crossed her arms, hugging the front of his shirt against her breasts. The shirt smelled of him, and that alone made her weak-kneed with longing. "I don't think I'd last long in a Cheyenne village."

Cheyenne laughed. "I don't think you'd last more than a day without getting yourself in a heap of trouble." He lifted the tent flap and motioned for her to go in ahead of him. As she did, he palmed her backside, getting a squeak out of her.

As Cheyenne ducked and slipped into the tent, Etta reached out for him, one hand sliding around the back of his neck, the other at his shoulders. She pulled him toward her, falling back on the soft pallet he'd fashioned for them.

The clouds released the rain to patter against the cloth walls. It was dark inside the tent, but Etta could see the sparkle of Cheyenne's eyes and the glint of his teeth as he smiled at her. She unbuttoned his shirt and stripped it away. He pushed off his trousers, and they embraced again, their mouths hungry, their hands bold.

As the power of the storm increased outside, so did their ardor inside the tent. Etta held nothing back, stroking him and loving him with her mouth. He tongued her nipples until she writhed. She gathered his straight hair in her hands and brought his mouth back to hers. She'd never dreamed kissing could be so involving. When he kissed her, she thought of nothing but giving him back as much pleasure as he gave. Her tongue tangled with his, and he moaned and ground his pelvis against hers. She cupped his hips in her hands, urging him to join her. He did, in a lightning-swift stroke. Thunder boomed overhead, charging the already sizzling atmosphere.

"I never thought I could feel so much," she told him, opening her thighs wider so that she could accommodate the full, pulsing length of him. "Umm, you fill me up."

He brushed his lips against hers and began his undulating rhythm. The rain seemed to come in torrents as his thrusts went deeper. Her breath sawed her throat. Bright bursts of sensation rocketed through her. She was dimly aware of the primal sounds he made, the cupping of his hands around her buttocks as he lifted her hips off the pallet and drove into her, hard and fast.

Etta almost screamed with ecstasy; then the world shattered in a blinding light of pure, undiluted passion. She felt him jerk against her, inside her, then release himself in a long, depleting shudder.

He relaxed upon her, his hand drifting through her hair, his murmurs buzzing in her ear.

I'm in love, she thought, and the words terrified her. Any woman who hitched her wagon to a shooting star was a damn fool, but it was too late. She was good and hitched, and glad of it. Etta closed her eyes against a frisson of regret. Her heart had led her into another box canyon. No way out. No way not to end up with her spirit broken again.

But this time would be different—not easier, but different. Brickman had set out to hurt her, to bring her to heel. Cheyenne meant only to give her pleasure, to ease her old aches and pains.

She ran her hands down his smooth back, telling herself to seize each moment and not worry about that day when he would ride away from the Flying H and resume his life as a wandering gunslinger. Oh, how could he want such a life? she wondered. It seemed so lonely and useless. Maybe he'd change his mind and want to stay.

Fool. She winced as the word blared in her mind. Yes, she was a fool even to entertain such a notion. He'd leave her, and she must let him. She must not beg or cajole. When it was time for him to go, she must put on a brave face.

Don't think about that, she schooled herself. *Love the moment. Love the man while you've got him.*

The rain had let up. Cheyenne sighed and lifted his head off her shoulder.

"Thank you."

He gave her a questioning look. "For what?"

"Not judging me too harshly. I expected you to keep your distance from me after I told you about Brickman."

"Now why the hell would I do that?" He pushed at a damp tendril of her hair with his forefinger.

"Because I gave myself to him." She hid her eyes from him with a sweep of her lashes. "I'm no lady."

"Ladies are good for pouring tea, and I've never had a taste for tea." His lips were cool upon her brow. "Etta, you're too hard on yourself."

"I've made some bad mistakes."

"Who hasn't?"

"Papa could hardly stand to look at me after he found out what me and Brickman did."

"That was his bad mistake."

"Maybe. I always wanted him to be proud of me, and then Brickman told him what happened, and I knew I'd lost Papa forever. He died about a year after that—sort of wasted away." She heaved a little sigh. "Anyway, you could have shunned me after hearing what I did."

He sprinkled kisses along her collarbone. "Sweetheart, in most eyes I'm lower than a snake's belly. If there is any shunning, it would be you shunning me. I'm still dumbstruck that you're lying here with me. I keep waiting for you to come to your senses and tell me to get my dirty paws off you."

She gathered his face between her hands and kissed his full, luscious lips. "You're a gift, Johnny. A gift."

The herd moved like a brown-and-white wave over the gentle rise toward another undulation of earth. Etta's mind traveled on ahead, seeing the big meadow beyond and the house and outbuildings of the Flying H poking at the horizon. She shifted her sore backside in the saddle, anxious to be out of it and planted in an easy chair for a change.

Southpaw snorted and lifted his front hooves off the ground. Etta held on with her knees and laid a hand against his neck to reassure him. She glanced around, but didn't spot a snake or other varmint.

"What's wrong with him?" Cheyenne asked, and had no sooner posed the question than he smelled something acrid in the air. He sniffed. Cutter pawed the earth and skinned back his ears. "Smoke. You smell it?"

Etta's eyes widened with sudden panic. "Oh, my Lord!" She popped her heels against Southpaw's sides and flung back over her shoulder, "Stay with the herd. I'm riding ahead."

She edged Southpaw around the herd and gestured to Bounder to keep herding. She whistled shrilly, and the herding dog returned to his normal maneuvering around the cattle and his sharp, warning yips. He leaped and bit a straying calf on

the backside, and the little heifer galloped to its
mother's side.

Southpaw raced to the next hillock and labored
up it to the crest. Etta let him race on, even as her
gaze gobbled up the wrongness of the sight before
her and her heart bumped against her ribs.

The meadow sprawled out like a green carpet,
but the house ... the house's charred and still
smoking silhouette was jagged, as if a monster
had taken a bite out of it. Her eyes hungered for
signs of life, and she released a cry when she saw
Andy emerge from the barn. She waved an arm
over her head, and he returned the gesture of welcome. She saw him glance at the house, then back
to her. His sympathy was almost palpable. It
seemed to take Etta an hour instead of a minute to
reach him.

She reined near him and looked down into his
sad, young eyes. "What happened?"

"Lightning struck the house, I guess. It's pretty
bad, Miss Etta. It ain't safe to live in, Whitey says."

She dropped out of the saddle, holding on to the
horn until her wobbly knees would support her.
"How ... how's Whitey doing?"

"He's got a cold. Me and him woke up to see
flames shooting through the windows of your
house. We tried to put it out; then the rains came
and killed it. Whitey got drenched and he took
cold."

"Where is he, in the tack room?"

"Yes'm. He's sleeping." Andy looked toward the
meadow and a big grin split his face. "I heard
them cows coming. The whole ground was rumbling. Lord have mercy, they sure looks good,
don't they, Miss Etta?"

"Umm-hmmm," she mumbled, barely listening as she crossed to her burned-out house. She stepped gingerly onto the porch. The chairs there were charred. Moving to the front door—which was no longer there—she looked inside, and the contents of her stomach threatened to surge up into her throat and mouth. "My books," she whispered, holding on to the blackened doorframe. "They're . . . they're all ruined."

Where there had been volumes, there were now piles of ashes. What had been her place of safety was now an acrid-smelling hole.

Andy placed a hand on her shoulder. "I wish we could've saved some of them, Miss Etta, but everything was blazing when we come up here. The fire was so hot, it singed off my eyebrows and eyelashes!"

Turning around to him, she was struck anew with horror when she saw that what he said was true. His face was hairless, and hot pink in places. She touched the side of his face. "Poor Andy. Here I am whining about my books when I could have lost you or Whitey in that fire! Are you sure you're all right? Did you put something on these tender places on your face?"

"Yes'm. Not your medicine, of course. It burned up with the rest of your things. But I smeared butter on them. I heard somewhere that butter helps burns."

She hadn't heard that, but patted his shoulder all the same. "I'm here now and I'll look after you and Whitey."

"What the hell happened?" Cheyenne yelled, leaping off Cutter as the horse pranced near the porch.

"We think lightning struck the house," Andy told him.

"You think?"

"Well, we didn't see the start of it," Andy explained. "We only got in on the finish."

Cheyenne clapped a hand on his shoulder. "You okay, partner?"

"Yeah, I'm fine." He fingered his hairless brow. "Lost all my face hair . . . and on my arms, too!" He extended his skinny limbs for Cheyenne's inspection.

"You sure as hell did." Cheyenne slapped him jovially on the back. "But at least you still got hair where it counts." He wiggled his eyebrows suggestively, and Andy chuckled and ducked his head, his brown eyes rolling in Etta's direction.

"Watch your mouth," Etta scolded Cheyenne. "You're embarrassing the boy."

"I don't know why," Cheyenne said, his tone as innocent as a saint's. He moved to the doorway. "I was only talking about the hair on his head. What hair was you thinking about, Etta?" He gasped softly as he spied the ruins inside. "Hell, Etta, you lost your books!" He turned, and would have placed an arm around her shoulders, but she shied away from him.

"I gotta check on Whitey. He's sick."

Cheyenne watched as she jumped off the end of the porch and marched, arms swinging, toward the barn. Andy followed her like a faithful lapdog, but Cheyenne stood his ground for a moment, trying to understand all the reasons for Etta's bad mood.

Why hadn't she accepted his shoulder to lean on? He knew her heart was broken at seeing her

vast library reduced to soggy ash. No doubt the
wound was too fresh and she didn't want anyone
touching it, or maybe she was just worried about
Whitey. Or maybe now that she was back on more
familiar ground and around the other two men
she cared about, she was ashamed of what had
happened between her and a half-breed gunslinger.

He shoved aside a charred front-porch chair and
went to see what ailed Whitey. In the distance, the
cows mooed plaintively and Bounder barked and
yipped, still keeping them under his guard. Butter
trotted out from the barn, her ears cocked forward,
then raced in the direction of the herd. Butter
barked, and Bounder leaped high in the air. The
two dogs met halfway and chased each other's
tails, chewed on each other's ears, and rolled in
the tall grass in joyful abandon.

Now *that's* a welcome home, Cheyenne thought
with a grin. Home, home for the hero. He thought
of himself riding over that gentle rise and seeing
Etta stepping out onto the porch, one hand shad-
ing her eyes. Then she was running to him, arms
outstretched, and wearing a smile so bright it rivaled the sun. He imagined himself sliding out of
the saddle and into her arms. And her kisses were
feverish, her words of welcome heartfelt.

Nice dream, he thought with a shake of his
head. But not likely any time soon. Another idea
struck him, and he turned on his heel and retraced
his steps to the house. He moved inside, dodging
lumps that used to be furniture, his boots sliding
on the slimy floor. The lower floor was badly
burned, the living room having taken the brunt of
the inferno. All the windows were gone, melted.

Chunks of charred wood crunched under his boots as he made his way to the staircase.

Part of it was hanging precariously, but Cheyenne managed to scale it. He jumped up the last three stairs to the landing, then wiped his blackened palms on his pant legs. The second floor wasn't so bad. He trod carefully to a room on the right. The big bed and dark furniture had been a man's, Cheyenne thought, then noticed the empty wardrobe. A saddle sat on a wooden brace, a rope looped around the horn. This must be Henry's room, he thought, backing out of it.

The room next door wasn't lived in either. No clothes, no personals. Hank's old room?

Lingering smoke stung his eyes as he moved to the last room at the far end of the hall. The doorknob was hot, stinging his palm as he gripped it and flung open the door. Etta's bed had a canopy of creamy Irish lace that matched the spread covering the double mattress filled with downy feathers. The lace was brown on the edges now, singed by the heat. The floor under his boots was covered by a soft carpet of forest green that made him think of her eyes.

Her wardrobe was as diverse as her personality. Dresses hung next to work trousers, high-necked blouses beside overalls. Her clothes smelled of smoke, but hadn't suffered permanent damage. Her shoes lined the floor beneath the clothes— high tops and boots. A handbag swung from a peg, a necklace of pearls and glass beads beneath it. The stench of smoke had chased away her usual scent of lilac, but her ownership was clear. The bed reflected her fanciful side and the desktop holding a ledger, inkwell, and writing pen reflected her practical side.

Cheyenne wandered around the room, examining the ledger, her string of beads and pearls, her tiny shoes. He took pleasure, even elation, in all her personals. He stared at the bed, wanting to make love to her in it. Would she allow him on that most private piece of her furniture?

Chiding himself for behaving like a lovesick fool, he inspected the items on her bedside table, then gave a hoot of jubilation when he spied the two stacks of books under her bed. He pulled them out and was relieved to see they'd suffered no damage. Well, at least there were these, he thought, noticing that one was her family Bible and another was none other than *Sweet Passion's Song*. He grinned and pushed them back under the bed.

Standing, he looked up at the ceiling. Nearly pristine. Odd. He went to the other rooms and examined the ceilings, finding no sign of a lightning strike. The strike could have hit and raced down a beam, then blazed in the lower floor first, but that was unlikely.

Downstairs again, he submitted the area to a more careful examination. The kitchen and dining room were mostly lost causes. The living room had suffered the worst, so that was where the fire had started. The roof over the porch was gone, making Cheyenne wonder if a lit torch had landed on it, setting it ablaze first. Or lightning, he supposed, though something in his gut told him that nature had had little to do with this house fire.

"Cheyenne?"

Andy's voice carried to him. The youngster

loped over to him, his long, thin legs swallowing up the ground.

"I don't suppose you know anything about medicine," he said, stopping before Cheyenne and running a hand down his gleaming face. He grimaced. "These tender places sting when sweat hits them."

"You want *me* to doctor you?" Cheyenne asked. "Why not ask Etta? You're the one who told me what a wonder she is around sickness and injuries."

"Yeah, but her medicine box got burned up. Besides, it's not me I'm asking for, it's Whitey."

"Whitey?" Cheyenne looked past Andy to the barn. "Is he bad off?"

"Pretty bad. He's having trouble drawing breath. Miss Etta says his lungs is all filled with water or something."

Cheyenne was already off the porch and striding toward the barn.

Chapter 17

Whitey lay wheezing in his narrow bunk, a game smile stretching his parched lips. "Hey there, head wrangler," he croaked out when Cheyenne entered the tack room. "I hear you rounded up enough beef to feed—" The rest of what he had wanted to say was stymied by a coughing attack that rattled the phlegm in his throat. His pale blue eyes leaked and his skin was as white as his hair. His splinted arm lay useless against his side.

Cheyenne looked at Etta and she tried to telegraph her concern with her eyes. He nodded, receiving the message, and sat on the side of Whitey's bunk. He pulled back the light blanket and laid a hand on the old man's chest, then touched the back of his other hand to Whitey's beaded forehead. Whitey's body shook with a convulsive shudder.

"Can't seem to get warm," he rasped out.

"You rest easy, old-timer. I'm going to fix something for you that tastes like coyote piss, and you're going to drink every drop of it. If it doesn't finish you off, it'll help slice through that mud you've got stuck in your craw."

"That'd make me grateful," Whitey whispered with a wan smile. "If it works, I'll drink a gallon of it."

Cheyenne patted his chest, then stood and

262

moved with Etta to just outside the tack room door.

"Do you know of such a concoction?" she asked, getting a quick scowl from him.

"Now, would I say I did if I didn't?" He waved a hand to dismiss the beginning of a quarrel. "I checked over the house. Your room didn't get much damage. While I work on Whitey, I think you and Andy should gather up your belongings and bring them to the barn. After I get Whitey taken care of, I'll take down your bed and set it up in here."

"In here?" She looked around at the hay-crowded building. "Here in the barn? Where?"

"I'll move some of these bales into the loft. This is where you're going to be living until something else gets built for you." He placed his hands on top of her shoulders and met her gaze. "The house is too far gone to live in. It should be torn down before it falls down and hurts somebody."

She could tell by the way he was looking at her that he expected her to puddle up and fall limply into his arms, but her breeding came to the fore. Shaking off his hands, she stood so erect her back popped.

"Fine. You see to Whitey. Right now he's the only thing I'm worried about. A house can be built. I can't replace him." Because she was afraid she might do as Cheyenne expected, she pivoted sharply away and marched to the house to see it for herself, and to be alone when her watershed of self-pity broke through.

Andy tagged along, jogging to keep up with her swift strides.

"Cheyenne's right," Andy said. "Most of your

things upstairs look pretty good. The downstairs is what's a mess. Everything turned to ash or melted to nothing."

Once inside the house, Etta averted her gaze from the piles of ash that had been her horde of books. She allowed Andy to help her climb the staircase, which now swayed and had gaping holes in the steps. The sight of her bedroom gladdened her heart and she immediately examined the Irish lace bedspread and canopy fringe. Some places were singed brown, but neither had been destroyed. She sighed with relief. The bedclothes had been her mother's wedding present from her grandmother.

Then her gaze fell on the corner of a book sticking out from under the bed. With a gasp of delight and gratitude, she knelt and clutched the volumes with trembling fingers. Her Bible, passed down to her by her father. Several books of poetry and verse. One of Shakespeare's dramas. And four of her favorite love stories! She picked up one and smiled. *Sweet Passion's Song.* Normally it wouldn't be up here, but she'd been reading the parts Cheyenne had marked with wildflowers. In a moment of joy, she clutched it to her breasts and closed her eyes.

"You found some books," Andy said.

She smiled up at him. "Yes. Some of my most cherished. So all wasn't lost." She looked around at her clothes, the furniture. "It's strange that this part of the house suffered so little damage. But I'm not complaining. At least I'll have more clothing to wear than what I've got on and what I packed in my saddlebags."

"Your papa's and brother's rooms are okay,

too." Andy moved to her desk. "You want me to start gathering up these things while you get an armload of your clothes?"

"Yes." She sighed, looking at what had been the only bedroom she'd ever slept in. The lowing of the cattle drifted to her, sounding as melancholy as she felt. "This wasn't the homecoming I pictured," she murmured, fighting her tears.

"You think Cheyenne can help Whitey?"

"I hope so, because I'm at a loss. He seemed to know what to do for him." She batted away her tears with the back of her wrist.

"You two have any trouble out there by yourself?"

She glanced at Andy, then turned away from him. "No," she said in a voice that sounded too shaky to be hers. "No trouble at all."

Her bed looked strange set up at the back of the barn along with her other bedroom furnishings. Etta stacked her remaining books on the bedside table, then lit a lantern. Darkness was descending quickly. The day seemed to have raced by, and she was bone-tired.

Listening, she couldn't hear Whitey. All day long she'd fretted about his rattling breathing. In between helping her and Andy empty out the remains of her house, Cheyenne had seen to the herd, gathered herbs and roots he needed to make medicine for Whitey, and administered the brews and poultices. She and Cheyenne had passed each other like ghosts, not wasting any energy on small talk or longing glances. There was work to be done. Serious work.

Etta sat on the side of the bed and fought the

temptation to simply fall back on it and snore like
a sailor. Nobody had eaten, and there was supper
to get. The livestock had to be seen to, the dogs
fed, the pigs slopped, the chickens rounded up
and put in their pen. Still so much to do before she
could collapse under the pressures of the day. A
day that should have been carefree, but had been
anything but that.

Deep moaning came from the tack room, and
Etta jumped to her feet. She stood swaying, her
knees and ankles suddenly weak and nearly useless. The low rumble sounded again, pulling Etta
toward it as flesh bumps dotted her arms and tickled her spine. Was that Whitey groaning in his
sleep? Had he taken a turn for the worse?

She crossed the barn to the door that led to the
tack room. It was partially closed, so she stopped
and looked inside. Cheyenne stood over Whitey's
bed, his arms held straight out in front of him. He
shook a gourd rattler in one hand and a talisman
of feathers and beads in the other. The sight made
her jaw drop, and her first instinct was to rush in
and scold him for practicing witchcraft or Indian
hocus-pocus on poor, defenseless Whitey. However, the spiritual cast to Cheyenne's face and the
whispered reverence in his voice stayed her impulse.

She was shocked that he would even practice
the ways of his Indian people. He had struck her
as a man who had turned his back on tradition.
But here he was, clearly reciting some sort of
prayer over Whitey. Prayer? She sucked in a
breath and had dashed inside the tack room before
she had time to think. Cheyenne jerked around to

face her, and embarrassment shadowed his eyes and pinked his lean cheeks.

"Is Whitey d-dead?" Etta would have flung herself on Whitey's prone figure if Cheyenne hadn't reached out and grabbed her around the waist.

"No, he's not," he whispered fiercely. "He's finally resting, so lower your voice. I don't want him roused up." He clamped a hand around her arm and manhandled her out the door and back into the barn.

"What were you doing in there?" she charged, moving a few steps away before whirling to face his scowling countenance.

"I wasn't killing him."

She released her breath in a sigh of aggravation. "Was that some kind of Indian cure?"

"It was a prayer. I've done what I can and I was asking the Great Spirit to help me. Anything wrong with that?"

"No." She hung her head, ashamed. "How's he doing? I noticed he isn't coughing like he was earlier."

"The tea is working, I think."

"What was in it? The smell was familiar, but I couldn't put my finger on it."

"Horehound."

"Of course." She nodded. "Horehound tea? That's what you gave him?"

"Among other things."

"You found these things out there?" She pointed to the doors leading outside.

"I had some herbs with me."

She tipped her head to one side. "I guess I had you figured all wrong. I thought you'd abandoned your Cheyenne heritage. I sure didn't expect to ever see you waving a bunch of feathers and a gourd."

"I like the old boy and I wanted to do everything I could for him. It didn't seem right not to ask for divine help."

"He's bad off, isn't he?"

"His lungs are full of fluid, but I broke his fever. If he can get some rest, he'll be able to fight off the worst of it. He told me that the night of the fire he'd been running around in his long underwear and got soaked to the skin. But he was so tired he didn't even bother to dry off. He fell asleep and woke up the next morning shivering and damp."

"Well, it's no wonder he's half dead. He knows better than to sleep in wet clothes." She walked past him to the open barn door and stared at her charred house. "I wish I'd been here."

"You couldn't have done anything, except get hurt." He stood near her, slightly behind and to the side. "I have my suspicions about this."

She turned her head to look at him, but his face was in shadow. "About the fire, you mean?"

"That's right." He fished a matchstick out of his shirt pocket and stuck it between his lips. "Did you look through the house?"

"Yes."

"Didn't you notice anything strange?"

She hesitated to speak, wondering if her observation would sound stupid to him. When he slanted her a curious glance, she made her decision. "I don't understand how the lightning could have started the fire downstairs."

He smiled, slow and cunning. "You're not just pretty, you're damn smart, too."

Despite herself, she felt herself blush.

"I noticed that, too. The lower floor was burned to a crisp, but the fire barely reached the second floor before the rain put it out. I figure if the rain hadn't come, it would have been perfect."

"Perfect?" she echoed. "The whole house would have burned to the ground and . . ." Her voice faltered as his cunning smile triggered a knowing inside her. "If the rain hadn't come, we wouldn't be talking like this."

He leaned negligently against the doorframe, his gaze traveling in the general direction of the Double B spread. "Any idea who might want to burn you out, Etta?"

"Don't play dumb with me. You know as well as I do that it was probably done on Brickman's orders."

"What do you want me to do about it?"

She looked at him sharply. "I don't want *you* to do anything."

He turned, no longer looking lazy and uncaring. His dark blue eyes bored into her. "You're going to lie down and take this?" He snatched the matchstick from between his lips and threw it aside. "If you do, then you're as spineless as that whole town of cowards called Clearwater."

"I'll get my comeuppance when I sell my stock and pay off my bills. Then the railroad will have no choice but to run their line through the Double B, and that will break Brickman's back."

"Like hell it will," Cheyenne said, almost snarling. "So they'll cut through his land. He has a lot more and will go on ranching. He'll also go on threatening you."

"You don't understand. If the railroad cuts through the Double B, it will be the first time

Brickman wasn't able to have everything his way.
I'll have bested him at last. A Hollister will best a
Brickman." She hitched up her chin, already feeling a gloating burst of pride. "He'll see that this is
one Hollister he can't bully."

Cheyenne shook his head and his smile was pa-
tronizing. "That might make you feel superior for
a few months, but you'll still have a skunk for a
neighbor—a skunk that is looking to spray you every chance he gets. He'll be more dangerous to
you than he is already."

She jammed her fists above her hips. "Okay.
What do you want me to do, order you to go over
there and kill him? Well, I won't do it! That's not
the way to solve problems."

"That's a sure way to get rid of skunks,
though." He spun on his heels, giving her his
back. "I hate that son of a bitch."

"I don't want you in the middle of this. It's
nothing to you. It's not your battle."

"Nothing to me? Did the shock of the fire rattle
your brain and make you forget that you and I
coupled—a whole bunch of times?"

"Lower your voice," she whispered, glancing
around.

"Why? You ashamed?"

"No, but that's private between a man and a
woman. I'm not ready to shout it from the highest
hill."

He turned and hooked an arm around her
waist, hauling her up against his chest. His mouth
blazed on hers, hungry and so demanding that all
her thoughts and troubles floated magically away.

Etta embraced him hotly, her body sagging
against his, her mouth flowering under his. She

made a desperate sound as she flattened her breasts upon his hard chest, and she felt him nudge her with the swelling evidence of his need. His hair was like black rain falling through her fingers. She thought of the bed only a few steps away, of their bodies joined in perfect bliss. His mouth lifted from hers and he drew in a shaky breath.

"Sleep up in the loft with me."

Her common sense returned and she pushed out of his arms. "No, we can't."

"I'll go up there first, and you can come up later when Andy is asleep."

"No, Cheyenne."

"I'm good enough out on the range, but not under a roof, is that it?"

"Of course not!" She ran a hand through her tangled hair. "Look at me." Holding her arms out from her sides, she delivered an exasperated frown. "I'm tired and dirty."

"You look beautiful to me." He touched her hair, his fingertips traveling along a golden strand. "Like sunshine," he murmured. "Your hair shimmers like gold when the sun finds it. Etta, Etta, curl up against me and I'll rock you to sleep tonight."

She found herself taking tiny steps toward him, not entirely of her own volition. It seemed that a force more powerful than her own formidable will pushed at her back, prodding her.

The silence was rent by a sudden hacking cough coming from the tack room. Cheyenne dropped his hand to his side and worry pinched the skin between his eyes. His gaze met Etta's briefly, regrettably, before he strode into the tack room to see to his patient.

Etta followed him. Whitey was sitting up, struggling for breath while a racking cough shook him. He held his splinted arm out stiffly from his body. Cheyenne placed a hand on his shoulder and kneaded it.

"Easy. You're going to cough your lungs up." He motioned toward the teapot simmering on top of the potbellied stove. "Etta, pour some of that tea for Whitey, will you?"

She obeyed, her worry for Whitey knotting her stomach. The strong-smelling horehound brew made her wrinkle her nose in distaste as she handed the cup to Cheyenne. He shook his head, refusing it.

"Your turn to sit with him. I'm going to find Andy. We need to ride out and check on the herd."

"Might try to stampede them," Whitey choked out. "Brickman."

Etta patted his whiskered cheek. "You don't fret about that. Your job is to get well. How am I supposed to run a ranch if my top cowhand is laid up with the sniffles and a busted arm?" She looked toward Cheyenne and smiled, then nodded as he gave her a wink before he ducked under the low door frame.

"You like him now, don'tcha?" Whitey managed to whisper before he began coughing again.

Etta got a swallow or two of tea in him, then answered, "Yes, I like him now."

"He's a good man," Whitey told her. "But . . ." He closed his eyes.

"But what?" Etta prodded.

"But . . . he makes the worst cup of tea I ever tasted."

Etta stared at him for a moment before she recognized the imps dancing in his watery eyes. She placed the rim of the teacup against his lips, making him drink some more of it.

"Well, I guess you're going to live after all," she said, and didn't try to hide her tears of happiness from him.

Sometime between midnight and dawn, Etta roused from a fitful sleep. She straightened in the rocking chair she'd drawn up beside Whitey's bunk and massaged the small of her back with stiff fingers.

Her throat ached with silent screams, and her eyes burned with unshed tears, all brought on by a vivid nightmare in which Blaine Brickman had gunned down Johnny Cheyenne while she watched.

It could happen, a menacing voice said inside her. She didn't want to consider it, but her mind kept returning to the nightmare like a tongue to a sore tooth.

Cheyenne was right. Brickman was obsessed with her, and he wouldn't want anyone else to have her. If it ever got out that she and Cheyenne had taken up together, Brickman would try to kill Cheyenne.

Etta brought her knees up and hugged them against her body. She blinked her dry eyes and stared at the flicker of flames around the closed door of the stove near her. The tack room was warm and safe, but she felt as jumpy as a rabbit sniffing bloodhounds. It seemed that every time she allowed a man to bed her, disaster struck.

Remembering the hatred emanating from Cheyenne earlier when he'd talked about seeking revenge for the fire, Etta trembled. She'd seen a dangerous glint in his eyes and she realized he was plotting something. Terror stormed her heart, and she knew the coppery taste of fear. Brickman really scared her now. Before, he'd made her mad, made her ashamed, made her wish him dead, but lately he truly frightened her. When she thought of Cheyenne pitting himself against Brickman for her benefit, she wanted to shout. If her troubles led Cheyenne to his death . . .

Whitey coughed and the congestion in his lungs rattled. Etta welcomed the intrusion, her feet hitting the floor and her hands snatching up the tea kettle by rote. She cupped the back of Whitey's head in one hand and helped him drink another cup of the nasty fluid. It seemed to be working some kind of magic, she thought, because his coloring had returned and his coughing spells were less frequent and not as severe.

However, she didn't intend to leave his side for the rest of the night, just in case he needed her.

"Where's Andy?" Whitey asked as she lowered his head back to the pillow.

"Out with Cheyenne. They're guarding the herd."

Whitey nodded and closed his eyes again. "Good. That cattle broker can't get here soon enough. We'll all sleep better once them cows is off to market." He drew in a wheezing breath, then hiccuped. "Think that tea's making me drunk."

Etta smiled. "Quit jawing and start sleeping. You're keeping me awake."

He turned onto his uninjured side, curved his spine, and dozed off as Etta watched his torso rise and fall. He was breathing easier, she noted with a sigh of relief. Come morning, he might be able to keep some food down.

Easing up from the rocker, she pulled her shawl more closely around her shoulders and went out into the barn. Butter lay near the foot of Etta's bed, her puppies sleeping snugly against her. Bounder was out with the herd, out with the other males.

Etta stood just outside the barn and looked across the corral and open field. The land had always been her lifeblood, her one true treasure. She'd inherited a love for it from her father, and he'd learned to worship land from his own Irish and English ancestors. But love taken to extremes could be destructive, she thought. Was this land worth the death of another good man?

She pressed her fingers to her lips to cut off a sob that sprang into her throat, catching her by surprise. The nightmare flashed through her mind again and she moaned, closing her eyes against the hurtful image of Cheyenne taking a fatal bullet and falling—falling, never to stand again.

By following her heart, was she leading Johnny Cheyenne to his death?

Chapter 18

◦◦◦

"**B**randing is the hardest job of cattle raising, isn't it, Miss Etta?" Andy asked, hauling his skinny butt up on the top rail fence.

"It's not easy, but you say that about every job. You said that rounding them up was the hardest, and you said that helping the mothers with their stuck calves was the hardest, and now you say that branding them and cutting the bulls is the hardest." She sat beside him on the rail and removed her dirty gloves. "I guess it's all hard."

"I reckon so." Andy sighed, then glanced over his shoulder at the barn. "I'm sure glad Cheyenne knew what to do for Whitey."

"Me, too." She took off her hat and fanned her face with it. The night of watching over Whitey had sapped her strength, but she'd rallied to begin the process of branding the new cows and cutting the young bulls. "Guess I'll fix us something to eat." She patted Andy's knee. "You hungry?"

"I'm *always* hungry. You know that, Miss Etta."

"You're a growing boy. In another year you'll be as tall as Cheyenne."

"You think so?" A grin spread across Andy's lips.

Etta smiled. It was easy to see that Andy looked up to Cheyenne and even tried to imitate him, she noted, eyeing the matchstick Andy chewed on. "You're going to be a fine-looking man, Andy."

He hung his head, still grinning. "Aw, I don't know about that. I just want to be as strong as Cheyenne. He's about the best cowboy I ever rode with. 'Course, I know I ain't ridden with nobody but you and Whitey, but— I hope you don't take offense at this, Miss Etta, but I do believe Cheyenne is a better cattle driver."

"He's good," she allowed. "I don't imagine he wants to make it his life, though." She'd been thinking about that, and about the possible danger she had placed Cheyenne in. He'd been hired to help with the roundup, not to tangle with Brickman. However, that was probably what Whitey had had in mind all along. Whitey must have known it might come down to a standoff.

Even though she and Cheyenne had become lovers, she didn't figure he was in love with her way of life. While she couldn't understand why he'd want to be a gunslinger, other than for the false sense of respect it sometimes afforded him, she knew he probably couldn't understand why she stayed on at the Flying H when she could sell out and go find herself a husband.

"You think you can hold on to the ranch, Miss Etta?" Andy asked, his voice suddenly soft and a little scared-sounding. "I like it here. The Flying H is the best home I ever had, and I'd hate to have to leave it. Me and Whitey, we've got faith in you, but after the fire and all . . . well, you think you'll rebuild?"

Doubt wormed its way into her head and heart. She wanted to tell him that he had nothing to worry about, but the fire had taken some of the wind from beneath her wings. Her home had been the jewel in her crown, and replacing it seemed a monstrous task, especially with just Whitey and Andy to help her. She sure couldn't hire anyone else. After she paid her bills and gave Whitey and Andy their shares, she wouldn't have enough to hire a carpenter. She planned to give Cheyenne wages, too. He'd earned them.

"Of course she's going to rebuild."

Both Etta and Andy jumped, taken by surprise at finding Cheyenne standing behind them. Andy's face lit up, but Etta couldn't point fingers because she was wearing a beaming smile herself.

Cheyenne stepped up on the bottom rail and leaned against the fence, his head now level with theirs. "Tell him, Etta. Tell him you're going to build yourself a house better than this one, and that the railroad will be laying track on the Double B come spring."

Etta replaced her hat on her head. "You heard him, Andy. How's Whitey?"

"Wanting something to eat."

"He is?" Etta slid off the rail and landed in the soft dirt of the corral. A fire smoked near the center of the arena, and two irons, bearing the letter H with wings on either end of the middle line, lay in the hot embers. "I'll make potato soup. He ought to be able to hold that down. Andy, go dig me up some spuds. Cheyenne, grab me a side of bacon from the smokehouse."

Andy sprinted toward the potato mound behind the house, but Cheyenne hooked a hand around Etta's arm.

"Whitey's going to be fine, Etta. He'll be up and about in a week or two, so there's no reason for you to be worried."

"I'm not. I could tell last night that the tea had

done the trick. I'm glad you remembered the teachings of the Cheyenne. That sure came in handy."

"Much of what I learned from them does. Especially when you're out on your own. I've doctored myself many a time. Once in Mexico I drank some bad water and was as sick as a dog. A gal there gave me some medicine that damn near killed me. If I hadn't took it upon myself to find my own cure, that little gal would have had to bury me within a week."

"Was she your ... you know."

"Friend?" he supplied with a wicked smile. "Yes, she's my friend. Her name is Rosalita and she runs a cantina. In fact, she's holding some money for me. I got lucky and won a hatful of currency one night. Didn't know what to do with it all, so I left it with Rosa."

Etta frowned. "It would serve you right if she's spent every cent of it. You afraid to put your money in the bank for fear that someone like Jeb Nelson will steal it?"

"No, but Rosa's just as good as a bank." He chuckled and nudged Etta's chin with one knuckle. "Don't be jealous. I've known Rosalita for years, but she's married now. Married to a pal of mine."

"I'm not jealous," she lied. "I only hope this woman honors the faith you've placed in her."

"If she doesn't ..." He shrugged. "Easy come, easy go."

His nonchalance infuriated her, and she had to fight not to scream at him. "Any money I've earned hasn't come easy. I guess you look at us working like mules for enough money to see us through the winter and just want to laugh in our faces." She started past him, but he stepped neatly in her path.

"Hey, what's wrong with you?" he demanded.

"Nothing." She bobbed her shoulders in an insolent shrug. "I know you're not cut out for this life, any more than I'm cut out to make my living in saloons and gaming houses." She felt her lower lip tremble, and she wrenched away from him. "I've got to get that soup on. Get the bacon, will you?"

"Etta . . ."

But she was gone, walking stiffly to the barn that had become their shelter. Cheyenne dragged his boots in the dirt as he strode to the smokehouse. The savory, tangy smells inside made his mouth water. He unhooked a slab of bacon. Only one other remained. The larder would be meager this winter.

Etta hardly glanced at him when he brought it to her. She pretended to be absorbed in chopping onions and potatoes. Cheyenne went back outside, leaving her to her mercurial moods.

Sitting under an apple tree, he stared at the burned-out house and blamed it for Etta's tenuous hold on her good nature. That fire was nearly the last straw for her, he thought. Just about did her in.

She was probably feeling prickly because of the change between them, too. He was feeling the same, not really knowing whether to kiss her or ignore her. He couldn't tell if Andy or Whitey had caught on that something was different between him and Etta, so he was careful not to be too demonstrative in front of them. But he wanted to show how he felt about her. He wanted to hold her close, stroke her soft, sunshine hair, and tell her to rest easy, because as long as he drew breath, he'd protect her and the land she loved. He frowned, squinting at the chicken coop, then shifted his attention to the big, boxy barn.

Funny, how the more familiar things became, the more he came to like them. Take this land and outbuildings. He hadn't been impressed the first time he'd seen them. In fact, he had thought them plain, even ugly. He'd seen better. But now he admired them. The barn was built with care and meant to outlast generations. And the chicken coop, well, it was functional, and the nests were kept clean by Etta's fastidious hands.

The Cheyenne had taught him that no one owned land. Land was tended. Land was shared. Only white men were foolish enough to believe that anyone could own land.

But living on the Flying H had made him understand what this land meant to Etta and Whitey and Andy—and to him. It went deeper than ownership or pride. It was home, memories, hardships, joys. It was a place for the familiar, a place where you were never a stranger and never turned out into the cold. No matter how you disappointed, no matter whom you wronged, the door was always open, the hearth ablaze, the lanterns lit.

Hank's face swam before his eyes, and Cheyenne cursed the young man for rejecting such a gift.

A dim memory from his own boyhood returned. He recalled Grey Wolf, one of the tribe's wisest men, who had taught him a valuable lesson.

Cheyenne had been given a black-and-white

puppy from a litter owned by Grey Wolf. The puppy required more time than Cheyenne was willing to give, since he was entering the age when females consumed his thoughts and made him hard with longing. He ignored the pup, and his cousin, Dark Cloud, befriended it.

When the boys gathered to go squirrel hunting months later, Dark Cloud took the dog along. He had named it Arrow, and the hound was devoted to him. Arrow proved to be a great squirrel dog, spotting the squirrels among the branches and leading the boys to the right trees. Cheyenne wanted to reclaim the dog, but Dark Cloud refused to give him up. Cheyenne and Dark Cloud fought, and the other boys pulled them apart. Grey Cloud intervened. He decided that Arrow now belonged to Dark Cloud. Cheyenne hadn't wanted the puppy, and now wanted it only because he saw the benefit of owning the canine.

"When you are given something, you should make use of it, be grateful for it, or someday you might find yourself admiring it in someone else's lodge," Grey Wolf had told him, laughing at Cheyenne's stony frown.

It had been a lasting lesson, and one that might have done Hank Hollister some good. He doubted Hank had ever looked at this ranch and counted his blessings. Hank had seen the Flying H as a prison without bars, a huge cell that couldn't contain his wild dreams.

Hank would laugh at him if he could see him now, Cheyenne thought, lounging back against the tree, one leg out straight, the other bent at the knee, a long stem of wheat bobbing between his lips. The feared gunslinger Johnny Cheyenne, pining for a life that Hank had gratefully exchanged for bank holdups and train robberies.

Maybe he wouldn't be laughing, Cheyenne considered, remembering that Hank wasn't chasing riches anymore. He was sitting in a prison cell, so the wide open spaces of Texas longhorn country might look pretty damn good to him now.

Like Arrow, Cheyenne thought, recalling how the dog had bounced along the ground, his nose up and sniffing, his sharp eyes sorting through the green leaves to find squirrels among the tree branches. Arrow had suddenly looked mighty damn good to Cheyenne that day. So good that he'd decided to claim ownership again.

Guess it was human nature to want what you once had, he figured, and his thoughts swerved from land and hunting dogs to women. Brickman wanted Etta because he couldn't have her again, Cheyenne thought, and he felt his temperature peak. God, he hated that skunk! The way he'd thrown that lit lantern on that hired man like he had a right . . .

Cheyenne spat out the wheat stem and stood up, agitated by the memory and the constant threat of what Brickman might do next.

He'd told Whitey yesterday that he thought Brickman had given orders to set fire to Etta's house, knowing full well that no one would be home and that lightning could be blamed. Whitey had nodded, and Cheyenne could tell that he had already figured it out for himself. The old man had reached up, using what was left of his strength, and grabbed a handful of the front of Cheyenne's shirt.

"Don't let him get to Etta," Whitey had rasped.

Cheyenne had nodded gravely, just as he nodded now, standing under an apple tree on land that had become familiar, owned by a woman who had earned his respect and made him care about something besides himself.

"If he so much as touches her, I'll kill him," he said, repeating what he'd told Whitey.

Whitey had closed his eyes and rested easy after that. The old-timer knew a solemn promise when he heard one.

Cheyenne saw Etta's silhouette in the barn doorway. She lifted a hand to shadow her eyes and must have seen him, because she beckoned.

"Supper's on!" she called, then retreated into the inky interior.

Cheyenne stood his ground for a few moments more, a sudden realization striking him immobile. For in that instant he knew: he'd die for her.

A few days later, the branding and cutting was finished. Cheyenne and Andy rode out to examine the herd and make sure all the cows had brands. Etta would ride out later to decide which cattle would be culled to make next year's stock. Once that was done, the rest of the herd would be placed in a holding pen to await the beef buyer.

Outside, behind the house, Etta hung wash on the line. She lingered over Cheyenne's shirts and trousers, feeling foolish but not able to resist hanging one of her shirts next to his just to contemplate the contrast in size and shape. She'd washed men's clothing for years without batting an eye, but today she took her time, examining each article of Cheyenne's.

Lovesick fool, she called herself, then smiled.

Ah, well. She deserved to be sappy and sentimental. After all, she hadn't been in love since Roy Powell, and what she'd felt for him was lukewarm compared with the white-hot desire that blazed between her and Cheyenne.

So she allowed herself indulgences such as dreaming of children's clothing hanging on either side of Cheyenne's and hers, instead of Andy's and Whitey's work clothes. And she dreamed of Cheyenne pulling on a freshly laundered shirt and thanking her for it, then giving her bottom a playful pat like a husband gives a well-loved wife.

Most people who had heard of or seen the gunslinger Johnny Cheyenne wouldn't be able to imagine him as a family man, but the image came easily to Etta. She'd seen his heart and knew that he wasn't as ruthless and bloodthirsty as she'd once thought. His gun was his shield from a world that had too often been cruel to him. She understood shields because she used them herself. After Brickman had ruined her reputation and destroyed her father's love for her, she'd built a wall around her heart, afraid to love again or even to attract a man, since such liaisons had been disastrous for her. But Cheyenne had scaled the walls, and she was glad he'd taken the trouble. He wasn't the type to hang around, but at least he was honest. He hadn't promised her anything he had no intention of delivering.

Butter, sitting nearby, growled, and Etta immediately whirled, her gaze sweeping the area.

"What is it, girl?" she asked, then spotted the rider in the distance. She shaded her eyes, then relaxed, recognizing Cheyenne on Cutter. "It's okay. You ought to be looking after your pups." She crouched to pet the dog. Butter rolled onto her back, begging for more attention. Etta laughed softly. Butter probably needed a break from the demanding litter. She petted the dog for a few more minutes, then straightened as Cheyenne rode into the yard. A white-faced young heifer tugged at the rope around its neck, the other end tied to Cutter's saddle horn.

"We missed one," Cheyenne said, dismounting.

"There are always one or two that slip past us," Etta said, strolling toward him. She wore a dress for the first time since returning to the ranch house, and the white apron she'd tied around her waist fluttered as a breath of wind flew past. The air was cooler, heralding an early winter.

"I left Andy out there, and he might cull out another or two. They're looking good, Etta. You ought to get top dollar." He wrestled the heifer into the corral.

Etta picked up her laundry basket and sauntered toward the barn, watching Cheyenne loop Cutter's reins around the fence railing and loosen the saddle. He hardly ever rode Lariat anymore. He and Cutter had become efficient working partners. Lariat, let out in the pasture, belonged to another life, another Johnny Cheyenne.

She wondered if Cheyenne was feeling restless. Was he anxious to be gone, back to his former life? She wanted to ask, but was reluctant to hear his answer.

Nearing the barn, she stopped to admire a clump of straw flowers growing against an old tree stump.

"Etta, get the rifle." Cheyenne's tone was as deadly-sounding as a snake's hiss.

The hairs lifted on the back of Etta's neck as she pivoted to see why she needed to arm herself. Three riders were coming from the direction of the Double B. She darted inside and grabbed one of the rifles from the rack, then joined Cheyenne outside again. She didn't hand the weapon to him, but kept it herself. Cheyenne gave her a questioning look.

"This is my ranch, and I'll defend it," she explained. She cocked the weapon when she was sure the riders were within earshot.

Brickman and two of his ranch hands trotted toward them. Etta lifted the rifle, anchoring the butt against her shoulder.

"That's far enough," she said, taking one step forward.

The riders reined in their horses. Brickman's gaze flitted from Etta to the burned-out house.

"I heard you had an unfortunate fire, so I came over to see if I could do anything for you." He tipped his hat. "I believe in being a good neighbor whenever possible."

"How'd you know about the fire?" Etta asked.

"I believe I heard someone talking about it in town."

"I haven't been in town since the fire."

Brickman smiled. "Someone must have seen the smoke and assumed something had burned."

When he adjusted his seat, Etta noticed the new, fancy saddle. It was remarkably similar to Cheyenne's, but it didn't have beads and feathers dangling from it. The lavish tooling and silver disks were of the same style.

"I picked this up in Mexico," Brickman explained, his gloved hand stroking the tooled leather near his thigh. "I had it made to my specifications. Lovely, isn't it?" He polished one of the disks with his thumb, then tilted his chin this way and that.

Etta sighed in disgust, realizing that he was admiring his reflection in the shiny disk. "It's okay, I guess. I know somebody who has a much prettier one." She glanced back at Cheyenne and grinned, then pressed her cheek against the rifle again. "You can go now."

Brickman tore his gaze from his reflection. "In a minute. I wish to discuss some business with you, Etta. Would you like to come over to my home tonight for dinner? We could talk in comfort. I know it must be a hardship not having a roof—"

"Stop your yammering, Brickman," Etta interrupted. "You know I'm not setting foot on the Double B, and I'd appreciate it if you'd return the favor by keeping yourself and your mangy bunch off the Flying H. I'm getting tired of telling you."

He narrowed his eyes menacingly. "Very well. You won't be civilized about it, so I must speak to you about this business out here. Now that your house has burned, you should set aside your stubborn pride and be practical. You can't pay your debts and rebuild. Even if you receive top dollar for your cattle—which I doubt—you won't have enough to accomplish both, Etta. You're intelligent, so act intelligently and sell the Flying H to me. Don't let the railroad take it and leave you with nothing."

Etta aimed the rifle to the side, just clear of the three horses, and squeezed off a shot. All three horses reared, nearly unseating their riders. Etta suppressed a grin of devilment. She knew

Brickman hated to appear graceless and out of control. As he brought his horse under rein again, he glared at her, fury stamped on his features.

"Etta, you try my patience. I'm trying to talk sense, and you're showing off for your . . . Indian friend." His glance was a slur on Cheyenne's character. "You're listening to the wrong people. I know you're fond of Whitey, but he's wanting you to hang on to this place for his own selfish reasons. He's old, and he wants to die here. As for that Negro boy, he's not long for this ranch. He'll leave before winter to seek his adventure elsewhere, just as Hank did."

Brickman ran the side of his glove across his thin mustache, and his gaze flickered over Cheyenne again. "I do hope you aren't listening to this hired gun. He's here only because his days as a legend are over."

Cheyenne had removed his gloves earlier, and Brickman stared unwaveringly at his scarred hand. Etta glanced back at Cheyenne. Tension fairly radiated from him. The muscles in his face were taut, pulling his mouth into a cruel, thin line. He looked murderous, but beneath that, Etta could sense a shadow of trepidation in him.

She looked at Brickman again, hating him all the more for making Cheyenne doubt himself. "I listened to you once, and you damn near ruined me," she reminded him, then gloated when his eyes grew icy cold. "You remember that, don't you?" She hadn't spoken to him openly about his tattling to her father since that day, but with Cheyenne standing slightly behind her, she found the courage to do so now. "You promised to keep your mouth shut about me and you. You said you'd never hurt me. I believed you were honorable. I trusted you. Then you talked about me to my father like I was no better than a whore."

"You exaggerate. I thought your father should know what we did."

"You thought to break him and me, and you nearly did. You've wanted to destroy the Hollisters ever since you were in knee pants. Your own pa instilled that in you. The Brickmans have always resented the Hollisters because we control the water source in this valley." She cocked the rifle again. "So let's quit acting like we're anything but mortal enemies. I won't rest until you're in Hell, and you won't be happy until I'm hell and gone from here."

"That isn't true, Etta. I don't want you to leave. It's common knowledge that I would very much like it if you would consent to be my wife."

"That's enough, Brickman." Cheyenne stepped up beside Etta. "Leave her alone."

Brickman's upper lip lifted in a surly sneer. "Ah, the mongrel yelps."

The two men with him chuckled, eyeing Cheyenne as if he weren't worth spit.

"I see you're still hiding behind this woman's skirts," Brickman said, getting another juicy chuckle from his cohorts.

"You think so? Climb down off that horse, and we'll see who is washed up and who isn't."

Etta didn't look at Cheyenne because she was afraid something in her eyes or her expression might reflect her misgivings. Why did men have to puff out their chests even when they knew the odds were good that someone might blow a hole through them?

"I'm not having a gunfight on my land," she said. "If there's going to be any shooting, it'll be me plugging one of you to get your attention and make you see that I've come to the end of my rope. You're going to ride like the wind back to your own place, or I'm going to put some lead in one of your men." She waved the rifle, pointing it at the man on Brickman's right, then at the one on his left. "Which one should I shoot first?"

Brickman patted the air with one hand and smiled indulgently at her. "We'll leave. I just wanted to see what had happened over here." He looked at the house again. "Your family home. Such a pity. There was a lot of lightning that night, though. You sure have rotten luck, Etta, dear."

Something inside her cracked like a dry twig. She aimed at the ground right in front of Brickman's horse and fired. Before the dust had settled, she cocked the rifle again and fired. Again, and fired. Again, and fired. The horses kicked and reared. The men cursed.

Cheyenne stepped forward, waving his arms and spooking the horses even more. The men had no choice but to give the animals over to their fright. The horses whirled and raced one another back toward the Double B.

The rifle heated Etta's hands and the acrid stench of gunpowder burned her eyes and nose. She held the rifle out to Cheyenne and he took it from her.

"You okay?"

"Reload that for me," she said, then turned sharply away from him.

"I asked if you're okay."

"I'm fine, and I'm tired of you asking," she

snapped, getting a look of surprise, then of aggravation, from him.

"Pardon me, boss lady." He touched a forefinger to his temple in a salute. "I'll get back to work, ma'am. Want me to brand that heifer, ma'am? Just tell me what to do."

Past his shoulder, she spotted Andy riding toward them, herding three more cows to the corral. "Here comes Andy with some more. I'll change clothes and help you with them."

Stalking toward the barn, she was so close to tears she could taste them on her tongue. Let Cheyenne be mad at her, she thought miserably. She wanted to be brave for him, not sag against him in a helpless heap. And just one touch, just one smile of sympathy, would dissolve what was left of her strength in a thousand bitter tears. Why couldn't he understand that?

Chapter 19

~~~~ᗡᑐᑐᑐᗞ~~~~

If he lived to be a hundred, he'd never figure out women, Cheyenne thought as Etta wrestled the strong, young heifer to the ground and tried to secure the animal's legs with a pigging string.

Andy started to help her, but was cut off at the knees by her glare of hostility. He backed off and looked to Cheyenne for an explanation. Cheyenne shrugged broadly, and Andy imitated the gesture. *Women.*

The wind had taken on a sharp edge and blew fiercely. They'd had to don their heavier shirts. Cheyenne looked at the gray sky and felt the nip of winter, the falling temperature. The morning had dawned with a blanket of frost, but the sun had come out briefly to melt it. However, as the day wore on, winter came with it. Cheyenne sniffed the air. Sleet, he thought. Might even snow by nightfall.

The heifer slipped the rope, scrambled to her feet, and bolted away from Etta. Cutter immediately backed up to bring the rope taut again. Cheyenne grabbed hold, making sure the lasso was secure and the end of the rope was wrapped tightly around Cutter's saddle horn. He looked at Etta, who was glaring at the heifer as if she were going to cut her throat instead of hog-tie her.

"Andy could help you get her tied if you'd let him," Cheyenne offered in a lazy voice. He knew that anything he said to her would be appreciated about as much as advice to a know-it-all.

"I can do it," she said, her voice sounding like an angry bark. Then she tackled the poor heifer again.

Cheyenne watched, shaking his head as she grunted and tugged and pulled. The heifer rolled her big brown eyes and bawled pitifully as Etta fell on her with fierce determination.

It occurred to him that she might have transferred her hatred for Brickman onto the heifer. He could tell that she was wound tight, that her emotions were simmering under the surface. What she needed was a good cry, and why she was depriving herself of it was a mystery to him. He would have gladly opened his arms to her and let her cry on his shoulder, but she spurned him and Andy and anyone else who got within a foot of her.

She pinned the heifer and grabbed the pigging string again. The heifer lay still while Etta struggled to wrap the string around the animal's white socks. But just when it appeared that she had finally subdued the animal, one of the heifer's back legs slipped free, then the other. Etta cursed, and the heifer kicked. Its hooves struck her jaw, sending her sprawling in the dirt.

Having learned his lesson, Andy stood back, eyes wide, fists opening and closing uselessly. He looked at Cheyenne again, and Cheyenne sighed laboriously. Cutter had backed up again to tighten the rope, but Cheyenne sent him forward to give enough slack so that he could unwrap the rope from around the horn. He set the heifer free, and Andy loped toward it and retrieved Cheyenne's rope from around the animal's neck.

Cheyenne dismounted and sauntered over to where Etta sat. She rubbed her chin and tears built in her eyes. He crouched beside her and craned his head forward to peer into her face.

"You hurt?"

She shook her head and a glistening tear rolled down her cheek, leaving a path in the dust there.

"Okay," he allowed. "Then are you mad?"

The dam broke. Her tears overflowed and her face crumpled with her sobs. Cheyenne leaned on one knee in the dirt and opened his arms to her. She flung herself against him, her hands balled into tight fists.

"Yes, I'm mad!" Her voice came out hoarse and broken. "I hate him, I hate him, I hate him!"

He knew she was talking about Brickman. He held her against his chest and let her wail. Andy slid through the rail fence and left them alone.

"I'm tired of fighting him," she mumbled against his shirt. "I'm even tired of hating him."

"I know, I know." He stroked her hair as she shivered and burrowed even closer against him. "But you're not alone. You've got Whitey and Andy, and you've got me."

"But I . . . don't want to get you killed."

"Killed?" He angled back enough to look at the tears sparkling in her lashes. "Don't you have any faith in me? I'm not the one facing death, Etta. If push comes to shove, Brickman's the one who will need a grave."

"But you . . . you can't shoot anymore. I know it and you know it, and I think even Brickman knows it."

He ran his gloved hands over her hair and

framed her sweet face, lifting it for his loving inspection. "I've been practicing."

"I know you have. Every day. I see you and Andy sneak off in the morning and evening. I hear you shooting. I've even looked at the cans you've been plugging, and lately you're hitting more often than you're missing. But Brickman is pretty fast himself and he has no honor. He'll shoot you in the back if he thinks he can get away with it."

"Don't you worry about me. I've been watching my back for as long as I can remember." He brushed her lips with his, his heart suddenly full of her. He wanted nothing more than to be her champion.

She drew in a trembling breath. "But this isn't your fight. It's mine. I don't want to drag you into it. I've been thinking about it, and it's just not right. I couldn't live with myself if you got hurt or ... or worse, because of me." She plucked handfuls of his shirt. "This isn't your fight!"

"You're wrong. He killed Lone Deer and he's challenged me to do something about it. What kind of man would I be if I let him get away with murdering my friend and running you off your land?"

A new batch of tears glimmered in her eyes and she gritted her teeth. "I want him stopped, but I don't want you killed. Stay clear of him. Do this for me. I'm scared for you ... so scared." Her breath came out in cloudy puffs, and she shivered against the cold, cruel wind.

Cheyenne bent his head and kissed her cool lips, lips that warmed beneath his and opened for the caress of his tongue. He pressed kiss after kiss upon her pliant mouth as his desire for her gathered force. Cold moisture dotted his skin and he opened his eyes to see a few snowflakes fall to tangle in Etta's long lashes.

She looked up at the pewter sky. "It's snowing. We'd better finish up here and ..." Her gaze collided with his, and a softness invaded the dark green depths. She ran her gloved thumb across his lips. "Oh, Johnny ..."

The way she said his name—that yearning, breathy, womanly way—shot fire through his veins and liquid iron to his loins. He took her in his arms and stood. She looped her arms around his neck as he carried her to the barn. Andy sat just inside the door, but jumped to his feet when they entered.

"Finish up out there and see to my horse, partner," Cheyenne said, then went to the loft ladder. He set Etta on her feet. "Go on up," he whispered.

She looked back at him, wrestling with the wrongs and rights of such an action. He pressed his lips to her temple and spanned her waist with his hands, helping her make the right choice. She scrambled up the ladder with Cheyenne in her wake.

Instinctively, they moved to a far, dark corner of the loft. Amid the sweet-smelling hay, they shed their clothing in a rush of enthusiasm. They said nothing, keeping their need and their pleasure as private as possible.

Etta lay back in the hay and Cheyenne moved over her like a wave of muscle and sinew. This was what she needed, she thought. This was what she wanted more than anything. She'd missed him. Night after night, she had strained to hear his soft snoring, had hugged her pillows and dreamed of him. Propriety had kept her in her bed while she longed to join him in the loft. She'd thought of telling Whitey that things had changed between her and Cheyenne so that he wouldn't be shocked if he caught them together. But she couldn't find the words, and didn't know if she should cavort with Cheyenne anymore. After all, the closer she got to him, the more it would hurt when he went away.

But rational thinking had no place among tangled limbs and soft, wet kisses. Guiding his mouth to her breast, Etta squeezed her eyes shut and let him drench her in lustful oblivion. She ran her nails down his back as he suckled her until her nipple throbbed almost painfully.

She reached between their bodies to fondle him. He was thick and long and ready. Etta parted her thighs wide to receive his first swift thrust. Her hips lifted out of the hay and she dug her heels into the straw. She gasped in sublime satisfaction as her body adjusted itself, accepted the invasion, tightened around him. He moaned and nipped lightly at her shoulder. His body movements were fluid and measured. With each plunge, he pushed her closer to her shattering climax. When she finally reached that point of no return, her breath sawed in her throat and her body trembled violently. Etta bit her lip to keep from crying out.

But he wasn't finished. He, too, had waited through the long nights without her. He had tiptoed across the loft to stare down at her small body curled up on the big bed. He had honored her decision to keep apart from him for as long as he could stand it.

In the afterglow of her ecstasy, her inner muscles fluttered around his thick shaft. Lifting his head, he traced the bridge of her nose with his lips and then flirted with her mouth, his tongue dipping into the corners. She sighed and her lashes lifted to reveal the emerald pools of her eyes. He laced his fingers through hers and brought her hands up over her head, then kept them there as he moved in and out of her. With each thrust, he drove his tongue deep into her mouth.

She arched against him, then slipped her legs around his hips. Cheyenne devoted himself to his own satisfaction. His body burned and a thin veneer of perspiration covered his skin as he drove faster and faster. Like a powerful locomotive, it came, rolling over him and through him, taking his mind and body. He heard Etta whispering love words urgently in his ear. It seemed that time went south as he released himself into her in a long, shuddering explosion.

Time returned with the erratic tick-tick-ticking of his heartbeats. He kissed dewdrops of moisture from her upper lip and chin as he relaxed. His fingers were still laced with hers. He disentangled himself with a light laugh and lay on his back. A hoot owl blinked at him from the rafters.

"You still mad?"

Her laughter sounded like the tinkling of bells. She stretched out on her side, close against him, and combed the hair on his chest with her fingers. "Mad about you, yes."

He grinned and pillowed his head in one hand. His other gravitated to her hip, then down to the valley of her waist. "I've been with some wild women. I've been with some tame ones. I've been with women who were dead below the waist, and others who would do anything but kiss me on the mouth. But you're the only woman I've ever been with who makes me feel like half of a whole."

She turned her face into his shoulder. "Don't go talking sweet like that to me," she said, her voice trembling with emotion.

"Why not? It's the truth."

She pressed three fingertips against his lips. "I don't want to hear the truth. Sometimes it hurts too much."

He moved his lips away from her damming fingers and angled back to see her face. She kept her gaze shuttered from him, but her mouth was set in a soft line of vulnerability. "Why does it hurt, Etta?"

"It just does." She sighed and rubbed her cheek against his shoulder. "Let's not talk. Let's just listen to each other breathe. Let's count heartbeats and sleep in each other's arms." She shivered suddenly. "I'm cold."

He stood up and crossed the loft to get two blankets from his belongings. Returning, he spread them under and over her.

Clutching the Hudson Bay blanket under her chin, she gazed up at him through the dimness. "Maybe we should dress. I haven't even fixed supper. Andy and Whitey—"

He slipped under the blanket and pinned her thighs with one of his. "They can take care of themselves," he whispered, nuzzling her ear, his tongue slipping over the outer shell of it. "And I'll take care of you. It's been too long since I've had you, Etta, and my body has a keen craving for yours."

"Your body has already been satisfied by mine," she said, snuggling closer.

"My body disagrees." He guided one of her hands to his burgeoning organ. Her fingers explored the tip of him, rubbing and massaging until a drop of liquid emerged. He spread a hand over her thigh and brought her leg over his body. She straddled him, then she took him inside her, and once again he was lost ... lost in the cradle of sweet wonder she made for him.

The stock for next year had been culled, and the rest of the herd were penned together in the big corral, waiting for the cattle broker's visit. Several beef buyers worked this section of Texas, but Etta expected Big Joe Simpson to show up first. Her pa had usually struck a deal with Big Joe after much hemming and hawing. Big Joe was tight with a dollar, but he was mostly fair.

When she saw the buggy rolling along the house road, Etta thought Big Joe might have traded his usual red wagon and two mules for the fancy black vehicle and splendid Irish red gelding. Cheyenne and Andy flanked the buggy on their cow ponies, giving him an escort, whether he liked it or not.

But as the buggy drew closer, Etta could see that the figure driving it was too slight to be Big Joe. The cattle broker topped three hundred pounds. Besides being thin, this driver was dressed in a suit and sported a derby hat. Dressed like a banker, she thought; then her breath caught painfully in her throat. Or a banker's son!

Instinctively, she removed her floppy hat and hit it against her chaps and shirt. Dust rose from her clothing, and she had no doubt that her face was smeared with it. Too late to look presentable, she thought. Besides, she could be the best-looking woman in Texas and that wouldn't sway Roy Powell from his mission.

Roy pulled back on the reins and the buggy rolled to a stop a few feet from Etta. She replaced her hat on her head and stepped forward, trying her best to look unruffled and unafraid.

"Hello, Roy." She was proud of the even timbre of her voice. "Got yourself a new buggy, I see."

He climbed out of the shiny vehicle, casting furtive glances at Cheyenne, who looked at him as if he were a scavenger that needed killing.

"I saw your herd as I came in. You've rounded up twice as many as I thought you would."

"Sorry to disappoint you." She eyed him openly. He wasn't nearly as handsome as she remembered. Even wearing boots with heels, he was only an inch or so taller than she. He had a boyish face, sprinkled with freckles. Fair-headed and fair-skinned, he was as white as a spinster's thigh. But his eyes were still the soft brown she had found so fetching, and his smile was just as shy and sweet.

"Henryetta Hollister, you know me better than that. I'm certainly not disappointed." He surveyed the area, his brown eyes growing sad. "Your house. Could you save anything?"

"A few odds and ends. I'll rebuild come spring," she asserted.

Roy looked back at Cheyenne, then edged closer to Etta. "Could we speak in private?"

"I guess," she conceded with a nonchalant shrug. "Come on. I was on my way to the chicken coop. I was so busy this morning I forgot to check for eggs."

Etta's gaze connected with Cheyenne's for a moment and she shared the private pleasure with him. Actually, she and Cheyenne had taken their time loving each other that morning and had gotten off to a late start with their chores.

Since the afternoon two days ago when she'd let go of her frustrations and they had made furious love in the loft, she had taken to sleeping with him at least part of each night. The cat was out of the bag, so to speak, and she didn't have to hide her feelings for Cheyenne around Whitey and Andy.

However, the feelings were still new and she wasn't willing to share them totally with anyone. When Whitey had teased her earlier that morning about being smitten, she hadn't been able to laugh or think of a quick retort. No matter how happy she was, she was almost afraid to show it. Life had taught her that happiness was a fragile, elusive thing.

"You've been working hard?" Roy said, walking beside her, his hands clasped behind his back. His derby hat was blatantly out of place.

"Ranching is a tough life," Etta allowed.

"That's what I'd like to speak to you about—as a friend."

"A friend who wants me to give up my land," she clarified.

"Not give it up," he corrected. "I'm hoping you will choose to sell it and realize a tidy profit. My father will be glad to help you get the most for your land as is humanly possible, Etta."

She opened the chicken coop gate and went inside the yard, closing the gate behind her. "I'll be right back," she told him. "I wouldn't want you to get bird poop all over your shiny boots." Then she escaped inside the small, stuffy structure.

Three hens covered nests. They clucked softly, their beady eyes following her movements as she went from nest to nest. She placed the eggs in a bucket, only seven this morning. Reaching under the hens, she ignored their fussing to gather the eggs they were trying to incubate.

"Don't you peck at me," she warned a red hen with a mean streak. "Last time you had chicks, they were mostly all roosters. I need pullets."

And I don't need advice from Roy Powell, she added mentally, glancing out the door at him standing where she'd left him. He looked around with the discomfort of a whore in church. Etta wondered if he'd come on his own, or if he'd been sent.

Stepping out into the winter sunlight again, she didn't return his smile. Setting the bucket down, she latched the gate. She wasn't wearing gloves and her fingers were stiff from the cold. The first snow had been a light blanket, already melted and gone, but the air remained chilly, the sky mostly gray.

"Did Brickman send you?" she asked point-blank.

"Brickman? No."

"Your father?"

"No. I'm here of my own volition, Etta. I'm concerned about you. When I heard about the fire, I wanted to come and see how things stand."

"Or *if* they're still standing," she said, smiling. "Don't worry about me, Roy. I figure that if you've lost any sleep, it's because you're anxious to see me fail so that the railroad can start laying tracks."

He smoothed his kid gloves more tightly over the backs of his hands. Hands, Etta knew, that showed no sign of hard work. Not like Cheyenne's with their scars and calluses.

"Etta, believe it or not, I'm trying to look after your best interests. If you manage to hang on here and that's what you want, then I'll be pleased for you. Although I don't think staying alone is a good idea. This is a big ranch, and you are one woman. Even your father had trouble paying his bills the last few years. Do you think you can manage this ranch better than Henry Hollister?"

Resenting his supercilious attitude, Etta confronted him with an icy calm. "Yes, as a matter of fact, I do. Just because I'm a woman doesn't mean I have a smaller brain than a man. My father was a pretty good rancher, but he wasn't any good at balancing books. I did that, and I could have done a better job of it if Papa had given me more responsibility. He rounded up only enough cattle to pay off his bills, and sometimes he was short of what he'd figured on getting. Sometimes he paid too much for feed because he didn't think it was Christian to haggle prices. I could go on, but most of it wouldn't make much sense to you because you don't know the cattle business."

Roy folded his arms against his chest, warding off the brisk wind. "I have never doubted your cleverness, Etta. I just wonder . . ." He looked out over the pasture, then swung his warm brown eyes back to her. "Are you happy out here? Whitey won't live forever, and then you'll be all alone. Have you thought about that?"

She picked up the bucket of eggs and started for the barn. "Yes, I've thought about it. I love this ranch, and I'm going to fight for it."

Roy clamped a hand on her arm, stopping her and swinging her around to face him. He placed both hands on her shoulders. His smile was tender and familiar.

"Etta, let's not quarrel. I'm here as a friend, honestly. I heard about the fire and I came to check on you and to see if there was anything I could help you with."

"Yes, you can do what you set out to do in the first place and run your railroad track on Brickman's land."

He sighed. "I wish that decision were mine alone to make, but it isn't. My boss thought that Brickman's idea had merit, so he agreed to ... well, to wait."

"To wait and hope that I fail and lose everything." Etta wrenched away from him.

A gust of wind tried to pluck his derby hat off his head, and Roy barely managed to hold it in place.

"Can we get out of this weather? I would like to visit with you if you can spare a little more time." He smiled winningly. "Please, Etta?"

She huffed out a sigh of resignation. "Very well. I guess I'm forgetting my manners. Would you like a cup of hot cider?"

He clapped his hands together with relish. "I would dearly love it, if we can drink it inside your barn."

Etta tucked her hand in the crook of his arm. "I can manage that, I imagine. Come along."

She escorted him to the barn and poured hot apple cider into two tin cups. Roy sat on her trunk, and Etta sat in the rocker. He removed his hat and gloves before tasting the cider.

"Ah, now, that is tasty." He crossed his legs and smiled across the space at her. "So you'll stay in here during the winter? Will it be warm enough?"

"Not as warm as my house, but it's right comfortable in the tack room." She nodded at the closed door. "There's a wood-burner in there, and I figure I can get used to Whitey's and Andy's snoring."

"What about that other man ... that Indian?"

"Johnny Cheyenne," she said, doubting that Roy wasn't familiar with the name and the man. "He's here only until after the roundup."

Roy wrapped his hands around the warm cup and blew at the steam rising from it. "Isn't the roundup over?" He glanced toward the barn door, closed against the elements. "I saw the herd as I came in."

Etta stared blindly at the barn door. Yes, the roundup *was* over, so why was Cheyenne still here? And why hadn't she stopped to think about it before? Maybe it was too painful. Maybe she didn't want to face the inevitable. It would hurt less if she awakened one morning to find him gone. Talking about his leaving would only shatter her heart. A clean break was always better.

"So when is he leaving?" Roy asked.

"Soon. I think he's waiting for the cattle broker. He wants to see how much we get for the beef."

Roy drew his brows together. "Is he trustworthy?" he asked, lowering his voice. "I mean, you don't think he's waiting around to rob you, do you?"

"No, I don't," Etta said succinctly. "I'd trust him with my life."

His brows shot up. "My, my. That's impressive, as I know how hard it is to earn your trust. But be careful, Etta. He might be looking to latch onto some of your land in exchange for wages . . . or by taking advantage of your gratitude, your generous nature."

Etta shook her head. "This land holds no interest for him."

Roy sipped the cider and dropped into a reflective silence. "You know," he said after a minute, "you're a very stubborn woman. I'm not sure it's wise for you to stay here and try to run this place on your own, but I can understand your attachment to the Flying H." He leaned back against the wall. "I'm not sure how I'd feel if you lost your ranch, Etta."

"I'd rather desert it, turn my back on it, than sell it to Brickman," she asserted. "But it won't come to that." She looked around and smiled. "I kind of like living in this barn. I don't have to worry any about keeping it clean or making it homey."

"That's true," he said, laughing. "But you deserve better. Can the house be saved?"

She shook her head. "No. The downstairs was gutted. It's unsafe. It'll have to be torn down. I'll start all over again."

He finished the cider and shook his head when she gestured toward his cup in a silent request to refill it. "Did you know that I married last year?"

"Yes, I heard about it in town. She's not from around here, is she?"

"No. She's a Virginian. We met in Dallas. She was visiting a cousin who works for the railroad.

I went to a party thrown in her honor and . . . well, I persuaded her to stay in the south as my wife."

When Etta had first heard of his marriage, the news had upset her, bringing with it memories of her own impending marriage to him. However, hearing him talk about it now had little effect on her. She experienced none of the melancholy or regret she'd suffered before. Perhaps that wound had finally scarred over.

"I hope you're happily married."

"Oh, yes." His eyes were bright with sincerity. "She's a fine lady. In fact . . ." He bowed his head briefly, shyly. "I learned a few weeks ago that we are to have a child by summer, God willing."

Envy knifed her heart. She pictured herself round with a child. At least she'd have something of his to sustain her, she thought, then drew herself up short, surprising herself with her own musings. She hadn't known until that moment the depth of her love for Johnny Cheyenne. She had never wanted any man's child until now. Not even when she had been engaged to Roy. Motherhood had seemed remote, something that happened to other women. She splayed a hand across her stomach and rejoiced in the possibility, however slight, that she might bear Cheyenne's offspring.

"Etta?"

She blinked, bringing Roy's face into focus again. "Yes? I'm sorry. What were you saying?"

"I was saying that I tried very hard to hate you for tossing me aside as if I weren't good enough for you, but I never succeeded."

"Tossing you aside?" she repeated, his meaning unclear to her.

"You led me on," he continued. "You made me believe you wanted to marry me. I never understood why you did that, Etta. Did your father make you accept my proposal, but you couldn't go through with it?"

"No, it wasn't like that at all." She stared at him, the fog in her mind beginning to clear. "I thought you knew, but you never did . . . did you? Nobody ever told you."

"Told me what?"

She wondered if she should confess to him. She'd assumed that the vicious gossip would have reached him, but maybe the people of Clearwater had talked behind his back and he'd never heard what had happened.

"Roy, I never thought I was too good for you," she said slowly, softly. It was still so difficult for her to talk about the choice she'd made in her girlhood. "I was the one who wasn't good enough for you."

"What nonsense is this?" he asked, smiling gently at her. "Etta, you're one of the finest people I've ever known."

She chewed on her lower lip, her emotions swimming to the surface. "Oh, Roy, don't say that." She looked away in consternation.

"But it's what I feel . . . what I've always felt."

"You're wrong about me." She smiled sadly. "I almost hate to tell you this, because I believe you're one of the few men left around here who doesn't think I'm soiled goods."

Roy set aside the cup and clamped his hands on his knees. "No one has ever suggested such a thing about you in my presence."

"They were protecting you, I suppose." She

looked at him directly, determined to put this to rights. "Roy, when I was fifteen I lost my virginity."

"No!" He swallowed hard. "You were ... forced!"

She closed her eyes. Just like Cheyenne, she thought. He, too, had given her the benefit of the doubt. "No, but I regretted my decision a moment too late." She opened her eyes, wanting to see his expression. "It was Blaine Brickman. I thought I loved him and that he loved me. I ... I was a silly girl with romantic notions floating around in my head. But it was wrong. I'm not making excuses for what I did."

His face went still, then his jaw dropped. "Blaine Brickman," he said, his voice hollow. "But he's twice your age. What was he doing seducing a girl of fifteen?"

"Papa didn't know about it. I made Brickman promise not to tell anyone, especially Papa. But years later, when I was betrothed to you, Brickman and Papa got into an argument, and Brickman blurted out what had happened between him and me."

"The cad!" Roy's pale complexion grew ruddy with his anger.

"Papa decided he had to tell your father about me. Of course, that changed everything."

"But I was never told!" He stood up and paced with agitation. "My father said you had had second thoughts. I was led to believe you'd rejected me." He slammed a fist into his open palm. "You should have said something to me about this, Etta. I deserved to know the truth. All this time I thought ..." He ran a hand through his blond hair. "Oh, never mind what I thought. I've been walking around with blinders on, and right now I feel like a huge fool."

"No, Roy, no!" Etta rushed to her feet and clutched at his coat sleeves. "You're no fool. You are one of the sweetest, kindest—" She stopped her profuse admission, fearing he might take it wrong. "What I mean to say is that you're right. You should have been told, but I was so ashamed I couldn't face you. I thought that your father or mine had told you the whole ugly story. I couldn't bear to have you look at me as if I were . . . well, tainted."

He tilted his head and moisture glistened in his eyes. "Darling Etta." He opened his arms and pulled her into his embrace. "I'm glad we talked, and I would never think of you as anything but a beautiful, honest woman."

His arms tightened around her and Etta felt his lips move against her hair.

"Hold on, Etta," he whispered fiercely. "Hold on until spring, and you have my word that the railroad will not touch the Flying H. We'll take a hunk of Brickman's land, I swear it."

Etta tipped back her head, smiling brightly at him. "You mean it, Roy?"

Smiling, he ran his hands over the top of her head, smoothing back wisps of blond hair. "Believe me when I tell you that we are friends, Henryetta Hollister, and that has not changed."

She turned her head to leave a quick kiss in his palm. "I believe you, Roy." Then she threw her arms around him and hugged his neck.

Standing in the loft, Cheyenne turned away from the tender scene below and walked with soft

feet to his pallet. He sat down and unclenched his
fists. He stared at the drops of blood in his palms
where his short fingernails had pierced the skin.

Lucky thing he hadn't had a gun in his hand, he
thought with a grin. Lucky for Roy Powell. That
smooth son of a bitch, walking back into Etta's life
as if years hadn't passed.

Of course, why shouldn't she respond to his
smooth ways? A banker's son. Educated. Lily-
white. Important job with the railroad. He could
solve Etta's problems without bruising a knuckle
or firing a gun.

Roy Powell was everything Johnny Cheyenne
was not.

Chapter 20

Humming happily, Etta put away the last of the supper dishes and dried her hands on her apron.

"I'm going outside," Cheyenne growled behind her. Then a gust of cold air circled her ankles and skittered up her skirt.

She whirled around. "Outside? But it's ... snowing," she finished, watching the barn door swing shut. Puzzled, she went to the window and stood on tiptoe to look out. Tracks led from the barn around to the back. Maybe he was answering the call of nature.

Crossing to the tack room, she knocked lightly before entering. Whitey was sitting up in bed and whittling, creating a bird in flight from a chunk of wood. Andy sat near the stove, a mound of leather reins and halters pooled beside him.

"Some of these need new rings," Andy said, lifting one set of halters. "Thought I'd fix 'em."

"You're as handy as a pocket on a shirt," Etta said with a smile. She perched on the edge of Whitey's bunk. "Do you know if anything in particular is bothering Cheyenne?"

"Can't say that I do," Whitey said, carefully slicing off wood splinters. "But he was unusually quiet at supper, and he hardly ate a thing. Think he's ailing?"

"I don't know. He just left."

314

"Where'd he go?" Andy asked.

"He didn't say. Maybe he's just taking care of necessary business."

"We all got to do that now and again," Whitey allowed. "If he don't come back in pretty soon, you might have to go check and make sure he didn't fall through the hole."

Andy giggled. "One of my littlest brothers almost did that once. If I hadn't grabbed him, he woulda slipped right through. We have two holes in our outhouse, and Daddy made them both too big."

"I worked for a ranch once that had a three-holer, all different shapes," Whitey said. "A star, a square, and a circle. I always liked to do my business a-sittin' on that star. Seemed like things came out better on it."

Etta placed her hands on her thighs and stood up. "This sure is interesting, but I've got important things to do, like brush my hair and stare at the moon," she teased, getting a chuckle from Whitey.

"Is the moon out? I thought it was snowing," Andy said.

"It was earlier. 'Night, y'all." Etta left the cramped but cozy tack room. Andy and Whitey were used to it, but she missed her more spacious house. It had been plain, but full of her personal history, her favorite things.

All gone now, she thought. Because of Blaine Brickman. She forced herself not to dwell on him. Roy had eased her mind a bit where Brickman and the railroad were concerned, and she wanted to hold on to her improved mood.

She waited for half an hour before slipping into her coat and going outside to find Cheyenne. She didn't have to go far. He was sitting on the corral fence, watching the herd jostle for space in the confined area.

"I was worried about you," she said, standing by the fence and looking up at his blue-limned profile. "Aren't you cold out here?"

"No."

She examined his stoic expression more carefully, thinking he looked more the proud Cheyenne than a white man when he glowered like that. "Is something wrong? You're making me feel like I should apologize, but I can't for the life of me figure out what for."

"I thought that railroad man got married."

"He did."

Cheyenne swung his head around to face her, and his eyes were blue steel. "It doesn't bother you to love up on a married man?"

"Love up . . ." She pressed her lips together in mute fury.

"I couldn't hear what you were saying to him, but I saw you hugging and kissing on him. Are you so desperate to save this place that you'll forsake all your morals?"

"You're certainly one to preach to *me* about morals, gunslinger that you are. And how many women have you slept with, pray tell? You remember any of their names? Did you make sure they weren't married before you rolled in the hay with them?"

"That's right." He swung his legs over the railing and landed lightly in front of her. "I'm filth. I'm dirt. But you're supposed to be more high-minded and pure-hearted. Etta, don't compromise yourself for this place. It's not worth it."

She poked a finger in the center of his chest. "You don't know what you're talking about, so you'd better button your lips."

"I saw with my own eyes—"

"Two old friends burying the hatchet," she interrupted. "That's what you saw. I told Roy about what happened between me and Brickman and explained to him about our broken engagement. I thought he already knew, but nobody ever told him. Anyway, he's on my side now, Cheyenne. He doesn't want me to lose the ranch."

Cheyenne showed no joy or relief. "What's he going to do about it?"

"About what?"

"Is he going to go ahead with his original plan and run the track on Brickman's land?"

"He can't. That's not his decision to make. But he said he hoped I could hold on until spring."

Cheyenne's mouth twitched in a quick, bitter grin. "And you hugged him for that? From where I was standing, you were sure grateful for such a small favor."

"Maybe you shouldn't have been standing there, then. Nobody asked you to spy on me."

"I wasn't. I just didn't think you'd be doing anything you wouldn't want me to see." He turned away and crossed his arms on the top rail to stare moodily at the sad-eyed cows. "He's more your kind."

Etta leaned sideways against the fence to glare at him, although he refused to look at her. "What does that mean—my kind?"

"He's white and rich. He's school-taught and well bred."

"He's married and he's part of my past." She

discovered a kernel of truth in her heart and she
voiced it. "I'm not sure I ever really loved Roy. He
was the first man after Brickman to court me, and
I went along with it because my papa liked him
and approved of the match." She shrugged. "I was
fond of Roy, and I would have grown to love him,
I suppose." She slanted Cheyenne a look. "Your
problem is you're jealous."

He made a disgruntled sound. "You've been
happy as a cream-fed cat since Powell left."

"Of course. I'm glad we're friends again. We
cleared the air, and I believe Roy when he says
he'll make sure the railroad leaves me alone if I'm
still here come spring." She wrapped her hands
around his upper arm, which was solid as a rock,
and squeezed hard. "Quit acting like a sulled up
possum."

He sighed heavily. "The Cheyenne believe that
land can't be owned."

"Well, I've got a deed that proves them wrong."
She sensed his anger had abated, so she leaned her
cheek against his shoulder. He was still tense, and
she wished she could understand him better. At
times like this, he seemed distant, foreign, impossibly complex.

"Ownership is man's curse. We even thought
we could own other people. Had to fight a war
over it. Nobody owns anyone else. If they think
they do, they're fools. It's not right to stamp a
brand on another person as if that person is a
maverick steer."

Etta raised her head, suddenly wary. Was he
telling her in a roundabout way that she shouldn't
expect him to remain at the Flying H much
longer? Her hands slipped away from him.

"Of course," she said, making her tone light. "It's downright stupid to claim to own anyone else." She stepped away from him, suddenly cold and lonely. So he didn't feel as deeply for her as she did for him. She'd known that. He wasn't the marrying kind. "Don't stay out here and catch cold," she murmured, turning toward the barn.

Butter trotted into the barn ahead of Etta, puppies running to catch up with her. Etta watched as Butter ignored their whines, lying on her stomach so that they couldn't nurse.

She's starting to wean them, Etta thought. Little by little, Etta knew that Butter would push the pups away, forcing them to be independent of her.

Etta looked up at the loft, where she'd been sleeping. Not tonight, she thought. Time to get used to being alone again, because he'll be gone soon. Too soon.

Big Joe Simpson drove his wagon into the porch yard, reined in the mules, and lumbered down from the vehicle. He started up the porch steps, then stopped, noticing that something was amiss.

"It burned," Etta stated simply, approaching him from the direction of the barn. "How you doing, Big Joe? I've been looking for you for more than a week. You're later than usual."

"Bust my britches, if it ain't little Etta!" He spread his hands across his ample stomach and grinned like a monkey. "I'm late 'cause I didn't figger you'd have any cows fer me." He spit tobacco onto the dead grass. "Winter's coming early, ain't it? I was gonna hit the cattle trail with what I done bought up when sumpin tole me to check in on you first." He eyed the house again. "What happened here?"

"Caught fire," she said, leaving it at that. Knowing in her heart that lightning had had nothing to do with the destruction, she couldn't bring herself even to repeat the lie. "I'm living in the barn now. Come on inside."

"Where's Whitey?"

"In the tack room." She waited for Big Joe to match her strides. "He's been sickly, so I'll be handling this by myself."

"Oh?"

She could have sworn that Big Joe's black eyes took on a green sheen. He thinks he can swindle me, she thought. Nerves tightened in her stomach. She'd never bargained by herself with cattle brokers. She'd watched her papa and Whitey haggle many a time, but she'd never entered into the back-and-forthing. Papa had deemed it a man's job.

But there was no man to haggle with Big Joe Simpson at the Flying H. It was Etta or nobody. She and Whitey had discussed it, and Whitey had schooled her a little in how to handle Big Joe. Whitey's strength hadn't fully returned, and Etta had insisted she could handle the cattle buyer alone. But she had her doubts—which she'd kept to herself.

Inside the barn, Big Joe sat at the table, and Etta sat across from him. She poured him a cup of coffee and sliced him a piece of warm raisin bread with honey poured over it.

"Much obliged." He swallowed the bread in three bites, then opened a small book full of penciled figures. He fished a stubby pencil from his pocket, licked the tip of it, and wrote down the name of the ranch, followed by the date and then Etta's name. He looked up, smiling; then his smile drooped and his eyes narrowed.

Etta turned in her chair. Cheyenne emerged from the shadows and walked toward them. He leaned against a thick support beam and nodded once at Big Joe.

"Uh . . . Big Joe, this is one of my hands, Johnny Cheyenne."

Big Joe almost swallowed his chaw of tobacco. "Ranch hand? I thought Johnny Cheyenne was a gunfighter."

Cheyenne held out his right hand. "I am, but I'm helping Etta out. I'm a friend of her brother's."

Etta sent him a puzzled frown. He'd never introduced himself that way before. She shrugged mentally. Maybe he thought Big Joe might believe the gossip about Cheyenne's gunslinging days being over. Of course, it wasn't just gossip, but Etta wasn't sure that Cheyenne had accepted it as truth yet.

"That right?" Big Joe pumped Cheyenne's hand. "Glad to know ya." He squinted, eyeing him carefully. "You ain't packing, 're ya'?"

Cheyenne held his arms out from his sides. "I'm peaceful today." He directed his attention to Etta. "Don't mind if I lend an ear, do you?"

"No, of course not," Etta said quickly, welcoming his participation. She had no inkling of his experience in such negotiations, but just having a friend in her camp would boost her self-confidence.

"You two partners?" Big Joe asked with a wily grin.

"No," Etta said, scoffing. "Let me get my own ledger. Excuse me for a moment." She went to the desk for the financial diary.

Cheyenne tipped his head, an idea sparkling, exploding. Partners. That didn't sound half bad. Him and Etta on equal footing. That's what they needed, he told himself. To be equals. Then he wouldn't feel like he had to answer to her, and she wouldn't feel like she shouldn't be leaning on him too much.

He'd be more like Roy Powell and less like brother Hank in her eyes.

Etta returned to her seat at the table and opened her ledger. "Very well." She looked expectantly at Big Joe.

"How many head?" Big Joe licked the business end of his pencil again and poised it above the blank page in his own book.

Etta squared her shoulders. "Three hundred and ten."

Big Joe raised his brows. "That many? Better keep some back for your stock next year—if you're planning on being here next year."

"I'll be here and I'm keeping plenty," she assured him.

Big Joe nodded. "You worked your tail off, didn't you, little gal?" He smiled, turned his head, and spit tobacco onto the hay-strewn ground. "Well, seeing as how you waited for me and all . . ." He tore off a corner of the paper. "I'll put down a number here and you can take it or leave it. It's a fair amount." He scratched out a figure and scooted the scrap of paper across the table to her. His beady eyes locked on Cheyenne, and Cheyenne knew in that moment that whatever figure he'd written was anything but fair.

Etta stared at the paper, and Cheyenne stepped up close behind her chair.

"Mind if I have a look?" he asked.

Wordlessly, she handed the triangle of paper to him. Cheyenne looked at the single digit, then lifted his gaze to meet Big Joe's. The cattle broker leaned back in the chair and divided his glances between Etta and Cheyenne.

"The market ain't as good as some think, and I've got a big herd bought up already. I come by here for old-time's sake, Etta. If I don't buy this cattle, it won't make much difference to me. I'm trying to help you out, is all."

Etta turned her gaze up to Cheyenne, and he saw desperation in her green eyes. He wished he could convey to her to be strong and not accept the cattle broker's fake charity.

"Well . . ." She swallowed hard and retrieved the piece of paper from Cheyenne. "I reckon we can . . ." Her brows dipped and her eyes questioned Cheyenne.

"We can return Big Joe's friendly gesture by thanking him kindly," Cheyenne put in, taking the lead that she had offered. He saw a flicker of disappointment in her expression. She thought he was siding with Big Joe. "Etta, I figure you'll want to talk with other cattle brokers since this is the best Big Joe can do."

Relief sparkled in her eyes, and some of the tension knotting Cheyenne's gut dissipated.

Etta faced Big Joe again. "That's right." She pushed the paper back at him. "Much obliged, but we'll see what other offers come in."

Big Joe looked surprised for a moment, then pinned on an expression that would have bluffed many in a poker game. "Fine, fine." He closed his ledger book and drained his coffee cup. "Like I said, I got all the cattle I need. Y'all did notice that snowfall, didn't you? When the flakes blow, the brokers head for the slaughter pens. There probably won't be any others come nosing around here after I leave." Big Joe smiled congenially. "Good luck to you." He lumbered to his feet.

Cheyenne sensed that Etta was prepared to leap up and grab Big Joe, so he rested a hand on her shoulder to keep her in place. He hoped to hell he hadn't made the biggest mistake of his life by calling Big Joe's bluff.

The cattle broker paused, looked from Etta to Cheyenne and back to Etta, then sat down again. "What number did you have in mind?"

Etta tore off a piece of paper, jotted down a figure she thought was fair, and showed it to Cheyenne.

Cheyenne branded it wishful thinking, but nodded. She extended it toward Big Joe. He didn't take the paper, but squinted at the number. His eyes widened.

"You're pulling my leg, little lady. Nobody's getting that price for beef." He shifted uneasily. "Some of them cows of yours haven't been on flat ground in three years, and their meat will be about as tender as jerky."

She gave a shrug of concession. "Most of them are fat and sassy."

Big Joe ran a hand down his face. "Tell you what. I'll add a penny to my offer."

Etta arched a brow at Cheyenne. He gave a half-hearted shrug.

"Might look better if you'd add two pennies to the offer," Cheyenne suggested, and Etta nodded.

"Two?" Big Joe chuckled. "Hell, you're both dreaming. No. That's my final offer, and I'm being awful generous at that."

Etta's gaze slid to Cheyenne again. He tried to convey to her that the offer still wasn't good enough, but he wasn't sure she wanted to receive that message.

Facing Big Joe again, she stared at the scraps of paper before heaving a weighted sigh. "You'd drive them to market?"

"From Clearwater, yeah. You'll have to drive them into town. I've got wranglers to take them the rest of the way."

Cheyenne cleared his throat to get their attention. "We'd have to get them into Clearwater?" he repeated, hoping Etta would take the bait and run with it.

"That's right. That's how I always do business. Your pa and Whitey always drove them into town. I set up pens out there by the blacksmith's. Ain't that far. Most ranches drive their cattle all the way to Amarillo for me. I only provide a few wranglers for the smallish ranches that ain't got enough men to herd their cows for them."

Big Joe's smile was strictly condescending. "See how accommodating I am for you, little gal? You ain't got much to bargain with—not like them big ranchers who can wrangle their own beef to market. I'm doing y'all a favor, if you look at it just right."

Etta sat back and folded her arms against her

chest. She stared at Big Joe, and Cheyenne couldn't read her next move in her taciturn expression.

"I never said we wouldn't drive them to Amarillo. We'll do it for a halfpenny more."

Big Joe spit tobacco again, then screwed up his face as if he'd sucked on a lemon. "How you gonna get them steers to Amarillo, little gal? You and Whitey can't—"

"Me, Cheyenne, and Andy will drive them there. Won't be any problem." She glanced at Cheyenne. He gave a quick bob of his head.

"You can't take a month getting them there, ya know."

"I know." She held out her hand to him. "Let's shake on it."

"Whoa!" Big Joe stared long and hard at her. "Half a penny more a pound? That's steep. I hadn't planned on paying anything near that."

Etta waited, hand extended, patient as Job. "I hadn't planned on taking anything less than that, Big Joe."

Cheyenne bowed his head and pursed his lips to keep from grinning. Pride in Etta's fortitude nearly burst like an exploding sun in his chest.

Big Joe gave Cheyenne the once-over. "You think you can depend on this man and that boy Andy?"

"I *know* that me and Cheyenne can do anything," Etta assured him. "There's no need for you to fret about it. Now, do we have a deal or don't we?"

The cattle broker let go of a face-splitting grin. "Why, sure. You drive a hard bargain, but I'm glad to shake your hand, little gal." He pumped her hand twice before letting go. "And I'm glad to have your business. You done good." He scratched at his stubbled cheek. "I paid too much, but—aw, hell! I ain't losing any sleep over it." He laughed, his belly shaking, then reached out and shook Cheyenne's hand. "Y'all take care, and I'll see y'all in Amarillo in a few weeks for the weigh-in. Don't run the fat off them, and don't fill 'em with water right before you get there, ya hear?"

"We won't," Cheyenne assured him.

Big Joe lumbered to the barn door. "I s'pose I'll see y'all at the Roundup Dance."

Etta's smile faded. "No, I'm not going."

"No?" Big Joe shrugged. "Well, I guess I can understand why. Ain't no love lost between you and Brickman, from what I hear." He released another stream of tobacco before pulling himself up into the wagon. He took up the reins and urged the two mules forward. "I'll buy y'all supper when you reach Amarillo. 'Bye, now!"

Etta stood on the beaten path and waved. When the wagon was a moving dot in the distance, she turned to Cheyenne and let out a squeal of delight. She threw her arms around his neck and laughed when he whirled around in a circle.

"I can't believe it!" she said breathlessly. "I never thought ... That's more money than Papa ever got for beef. Even in a good year!"

Cheyenne laughed with her, sharing her joy, her pride.

"You're not mad, are you?" she asked when he set her on her feet again.

"Mad? Why should I be mad?"

"Well, I enlisted you on a cattle drive to Amarillo." She clutched the sides of his Indian blanket

vest. "I need you to help me on that drive, Cheyenne. Will you do it? I'll pay you fair wages."

He covered her fists with his hands. "Like you
told the man, we can do anything. Hell, yes, I'll go
with you to Amarillo. I wouldn't miss it."

She closed her eyes for a moment in relief. "You
were wonderful. I couldn't have held out if you
hadn't been there, giving me strength, guiding me
when I floundered."

He could have stared into her eyes forever, for
in them he saw respect. He held no gun in his
hand, uttered no threats, and this woman respected him. This beautiful, trusting woman.

Etta grabbed one of his hands. "Let's go tell
Whitey."

"Wait a minute. What's this about a Roundup
Dance?"

"Oh, that." She wrinkled her nose. "Brickman
holds a dance every year to celebrate the end of
roundup. Everybody in town shows up to kiss his
boots, and he presides over the whole thing like a
king. It's disgusting, and I'm not going anywhere
until the cattle are delivered."

"I understand. I was just thinking it would be
nice to dance with you."

She blushed prettily. "Yes, but not there. Not in
front of Brickman." She tugged on his hand again.
"Come on. I'll need you to back me up again, because Whitey won't believe me."

She led him to the barn, but she stopped short
of the door, spun around, and embraced him
again. He laughed lightly, his hands spanning her
waist.

"What's this?" he asked, moving her back to
look at her shining eyes and bright smile.

"I'm so happy!" Her voice was light and young, her laughter as bubbly as champagne. "I really think I can beat Brickman now. I'll even have enough money left over to buy some lumber to build myself a house."

Cheyenne traced her smiling mouth with his thumb before he kissed her. She moved closer, her arms sliding up his back, her hands hooking at his shoulders. He outlined her hips with his hands. He finger-walked against her thighs, hiking up her long skirt. She thwarted him, slapping playfully at his hands.

"Stop that!" Laughing, she tipped back her head. Her eyes searched, caressed, adored his features, bringing a lump to his throat and fire to his groin. Her eyes changed from limpid to lusty. Her fingertips buried through the hair at the back of his neck and massaged his nape. "Maybe we should celebrate alone before we tell anybody else." Her mouth flowered against the skin exposed in the V-shaped collar of his shirt. Cheyenne locked his knees to keep from falling to them. "Then we'll tell Whitey and Andy and have another little celebration with them. But first . . ." She smiled and stood on tiptoe. Her tongue circled his mouth. "Mmm, you taste good."

The hungry animal in him growled, and Cheyenne responded by gathering Etta into his arms and striding inside with her. He let go of her just long enough for her to climb the ladder. Once in the loft, he pushed her into the soft hay and slid his hands up her skirt, along her satiny thighs.

She pushed the vest off his shoulders and down his arms. With impatient fingers, she unbuttoned his shirt, and he helped her by pulling his arms roughly from the sleeves. Her mouth was hot and moist upon his chest, moving restlessly, kissing and sucking and biting.

His devotion to her, his pride in her, were overflowing, and he couldn't hold himself in check. Already hard and near bursting, he struggled with her underclothes until he could at last drive himself into her . . . home.

His release came quickly, wildly, blessedly. Flinging back his head, he let it come in short jolts. Etta writhed beneath him, clutching, moaning, asking him to go deeper, faster, higher, longer.

"I'm sorry . . . I'm sorry." He shook his head and droplets of sweat sprayed from the tips of his hair. "I wanted you so bad, I couldn't stop myself."

Lacing her hands behind his head, she brought his mouth down to her straining nipples. He tongued them, washed them thoroughly and lovingly. Her breathing grew rapid and ragged. He knew she was on the brink of a shattering climax as he moved from one taut, throbbing nipple to the other. He kneaded her soft flesh, filling his hands with her breasts, pulling them up so that he could take as much as possible into the hot cavern of his mouth.

He began to grow hard again inside her. He ground his pelvis against hers, then let go of one breast to palm her mound. She moaned, opening her legs wider for him. He located the hard bud of flesh in her moist folds and chased it around and around with his thumb.

She gasped, and came in a long spasm of ecstasy. Her climax triggered his own, this one not as wild, but twice as sweet.

He held her in his arms, limbs tangled, clothing

bunched between them, skin slick with sweat, and felt her heart leaping against his. Closing his eyes, he tried to remember any other woman's face. He couldn't.

Chapter 21

The crack of gunfire lured Etta behind the burned house. The morning was chilly, and she was glad she'd thought to slip into a heavy jacket.

Cheyenne and Andy stood shoulder to shoulder, and on Cheyenne's mark they drew and fired on tin cans and brown bottles. Andy had gotten as fast as Cheyenne, which proved to Etta that Cheyenne certainly hadn't returned to his glory days. She wondered if he had finally realized that those days were over. She didn't talk to him about it because she sensed it was a subject he would rather avoid.

The two drew their guns again. Cheyenne was a second faster than Andy. Etta watched as Andy holstered his gun again, a big smile on his face as Cheyenne complimented him. Etta advanced on them, suddenly seeing red as thoughts of her brother rose in her like an evil mist.

"I thought you wanted to be a cowboy, Andy," she said, eyeing the youngster with a critical eye. "Being the fastest gun has nothing to do with riding the range."

Andy's joyful grin slipped sideways. "Aw, Miss Etta, we was just practicing."

"For what?" She switched her critical glare to Cheyenne. "Can't you teach him something useful? All this will do is get him killed or in the same prison as Hank."

Cheyenne loaded the chambers of his six-shooter again, effectively dismissing her complaints. "Thought I'd see how limber my hand is getting, and Andy challenged me to a draw. Simple as that." He slipped the gun into the holster and his gaze lifted to hers. His long lashes threw shadows across the broad planes of his cheekbones.

"Is Andy faster than lightning, or are you slowed up some?" she asked, moving closer to glimpse his hand. He usually wore gloves, but not today. The stitches had been removed and the wound was red, but healing.

"I'm slower." He stiffened his fingers, then relaxed them. "I suppose I'll never be as fast with this hand again."

"But you can shoot whatever you aim at," Andy said. "I never seen such accuracy."

"And you've seen 'em all, haven't you, pal?" Cheyenne grinned and cuffed Andy lightly on the shoulder. Laughing, Andy ducked and dived and put up his dukes.

Etta smiled, watching the two posture like bantam roosters. They circled each other, dodging playful fists, jabbing at the air, laughing at their near misses, their breath escaping in clouds. Andy was limp by the time he called a truce.

"Gimme your gun and I'll clean it," he said, holding out his cream-colored palm for Cheyenne's weapon. "I'll challenge you tomorrow using your left hand."

Cheyenne unbuckled and untied his holster. "You'll draw left-handed with me?"

"No. That won't be fair. Gotta make it fair."

"Here, partner." Cheyenne gave him the pearl-handled weapon. "Much obliged."

When Andy had left them, Etta touched Cheyenne's arm. "Have you been practicing with your left hand?"

"Sure." He reached behind her and gave her buttocks a squeeze. "Practicing on you."

She jumped away from him, slapping at him. "You!" After looking around to make sure they were alone, she wagged a finger at him. "That's not what I was talking about, and you know it." She captured his hand to more closely examine the red skin. "I've done all I can do for it, Cheyenne. You should be getting back to normal by now." She pressed on the flesh around the scar. "Can you feel that?"

"I feel a tingling sometimes. That's all."

"A tingling? Maybe that's the nerves knitting."

"Doesn't matter."

"It doesn't?" She gave him a perplexed look. "Since when? You were fretting something powerful over it just a few weeks ago."

"Well, that was a few weeks ago. I don't have the reflexes in this hand anymore. Maybe it's for the best."

She kissed the scar, then let him go. Clasping her hands behind her, she studied his resigned expression as an idea formed in her mind and clogged her throat. "It might be time for you to think of hanging up your gun belt, Johnny Cheyenne."

He chuckled. "And do what? Be a cowboy?"

Was that mockery in his eyes, in his voice? she wondered. "Would that be so terrible?"

"You mean I could take Whitey's place?" he asked, squinting at her as if she had angles he couldn't figure out. "Be your faithful friend. A younger Whitey. An older Andy."

Etta squeezed her hands together so tightly behind her back that her shoulder sockets began to burn. "That's not exactly what I was thinking."

"Well, no, thanks."

His words tarnished the bright idea she'd had about him staying on and working beside her. "Forget it. I was only thinking you could do a lot worse."

"You want me to work for you."

"You *are* working for me," she reminded him. "But if you stayed on, I'd pay you wages."

"Oh, would you?" He propped his hands at his belt and reared back to give her a long, frank look. "As I said, no, thanks. I won't work for wages. Not for you." He leaned forward, a foxy smile slanting across his mouth. "But I might consider a partnership."

Now she reared back to examine his twinkling blue eyes and naughty smile. Just what was he up to? Distrust crept around her heart and seeped into her mind. He surely didn't think she'd divide the ranch with him. "What do you mean, partnership?"

"I mean partners. Equals. Me and you and the Flying H." He stuck his thumbs in his belt. "That's the only way I'll stay here."

The wariness that had once been her shield sprang up around her again. She'd been taught not to trust men outside her family and family-like friends, and the teachings were as strong as a prison's iron bars. While her cell was lonely, at least she was protected.

But this time her wariness was mixed with bitter disappointment. She had hoped Cheyenne would want her only for herself and not for her ranch, Clearwater Spring, or to gain some other foothold.

"I told you I have some money in Mexico. I can get it and—"

"This ranch is not for sale, Cheyenne," she broke in, her voice hard and rasping. Suddenly his discussion about how she could own land but not him resurfaced. He'd been priming her for this, explaining to her that he was interested in sticking around to be a partner in the ranch, not to be a partner for her. "No part of it is for sale. You think I'd fight tooth and nail against the likes of Brickman and the railroad, then sell you a chunk of my land just because we've slept together?" She laughed hollowly. "You're good, Cheyenne, but not that good."

His face went still, and then chaos reigned. In an instant she saw that he was furious. His eyes blazed blue fire, his mouth thinned to a dangerous line, and he struck out, punching the air between them with an angry fist to punctuate his words.

"You think I'm offering to *buy* your ranch? I was going to loan you the money to build your damned house!"

She blinked, unsure whether to believe him. Maybe he was trying to repair the damage he'd done. Maybe he was sincere. Maybe . . . no . . . yes. She couldn't be sure of anything except that he was more angry than she'd ever seen him. Hot color scalded his neck and tendons strained against his taut skin.

"I didn't ask for your money," she mumbled, re-treating from the heat of his fury.

"I know you didn't, and I'm damn well not go-ing to give you a cent of it now. After what we've been through, I thought you trusted me, but you think everyone is scheming to get this ranch. Well, I don't want your damn ranch!" He was shouting now, advancing slowly, forcing her to retreat. "My notion of a great life isn't a view of the backside of a cow."

"Nobody is asking you to stay if you don't want to. I was doing you a favor by letting you bunk here." She heard herself babbling and couldn't stop herself. His words hurt and she could do nothing but strike back.

"Doing *me* a favor?" he repeated, incredulous.

"Yes." She pushed out her lower lip in a pout. Why was he being so belligerent? Why couldn't they both just shut up before this went too far?

"If that's the way you feel, then you don't need me to ride with you to Amarillo."

The threat hung between them like a sword. Cheyenne stood, feet braced apart, hands clutched in fists at his sides, his whole posture daring her, taunting her. For an instant Etta started to surren-der, to beg for reason and peace offerings. But her pride, both her sustenance and her poison, ruled.

"Suit yourself," she said with a bob of her shoulders. "I don't expect you to keep your word."

An unpleasant smile curled his lips. "I guess neither one of us should expect a damn thing from the other." He chuckled, but the sound was sor-rowful. "Your ranch is safe from me, Etta. And so are you." Then he turned sharply on his bootheels and moved away from her with long, angry strides.

Etta bit down on her lips to keep from sobbing aloud as her eyes filled with tears. Go, she thought, go! She'd given him her heart and her respect, and he'd waved money in her face as if she were a whore! She'd never forgive him for that, and she'd never forgive herself for trusting him.

Whitey sat at the table in the makeshift living room. He moved a black checker piece and grinned at Etta.

She moved a red piece without considering any strategy. Whitey whooped with glee and jumped three of her men to land at the end of the board.

"King me, sister girl!"

Etta placed another checker on top of his. She slid another of her red disks. Whitey frowned and jumped her.

"You letting me win just 'cause I've been sickly?"

"What? No, of course not." She stared at the board. "Is it my turn?"

"Yep."

She touched a checker, but Whitey cleared his throat with alarm.

"I'm black. You're red."

"Oh." She moved a red playing piece nearest the black one she'd tried to claim.

Whitey sighed. He jumped her piece. "Did you forget how to play this game? I'd be glad to go over the rules for you."

Cheyenne's footfalls sounded in the loft, and Etta's gaze flew to the shadows up there. He ap-

peared, buttoning a clean shirt. Descending the
ladder with the agility of a cat, he didn't spare a
glance in her direction.

"Where you going, stud?" Whitey asked, and
Etta could have kissed him for that. She'd wanted
to ask but couldn't, since she wasn't supposed to
care.

"To town," Cheyenne said, wrenching open the
barn door. "I hear there's a party there tonight."
He pulled a red handkerchief from his back
pocket. Holding it by opposite corners, he twisted
it into a rope which he tied lengthwise across his
forehead. He stepped outside and shut the door.

"You two have a ruckus?"

"No," she said too quickly. She moved her final
piece and shrugged when Whitey jumped it. "You
win."

"If you didn't have a ruckus, how come you
two stayed out of each other's way all day? Cheyenne didn't even come down for supper."

She shrugged. "I'm not his keeper."

"You're his woman, aren't you?"

Etta flinched and quickly began gathering the
wooden disks. Whitey's gnarled hands clamped
down on her wrists, pinning them to the checker-
board.

"Etta Lou, look at me."

She hauled her gaze up to meet his.

"Well, are you his woman, or ain't you?"

She gulped. "Ain't."

Whitey let her go. "Since when?"

"I never was."

"Don't lie to me, sister girl."

"It's none of your business." She slapped the

disks into a can, one after the other, and they sounded like buckshot.

"It *is* my business, because I love you like I would a daughter."

"He's just like Hank," she blurted out. "He's gone and he probably won't be back." She swiped angrily at the tears leaking from the corners of her eyes. "Just as well. We don't need him."

"We sure as hell *do* need him! We got cattle waitin' to be driven to Amarillo."

"We can do it without him."

"Quit talkin' like a spurned woman, and tell me what happened between you two. He's takin' hisself to town for a reason, and I'd like to hear it."

"All he wanted was a piece of this ranch," she said, trying hard not to sob. She stared at her entwined fingers and concentrated on keeping the pain out of her voice. "He offered me money for it, and I told him I didn't want his stinking money. I'd rather die than sell one acre of this ranch, and now that he knows it, he's heading for greener pastures. He's out looking for his next fool or floozy." She spun her thumbs around each other. "Guess I'm both."

Whitey stowed the board and the can of checkers under the table. He scrutinized Etta while he wedged a clump of tobacco at the back of his left cheek, just behind his molar.

Etta hid her eyes from him behind a scrim of dark brown lashes, waiting for one of Whitey's succinct observances. The wait lengthened until she couldn't stand the loud silence another moment.

"Well? Tell me I'm a self-pitying, prideful mule!" she demanded of him, hammering a fist on the tabletop. "Tell me! I know you're busting a gut to give me a tongue-lashing."

He smiled congenially. "No need in telling somebody something they already know." He picked up his stained, smelly cuspidor and held it close to his mouth. The juice pinged against the bottom of the can. Setting it down within easy reach, he folded his arms against his black suspenders and brown shirt. He'd lost weight, and the shirt sagged over his narrow shoulders and scrawny chest. "Thought you'd start for Amarillo tomorrow."

"I was going to . . . I need to. I don't like keeping these cattle here. I should move them away as soon as I can."

"Yep. The longer they stay penned up, the more restless they get. Won't take much to spook 'em." He scratched his upper lip with his lower teeth. "If Cheyenne ain't gonna help you drive 'em, how you gonna get them there?" He raised his bushy brows at her. "Sister girl, you know I'd help you if I was able, but I ain't. My old lungs is weak and still rattle at night. I ain't got my gumption back, and maybe it won't come back."

The truth of what he said subdued her anger and worried her. Whitey had been her solid rock since her pa had passed, but that chest cold had shaken him, weakened him. She couldn't lean on him anymore. It was time for him to lean on her.

"I'll ride into town and tell Big Joe that I changed my mind. He'll have to drive them to Amarillo."

Whitey scratched at his whiskers. "That won't do. You got yourself a good price for your beef, but once you tell Big Joe that you can't deliver, he'll see that he's got you over a barrel, and you'll have to take whatever he offers. And what he offers won't amount to spit."

"I'll deal with someone else."

"Too late for that. Other buyers will get wind that you've reneged on your deal with Big Joe and they'll be looking to take advantage of you."

Etta stood up and paced to her bed, then back to the table. "Well, what do you want me to do, crawl on my belly to Cheyenne and beg? He wants my ranch, Whitey!"

Whitey shook his head. "I'm having trouble swallowing that one, Etta. What would a gunfighter want with a piece of a cattle ranch?"

"He's not a gunfighter anymore. His hand isn't ever going to be right again and he knows it. He's looking for another way to make his living."

Whitey screwed up one blue eye. "I figured him for a smart fella, but only an idiot would think a ranch would make him some money. Hell, ain't he been listening while you've been squawking about being dirt-poor?"

"All I know is that he offered money. Said he had some put back in Mexico. Of course, after I told him off, he said he was going to loan me the money to build me a house, but I'd already seen his true colors."

"I wish I'd heard the conversation from beginning to end, 'cause something's not right. One of you wasn't listening too good."

Etta sliced him with a glare. "Well, it wasn't me! I know what he's up to! I should have known better than to take up with him. He's just like Hank."

"He ain't nothin' like Hank. Hank's an overgrown boy and Cheyenne's a man."

"And neither one is interested in hard work or staying anywhere long enough to put down roots."

Whitey pushed himself up from the chair slowly and with an old man's stiffness. "For a man not interested in hard work, Cheyenne sure does lather up a sweat. I'm going to bed, and for your sake, I hope Cheyenne's back by morning and in a forgiving mood."

"Forgiving? He should be seeking *my* forgiveness!"

Whitey ambled toward the tack room. "Say your prayers tonight, sister girl. If you ain't gonna take human help, then you'd be wise to seek divine counsel." He shut the tack door quietly so as not to awaken Andy.

Etta fell across her bed, her head throbbing, her eyes scratchy from too many unshed tears. Doom settled on her chest like a lead weight and she struggled to breathe. She stared up at the loft, recalling the paradise she'd found up there. How could she have been so wrong about him? Every time she let a man close, he knifed her, cutting out a chunk of her heart. After Cheyenne, she doubted she had any left.

Chapter 22

The Scarlet Rose Saloon was the center of activity, and it seemed to Cheyenne that everyone in town was crammed into the long, narrow tavern. Over the roar of the crowd, he could barely hear the tinkling of a piano and a tenor singing slightly off-key.

He'd secured himself a corner in the front of the saloon, only a few steps from the bar. He propped a hip on a windowsill and took another swig of his second glass of whiskey. The potent alcohol did little to improve his mood.

He didn't see Meg O'Rourke until she was only a few steps from him. Too late to duck and run.

"Where have you been, big gun?" she asked, gathering her mouth into a red bud.

"Right here. Where have you been?"

"I don't mean tonight. I mean for all these weeks." She rested a hand on her jutting hip. "I heard you was out at the Flying H, but I couldn't figure what you'd be doing out there."

"It's a mystery, all right."

Meg studied his face, trying to read it. Finally she smiled and flipped her red hair back over her shoulders. "You're tight-lipped, is that it? You're not going to tell me nothing about nothing." She shrugged a pale white shoulder, exposed by her daringly cut gown of black and red. "I'm glad you came back into town, especially tonight." She glanced behind her, where a few dozen couples were trying to dance to music they could barely hear. "How about me and you taking a spin?"

"I don't ... spin."

"You never learned how?"

"Only around a bonfire before a big hunt," he teased her. "Or before we rode out to scalp some white men." He eyed her flaming hair. "I got a scalp once almost the color of yours. Wore it on my belt for years."

Her smile faltered, faded. "You're having fun with me, aren't you?"

"Am I?" He took another drink, enjoying her discomfort more than the whiskey.

Just then a group of men hefted someone from the crowd, and everyone stepped aside as they carried the man to the bar, where they set him on his feet, atop the gleaming surface. The bartender swept aside glasses, giving the gent room to stand without breaking glass.

"Speech!" someone called, and others chimed in.

That's when Cheyenne realized that the man singled out was none other than Blaine Brickman.

Holding on to either side of his black suit jacket, Brickman smiled benignly at the sea of worshippers. Dressed all in black, he was his usual dapper self. He wore a flat-topped hat of beaver skin. While he waited for the chatter and cheers to die away, he admired his reflection in an oval mirror directly across from him.

The man just can't keep his eyes off himself, Cheyenne thought with revulsion. His hatred for Brickman was so trenchant that he drew in a swift breath. What kind of woman would Etta be if it weren't for Blaine Brickman? he wondered. Her heart wouldn't be so sheltered, for one thing, and her trust wouldn't be so impossible to secure. Had Brickman ruined other women and men along the way? Was there a whole line of broken spirits, bruised hearts, and gray souls in his wake? Someone had to stop him. Someone had to revenge the lives Brickman had ruined or taken.

"Thank you all," Brickman intoned in his oh-so-perfect diction. "You're all so very kind. Too kind." He smiled again, his gaze locked on his image in the mirror. It took a lot for him to yank his attention away from his own dazzling smile. "I'm only too happy to set up drinks for you and provide a night of frivolity after yet another roundup. We all have much for which to be thankful." He took the glass of amber liquid the bartender handed him and lifted it toward the light and his reflection. "Here's to the land that binds us and sustains us. Here's to Texas!"

"To Texas!" others chorused, and elbows bent, heads tipped back, and mouths fell open.

Cheyenne turned his glass over and emptied it onto the floor.

"What'd you do that for?" Meg asked, staring at the puddle. "Hey!" She retreated from another stream of whiskey splashing on the planked floor.

Cheyenne regarded the man who had followed his lead by also pouring out his drink. He couldn't place him until he noticed the man's stubby eyebrows and almost hairless eyelids.

"You remember me now, don't you?" Barney Timmons said, grinning. "I used to work for him." He jerked his head toward Brickman, who was being helped down from the bar top.

"Somebody's going to step in this and break his neck," Meg complained, staring at the spilled whiskey.

"Honey, why don't you take yourself somewhere else?" Timmons said. "Me and this fella want to jaw, and we don't need an audience."

"Why don't you stuff your drawers in your mouth?" Meg rejoined.

"Go on." Cheyenne slipped a coin down the front of her dress, nestling it in the warm V between her breasts. "Find me later."

She ran a fingertip down his cheek and fluttered her lashes at him. "If you say so, big gun." Hips swinging, she glided away, making a beeline for Brickman.

"Look at all these sheep," Timmons said, his gaze moving around the room. His upper lip curled in distaste. "They follow whoever's ringing the biggest bell. And that's Brickman. But after that bastard flung that kerosene lamp at me, I'd sooner work for a one-eyed Injun— Oh, sorry. Didn't mean no offense." His pasty face gleamed with nervous sweat.

Cheyenne stared at him, saying nothing, giving nothing. Timmons wanted to talk, and Cheyenne wasn't going to get in his way.

Timmons looked at Brickman again. "That Meggie didn't waste no time. She's all over Brickman like syrup on a waffle."

Cheyenne slid his gaze in that direction, confirming Timmons' observance. Meg hung on to Brickman's arm and stared up into his face as if he were a golden idol and she a pagan worshipper.

"You ain't riding for the Flying H anymore?"

Timmons waited a few seconds, but when Cheyenne didn't say anything, he forged on. "Guess not, or else you wouldn't have left the herd. I noticed I didn't see Whitey or Etta or that darky boy in town. Etta's smart. She knows Brickman will try something tonight, since he's got witnesses."

Cheyenne furrowed his brow, having trouble following the man's circuitous route toward a point.

"Yeah, Brickman can say, 'I haven't the foggiest idear what you people are speaking about.'" He chuckled at his poor imitation of Brickman. "'I was in town all evening. Ask anyone! I spent the night upstairs at the Scarlet Rose, as I do every year during the Roundup Dance.'" Timmons chuckled again and slapped his thigh. "I can just hear him. Can't you?"

Cheyenne looked from Timmons to Brickman and was disconcerted to find Brickman staring steadily at him. A pernicious grin spread over Brickman's lips before he gave Meg his full attention once again. Cheyenne felt the skin crawl between his legs. He whipped his gaze back to Timmons, who had seen the silent exchange.

"There's bad blood between you two. If you want to get his goat, you ought to help out Etta at the Flying H. Brickman's hoping that after tonight, she'll cave in and sell her land and herself to him. He's running hot and wild for her. Has been for years, so folks say. He had her once and it was so good she spoiled him for any other piece of—hey!" Timmons' eyes bulged as Cheyenne twisted the material of his shirt collar in his fist, tightening it around his neck like a hangman's noose.

"If I ever hear you talk that way about Etta Hollister again, I'll cut your tongue out," Cheyenne said in a near hiss, then set Timmons from him.

Timmons jerked his shirt back into place. "Fine with me. Hell, I didn't figure you cared, since you ain't out there no more."

"Who says?"

"If you worked for the Flying H, you'd be watching that herd tonight. Brickman ain't gonna let them cows get to market, and tonight's his best shot at making sure they get scattered to the far winds."

A chill passed through Cheyenne as Timmons' logic registered. He swung around to look at Brickman. Once again, Brickman's gaze hunted his and found it. He lifted a whiskey glass in a salute, then drank the liquor. Cheyenne looked around the crowded saloon at all the happy revelers—witnesses.

"I don't see Clyde Smith," Timmons said. "Guess he's out with a couple of the other men doing Brickman's dirty work."

"Sheriff Craw!" Brickman's voice rode above the others. "Come over here and let me buy you a drink! Let our sheriff through, folks."

Suddenly Cheyenne felt as if he were in a nest of snakes. Shoving Timmons aside, he burst through the swinging doors and outside into the chilly air. The silver disks on his saddle glinted in the pale moonlight as he approached Lariat. His bedroll and parfleches were strapped on. He'd

been ready to hit the trail, but thoughts of Etta had
kept him lingering in town.

Not that he owed her anything ... It was just
that he'd invested too many saddle sores on that
damned herd to stand by and let Brickman's
men stampede the cattle back into the piney
woods.

He swung up onto Lariat and gave him the
spurs. Glancing up at the moon, he noticed it had
a yellow cast to it. A bad moon, the Cheyenne
called it.

Bending over Lariat's neck, he urged more
speed from the horse, but the night seemed to
hold them back as the bad moon smirked down at
them.

When he finally reached the fence line of the
Flying H, he relaxed. But only for a few moments.
He heard the rumble and tasted the dust.

He was too late. The herd had been stampeded.

Etta was riding flat out, halfway to the front of
the wild herd, when she saw him. At first she
thought her eyes were playing tricks on her. He
looked so wonderful—an answer to a prayer.

His black hair flew out behind him and he
rode with his characteristic grace. The silver
disks on his saddle flashed, and Etta knew he
was no vision. He'd come back, and in the nick
of time.

Her spirits lifted as he faced the herd, racing
Lariat back and forth, yipping and waving his
rope as he held his ground and tried to force the
herd to turn back. She had seen herds run right
over a single rider, especially when they were as
terrified as this one. The explosion of gunfire and

what sounded like a stick of dynamite had sent the cattle into a blind frenzy. They'd smashed through the fence as if it were made of matchsticks. She'd seen two steers go down, and she didn't want to think about how many others had fallen.

Whitey rode behind her somewhere. She could hear him hollering hoarsely. Andy rode on the other side of the herd, waving his hat like a madman and whooping like an Indian on the warpath. Etta's throat was already sore as she tried to yell above the roar of the herd. She clutched a whip in one hand and she popped it over and over again in the air above the steers' heads. So far, none had given her much notice.

She blinked against the sting of the wind and looked ahead again. The herd was nearly on Cheyenne, but it didn't seem to be moving as fast.

Part of her wanted to shut her eyes and not watch the cattle engulf him, while another part forced her to keep her eyes open just in case . . . by some miracle . . .

Please, please. Turn, you stupid beasts!

Miraculously, the wall of cowhide began to curve south toward Andy. Although Cheyenne wasn't riding a cutting or herding horse, Lariat did him proud. The big stallion dashed back and forth, responding to Cheyenne's deft touch. Dust clouds rose up as the herd turned, obliterating Cheyenne from Etta's view. She popped the whip and jammed her spurs into Southpaw's sides. The spunky horse found extra speed, bringing them closer to the cloud at the front of the herd.

She checked over her shoulder and saw Whitey galloping not too far behind. If anything happened to him because of this, she'd ride over to the Double B and shoot Brickman herself. Whitey should be in bed, getting well, not out chasing wild cattle. Wrestling with guilt, she rode near enough to Cheyenne to exchange a speaking glance. He gestured for her to help him veer the herd ever southward, and she reined Southpaw into the slowing animals, dividing them. Seeking control, she singled out a massive long-horned bull and pitted Southpaw's quick reactions against the bull's hot temper.

After a few charges and retreats, the bull stopped dead, and Southpaw pranced toward him. The bull eyed Southpaw, then turned on a dime and headed back the way he'd come. A number of heifers followed blindly, just as Etta had hoped.

Looking around to share the triumph with Cheyenne, she spotted Andy instead. He seemed to be having some trouble. He jerked at the reins. Nugget whinnied in fright. Then he and the horse disappeared. Etta screamed. Andy's horse sprang back up without Andy in the saddle and trotted a ways from the herd.

"Andy! Andy!" Etta yelled across the herd. She could do nothing, separated by a river of cattle spines and long horns. She saw Cheyenne and gestured wildly. "Andy! He's down!"

Cheyenne looked to where she was pointing and spurred Lariat in that direction. Whitey rode alongside Etta, then past her. She realized that he was taking over for Cheyenne at the front of the herd. She tried to concentrate on controlling the cows, but it was useless, so she let Southpaw guide himself around them while she tracked Cheyenne with her eyes.

She'd had her share of falls, but only one in the midst of runaway cattle. She'd been lucky, falling at the edge of the herd and escaping with scrapes and a sore right hand where a steer had stepped on her. But Andy had been near the center, engulfed by the herd as it had turned toward him. Cheyenne was having a devil of a time forcing Lariat into the throng. He searched, his head twisting from side to side as he peered amid the moving bodies for glimpses of the ground. The moon slipped behind a cloud, throwing the world into a darker night and making Cheyenne's search even more futile.

Etta felt tears block her throat and swallowed convulsively as whimpers of fear escaped her. If Cheyenne didn't see Andy in a minute, she'd go into the herd, too. If the animals stampeded again, to hell with them. She had to get to Andy. Even if it was too late, she had to find him and pull him out from under the sharp hooves and—

A black hand shot up from the herd. Cheyenne reached out and grabbed it, hauling Andy up from the ground and onto Lariat's back.

Etta bowed her head, limp with relief. "Thank you, thank you," she whispered, then looked at Andy again. His shirt was torn and bloody, but his limbs were straight, and he showed enough strength to hold on to Cheyenne.

Winding through the herd, careful not to spook it again, Cheyenne guided Lariat out of it and over to Nugget. Andy's horse stood quivering, bereft without his rider. Cheyenne grabbed Andy's arm, steadying the youngster as he slid to the ground. Etta watched Andy limp toward his horse before she returned her full attention to the herd.

By the time the moon escaped from the cloud cover, she and Whitey had the cattle moving at a slow walk toward home paddock. Andy joined them, his face streaked with dirt and blood.

"Are you okay?" Etta asked, reaching out to touch a scraped place on his chin.

"I will be. I'm just shakin' all over."

Whitey jerked a thumb backward. "Take the rear, son."

Andy nodded and fell back.

"Him and Cheyenne can give their hosses a rest by pulling up the rear," Whitey explained. "Me and you got things under control up here."

Etta smiled. "Old man, you're really something. You were riding like a twenty-year-old tonight. Guess you've just been lazing around, making us think you were ailing when you weren't."

Whitey tipped back his head and laughed. The moon bathed his face in pure light. "Sister girl, don't you know there's nothing like a stampede to start a fire in a cowboy's gut? Shoot, that was more fun than I've had since Hettie got me hemmed up behind the barn."

Etta laughed with him. "Who's Hettie?"

"Who's Hettie?" he repeated, aghast. "Why, she was only the purtiest gal in Tucson, and the friendliest, too." He smacked his lips. "That's a right wonderful combination for a girl to have, especially to a boy of sixteen."

She twisted around to look behind them. The moon spilled waves of pale blue over the cattle's wide backs. The cows had been an unleashed evil a few minutes ago, but now they were docile lambs. Etta could see Andy's figure in the distance, but not Cheyenne's.

"I don't see him."

"Who?"

"Cheyenne."

"You see Andy?"

"Yes."

"Cheyenne's back there. Maybe he spotted some strays and he went to muscle them back where they belong."

"Yes, that's probably it."

"Or he might be checking for injured steers. I know I saw a couple fall."

"Me, too. They should be on up here . . . if they stayed down."

"Maybe we was lucky, sister girl. Maybe we didn't lose any."

"Maybe, but they ran a pound off. I'll have to feed them good and let them rest another day or two before I start the drive to Amarillo."

Whitey slanted her a peculiar glance. "You still figuring to drive them there by yourself? Just you and Andy? I ain't able to go, sister girl. No matter how much I wish it or want it, I just can't."

"You need to stay here and keep the home fires burning." She sent him a gentle smile. "Cheyenne's come back. Me, him, and Andy can get the herd to Amarillo without hardly breaking a sweat."

Whitey stroked his whiskered chin thoughtfully. "That's true, but before you go counting on Cheyenne, you'd better ask him nice if he'll go on that drive, Etta. Ain't nothing worse than to be taken for granted."

Etta wobbled her head in a halfhearted acceptance. "I'll talk to him."

Whitey sighed. "Well, that's a start, I reckon."

Chapter 23

Morning stained the sky pink and violet. Etta held a board in place while Andy hammered nails into it. They worked quickly and quietly to repair the corral fence. Whitey sat astride Cannon, the Appaloosa he'd named, and guarded the opening against another breakout by the nervous cattle.

After getting them into the paddock, Etta had given a few clipped orders and work had commenced. With dawn's appearance, the work went easier because they had more light to see by. Etta hoped Andy wouldn't bring the hammer down on her thumbs and fingers anymore.

She looked along the fence line. Only a few more boards to lift into place and the corral would be secure again. They'd scavenged lumber from her house. The porch was no more, having become part of the cattle pen. Etta glanced over Andy's shredded shirt and numerous bleeding cuts.

"You sure you're okay? Looks like you got trampled pretty good."

"I got a headache and I'm sore, but I'll be fine, Miss Etta."

"Were you kicked in the head?"

"Not kicked. More like stepped on."

"Is your noggin' bleeding anywhere?"

"No, ma'am." He hammered another nail. "That's enough to hold that one. We got one more, and then we can all rest a little easier." He moved down the line while Etta selected a final piece of lumber; then he aided her in placing it against the post. "That looks good. Hold it right there." He plucked another nail from the pouch hanging on his belt and wielded the hammer again.

"Wonder if I should go see what's keeping Cheyenne," Whitey said, climbing down from Cannon. "He's been gone a long time to be rousting mavericks. Maybe he ran into trouble."

Etta straightened upright and patted her gloved hands together, letting dirt fly. "He's not coming back," she stated flatly, revealing the painful realization she'd struggled with for the past two hours as they'd repaired the fence. "He's long gone. Probably headed for Mexico."

"Did he tell you that?" Andy asked, his dark eyes wide with disbelief.

"Not in so many words." She looked around to make her point. "But I don't see him here, do you?"

"Don't get sassy," Whitey admonished, ambling toward her on his bent legs. "An hour or so ago you was happy as a lark because you was sure he had come back to ride with you to Amarillo. Just what changed your mind?"

Etta sighed, extending her arms out from her sides. "Because he's not here! And he's not rounding up mavericks either. He would have been back an hour ago if that were the case. He helped us with the stampede—probably rode up on it by accident—but he's not staying."

"Well, why not? I thought he liked it here," Andy said. "I thought you and him were ... well, talking up marriage."

"He wanted the Flying H, not me, Andy." She toed the dirt with the rounded tip of her boot. "When I told him I wouldn't sell him one acre of my land, he lost interest in all of us. He's an opportunist."

Andy removed his hat and scratched at his dust-covered black head. "That don't sound right to me. He never struck me as a man interested in buying up ranch land. Did he you, Whitey?"

"Hell, no," Whitey growled, spitting tobacco juice with enough force to send a pebble skittering. "None of this washes with me. I wish I'd been a fly on the wall and could have heard this tiff you and him had yesterday. Something about it just don't add up."

Etta bristled. "You're taking his side."

"I ain't taking nobody's side, sister girl. I'm tryin' to make heads or tails of this here mess." He waved an arm, indicating the torn-up earth, the aftermath of the stampede. "Why would he help us out . . . what was he doing back here? He wouldn't be hanging around for old-time's sake. He was in town, remember? And then he came back here. What for?"

"Maybe it's on the way to wherever he's headed. His gear is gone. I checked earlier." Hopelessness swamped her. "He's not here anymore. He's gone. We'd all better get used to that and get on with our lives." She began picking up the splintered boards and piling them in a heap. Expecting Whitey and Andy to fall in beside her, she looked up curiously when they didn't move. "Well? We've still got work to do, you know."

"I ain't finished thrashing this out." Whitey delivered a stubborn glare.

"Well, I *am*," Etta rejoined, matching his attitude.

"Good. You go on with what you're doing. Me and Andy will chew on this here bone until we're satisfied." He motioned Andy closer and hung an arm around the boy's narrow shoulders. "You and Cheyenne had some good talks, didn't you?"

Andy nodded, smiling. "Sure did. He talked to me like I was somebody. Like he wanted to hear my ideas on certain things. He told me his dreams, and I told him mine. We're saddle pals, that's what he said. Saddle pals."

Etta went on with her busy work, pretending to ignore them, but having no luck at actually doing so. Afraid she might cry from the heartbreak she was nursing, she dropped the boards she was holding and turned on the two men.

"This is hopeless!" Her voice emerged loud and strident. "Brickman's in town asleep. You know he is. He's curled up on a bed upstairs at the Scarlet Rose—probably with that tart Meg O'Rourke. That way, when we tell the sheriff about this and he tells Brickman, Brickman can say he doesn't know a thing about it. He was in town all night celebrating."

Whitey nodded. "True enough." He sounded as if he were discussing the weather instead of the end of their world.

"I can't . . ." Etta sat down in the dirt, dejected, defeated. "I can't keep fighting him. I'm so tired." She leaned her forehead against her bent knees and her muscles turned to jelly.

"Andy, did Cheyenne ever say anything to you about wanting a piece of this here ranch?" Whitey asked, as if Etta's announcement meant nothing. Nothing at all.

Etta brought her head up. She looked toward the pile of lumber, thinking it might be nice to pick up one of the boards and connect it to Whitey's empty head. "Didn't you hear me? I'm at my rope's end!" she shouted.

"Andy?" Whitey repeated. "Did he?"

Andy wrenched his big-eyed gaze from Etta to Whitey. "Uh, no, sir, no. I don't recall him ever saying nothing about wanting a ranch. This one or any other."

"Me neither." Whitey's arm slipped off Andy's shoulders. "Why would a gunfighter want a piece of a cattle ranch? Just don't make any sense."

"He's not a gunfighter anymore," Etta said without emotion. She was drained and her voice came out hoarse and flat. "He said his hand hadn't healed and he'd have to find another way to make a living. He'll probably join up with that outlaw gang again, since he can't finagle my land out of me."

"I don't think so," Whitey said. "He told me more than once that he would never join up with outlaws again. He never liked 'em all that much, especially after they deserted Hank like he was worthless."

"That's right," Andy chimed in. "He told me the same thing."

"Well, he told me he cared about me, and that was a lie." Etta faced them. "What makes you think he wouldn't lie just as prettily to you?"

"Miss Etta, I truly believe he was happy here and I don't think he'd do anything against you. He loves you."

"Ha! Andy, you don't know what you're talking about. He does not love me."

"Why, it's as plain as bristles on a hedgehog," Andy persisted. "Even when he wasn't in love with you yet, he respected you. He told me you had more grit and gumption than any woman he'd ever known. I knew then that he was falling for you." Andy ducked his head for a moment. "I'm green and don't know much about them things, but it was easy to see that Cheyenne was smitten. You, too."

Etta hugged her knees and hid her face against her crossed arms. She rocked back and forth, trying to contain her sobs of remorse.

"Sister girl, I do believe you're so full of hate for one man that you can't see the love and goodness in another. The only reason Cheyenne would be interested in this ranch is because it's part of you. And if you can't see that clear as day, then you're blind."

"So where is he?" she said on a sob. "If he loves me so damned much, why'd he pack up and go?"

"That's what I'm trying to figure out," Whitey said. "And I don't much cotton to the answer I'm coming up with."

Etta forced her head up and studied the worry lines etched on Whitey's face. "What? What are you thinking?"

"That he's a man of action. If you're at the end of your rope, Etta Lou, where does that put him, you reckon?"

She closed her eyes, trying to sort through the jumble in her head. Suddenly a dark vision loomed—a vision of a wide, dusty street and two men standing facing each other, twenty paces apart. Gunfire bloomed from their drawn weapons and one man crumpled to the ground, his long black hair wet with blood.

"No!" She was on her feet before she knew it, swaying with the violent movement, squeezing her eyes shut against the terror in her mind. "He wouldn't . . . he can't beat Brickman and he knows it. He's too slow now. He wouldn't clear his gun from the holster before Brickman shot him dead." She heard herself babbling, but couldn't stop. "He's gone to Mexico. He's safe there. He wouldn't call Brickman out . . . not when he . . . he's not as quick, not as accurate."

"But he's crazy for you, and he's got a long memory," Whitey said. "You forgetting Lone Deer? Well, he ain't." Whitey stepped in front of Etta and grabbed her by the shoulders. "I saw him out there, saw his face. I should have known right then that he was planning his own death. He had a look in his eyes—that cold, blue-steel look a gun-fighter gets when he's been challenged. Only one person might be able to stop this, and that's you. He might listen to you, Etta."

"If he's out to revenge Lone Deer, then I'm not sure Cheyenne will pay any heed to—"

"Not Cheyenne," Whitey cut in, his stubby fingers biting into her shoulders. "Brickman."

"Brickman?" she repeated before the sense of that landed like a rock in her mind. Yes, of course. She'd have to appeal to Blaine if she had any prayer of saving Cheyenne's life.

Whitey shook her a little and glanced up at the bright sky. "We gotta ride if we hope to get into town before they face each other."

"Yes, yes." Etta jerked out of his grasp and ran toward Southpaw. "Let's go!"

"What about the cattle?" Andy yelled. "Should I stay with them?"

"To hell with the cattle," Etta shouted. She reined Southpaw in a tight circle and rammed her bootheels into his flanks.

The sky was robin's-egg blue. It was a beautiful day for a killing.

Etta stowed that thought to the far recesses of her mind as she rode into town atop a sweat-laced Southpaw. An ominous quiet shrouded Clearwater, and Etta feared she was too late. Businesses were locked up tight. No flags fluttered from the poles in front of the school or the sheriff's office.

Whitey and Andy flanked her. She glanced at them and saw the worry plain on their faces. Were they too late? Was Cheyenne already at the undertaker's? Etta clucked her tongue and Southpaw responded by picking up his pace. She pointed him in the direction of the saloon, figuring that was where Cheyenne would have found Brickman.

Turning into the main street, she saw the crowd gathered on either side under the overhangs of the businesses. Two men stood in the middle of the street, right in front of the Scarlet Rose. Etta's blood ran cold. No, no! She slid from the saddle and ran toward the standoff. Brickman's back was to her, but she saw Cheyenne's face register surprise. He stood nose to nose with Brickman.

"Stop!" Etta grabbed Brickman's white shirtsleeve. "Don't do this. Please, don't do this." She looked into his eyes and saw nothing but black malice.

"Begging me to spare his life?" Brickman asked, a chilling smile creasing the corners of his mouth. "How touching."

"Stand back, Etta," Cheyenne ordered, and his eyes were nearly opaque, unreadable.

"No." She fastened her gaze imploringly on Brickman. "You still want me? You can have me. Just walk away from this. If you go through with it, I'll never speak to you again. I swear it."

"Etta!" Cheyenne's voice lashed out like a whip. "Stand back. I'm going to kill this devil. It's too late to sell your soul to him."

"Blaine . . ." She swallowed, not having used his first name to address him since that day when he'd told her father about them. "Blaine, please? Do this for me."

Brickman looked from Etta to Cheyenne, then back to Etta. He shook his head slowly, then pried her fingers off his sleeve. "I don't believe you'd keep your part of this bargain, Henryetta. I think this half-breed has turned your head. Otherwise, he wouldn't be here, would he? Do as he said, dear, and step aside. You're in the way, and I would be so distressed if a stray bullet found its way into your duplicitous heart."

She looked at Cheyenne again. His eyes were now blue-black, like his hair, and she knew there was nothing she could say to stop this senseless act of violence. The two men were determined to draw first blood. Glancing around, she saw Whitey and Andy among the crowd of onlookers. It seemed that the whole town had gathered to watch the gunfight. Whitey rocked his head back, beckoning her. He, too, understood that her pleas were falling on deaf ears. With a sound of futility, she retreated to stand between him and Andy on the boardwalk.

Her mind went back to the day she'd stood almost in the exact same place to witness Ben Brickman's death by the hand of the infamous gunslinger Johnny Cheyenne. Now it had come to this. Fate had played its final hand, bringing another Brickman forward to challenge Cheyenne's gun once more. But this contest wasn't fair, because Cheyenne wasn't the shooter he'd been when he'd faced Ben.

The people around her pressed back against the wall of the saloon as if trying to become part of the wood. Cowards! she thought. No doubt they hoped Cheyenne would gun down yet another Brickman, but they wouldn't show it. They wouldn't take bets on Cheyenne winning, just in case he didn't and they'd have to deal with Brickman again. They wouldn't show their support for fear they'd draw Brickman's disfavor. God, how she hated the yellow-bellies of Clearwater!

She looked down at her dirty clothes and knew that her face was streaked with grime and dried tears, and that her hair was in wild disarray. She'd been fighting for her life the past hours, fighting Brickman from a distance. Well, now she must fight him where he could see her and she could see him. No more hiding behind polite words and empty threats, terrible secrets and private shame. No more!

Taking a deep breath, Etta took one step forward. She stood erect and proud. Hearing the murmur of people behind her, she cleared her throat, wanting her voice to be as clear as a church bell.

"Shoot straight and true, Cheyenne," she called out. "You rid this town of one Brickman varmint, and I'm counting on you to rid us of the other one."

Brickman snickered, then tipped back his head and laughed. He swiveled around to stare malevolently at her. "Varmint, you say?" His voice was as clear as hers. "That's not what you called me that day in the clover when you spread your legs for me, Etta, dear."

She felt faint for a moment as his words pummeled her. Cheyenne emitted a low, primal growl, and stretched his fingers as if he were anxious to pull the trigger.

"Let's get this over with," Cheyenne said, his tone brusque and deadly. "Twenty paces."

Etta glanced around. Now the whole town knew of her shame, if it hadn't known already. Whitey's eyes gleamed with tears. Andy wore a look of dismay. Etta's breathing came in short gasps and her face flamed. She felt small and weak, a dirty spot on the street.

Then suddenly she wasn't alone. Whitey and Andy stepped forward, one on either side of her, standing tall and strong as pillars. She looked from one to the other, soaking up their strength, their kindness, their unquestioned support.

The others had grown quiet, watching the display of unity.

"Steady as you go, Mr. Brickman!" someone shouted from across the street, and Etta recognized Dan Pitch, the dry-goods-store owner.

That's right, she thought fractiously. Kiss his butt, Pitch. He's got money, so he's your man.

Hester Pitch was beside him, staring at her husband with open contempt. Etta could hardly believe her eyes when the usually dutiful wife stepped forward, her narrow-eyed gaze moving to Cheyenne.

"If one must die, let it not be Mr. Cheyenne," Hester said, and although she held her chin high, it trembled.

Etta's estimation of the woman towered.

"Hester," Dan hissed. "Step back here, you fool!"

But Hester ignored him, standing her ground. From the corner of her eye Etta saw movement. To her utter amazement, she observed one after another take one step forward to stand even with her, Whitey, and Andy. Across the street, others joined Hester to show their support of the gunslinger and their hatred for Brickman.

"Well, I'll be damned," Whitey breathed beside Etta.

Pride for her town—a pride she hadn't felt since she was a girl—spiraled through her. She stood taller, stronger, as she met the gazes of her compatriots: Gerald Powell, Roy's father; Clarence Allred, the owner of the general store; Jessup, the blacksmith; Lester Craw, the sheriff; Big Joe Simpson, the cattle broker; and Barney Timmons, a man who used to work for Brickman. Others took the fateful step forward, until almost half the onlookers had thrown their support to Cheyenne. Etta figured that half of the other half wanted to, but couldn't muster the courage.

Andy captured Etta's hand, and on impulse, she

grabbed onto Whitey's hand in turn, physically linking them. The others followed suit, until all those in front formed a human chain. Silence descended. Etta saw Andy's lips move in a prayer, and she bowed her own head.

She heard the men's boots biting the dirt, and she raised her head to stare with tear-glazed eyes at the inevitable duel. Her loving gaze caressed Cheyenne. Would these minutes be his last? Would he lie dead soon? Of course he would. Brickman was as quick as a snake with a gun, and Cheyenne ... Cheyenne's hand hadn't recovered—wouldn't recover—from Ben Brickman's lucky shot.

Her gaze tracked to his injured hand. A gasp of surprise shook her body as she stared, disbelieving, at his strange holster. He wasn't going to draw with his right hand, but with his left! The specially designed holster's leather was unscarred, cut from new hide. Etta looked at Andy, and his smile spoke volumes.

The scamp! Andy had fashioned a left-handed holster for Cheyenne, and the two of them had been practicing—or so she hoped. But how fast could he be, using his other hand? He hadn't been allowed much time to practice. Her gut twisted with agonizing dread. Sweat beaded on her brow, even though a wintery wind flowed from the north.

Time slowed and the expressions on each of the men's faces were clear, etched in Etta's memory. Brickman, ever the smiling gent, looked relaxed, as though he were facing a friend instead of an enemy. His hands were held out from his sides, his right one hovering near an ebony-and-silver-handled Colt. Etta suspected that Brickman's casual stance was deceptive. Even though Cheyenne was at a disadvantage, he still had a reputation as a gunfighter. No one could say for certain that he wasn't just as fast with his left hand, and that doubt would naturally eat at Brickman's cocky self-confidence.

Cheyenne's expression gave away nothing. Only the vitreous sparkle of his eyes hinted at his intense readiness for the task ahead. His classic gunfighter's stance lent its own brand of danger. The wind hit him in the face, blowing his hair back, making him squint slightly.

Silence, broken by the honking of wild geese flying in formation overhead. Then movement. Brickman's hand twitched. Guns cleared holsters. Fire shot from the barrels and curling fingers of smoke lifted into the sky. Bullets divided the air to find bone and flesh and vital organs.

Etta's muscles twitched, and she realized she'd jerked all over and that she clutched Andy's and Whitey's hands so tightly it was a wonder she hadn't crushed their bones.

Both gunmen remained standing, staring at each other, each face registering shock. They clutched their guns in their hands, ready to fire again. Etta whipped her gaze back and forth. Was anyone wounded? Had both bullets gone wide?

Slowly, tellingly, the tip of Brickman's gun dipped, like a flower's head drooping under a hot sun. He looked a bit stunned; then he fell heavily to his knees. That was when Etta saw the bloodstain on the back of his shirt and the blooming circle of red on the front. She knew he was mortally wounded and was stunned that he'd been bested by a man he considered a has-been.

His head swiveled around and his eyes found Etta. His mouth struggled to form a smile. Lifting his free hand, he touched his fingertips to his lips, then blew her a kiss. She shuddered. How in heaven had she ever found Blaine Brickman attractive? she wondered even as he dropped dead, face-first, in the dirt.

"He's hurt!" someone yelled.

Hurt? Etta stared at Brickman's inert body. Hell's fire, he's dead, she thought. Whitey and Andy let go of her hands and stumbled forward. She blinked, feeling as if she were rousing from a long sleep. Hurt? She looked toward Cheyenne, but couldn't see him because others were in her way.

"You okay, sir?" a man asked.

"Anybody know anything about doctoring?"

"Got to get that bleeding stopped. We can't let you get away from us. You're the town hero!"

Etta's heart thumped painfully. They were talking about Cheyenne!

Chapter 24

He was Clearwater's fair-haired boy, this Cheyenne gunslinger who had spent his whole life fighting for respect, both from others and from himself.

His back was probably sore from being slapped and pounded, Etta thought. She wound her way through the crowd gathered at the bar of the Scarlet Rose. Cheyenne had been hustled inside, while a couple of the Double B men had loaded Brickman's body into a wagon and taken it to the undertaker's.

Cheyenne's shoulder wound was dressed, and Etta had gathered from the excited voices around her that it was only superficial, nothing to worry about. She heard Cheyenne refuse further assistance as she approached, the tortuous route to him seemingly endless. Whitey was ahead of her, Andy somewhere behind.

"Pour him a drink!"

"Sure thing. I'll buy."

"Drink, hell! I'll spot him a whole bottle of the best stuff you've got."

"Right! He deserves the best. Look what he's done! No more kowtowing to the Brickmans!"

"No, please." Cheyenne's voice rumbled. "I don't . . . no, I don't want a drink. I just want . . . that is, thanks, but—"

"He wants to get home. Can't you see he's as

372

weary as a tomcat high-stepping in mud?" Whitey demanded.

Etta dodged around the last human obstacle. Cheyenne leaned against the bar, one boot propped on the foot rail, one elbow keeping him from slipping to his knees. Indeed, he did look frazzled. His shirtsleeve had been ripped off to expose his gunshot wound, now covered with a bandage that had a lacy edge—some woman's petticoat, Etta figured.

Drying blood splattered the front of his shirt. His eyes seemed to have sunk deeper into their sockets. He reminded Etta of a knight victorious: weary, but at ease; confident, but shaken by what had transpired.

He spotted her among the sea of faces, and the skin around his mouth tightened. He looked away in a reflex action that tore at Etta's heart. He had not forgiven her. And just like Papa, he never would.

She turned away and moved trancelike through the crowd of well-wishers. Outside, she watered the horses and waited for the others. Her heart felt like a stone in her chest.

The tub was set up in the tack room for privacy. They drew straws. Whitey got his bath first, then Etta, Andy, and Cheyenne. Whitey offered to trade places with Cheyenne, but he declined. He didn't mind waiting.

They ate in rounds. Etta made a chicken pot pie and stirred up a batch of fudge. She had to admit the simple meal was one of the best she'd ever prepared.

Sitting in the rocker, she sewed a button on one

of Whitey's shirts. Whitey and Andy sat nearby, each partaking of another wedge of fudge. Occasionally, the sounds of splashing water floated in from the tack room, where Cheyenne bathed.

Etta had only to close her eyes to see him naked. She'd memorized his body—the long limbs, powerful shoulders, wide chest. She knew his skin texture, the taste of him, the smell. She'd spent hours adoring his physique, marveling at the leashed power in his upper arms and in his thick thighs. Could he recall every curve of her body as well? Or did she blur into a composite of the women he'd had, the women who had pleasured him and been pleasured by him?

"Sure feels good to get clean and fill my belly," Andy said. "I didn't know how tired I was until I sat in the tub. My muscles turned to water!"

Whitey chuckled. "I know what you mean, son. My old bones feel like they're rubbing together. This day has been so long, I wouldn't be surprised to see signs of spring tomorrow."

"Speaking of spring . . ." Andy looked toward Etta. "When we going to drive those cattle to market?"

"*Where* we gonna drive them, that's what I'm wondering," Whitey added. "Clearwater or Amarillo?"

Etta sighed. "Amarillo," she said with more determination than she felt. "Let's see . . . today is Friday. We'll set out Monday, bright and early. Tomorrow we'll start getting things ready for the trip. Whitey, you'll stay here. I'll take Bounder, but we'll leave Butter here to see to her pups."

"They ought to be weaned by the time you get back," Whitey said. "We gonna keep all of them?"

Etta shook her head. "I'll ask around and see who wants one. They won't be hard to place. Lots of folks need good stock dogs. I'll keep two. Whitey, you can pick them out while I'm gone."

He nodded. "So you're going to Amarillo. You and Andy."

Etta lifted her lashes to meet his gaze. She knew what he was really asking: *have you spoken with Cheyenne?* He knew she hadn't, and that she was taking a hell of a lot for granted.

"I'm hoping Cheyenne will go with us," she admitted. "I'm going to ask him."

"I sure hope he does," Andy said, popping the last bite of fudge into his mouth. "Me and you will have a devil of a time tryin' to drive them cattle, Miss Etta. We sure enough do need one more trail driver."

Etta studied the button she was sewing on, although her thoughts wrestled with a problem of a different sort. Cheyenne had been his silent self on the ride home, revealing little except that, like the rest of them, he was dog-tired. He'd insisted that his wound was nothing. Even Whitey had been unable to pry him loose from his dark mood. Finally, they'd all ceased trying to converse with him.

The sight of the penned cattle hadn't even lifted Etta's spirits. In fact, she hated the sight of them. For months the roundup had consumed her, but now that it was over and Brickman was dead, she felt no jubilation. Only numbing relief—and trepidation. What if Cheyenne left her? What would she do?

"Sure hope old Cheyenne decides to stick with us through the cattle drive," Whitey said, then released a sigh. "Having him along is like having two men instead of one. He's the best cattleman gunslinger I ever did see."

"I don't care about the cattle drive!" Etta blurted out. She tossed the repaired shirt at Whitey and glared at him. His pale blue eyes glistened with interest and surprise.

"Since when did you stop caring about the cattle drive?" he asked, humor twitching the corners of his mouth.

"I do care, but that's not the only reason Cheyenne should stay here. You make it sound as if he's nothing but a hired hand. Like the only reason we want him around is to work the cattle."

Whitey exchanged an amused glance with Andy. "Sorry, but I thought that's what he is—a hired hand. 'Course, he's a different sort. Him working here was a trade, if you'll remember."

"I remember." She clutched the chair arms and rocked back and forth, making the rocker creak with the exertion. "But he's become more than a cowhand." She knifed Whitey with a keen glare. "And you know it, so don't keep on acting like Cheyenne's not special to me—to all of us."

The tack room door opened. Cheyenne wore a clean pair of brown trousers, no shirt, no boots, no headband. His hair hung damply against his neck and across his forehead. The clean scent of him pierced the air. Longing curled in Etta's stomach. She almost moaned aloud, she wanted him so. A strip of white cloth dangled from his fingers.

"I was wondering if you'd be kind enough to dress my wound." He lifted the cloth and looked at Etta. "If I recall, you're pretty good at this kind of thing."

She fairly flew across the space to him. A chink in the armor! Thank heavens! She took the cloth from him. Shyness stole through her when she realized she'd reacted like a love-starved young maiden, leaping at the slightest encouragement from her first suitor.

"I'd be happy to help." She looked into his eyes, searching for a sign of forgiveness, but as usual, he gave away little. "Come over by the light so I can see what I'm doing."

"If you've finished your bath, me and Andy are going to put ourselves to bed," Whitey said, grabbing Andy by the arm and hauling him to his feet. "Let's go, son."

"But I'm not—"

"Let's go," Whitey cut in, and pulled the startled youngster along with him to the tack room. " 'Night, y'all. See you bright and early."

"Good night, Whitey, Andy," Etta called cheerfully, glad to be alone with Cheyenne. There was so much to say, so much to explain—if she could.

" 'Night," Cheyenne said, already approaching the glow of the lamplight. He sat on Etta's trunk and propped his hands on his hips, waiting for her to dress his wound. "I suppose if you make sure it's clean, that will be plenty."

"Yes, of course. We don't want it to fester." She examined the gash, which had been stitched up in town by the barber, who also doubled as the town dentist and occasional doctor. "The barber did a good job. These stitches are even. Neat."

"As good as that doctor who sewed me up the last time?"

"Not quite. The wound looks more ragged. It will be a bad scar."

"I don't care about scars." He examined the one on top of his right hand. "It's what's under those scars that matters."

She cleaned the wound and dressed it while he sat silent, immobile as a statue. When she'd finished, she sat in the rocker and released a short, poignant sigh. "We need to talk."

"No, you need to listen." His dark blue eyes challenged her to question him, to argue. When she didn't, he nodded in satisfaction. "You haven't really listened to anyone since the day Brickman told your father what happened between you and him. Since that day, whenever things became too unpleasant or when someone came too close, you shut yourself up like a turtle retreating into its shell."

She smiled weakly. "There have been times when I wish I did have a shell like that."

"Eventually, even the turtle must emerge if it wants to continue living." He leaned back, propping his elbows on the foot of her bed. The broad expanse of his chest drew her gaze, and he let her look, loving the feel of her lambent gaze on his fevered flesh. "When I first met you, you fooled me as you fool so many people. I thought you were a dried-up, bitter woman with not one drop of tenderness in your heart. Then I saw your home."

"My home?" she repeated, puzzled. "What about it? It's just a farmhouse. Nothing fancy."

"Ah, but inside your house I found you. The real you." He smiled, remembering. "Your books, Etta. All those thousands of pages of romance and love and flowery poetry. Why, you could have knocked me over with a good puff of breath! I thought, this woman is hiding herself from the world. This woman has passion inside her." He lowered his brows for emphasis. "And that's when I decided I would tap into that passion. I never back away from a challenge, and you, Etta, were a glove slapped across my cheek, a red cape waved in my face, a lance buried at my feet."

"A challenge," she murmured. "That's what I was? A challenge?"

"At first, yes."

"Another notch on your belt." She stared off to the side, dealing with her pain and fighting not to show it. She didn't want to cry, to melt in front of him, a weak, long-suffering female for him to push away as gently as possible.

"You're talking when you should be listening," he admonished.

"I'm sorry. Go on." She wanted him to talk all he wanted because it kept him with her. His voice rolled from his chest like a purr, warming the room, creating an intimacy she had worried would never exist again between them.

He averted his gaze, staring sightlessly at the straw covering the ground between his bare feet. "I can see that you're worried, although you're too damned stubborn to tell me, so I'll ease your mind. I'm going on the cattle drive, Etta."

Sweet relief beamed through her, followed swiftly by anger at herself and with him. "I'm glad," she admitted in a tight voice that brought his gaze back to her. "But those cattle aren't the most important thing in my life, you know. Everybody's acting like that's all I care about, that I'm only interested in you staying just so I can get my cattle to market. It makes me mad." She began rocking furiously again, the chair squealing and squeaking.

"With Brickman dead you don't have to be as worried about the market price. The railroad's not going to bother you anymore. They'll run that track across the Double B, which is what they should have done all along."

Etta stopped rocking. Brickman was dead. She knew it, but hadn't actually accepted it until that moment. "I wonder what will happen to the Double B."

"It'll be sold off." Cheyenne managed a quick smile. "Hope you get along with the new neighbors better than you did with the Brickmans. Maybe you can buy some of it."

She let go of an ironic laugh. "That'll be the day. Once I pay my bills, I'll have just enough to throw up a house and put in a garden."

"Maybe I'll buy some of it, then. We can be neighbors."

Etta looked at him sharply, hoping he was kidding her. She couldn't be sure.

"I told you I had some money put back," he reminded her. "I should spend it on my future."

"You want to ranch?" she asked dubiously.

"Yes. Much to my surprise, I like it. I don't care which ranch, mind you." He sent her a frosty glare. "I know you think that every man in the county wants the Flying H, but you're wrong. I don't want your ranch, Etta. I never did."

"Then why did you offer me money?"

"Because I wanted to see you happy. I wanted to buy you smiles and laughter, carefree days and peaceful nights. I wanted you to live in a house filled with books again because that's where you were happy." He ran a hand roughly through his straight blue-black hair. It fell damply across his forehead. "But I don't want to take this place from you."

"What did you mean by a partnership?" she asked. "Exactly."

He viewed her through thick, stubby lashes, then got up from the trunk and strode toward the barn door. He yanked it open a few inches and stared out into the wintry night. The cold breeze swirled around Etta's ankles and up her skirt, but she didn't voice a complaint. Starlight limned his shoulders and caressed his smooth back.

"Me and you are a lot alike, you know," he said after a while, keeping his back to her. "Maybe that's why we have trouble making the other understand. We both learned to shield ourselves, to hide our feelings under hard glances and sharp words. But you earned my respect, Etta, and more importantly, I earned yours. I didn't even have to hold a gun on you to get it either." He laughed softly. "That was the first time I was ever respected for just being me."

The revelation gave her insight into the deepest part of his soul. She stared at him with new eyes, knowing his pain, feeling the years of rejection and the frustration of not truly belonging anywhere or to anyone.

"You like it here," she stated, the simple truth having eluded her until that moment. He turned his head to the side, not looking at her, but seeing her at the edge of his vision. "You wanted to stay, so you offered me a partnership."

"Yes, I wanted to stay, but not as a hired hand with you as my boss lady. That wouldn't work anymore. I had become your equal, and I liked it. I won't go back to being on your payroll."

"I never thought . . . that is, I figured you had been using me to get a foothold here."

"I know that's what you thought, and I can't begin to tell you how much it hurts me."

She winced. Her heart boomed in her chest, so full of woe that it swelled painfully to contain it all. "Cheyenne, I am sorry. Every time I've reached out to a man, shown him my heart, I've been made to pay. I thought this was the same story. I loved and I was being punished. I followed my heart, only to have it stomped on."

"I've never wanted to kill a man until I met Brickman and learned what he'd done to you." He leaned a forearm high on the doorframe and cocked one hip. "I've killed men, yes, but never because I wanted them dead. I just defended myself. Brickman's the only man I've called out. The only man I wanted dead."

"He needed killing. After what he's done . . . after Lone Deer . . ."

"I didn't kill him for Lone Deer." He turned around slowly, his gaze landing like a beam of light upon her. "I killed him for you, Etta."

With a sob of gratitude and regret, she left the rocker and ran into his arms. He embraced her, holding her so tight that she struggled for breath. But she clutched him just as desperately, yearning to melt into him, inseparable. Her hands sought his face, found it, framed it, and then her lips traveled over it in quick, hot, desperate kisses.

"Johnny, Johnny," she whispered against his skin, "I wanted you to kill him. God knows I shouldn't have wanted such a terrible thing . . .

that you should do such a grievous deed for me . . . oh, but I wanted it! I knew you were the only man who could stand up to him and defeat him. He's dead now, and I should be happy, but I'm not."

He grabbed her hands and pushed her back from him. "You're not?"

"No."

Exasperation pinned down the corners of his wide mouth. "Why the hell not? You've got your land and your cattle and your peace of mind!"

"But I don't have you," she wailed, tears choking her. "I've lost you." She wrenched her hands free and pummeled his chest with her fists. "Why can't I have you, Johnny Cheyenne? Why? Why!"

Her tears came in a flood. He let her lean on him. Holding her lightly, he stroked her long hair and listened to her broken sobs.

"I didn't want to fall in love with you," she said, her words muffled against his chest.

"I know," he said, smiling. "You made it clear you thought I was one rung below a stinking coyote."

"I was wrong. So wrong." She rubbed her cheek against the center of his chest where the slick hairs tickled her nose. "I was so mad at Hank for getting caught up in that gang of outlaws, and you were one of them."

"I knew them. I wasn't one of them," he corrected her. "But you never believed that."

"I believe it now," she said, turning her tear-stained face up to him. She wrinkled her nose. "Too late, I know. Oh, why am I such a sob sister? I never cry, but that's all I've done lately. Cry, cry, cry." She turned away from him and retrieved a handkerchief from her skirt pocket. She dried her tears and blew her nose. "I didn't even cry at Papa's funeral or when Hank was sentenced to prison."

"Then you're way overdue." His voice was as soothing and as deep as Clearwater Spring. "And you *can* have me, Etta. I've been yours for the taking since that day you threw *Sweet Passion's Song* at me. *You're* the one who's hard to rope."

She spun around, unsure whether to believe him. The soberness of his expression sent another blur of tears to her eyes. "You never cared, did you?"

He blinked, flummoxed. "Never cared? Woman, I just told you that I'm yours!"

"No, no." She laughed softly. "I mean, you never cared that Brickman and me . . . that I let him—you know."

"Etta, did I make love to you like a man who cared about any other thing in this world except me and you?" he asked, kindness radiating from his blue eyes like warm sunshine.

"No, but I couldn't believe it." She stared at her clasped hands, mining the words from her most secret heart. "I had thought you unworthy, lower than low because you killed for a living—"

"I didn't. I'm not a hired gun. Never was, never would be."

"I know, I know," she said, appeasing him. "But that's the way I had you figured. I was looking to blame someone for Hank leaving the ranch and landing in prison, and you were handy." She sent him a quick smile, which he returned. "I see the errors of my ways, but I was blind to them before.

You gave me back my self-respect. Something I never hoped to retrieve."

"But you didn't trust me."

"No, not then."

"How many times must I prove myself to you, Etta, before you finally believe I'm worthy of your trust?" He folded his arms against his chest, closing himself off from her.

Etta sensed an edge of anger in him, and she knew it was well deserved. She closed the distance between them, standing so near to him that her breasts pushed against his folded arms. Looking up into his face, a face that reflected the marriage of peoples, she was nearly overcome by his fierce beauty.

"If you still want to be my partner, I accept." She lifted a hand to her hair and untied the blue ribbon at the tail of her braid. She dropped the strip of grosgrain at his feet, then pulled her braid around to untwine the thick strands, to loosen them as she loosened her hold on her emotions and unlocked her heart.

Cheyenne watched. The only thing that could have taken his gaze from her would be death, he thought with a grimace. The hold she had on him was almost shameful. He'd never imagined that a woman could stamp her brand on him, until her. With Etta, he was the man he'd always wanted to be. Without Etta, he was once again stuck in a twilight between two worlds. He had found sure footing on the Flying H Ranch. He belonged.

Her hair shimmered through her fingers in waves. She tossed it back over her shoulders. Her green eyes spoke to him, and his body tightened below his belt. She smelled of lilacs. Leather and lace, he thought. His Etta.

She curled her fingers around his forearm, leaned into him, and pressed her mouth lushly in the center of his chest. His manhood stirred, thickened.

"I don't need a gunslinger anymore or a shadow to hide in from Brickman," she said against his hot skin. "What I need is a husband who knows cattle, can build me a new house, and can make good love to me." Her tongue flickered over his nipples. "You interested?"

He liked this game, but his body was quickening and his blood coursed like a floodwater through his veins. "I'm interested," he growled, swinging her off her feet. He strode to her bed. Glancing up at the loft, then at the tack room door, he shook his head and laid her on the bed.

"I've wanted to make love to you here—in this bed—and, by God, I'm going to."

Her eyes were pools of green passion. "You've earned the right." She motioned to the curtain she'd strung up to separate her bed from the rest of the barn. "Pull that across the line to give us some privacy."

He did before turning around to her. He unfastened the buttons on his fly. His member sprang out, long and tumescent. Sliding his trousers down his legs, he kicked them aside and settled one knee on the feather mattress.

"You always did like to look at me," he teased her, reaching up under her skirt to caress her soft thighs.

"I never can get enough of you," she admitted, unbuttoning her own blouse for quick removal.

He helped her out of her skirt, then took his time unfastening her chemise and discarding her underpants. She squirmed, eager for his union. He smiled, in no hurry.

"I was afraid you'd never love me again," she murmured. "I was sure you'd ridden to Mexico and wouldn't even look back, wouldn't miss me one moment."

"That wasn't your heart talking, Etta."

"No, it wasn't. My heart believed in you." She curved her hands at the back of his head and brought his mouth to hers. His tongue slipped between her lips at the same moment his arousal slipped between her moist folds.

Moaning almost deliriously, she parted her legs wider, giving him all the room he needed. The union was wild and wonderful, unleashing groans and urgent kisses. His hips bucked and he ground himself into her. She accepted him, gloved him in her hot, tight cavern. Like a flash of sizzling lightning, he sent his seed into her as she quivered with her own sweet surrender.

"Do I have a partner?" she whispered.

"Forever," he whispered back. "Forever, sweetheart."

She smiled. Trusting. Loving. Being loved.

He smiled. Peaceful. Comfortable. Belonging.

They held on to each other, reluctant to let go.

Johnny Cheyenne was finally home.

Avon Romantic Treasures

*Unforgettable, enthralling love stories,
sparkling with passion and adventure
from Romance's bestselling authors*

COMANCHE WIND *by Genell Dellin*

76717-1/$4.50 US/$5.50 Can

THEN CAME YOU *by Lisa Kleypas*

77013-X/$4.50 US/$5.50 Can

VIRGIN STAR *by Jennifer Horsman*

76702-3/$4.50 US/$5.50 Can

MASTER OF MOONSPELL *by Deborah Camp*

76736-8/$4.50 US/$5.50 Can

SHADOW DANCE *by Anne Stuart*

76741-4/$4.50 US/$5.50 Can

FORTUNE'S FLAME *by Judith E. French*

76865-8/$4.50 US/$5.50 Can

FASCINATION *by Stella Cameron*

77074-1/$4.50 US/$5.50 Can

ANGEL EYES *by Suzannah Davis*

76822-4/$4.50 US/$5.50 Can

Avon Romances—
the best in exceptional authors and unforgettable novels!

FOREVER HIS   Shelly Thacker
77035-0/$4.50 US/$5.50 Can

TOUCH ME WITH FIRE   Nicole Jordan
77279-5/$4.50 US/$5.50 Can

OUTLAW HEART   Samantha James
76936-0/$4.50 US/$5.50 Can

FLAME OF FURY   Sharon Green
76827-5/$4.50 US/$5.50 Can

DARK CHAMPION   Jo Beverley
76786-4/$4.50 US/$5.50 Can

BELOVED PRETENDER   Joan Van Nuys
77207-8/$4.50 US/$5.50 Can

PASSIONATE SURRENDER   Sheryl Sage
76684-1/$4.50 US/$5.50 Can

MASTER OF MY DREAMS   Danelle Harmon
77227-2/$4.50 US/$5.50 Can

LORD OF THE NIGHT   Cara Miles
76453-9/$4.50 US/$5.50 Can

WIND ACROSS TEXAS   Donna Stephens
77273-6/$4.50 US/$5.50 Can